Keeping Faith

A Novel

2011—
Happy,
Mothers Day

Cindy Bradford

ISBN: 1-4392-6105-9
ISBN-13: 9781439261057

In Memory of My Parents,
Who Thought I Could Do Anything

Acknowledgements

Writing a book is primarily a one person endeavor, but bringing it to life takes many others encouraging, pushing, prodding and lending support. My gratitude goes to my two closest friends, Carlene and Judy, for doing all the above and more. You're the best!!! And to Chris, my agent, who made it happen. Most of all, I thank you, the reader, for taking a chance on this book.

prologue

East Texas, 1991

Faith O'Brien had been looking for her father for as long as she could remember. From a slight glance out of her upstairs bedroom window at a lone passerby to a concentrated scrutiny of familiar faces she saw each autumn Friday night in the crowded wooden bleachers of the high school stadium, she searched. With a single, faded black and white photograph that she took often from a worn little box that held her only other connection to him—a tiny gold ring he had given her mother the first year they dated, she had tried to picture him, studying every tiny detail of the handsome nineteen year old boy with a crooked grin, leaning against an old, but shiny Oldsmobile.

When she pressed her aunt Alice, as she often did, to describe him better, Alice's answer was always hesitatingly the same with her reflective voice trailing off at the end. "He was tall, lanky and athletic, with hair the color of a cinnamon stick and eyes like the sky on a cloudless day. Yet even when he smiled, he had a haunting sadness in those eyes that I never understood and can't explain."

In sharp contrast, Alice talked easily and often about Sue, Faith's mother, and there were photographs of her in assorted old fashioned frames displayed on small tables at either end of the couch and one atop the mantle. A grouping hung prominently on a wall in the small formal living room with pictures of a pudgy two year old mischievously sticking four chubby fingers in the sugar coated frosting of a lopsided birthday cake, a skinny preteen striking a silly pose with girlfriends and a serious young lady accepting her high school diploma at commencement. Together they depicted a sequence of growing up in a long ago life, yet they also portrayed how strikingly similar a daughter now

looked—the resemblance, pronounced, straightforward and unde-
niable except for one distinctive difference—her eyes. No question, Faith had her father's gentle, searching, telling blue eyes.

The pictures were a constant reminder to Faith of her mother's indirect presence in their lives, but they also made it painfully
obvious that she was not really there, that she was gone forever.

Her disappearance and apparent death and her father's be-
trayal of the woman who loved him had not been something
Alice had kept from Faith even as a toddler, instead explaining
all the circumstances, everything. Everything, that is except why
the young man who was her father chose to be a Priest rather
than return for his child. That was mystery even she, the adult,
couldn't solve.

And so it was early in Faith's life that she knew her mother
wasn't coming back, couldn't come back. But he was out there…
somewhere. So Faith kept pursuing, probing, chasing after a
shadowy, silent figure from a tattered snapshot and a sketchy past
she heard about late at night when she climbed into Alice's lap
with questions only a child could ask. Often after their conversations, she dreamed about him, seeing him clearly, vividly, matching the description Alice had patiently repeated. And always she
imagined him holding her hand while she clumsily took her first
awkward steps or demonstrating how to shift gears and ease off
the clutch as she practiced for a much anticipated driver's per-
mit and someday at her wedding, walking her down the aisle
to give her away. It was always then that she woke up, remembering it was all a dream because one can't give away what he
never claimed.

Though she never mentioned it, Alice also looked for Patrick,
making phone calls, checking police records, reading newspapers
from far flung places at the local library and contacting state
and national politicians, even the Vatican, with no success. It certainly wasn't because she wanted to see him, but her love for Faith

compelled her. Actually pleasing Faith was what drove most of her decisions, and going to the class reunion was no exception.

"You simply have to go," Faith pleaded.

"Give me one good reason."

"Because Teresa and Jane are expecting you; probably a lot of people are. Besides, you might even enjoy yourself," a tinge of exasperation in her voice.

"I'm a mess. Look at me. My hair needs cutting and I've gained weight." Pausing, she continued, "I don't know, Faith. I haven't seen some of those classmates in so long, I'm not sure we would have anything to talk about."

"You look great, and you know it! I'm sure you'll think of something to say. Haven't noticed that being a problem for you before now," she added teasingly, grabbing a diet coke from the refrigerator. "I'm off to Lisa's. We're going shopping. You better do the same. You know; something sexy to knock them off their feet."

Rolling her eyes, Alice acquiesced, "Oh, you're impossible; I'll go, but I'll bet I'm home before you are."

Whether it was a stroke of luck, a fluke of coincidence or perfect timing, Alice, mellow from the rum and coke, found herself staying long after the official reunion, reminiscing with friends about babies and divorces, career achievements and set-backs, dreams satisfied and goals unmet.

As she had expected, everyone in the little group who sat huddled around the picnic table in the same city park where they had played as children, had had their ups and downs. Tears filled Teresa's eyes as she talked about her fifteen year old son who had died four years earlier in a hunting accident.

Sparing no expletives, Jane related how she discovered her husband was having an affair with his secretary. And the dark circles under Joey's eyes told his story before he began. Twenty plus years of binge drinking had taken its toll on the once ambitious student body president. Tapping his foot nervously against the wooden bench, he sipped a 7-Up and looked away from the others, as if remembering the happier times when he was co-captain of the football team and Homecoming King.

"I lost my job and my family. This AA deal is my last straw. I just hope I can hang on."

The only one apparently unscathed by the years was David, now a research scientist and professor in Minnesota who from all indications had fulfilled the old yearbook prediction of "Most Likely to Succeed." He sat quietly, silently assessing the casualties and wondering if Alice knew he still loved her. He had since sixth grade when they began walking to the corner drugstore his uncle owned. Every day after school, they slung their books on the counter and drank a coke float before Alice walked the remaining four blocks home. One afternoon he bashfully admitted he had a crush on her, but she had responded only with a whimsical smile and asked to copy his math homework.

David knew even then she would never feel the same about him, but it didn't stop him from caring, though he never mentioned it again. He knew too well it wasn't going to happen now either, yet he still enjoyed smelling her perfume as it wafted toward him when the gentle summer breeze filtered through the tall pines. He watched the corners of her mouth turn up when she giggled and thought how much some things never change. But, now he listened intently as she somberly related Faith's interminable, but fruitless search for her father. After a long pause, he said softly "I have an idea," stroking a stubby salt and pepper beard that fit his craggy face perfectly. "There's a colleague of mine at the university who is experimenting with a new computer search engine, Gopher, as in our mascot. It might just open up some leads," he added, wanting desperately to help.

☙❧

When the call from David came two days later, Alice's voice quivered as she thanked him and said goodbye. She turned slowly, reaching to place the phone back in its cradle, but her shaking hand missed its mark, and the receiver dangled as limply as she felt. She was torn; relief and apprehension overwhelmed her, and for a minute she felt old and tired and wished she hadn't pursued this. What if he turned his back again, rejected Faith after all these years? What good could possibly come from finding a man who had tossed aside his own child like a throwaway toy—a man who was seemingly more interested in the souls of others than the heart of his offspring? The answers might not be easy to accept, but she knew Faith O'Brien was determined to get them. She called out to her, "Hon, your search is over; your father is in Maine."

PART ONE
Making Mistakes

God sent us here to make mistakes,
To strive, to fail, to rebegin
To taste the tempting fruit of sin
And find what better food it makes...

chapter I

Boston, 1962

Patrick woke, startled, hearing a rustling noise. Reaching quickly to push back the heavy canvas, he found it zipped closed. Darkness swallowed him. In the airless, musty pup tent, he felt trapped. Sweat beaded on his forehead, when suddenly he heard another sound and felt the presence of someone.

"Shh."

Then Patrick felt a body pressing against him and a clammy hand cover his mouth.

"Patrick, you're a very special boy to me," and breathing heavily, the whispering voice continued, "Turn this way and be very still," nudging the youngster forward.

Trembling, Patrick recognized the voice of his priest. *Why is he doing this? What is happening to me?*

Patrick's mind was reeling and he found it difficult to breathe as Father Michael slid a hand over his boyish, gangly frame, fondling him for what seemed an endless time. Nauseated, his stomach churning, Patrick lay lifeless when the priest moved away.

"Paddy, this makes a special bond between you and me. You can't tell anyone. Do you understand?"

His head was pounding as Patrick nodded although he knew it was too dark for the priest to see it move.

Without another word, Father Michael unzipped the tent and left as quietly as he had approached. Patrick lay in his sleeping bag, shaking and hurting, unable to comprehend why this had happened to him. A single salty teardrop fell on his upper lip, followed by a steady stream. He suddenly felt sick, like he was going to throw up. Pushing his head into his pillow, he sobbed until he fell asleep. When he woke he remembered the ugliness of the night. *What if someone had seen Father Michael crawling into or out of his tent or heard him crying after the priest left? His priest—the man Patrick's dad called their spiritual leader—who his dad described as a gentle spirit.* There had been nothing gentle about him the night before and Patrick knew he would never see him again as anything close to spiritual. *This man had christened him, blessed him and now done this to him. How could a priest be a man of God and Satan all in the same robe?* It was so hard for him to think about.

Patrick lay in the tent for a few minutes, not wanting to dress for the day. Yet, desperate to escape the confinement, he pulled on his shorts and shirt and drug himself out. Looking around the camp ground, he saw lines of tents, along with old log tables, scattered with cooking utensils. Beyond that were stretches of nothing more than acres of green wilderness circling the camp. Through gaps in the tall trees and wild foliage, the orange glow from the sun was just appearing in the east, and he was grateful for the break in the darkness. He didn't see the priest at first and was startled when he heard his voice.

"Good Morning, my lad," Father Michael said, shifting to look at Patrick as he gave a cursory turn of the bacon just beginning to sizzle in the heavy iron skillet.

"Good Morning, Father," Patrick murmured meekly, diverting his eyes.

"And how did you sleep, Paddy O'Brien?" the wan, small framed priest asked without emotion. His clerical collar was slightly askew and he looked tired and like he had not been awake long.

Patrick hated being called Paddy. His brothers, knowing how much he despised it, occasionally used it teasingly, but he knew the priest was taunting him, testing his reactions. He looked down again, but not before catching a glimpse of Father Michael's beady gray eyes that always appeared weak behind his black square framed glasses. His scars from teenage acne had deepened over the years and this morning looked more pronounced than usual.

"Okay, I guess," Patrick answered, struggling to be polite but wanting to escape. Other boys were beginning to gather and Patrick saw his chance to move away.

Noticing, the priest loosely grabbed Patrick's arm, "Come, help me make the coffee, lad" he instructed, playfully tousling Patrick's thick uncombed hair.

As much as Patrick had looked forward to this day, now he just wanted to go home.

He thought back about how excited he had been the day before waiting for the bus to take him and the other new altar boys to Camp Timbers in a small rural area west of Boston.

He had checked his packing list at least three times and recounted the items he was required to bring, carefully placing his clothes and supplies in a small duffle bag that had been his older brother Robert's when he was Patrick's age. Although he had wanted a new backpack he knew there wasn't money so he marked through his brother's name and with a black magic marker printed his.

But to his surprise his parents had bought him a Timex watch with a brown leather band. Although he had learned to tell time long before starting kindergarten by staring at the kitchen clock while he waited at the window, watching for his father to come home from the fire house, he had never had a watch of his own. Throughout the week before wilderness camp, his dad had cautioned him not to wear it in the lake. "Your mother and I saved for this, and we want you to take good care of it, okay?" They need not have worried because even at ten, Patrick was proud and responsible, and knew finances were tight at home.

The ringing of the giant bell, announcing breakfast, brought Patrick back to the present. Father Robert, the white haired senior priest whose mild manner radiated calm confidence and reminded Patrick of his grandfather, called "Come and get it!" Dispirited, Patrick looked down at the bacon, scrambled eggs and fried toast that filled the oversized pans. Gingerly, he put a piece of the crisp buttery bread on his plate and then a spoonful of eggs as he eyed a vacant seat at the long table. He had to admit that the food smelled good, but he wasn't hungry and wished he were home in the small, cramped kitchen, dotted with a collection of pictures of fruit in oversized vases hanging strategically over the peeling wallpaper. He knew his mother would have on her old worn yellow checkered apron smudged with flour, bent over the dented stainless steel counter, making Irish soda bread. He could see his dad at the round pock marked wooden table reading the sports section of the daily paper, complaining about missing another Red Sox game.

When the pots and pans and leftovers were put away, Father Andrew stood and announced, "This morning we are going to have a scavenger hunt. Each boy needs to choose a partner".

Patrick looked around, searching for his best friend Stephen, but before he could say anything, Mikey Kennedy shouted, "Hey Patrick, let's be hunting buddies."

"No, come on Patrick, his friend Casey called.

Randy shouted louder, "We'll make the best team, Patrick."

Patrick paused, eyeing all three boys, wishing Mikey hadn't asked first and still looking for his best friend Stephen. "I guess I had better help Mikey," his voice trailing off. Then in his typical competitive spirit, he added, "And we're going to beat your butts," trying to sound more confident than he was feeling.

"Yeah," Mikey gloated, unable to hide his excitement that Patrick had agreed to team up.

Father Andrew handed each set of boys a list of items to find: a maple leaf, one edible item, a piece of birch bark, three shades of granite rock, an arrowhead, proof of wildlife, a pine cone, a twig of blue spruce, a bouquet of wild flowers and a sign of previous campers. "You have an hour and a half to search. If you're late, you'll be disqualified. When you've found everything on the list, bring it all back for checking. The winning team will be released from chores for the day and each boy will receive a prize."

Feeling doomed, Patrick looked at Mikey, who was chubby, all milky white and soft as a marshmallow. On top of that, Mikey usually acted like a big baby. Yet Patrick could understand why. Mikey's mother hovered over him, some days even bringing his lunch to school and eating with him in the cafeteria. Patrick thought how much he loved his mother, but admitted he would have wanted to die if she had ever brought his lunch and sat down with him and his friends.

After blowing his whistle, Father Andrew shouted, "Take off!"

The boys ran into the woods in all directions. Mikey found a feather and beaming proudly shouted to Patrick, "I got something" holding up a beautifully formed crimson feather.

Maybe this wasn't going to be so bad after all Patrick thought. Next, Patrick found berries and then the biggest maple leaf he had ever seen. "Look for rocks, Mikey, over there. There are some by that little stream."

"I just found a can," Mikey responded.

Almost 45 minutes had passed when Patrick looked at his list. They still needed birch bark, some blue spruce and a pine cone, which seemed easy enough and there were plenty of wild flowers scattered among the tall grasses, but finding an arrowhead seemed like a stretch.

"I've got the tree stuff, Patrick" Mikey yelled.

"Good, now start looking for a mound or heaps of dirt. We're probably going to have to dig if we're going to find an arrowhead."

"Do you really think there were Indians here, Patrick?"

"Well, the Pilgrims were here so there must have been Indians," Patrick said with confidence.

"Don't you think all the arrowheads are gone by now, if there ever were any?"

"Who knows, but if it's on the list there must be some or they are just trying to trick us."

"I don't think a priest would do that, do you, Patrick?"

Patrick didn't respond, "Just keep digging Mikey; we only have about thirty minutes and I'm not hopeful."

There were four large mounds of dirt and the boys probed with their bare hands, but found nothing. Just as they were about to give up Mikey cried, "Ouch! That hurt; something stuck me."

Patrick thought *he's whining again*, but joined Mikey and quickly began scooping the soft soil. There, jutting out was a grayish arrowhead with one jagged edge.

"All right, we may win!" Patrick exclaimed, but wondering what would happen if another team found one in better shape.

"Hurry, let's go. We don't want to be late." Running ahead, Patrick almost forgot the wild flowers.

"Grab that purple stuff, Mikey," Patrick yelled as he caught hold of two yellow flowers.

Panting, the two boys ran into camp where several of the older boys stood, looking disgusted, their mouths formed into smirks. From a distance, Patrick heard one say, "There weren't any damn Indians here."

When the whistle blew signaling time was up, the boys formed a line, each team dropping their findings on the ground in front of them. As the judging began, it looked promising for Patrick and Mikey until they saw two other boys who also had everything on the list; their arrowhead, though a little larger, looked to be in about the same crooked shape as Patrick and Mikey's.

"We have a tie, boys. We only have two prizes so you'll have to vote," said Father Andrew. He was tall, athletic and muscular, and looked to be in his late twenties. Of all the priests, he was Patrick's favorite. Smiling, he pointed to a long table, "We're going to place all the treasures for both teams over there, and then you will have to choose which team has the overall best finds. Everything is basically the same between the two teams so your decision will probably depend on the arrowheads and feathers."

Patrick looked at Mikey wiggling with excitement and was afraid he was going to wet his pants. Both boys chewed their fingernails as the line of boys passed by the piles of twigs, rocks, flowers and feathers. Patrick watched, shifting his weight back and forth, as he did when he was nervous.

"Okay, this is it boys. Let's see a show of hands," Father Andrew called, first holding up the arrowhead and long gray feather belonging to Mark and Javier. When he lifted the other arrowhead and crimson feather, Patrick began counting the raised hands.

"The red feather wins!" shouted Father Andrew as Patrick and Mikey whooped and hollered, jumping up and down. "Come forward and get your prizes."

They walked erect, chests puffed out, straining to look taller than they really were to the front of the group where the priest stood smiling, reaching to hand them their prize.

Patrick slowly opened a wooden box to find a small gold cross on a tiny chain. Like a bolt of lightning, the night before came crashing back as he remembered the shiny, gold cross hanging from Father Michael's neck.

Trying to hide his anguish, Patrick managed a smile and a mumbled "Thank you," as he crushed the box into his pocket and started to walk away until Stephen hit him hard on the back.

"Good job! What did you do to Mikey? His eyes are all puffed up." Patrick turned to look and saw Mikey rubbing his eyes, now red and swollen.

Patrick couldn't help but smile as he looked over at the wild flowers lying wilted in a heap by Mikey's feet. "Guess, Mikey has allergies too. Poor guy, he can't win for losing."

"Who wants to try archery?" Father Robert asked, picking up a bow and demonstrating how to position it. As he let the arrow fly it missed the bull's eye by half an inch, tempting the boys to try. Each boy claimed a bow and quiver of arrows and ran to the practice targets. Arrow after arrow flew, the swishing sounds reverberating in the open setting, but no one hit the bull's eye. When the scores were tallied a short squat boy named Jack from Millsport Parish won the contest, narrowly edging out Patrick who had competed vigorously. Though disappointed, he quickly rebounded when swimming was announced. From the sound of the whoops of the boys, this appeared to be the favorite activity for everyone except Mikey.

Today, like yesterday, he sat on the bank, but this time he was clutching the crimson feather. Watching him, Patrick thought, *well, at least something good happened to Mikey today.*

Although there was a shallow part of the lake where Mikey could stand, his mother had told him not to go in. Patrick had heard her repeat to Father Michael at least four times, "Do not let Mikey go near the water, and be sure that he has on his cap. I don't want him to get too much sun." Mikey's skin looked so translucent that Patrick wondered if she ever let him play outside, plus his cap was shaped funny, the beak too long, making his head look lopsided. *Why couldn't he just wear a normal baseball cap?* Patrick wondered, knowing that Mikey's mother probably picked it out. Feeling a little sorry for Mikey, he almost stopped, but wanting so badly to swim, he jumped in instead. "Yikes," he yelled, gulping and spitting water as he came to the top. "Man, this water is like ice."

Joey Sinclair, who had leaped in first, was bobbing up and down. "You'll get used to it; don't you remember yesterday?" he asked, sarcastically. Joey was a year older than Patrick and liked to act tough. Although their dads were both cops and friends, Patrick didn't really like Joey.

Boys crowded the diving platform like ants. When Patrick's turn came, he flung his body as high as he could and grabbed his bent legs beneath him, "Cannon ball," he yelled, right before his face hit the water. When his head popped out of the water, his skin was still stinging. He rubbed his eyes and looked at a group of boys clapping and yelling.

"Let's see that again. I dare you to start back there and run," a skinny kid shouted, pointing to a tree more than ten feet from the board. Without hesitation, Patrick pulled himself up on the rickety wooden ladder and raced to the spot, touched the tree and ran back, this time, bounding off the board on one leg, flying high until...splat! His body cut through the water and back up in seconds. Head bobbling, he caught his breath, grinned and glanced over to the bank. Immediately he saw Mikey, watching earnestly but forlornly at the action in the lake. Patrick swam over and asked, "Are you okay?"

"I guess," Mikey answered in a pitiful voice.

"Hey, at least put your legs in the water," Patrick encouraged, pulling himself out of the water and standing up said, "You surely can't drown doing that."

Mikey smiled meekly, and complied by gingerly dipping first one and then his other foot into the water, obviously glad that someone was talking to him. Then, Patrick moved to stand as close to Mikey's body as he could, and jumped in, splashing water everywhere and soaking Mikey's clothes. Seeing him drenched, Patrick laughed so hard he could barely stay afloat.

Grinning and reaching down to the water to splash at Patrick, Mikey lost his balance and fell in. When he came to the surface, he began slapping the water hysterically and screamed as soon as he caught his breath.

Patrick yelled for help and cautioned Mikey, "Be calm and you'll be okay," trying to hold onto him with one hand and to the bank with the other. Now, Mikey was jerking his arms and fighting so hard that Patrick lost his grip and thought both of them might drown. Finally, two boys ran over, reached out and caught Mikey as Patrick pushed him toward them. Once they had dragged him up he sat on the hard dirt of the lake's edge looking paler than ever and sobbing uncontrollably. *So much for Mikey's already poor image*, Patrick thought. Feeling a little responsible, but tired from the effort, he dog paddled out into the middle of the lake and floated, trying to clear his head.

When the whistle blew for time out, Patrick swam to the shore, pulled himself out and dried off. Back at the camp, he dressed and sat on one of the benches by the campfire, trying to find warmth. Although it was summer the air was cool when the sun started to set and a light breeze added more chill. Hungry, Patrick walked over to Father Robert, "How much longer until dinner?"

"About thirty minutes, but it will be worth the wait," Father Robert replied, stoking the coals and blowing into his palms.

Patrick looked at the aluminum foil shapes nestled among the grayish-white coals. The menu, written on a weathered, thin piece of poster-board tacked to a blue spruce, read: Roasted Potatoes, Roasted Corn and Brisket. Without that it would be hard to tell what was hidden in the belly of the fire-pit.

"Those look like something that fell off a space capsule," Patrick said to the group of boys huddled around the smoking pit.

"Yeah, maybe we've been invaded by aliens," Randy chimed.

"Hey, look at the sky. I think I see something," Mikey added excitedly.

"You dope, that's an airplane," Joey exclaimed, rolling his eyes and moving to be further away from Mikey.

"You don't know that for sure," Patrick said, defensively.

"Okay boys, grab your plates. We're just about ready," Father Robert announced.

Quickly forgetting about their argument, the boys jumped up pushing and shoving, to be first in line. Patrick reached over to the rusted metal cooler, and dug in the ice until he found a Dr. Pepper. Then popping the top, he flicked the pudgy kid in front of him with the cold water on his hand.

"Hey, watch it," he said, grinning.

"Watch what?" Patrick answered, feigning surprise and innocence.

❧❧

Around the campfire the boys ate, told ghost stories and listened to a short devotional led by Father Robert.

"Lights out," Father Robert shouted, shortly before 10:00. He then began blowing out the lanterns and scattering the remaining ashes of the campfire. Sleepy and tired, Patrick crawled into his tent, careful to place his pillow in the opening. Falling onto his sleeping bag without undressing, he was asleep as soon as his head hit the pillow.

A noise woke him. When he looked at his watch in the dim light coming through the small opening in his tent, he noticed it was 1:00 a.m. Not seeing anyone, he sank back into his sleeping bag, and within a few minutes drifted back to sleep.

But, like the night before, Father Michael eased into Patrick's tent, waking him.

"Move out of the sleeping bag" Father Michael commanded, tugging and pulling at him. Suddenly, the muffled sound of something outside the tent caught Father Michael's attention and he froze, covering Patrick's mouth with his hand, afraid the slightest sound might bring someone to the tent. Minutes seemed like hours. It was now dead quiet.

More time passed and Father Michael whispered "Open the tent, Paddy, and see if anyone is out there."

Patrick edged forward and looking out saw only the glow of a full moon on the tranquil campground and a lone raccoon scampering off into the trees.

"There's nobody," he whimpered, wishing the priest would just go away. Father Michael started, and then stopped.

"Remember you are a special gift from God to me, Paddy, my lad." Then he slithered out of the tent.

Patrick lay awake for the longest time, trying to swallow his tears. He could hear his heart beating, afraid the priest might return. Thinking about what had just happened, he felt dirty and lonely, trying in his ten year old mind to put reason to the unreasonable. *Why had the priest come back? Why him? Was he the only one?*

The next morning, Patrick stayed in his tent until the whistle announced the last wake-up call. Sitting, his head touched the top of the tent. It smelled like his first puppy Daisy when she played in the little lake behind his house and then ran in the cool wind until her short legs could run no more. His thoughts went back to home, where he would soon be away from this horrible place and this horrible man—at least until the next mass. Breaking the silence, Father Andrew called out to the boys, "Finish your breakfast, and get your tents broken down and your sleeping bags and gear ready for the vans."

When Patrick finished putting his away, he noticed Mikey having trouble, "Hey, do you need some help?"

"I just can't get this one stake."

"Okay, move, I think I can get it," Patrick told him as he wrestled the stubborn piece of metal pipe.

"Whew, that wasn't easy was it?" But before, Patrick had time to answer, Mikey said, "Were you homesick last night?"

Patrick turned quickly and looked at him, surprised, "No, why?"

"Oh, I just wondered."

Patrick turned away so Mikey couldn't see the anguished look on his face and walked toward a group of boys gathering around Father Andrew who was just beginning to explain the morning schedule.

"This morning you have a choice of fishing or canoeing before reporting back to camp at 11:30 for a quick lunch and trip home."

Quickly, Patrick yelled to Stephen, "Hey, you wanna fish?"

"Sure, but I hate putting those gross worms on the hook."

"Oh, you big sissy, that's what happens when you have a bunch of girls in your family! What if you catch a big fish? You want me to take it off your hook, too?"

Stephen shrugged and grinned, "Maybe."

Gathering gear and an empty aluminum bucket, the two boys headed to the smallest of the three lakes where Patrick dug in the soft dirt until he found six long, wiggly earthworms. Slowly weaving the worms onto the hooks, Patrick handed a rod to Stephen. After tossing in their lines, they sat patiently waiting for a bite, but the cork never moved. When they reeled in their lines, they saw that something had nibbled part of the worms so Patrick carefully baited the hooks and each tossed their lines into the dark water. Almost immediately, Patrick watched his cork go under.

"I've got one, I've got a fish." He jerked, and the fish jerked. The line went out whining, but Patrick kept the tip of his rod up and continued reeling like his dad had taught him. Finally the line was taut and it seemed that the fish had given up, but as Patrick relaxed, it took off again.

Jerking his line, Patrick heard a snap. His shoulders drooped as he realized the fish and his hook were gone. "I had a huge fish, my very own, Stephen. I'll probably never have one like that again." He was about to try again when he looked at his watch and decided they had better start back. Trudging along the narrow path carved through the thick underbrush Patrick kicked at a lone rock. He looked around at the campsite, now cleared of the boys' belongings, void of purpose and spirit, much like he felt. The others were lining up to board the bus as Patrick lingered for a minute, glancing back at the lake, wishing he had been as lucky as the fish.

☙❧

Standing near the altar in his white surplice, Patrick, with candle in hand, looked like a cherub, but inside he didn't feel angelic. Feeling choked, he wanted to tear away the tight black satin bow that scratched and tickled his neck. The thigh length robe with wide, full sleeves reminded him of costumes he had worn as a younger kid when he pretended to be a character he wasn't, almost like today. A month ago he thought this day would never come, his first mass as an altar boy. Now as Patrick watched his brother, John, carry the cross while walking in front of Father Michael, suddenly he felt sick. With the memories so fresh and raw, the sight of the priest terrified and disgusted him. Seeing his parents gaze admiringly at the clergyman, he felt abandoned and alone again. As Father Michael turned to face his followers, Patrick exhaled so hard his breath extinguished the candle's flame.

After the service, the priest invited the new altar boys to the Parish House for lunch. Making excuses, Patrick hurried to the car, careful not to mention the invitation to his parents. He knew that if he did, they would make him go. They would never understand, never, and thus began a pattern of omission that was to define his life and that of those around him.

Over the next months, Patrick became withdrawn and irritable, sleeping fitfully and even wetting the bed on occasion. His mother's face showed concern when she noticed the change in the son she always said was her most playful and full of pranks. She would pat his head and ask him where he hurt. He avoided her gaze because he could never explain his pain. His dad had less patience and threatened to take him to the family doctor if he didn't straighten up. Patrick worked at forcing himself to put the events of the awful nights behind him, and began tricking his mind to think of other things. The basketball court became his escape. He was in control there and his mind was focused on that orange ball spinning between his hand and the ground, but at night the past has a way of creeping back.

chapter 2

The bus ride from Boston to East Texas gave Patrick plenty of time to think. Night had come shortly after he boarded and the darkness left him feeling lonely, empty and a little apprehensive. He had never been away from home for more than a week and now he was going off to college to a place he had never seen, eighteen hundred miles from home. The steady buzz of the air conditioner had lulled many of the passengers into various stages of sleep, but it didn't come so easy for him. Watching the distant lights of an occasional town, he thought about the big universities in the East and Midwest whose coaches had promised him scholarships. Now those assurances were as limp as his old duffle, wedged beneath his seat.

The bus stopped once around midnight and a young woman, carrying a crumpled sack and a dirty little boy in diapers, climbed on barely grabbing a place to sit before the driver slammed the gears, and waking the few passengers who had managed to sleep through the stop. A baby cried and Patrick wished he could.

Around Washington, D.C., he drifted off, dreaming he was playing in the Final Four Championships for Ohio State. Rain hitting his window woke him, bringing him back to the reality of his situation. No big time coaches were willing to take a chance on him, although his doctor said his knee was healed. Instead he was going to a piddly-assed junior college where his brothers had played. And that was the only reason Cherokee Junior College was even giving him a chance. There had to be more to all this but just his bad luck, yet he wasn't sure what. Maybe he needed to rethink his future.

Morning turned into midday as Patrick pressed his face against the window to see the Blue Ridge Mountains. He could be, should be, riding the bus to Duke.

Now the bus was stopping more often, making the day seem even longer. An old man got on in Charlotte with a small tattered suitcase. He took the vacant seat next to Patrick and mumbled a soft hello. Patrick returned the greeting as he studied him. His face was weathered by endless summers in the sun and his clothes as worn as his luggage.

"Where you headed, boy?" the man asked.

"To a small college in East Texas. I'm going to play basketball."

"Look like a ballplayer. You any good?"

Smiling now for the first time since he left the station in Boston, Patrick answered, "I think I am, least I hope so. I thought I was going to get to play for a big school, but I blew out my knee."

"Yeah, sometimes life just don't give us what we expect," he said, glancing down momentarily. "Didn't think I'd lose the farm either, but between bugs and drought the bad years added up quicker than the good. Just had to let it go. Sometimes that's easier than holding out hope for something that's not going to happen. Now, I'm going to live with my daughter in Houston. She's a school teacher and her husband sells cars. Don't know how it'll be for me, living in the city, but I don't have anywhere else to go."

Patrick found himself feeling sorry for the old man and for the first time in a long time not thinking about his own circumstances.

A bit embarrassed, he pointed to the overhead compartment and asked, "Is that all you're taking? I mean I noticed you only had one suitcase."

"All I got left. Sold what few things the bank didn't take. Never been one for a bunch of extra belongings. Since my wife died five years ago, hadn't needed much." He reached in his wallet and pulled out a worn photograph. "She was the prettiest gal in the county." His eyes brimmed with tears that he struggled to hold back.

"I'm sure she was," Patrick said quickly, wishing he could think of something to make the old fellow feel better. "Have you been to Houston before?" he added hastily.

"Nope, my daughter usually came to visit me a couple of times a year so I never made the trip. They've only been there since '65. Before that they were in Virginia, lots closer."

"I've never been to Texas," Patrick said, and I can't say I'm really excited about it."

"You a city boy?"

"I guess you could call me that. I've lived just outside Boston all my life."

"Umm, a city boy and a Yankee to boot," the old man said teasingly. "You'll be okay. Just relax and be patient with folks. Things run a little slower down here."

Frowning, Patrick replied, "That's what I've been told."

"Well, things might be a little different at first, but people, people are all the same if you give them a chance," he said, looking at his watch. "Bout time for my nap. I've taken to dozing about an hour this time of day." And with that, he leaned his head back and began to snore in rhythm with the droning of the engine.

When he awoke, the sun was beginning to set. He shook his head as if to shake off the sleep. "Where are we, boy?"

"According to my map and route info, I think we're almost to Montgomery. You slept a lot longer than an hour."

"I guess all the motion rocked me like a baby. Now I'm hungry."

"I think we're supposed to make a stop here to change buses. My mother packed me food, but I finished that before noon, so I hope we have a chance to grab a sandwich. I'm starved"

"Should be plenty of time. Don't think we connect 'til 9:00. We should be in Houston by daybreak."

The old and dingy bus station smelled of sweat and stale newspapers, with people crowded into whatever space they could find, many looking like they had been traveling for days, their rumpled clothing just one clue to the duration. He had been gone only a little more than 24 hours, but it felt like a year. His spirits were as crushed as his shirt was wrinkled. He glanced around for an attendant or an open ticket window, but everything was closed for the night except two vending machines. Eyeing a spot in line, he made his way over to the first one. Rummaging in his pockets he found only enough coins for a sandwich and coke and was thankful when after a pause they dropped into the bottom of the rusty machine. As he turned and stepped away he almost bumped into a light skinned black woman, dark circles under her eyes, with a baby hanging precariously on her hip. The baby was clutching an empty bottle, and a slightly older, grimy little girl held tight to the woman's hand. Tears streaked the little girl's face already smudged with a substance Patrick couldn't make out. He noticed that the woman who couldn't be much older than him walked with a slight limp, and he couldn't tell if the pained look in her eyes was from that or something less obvious.

Though she whispered, Patrick overhead her say, "I know you're hungry sweetheart, but we have to wait 'til we get to grandma's. I don't have no money."

The little girl seemed not to understand and stood pleading with her mother.

"Here, I'm not hungry. You need this," Patrick said, handing her his sandwich and drink.

She looked up stunned and stammered a weak but quick "Thank you," as if she were afraid he would change his mind. Quickly she tore open the cellophane and began breaking small bites off for the child.

Patrick turned and reached down to pick up his belongings, anxious to get outside in the open air.

When he boarded the bus he began looking for the old man, suddenly remembering that he hadn't asked his name. He eyed him midway to the back already sitting next to a young boy who was munching on a candy bar and talking between bites. Taking the first open seat, he told himself it would be nice to have the extra room to stretch his long legs, but it wasn't any time until the loneliness took over. He pressed his cheek to the window and felt his stomach growl. A long night lay ahead.

❧❧

Riding into town, Patrick looked out the window of the Greyhound and decided he had stepped back in time. Along the main street were three clothing stores, all adorned with faded awnings of various colors and styles, but inside each window were mannequins dressed in plaid dresses or paisley jackets, several tilted or slightly askew probably as a result of unwatched children crawling through the tempting displays. All manner of plastic decorations lined the windows along with footballs and pompoms, a couple of used helmets and an occasional red and white jersey. Back to School banners hung on outside posts, announcing special sales. Across the street stood what appeared to have once been a Woolworth's, its lettering still visible under a thin or worn coat of paint. On top of the flat roofed building stood a giant sign, flashing red in the shape of 5¢. Hand drawn in shoe polish on the window of the front door were the words, *Under New Ownership. Come see what you can get for a dime. Fountain open daily 11:00 'til 4:00. Best sodas and grilled cheese sandwiches in town.*

A chalk board announced the day's special of chicken-fried steak, gravy and black-eyed peas out front of the Mom and Pop Café, located in the center of town, next door to an Esso gas station and First National Bank. Around the corner the bus drove by the First Baptist Church which filled the city block and passed the Piggly Wiggly grocery before finally coming to a stop at the bus station, which Patrick determined had seen better times.

He stood up stiffly and stretched his long legs. Grabbing his duffle bag and suitcase, he stepped down to the concrete of Townsend, population 9,038. The air smelled faintly sweet, like gardenias or fresh magnolias; he wasn't sure.

He looked around to get his bearings. Only two other people, a young woman who looked in her mid-twenties and a little boy, had gotten off the bus and they were met by an older man and woman who Patrick figured were grandparents by the way they hugged the woman and swept the boy up into their arms, taking turns to smother him with wet kisses. Only when he reached for the bright blue package and took it in his hands was he able to squirm his way out of the man's arms and land on his pudgy feet. This scene and similar ones Patrick had seen from inside the bus along the long journey reminded him that there would probably be no one meeting him. He had hoped the coach might be there, but there was no mention of it in his letter and no other person except a ticket person and janitor sweeping the concrete steps was anywhere in sight.

Remembering that his brothers had given him directions to the college, he headed south for what he figured would be less than a mile. He wanted to be excited about being here, but looking around he saw nothing to encourage those feelings. Across the street was a park, surrounded by pine trees that he swore touched the sky. Like many years ago in a place he willed his mind to never go, he felt suffocated. Trudging onward he had walked less than two blocks when a pretty girl in a shiny Oldsmobile cutlass pulled up to his side.

"Hi, I don't normally pick up strangers, but I thought maybe you could use a lift," she said in a slow friendly drawl.

He returned her smile, "That would be nice. This one is heavy," dropping his duffle. He was beginning to perspire, not used to the heat and humidity.

"Then hop in. Where you wanting to go?"

Patrick opened the door and set his luggage in the backseat, careful not to touch two shopping bags. "To the college, Parks Hall"

"Oh, so you're an athlete, huh? We call that the animal dorm."

Patrick smiled "Yeah, basketball player or so they say."

"Well, since you were walking from the station, I guess you are from somewhere faraway. You sound like it, anyway."

Laughing, Patrick replied, "Boston."

"Massachusetts?"

"Is there any other?" he answered with a surprised look.

A little embarrassed by her own question, she said, "Well, that is just so far away. By the way, I'm Sue. Sue Little. I've lived here all my life. Never been further north than the Mason-Dixon Line. Well, here we are."

"My name is Patrick O'Brien and I really appreciate the ride. You go to college here?"

"A freshman. I can't wait."

"I wish I were that excited," he said, opening the car door. Turning, he smiled faintly. "Thanks again," as he reached for his bags.

After dropping off his belongings in his dorm room, he walked over to the gymnasium where he was pleasantly surprised at the modern facilities and plentiful bleachers. Two young boys were dribbling haphazardly. He smiled and waved to them. His thoughts drifted back to his first lopsided, wobbly attempts to sail down the court, ball bouncing, his mind on that rhythm, and his eyes on the other players. He was a hustler, a ball shagger, even then.

Seeing the gym bolstered his spirits and gave him the energy to venture across campus. Tall pine trees shaded many of the older one story buildings. Pine cones littered the thick St. Augustine grass that carpeted the plaza, lined with concrete benches. Patrick lingered there in the shade, trying to keep cool. Dodging a sprinkler spraying water on late summer begonias, he sprinted across the pathway leading to the newer two and three story structures close to the Student Union Building or "SUB", as the sign indicated. Thirsty, he went in to buy a Coke, stopping first to look at a bulletin board, splattered erratically with messages, notices and an occasional photo: **"For Sale: Good Bicycle $15.00. Call Nancy 986-4446"** or, **"Never-Used Book, History 101 Brooks Dorm, Rm. 206 Ask for Paul"**. There were hundreds of papers tacked, one on top of the other. To Patrick it looked like perhaps three years of accumulation. One caught his eye: **"Holy Spirit Catholic Church welcomes you. Two blocks from campus. Mass 7:00 a.m."** Finally, a welcoming and familiar invitation that made him feel a little more at home.

∾∾

Patrick might have been disappointed to be at Cherokee Junior College, but Sue Little was excited to be in the audience at freshmen orientation. She was lonely, so being surrounded by other students and the accompanying noise was a welcome respite. Even the voices of strangers were better than the silence at home.

Her parents had settled in Townsend years ago when they married because it was small and quiet, a good place to raise children. In the midst of towering pine trees, hidden from the closest big city by more than 100 miles, life was easy and carefree.

But life and death, as Sue learned as a teenager, is often not that simple. Her idyllic and happy childhood had come to a halt three years ago, the night her father died. A successful insurance agent, James, was also committed to helping his community in as many ways as he could. He coached little league, was a deacon in the Baptist church and served as a volunteer fireman. He wasn't supposed to be on call that night, but when he heard about a fire burning the local hardware store that belonged to one of his best friends, he rushed over to assist. James was distraught when he came out of the smoldering front door, knowing it was going to be a total loss. Just as he was ready to leave, someone yelled that the owner's German Shepherd was still in the burning building. Knowing how much the dog meant to his friend, James went back in. Minutes later, they found her dad just inside what was left of the door, clutching the dog, both charred almost beyond recognition.

Sue's mother, Sarah, who taught second grade, and sang in the church choir, never adjusted to life without James and withdrew from everything after his death. When she lost weight, her family and friends assumed she was depressed and still grieving and no one suspected a terminal illness. Within a year she was diagnosed with stomach cancer and shortly after Sue's seventeenth birthday, on a morning so hot and sticky that the trees drooped and the birds didn't sing, Sarah took her last breath.

This left Sue with no one but her older sister Alice, who had married three years before and moved a few streets over, into the new part of town. Because Sue begged to stay in the small two-story house where they had grown up and lived while she finished high school, Alice acquiesced. Although worried that Sue was too young and vulnerable, and much too lonely to live alone, Alice trusted her, knowing that it was Sue who had always been the dependable one. She was the one with the good grades, whom her parents counted on and who never disappointed them by running around town, staying out too late or sneaking around with boys. The sisters were close, even though their personalities and looks could not have been more different.

Sue's hair was jet black, like her mother's. She was tall and trim and her olive complexion set off the unusual color of her eyes. To her delight, people often told her that her eyes reminded them of Liz Taylor, the movie star. She was the more reserved of the two girls, and held many more aspirations. If someone were describing the All-American Girl, Sue could have fit the description.

Those who knew Alice, however, were not fooled by her tiny frame and blond hair. She was certainly not an airhead and neither a pushover or witless, but rather a "spirited, animated and outspoken spitfire," as her dad had proudly described her. She favored his appearance and he admired her spunk, so when her mother had said she lacked ambition, he had always come to her defense, saying it wasn't missing; it was just misplaced.

The sisters wore fashionable clothes, with just the right amount of make-up to complement their striking features and up-to-date hair styles. Both had been cheerleaders in high school and in as many clubs and activities as time allowed. Friendly to everyone, thoughtful and caring, their parents had taught them well. But now their parents were gone.

At freshman orientation, Sue listened as the vice president discussed the college's rules and expectations, all the while scanning the audience, looking for a certain shock of sandy red hair. She easily identified the football players sitting in a group down front, squirming and whispering while the speaker pointed to a diagram of the campus and rehashed guidelines. Finally, after what seemed like a litany of do's and don'ts, the coaches began introducing their teams. When Patrick's name was called, he stood up quickly, making his way to the stage without a waste of a minute. She remembered him being tall and muscular, but seeing him with his teammates, she was surprised how tall. He was a full head taller than most. His smile looked forced, almost sad, but all Sue really saw now were is his blue eyes that softened his angular features and matched his wrinkled shirt. He practically sprinted off the stage, agile and smooth in movement. Sue could visualize him on the basketball court as self-assured and in charge.

"I want that one," she said, turning to her girlfriend and pointing to Patrick.

"But he's redheaded. You always date guys with dark hair."

"Yes, but there's something about him that intrigues me. I think it's his eyes. They're gorgeous. And, he just seems so different from the guys here."

"How do you know that? You've just seen him two minutes."

"I met him yesterday. I was leaving The Toggery and he was walking from the bus station. So I offered him a ride."

"I can't believe you. Sue, you are so naïve and trusting. He could have been a serial killer."

"Oh, don't be so dramatic. I could tell he was a nice guy. Wouldn't hurt a flea."

"Yeah, Yeah, famous last words."

৵৹৵

As the bell rang announcing the start of English 101, Patrick dashed to grab the last available seat, only to find Sue sitting across from him. He smiled and nodded.

"We meet again," he mouthed, careful not to interrupt the instructor who had already begun spilling her welcome to grammar and composition speech that he figured she must had reiterated for at least the last twenty years. There was scarcely time for conversation as Ms. Bigsby explained prefixes and suffixes as if she were unlocking the secrets of an unknown language. She was still talking when the bell rang and students began to gather their books to leave.

"Well, what do you think of Cherokee so far?" Sue asked, turning to Patrick.

"It's okay for a *foreign land*," he teased. "Not exactly the hot spot of the world. No, I take that back. It is the HOTTEST place I've ever been."

"You'll get used to it. Should have been here in July."

"I was working the lobster boats in July," he said wistfully thinking about New England. "See you tomorrow and he took off toward the plaza.

The next two times the class met, Patrick slid in as the bell rang and left as hastily when it was over, but on Friday, he seemed to notice that Sue was in no rush to leave so he lingered also.

"Do you not have a class after this one either?"

"No and I hate my schedule. I registered early, but still couldn't get the classes I wanted back to back. I have a quiz in biology today, so I guess I'll use the time wisely and study."

"Oh, no need for that. Would you like to get some coffee at the SUB?"

"Yes, that sounds good. What's your next class?"

"Algebra. I'm not sure studying will help. I'm already lost and it's only the first week."

Walking into the SUB, Patrick glanced around, "Grab those seats. I'll get the coffee. It's not the best coffee in the world, but this place isn't in the real world anyway," he teased Sue, handing her a cup. "Sugar and cream?"

She shook her head no and before he even sat down, asked, "Do you not have an alarm clock or are you just a sleepyhead?"

"Pardon me?"

"Well, you're almost late to class every day."

"Oh, no, I'm actually a very early riser. That's when I study and then I go to mass."

"Every day?"

"Yes. Every day, well mass that is. I'm not so regular about studying. You're not Catholic, I take it."

"No. I was raised Baptist, very Baptist," she said, twisting her mouth to a half smile, and then half frown.

"Oh, one of those teetotalers! I'll bet alcohol has never touched your lips, or your parents don't know, it if it has."

"My parents are both dead," she offered.

Embarrassed, Patrick blushed and stammered, "Oh, I'm sorry. They must have been really young. How long ago was it?"

"Yes, they were. My dad died three years ago, and my mom's been dead almost two. It's just my older sister and me now, and she's married."

"Do you live in the dorm?"

"No, I have the family home, here. My sister and I agreed not to sell it until I finish college, then I guess there won't be any reason not to."

They talked easily pausing only to drink their coffee or to laugh at Patrick's sarcastic descriptions of Townsend.

Patrick shifted in his chair and looked serious, "Sue, I wanted to ask you out, but I don't have a car. I may be able to borrow one, but I'm not sure yet."

"That's okay, Patrick, I'd love to go out with you. I have a car, and although it's not East Texas tradition, I could pick you up," she offered.

"Great. How about tomorrow night? We could go get a pizza and then take in a movie."

"That sounds good! We better get to class. I don't think Mrs. Kloster would be as understanding if I'm late to her frog lecture, as Ms. Bigsby is to your sliding in as the bell rings every class. But then, I'm not a big basketball star," she teased.

Ms. Bigsby, who was single and at least forty years old, had quite a reputation on campus for liking the athletes. Although the English teacher was attractive, Sue could not imagine any freshman or sophomore boy going out with her, even if it were a one-time clandestine event. But she had heard the rumor more than once. Everybody at the college probably had.

Sue thought Saturday night would never arrive. She couldn't remember ever being so excited about a date, nor had she ever picked up a boy for one, but he promised to be standing out in front of the dorm waiting for her, at 7:00 p.m. sharp.

He waved when he saw her turning into the parking lot.

Rolling down the window, she said "Hi," blushing slightly as she scooted over enough to let him drive. After a few minutes of uncomfortable silence, Patrick finally spoke, "Well, what did you do today while I practiced my heart out to keep my scholarship in this *foreign land*?"

She laughed, "Not really much. I went shopping for this new outfit and ran by my sister Alice's house for awhile. She's sorta having husband problems. I always liked Dwayne when they were dating, but lately he's being a real jerk."

"What's the deal?" Patrick asked, glancing quickly at Sue's short plaid skirt while still trying to concentrate on navigating the unfamiliar streets.

"Well, he was always a little bit of a ladies' man. All of Alice's friends knew he was cheating on her while they dated, but everybody, especially Alice, thought he was serious when he decided to get married. I've wondered a thousand times why he even wanted to get married. They were both so young. She was barely eighteen and he was just a year older. Maybe he thought Alice would settle him down. I know that's what *she* thought. It certainly didn't work, though." Sue caught herself talking more than usual and stopped.

"And, so now what?"

"Well, he's staying out a lot and not always coming in until after the sun comes up. Alice is so hurt," she paused. "So, Patrick, tell me more about your family."

"There is a lot of it. I'm the third of six kids, four boys and two girls, a very Irish Catholic family." He assumed that Sue recognized the last name and knew of his older brothers, when they played at Cherokee, but she gave no inkling of it if she did when he began explaining. "John played at DePaul, after here, and now is working in Boston, in hopes of getting in Law School. Andrew is at Duke. He was never much of an academic star, so it's taking him a little longer. Because of that, he hasn't been able to play much. He's usually on scholastic probation. I'm afraid he won't have a scholarship next year. My sisters, Mary Margaret and Rose Marie are still in high school and Joe Jr. or "Joey", as we call him, is in junior high school."

"Does your little brother want to play basketball?"

"No, he rarely even gets out of the house. I'm afraid my mother and sisters have spoiled him, rotten. He has a slight learning disability, so they baby him. He sits in front of the television and snacks, which drives my dad crazy. Plus, he's getting pudgy, but he's a great little guy and I miss him. He plays a mean game of Monopoly."

"It must be interesting, having such a big family. I didn't put your name together with your brothers until you mentioned it. They were quite famous here; I remember hearing of them. Of course, everyone knows about everyone and his business in this town," she said, smiling slyly.

☜☞

The Pizza Joint looked crowded. Small, dark, and smoky, the main room was quaintly furnished with small tables, each covered with a red and white checked tablecloth. No two coverings had the same kind of checks, or the same faded red color. Three old photographs of Townsend's own sports heroes hung crooked on one wall, yellowed by smoke and age. A poster of an Italian countryside and a worn map of Italy were tacked with pushpins to another wall.

Squinting from the smoke, Patrick searched for a seat. "I guess I should have checked this place out before I brought you here."

"Don't be silly. This is the hot spot; the locals love it. Sure better than the Dairy Queen!"

He noticed a table for two in the corner and guided her toward it. "Okay, if you say so."

"Check out that candle, pretty colorful, huh?" he said as they both sat down. Red and green melted wax oozed down the straw basket surrounding the old wine bottle. The sullen waiter rammed another red taper into the waxy opening, lighting it with not so much as a hello. Patrick looked at Sue incredulously.

She laughed, "Welcome to Townsend's finest Italian restaurant."

They talked non-stop, over pepperoni pizza and Cokes. Finishing off the last gooey piece, Patrick asked, "You ready for a sappy, sad movie? I noticed the only movie showing at the Majestic is 'Love Story'."

"I can't wait." She knew there was a B-rated western, at the drive-in theater, but nice girls didn't go there on a first date.

Being Saturday night, she also knew what to expect at the theater. All the local junior high kids had spent the day there and even though the management did their best to clean it for the evening showing, it was futile. No matter how many popcorn kernels and empty cups they picked up, it didn't keep someone's feet from sticking to the floor. The theater had been built in the early fifties and there had been so many soft drinks spilled that nobody could ever scrape it up. The aisles weren't too bad, because they used machines to clean them. The floor around and under the seats, however, was a different story. There must have been an inch of caked, sticky, gummy *Graveyard* on the floor underneath the seats. This orange, grape, Dr. Pepper, cherry coke mixture was a favorite drink among the seventh and eighth graders; hence, every Saturday, a new layer was added to the theater floors. That, along with the junior mints, malted milk balls, chocolate covered raisins and popcorn, that they threw as soon as the lights were dimmed, made a royal mess—about twenty years of mess. Sue had been sticking to that floor for years, as a young kid and then as a teenager. She was anxious to hear what funny remarks Patrick would say, and just as she predicted she saw him grimace and look down at his feet.

"What's on the floor?" he asked when he stood up to leave. He had noticed it some, when he came in, but once his feet were in one place so long, they squeaked when he tried to move them. "Ugh!"

Sue laughed and tried explaining until she realized it was just something one had to have experienced on a Saturday when young and silly in a dark little town theater where the movies weren't good, but the action was. She stopped mid sentence.

"Oh yes, I knew I wasn't in the real world," he laughed.

They drove back to the dorm, casually discussing the movie, as Sue wiped her eyes.

"Sorry, but that was so sad."

Patrick sighed, "I warned you," rubbing his eyes mockingly. When he parked out front of the dorm, he cut the engine and following a long pause said, "I had a great time, Sue."

"Me, too," not wanting the night to end.

"Hey, you see that guy over there in the white T-shirt?" Patrick asked pointing to a bulky guy with his cotton sleeves rolled up to the top of his arm, sitting on one of the dorm steps. Muscles bulged from his huge arms. Then before Sue could answer, he added, "That's Hank, my gargantuan roommate. He calls himself Hank the Hunk from Henderson."

Sue snickered. "Looks more like a simple slob from some-where small."

"You're right on target. Dumb," Patrick said, laughing.

"Is he really from Henderson?"

"That's what he says, why?"

"Well, it's only about twenty miles away. I was just wondering why he lives in the dorm."

"To torment me. Actually, all the football players are re-quired to live here. He loves it. Runs around in his underwear, burping, farting and flexing his muscles." He stopped quickly, then stammered, "I'm sorry, Sue, that wasn't a very nice thing to say in front of you."

Blushing slightly, she said, "That's okay, Patrick. You're the one who has to sleep in the same room with him."

"Well, I'm used to having a roommate. When you have three brothers, that's a given."

His face turned more serious. "Can we go somewhere next week? I promise to put some gasoline in your car."

"That's not necessary, Patrick, but I'd love to go out again."

"Okay, so that's a deal!" and then he leaned over and kissed her on the cheek.

"See you in English, Monday, and be on time," she reminded him, patting his arm as she moved over to drive.

As he was jogging toward the front door, Sue could hear Hank yelling, "Hey man, you got a chauffeur?"

❧

Summer finally gave way to fall, ending the scorching tem-peratures and bringing rain. The air began to smell of damp pinecones and homecoming mums, a strange mixture but one everyone who lived in Townsend was used to breathing and even savoring. Autumn was always exciting here. Football games were the dominant theme that gave the town its focus. Parades before and dances afterwards capped off the months of October and November. In between, the county fair and Halloween carnival brought the chance for old and young alike to eat all the candied apples and cotton candy they could hold. It also provided opportunities for teenage boys to impress their girlfriends with giant stuffed animals, won by tossing little round plastic circles over cases of coke bottles.

And Patrick was no exception. Handing Sue an over-stuffed black and white bear, he beamed. A smile sprang to her lips. "You are my knight in shining armor."

He took her hand in his. "Let's ride the Ferris Wheel so I can steal a kiss."

She leaned into him and he could smell her perfume.

"What are you thinking, Patrick?"

It caught him off guard for a minute and he fumbled for an answer. After a long pause, he answered, "I'm glad I came to Cherokee. I never thought I'd say that, but it's beginning to feel...well, not like home, but comfortable." Catching himself, he stopped as if he were sorry he had offered a part of himself.

Sometimes, Patrick's moods were a complete mystery to Sue. It was as if he wanted to share his inner self, but there was always a part of him he wouldn't let go. Squeezing his hand, Sue broke the stillness. "I'm glad you came to Cherokee, Patrick."

Since their second date, Patrick and Sue had been together almost every night. At first, Sue had hesitated about Patrick staying at her house so much, especially after midnight. "What would the neighbors think?" she had asked him, but relented almost as soon as she had said it. Still, if they went out for awhile and came back, he always parked in the garage, so as not to arouse any suspicions from the Taylors on one side and the Blackwoods on the other.

"I don't get it," he had said, the first time she had told him where to park.

"Oh, Patrick, remember this is not Boston. Everyone watches out for each other in a little town like this plus, the neighbors feel responsible for me living here alone."

"Yeah, they watch out all right, right out their windows. Look! They're probably looking right now." He pushed the drape back from the den window and pointed across the street. Tugging at the back of his pants as if he might moon them, he grinned devilishly at Sue.

"You're terrible. I think a young couple lives there, anyway. Old Mrs. Waters died not too long ago, and the For Sale sign is gone. I saw a young woman pushing a baby stroller there the other day."

"But of course you weren't snooping, just watching out for your new neighbor." He fell over the back of the patterned blue couch, onto the cushion next to Sue, and slapped a big wet kiss on her cheek.

She pulled out her high school yearbook. "You want to see some big hair?" showing him the section of senior photos. "Why we felt the need to get our hair fixed at the beauty shop and wear those feather boas is a mystery to me," Sue giggled.

"This doesn't even look like you. Let me see the basketball team," he said, beginning to flip the pages, but stopping to look at a picture of Sue, holding two red and white pompoms high in the air. Finding the team picture, he said, surprised, "Look at those wimpy guys. They're little."

"Hey, I used to date that guy. He's not so little."

"What part are you talking about?" Patrick teased.

Blushing, Sue slapped him on the arm. "You know I'm not that kind of girl."

"Do I ever! I've been meaning to talk to you about that." He leaned over to kiss her.

Sue's stomach churned slightly. She knew Patrick had been exasperated several nights when she had stopped him from going too far and told him she wanted to wait. Although he appeared to accept her decision it was not without some consternation.

Sue shifted her position to be nearer and kissed him back. He drew her even closer and she could feel the warmth of his body and the smell of his aftershave. She knew that resisting him was going to get more difficult.

৵৽৻

Though usually a second-level sport, this basketball season even the visitor bleachers were packed. Some of the overflow hometown backers were forced to sit across the gym, just to gain a seat. Students had to be posted to help reserve the front rows behind the clock keepers for the university recruiters. And the crowd was getting there earlier and earlier. Concession sales were up for the first time in four years because the Cherokee Indian basketball team had the town in a frenzy and Patrick was having his best season yet. If next year was anything like this, he knew he might have a shot at going to a powerhouse university.

Tonight was an especially important game against rival Ranger College who had gone to the Junior College Super Tournament last year in Wichita, Kansas. If the Indians could win tonight they would strip the opposing team of the title and be on their way to represent the conference.

But more than even winning the game, Patrick was excited because Father Andrew had flown in from Boston just to see him play. He had hoped his dad could come also, but he had said he needed to stay home. A couple of guys had quit at the station and they were shorthanded. Patrick knew it probably had more to do with the cost of a plane ticket.

Now, Father Andrew sat high in the bleachers next to Sue. As always, he looked relaxed, self-assured and boyishly handsome. Sharing a box of popcorn, he and Sue talked easily, sharing stories about Patrick as the team warmed up.

"Patrick said you have always been his role model. He thinks a great deal of you."

A pink tinge came to the Priest's face as he smiled. "He's always been my favorite kid in the parish. He's from a great family. All the boys are good boys, but Patrick is special. You know he's the third born and according to Irish tradition, the third child is dedicated to God while he's still in his mother's womb. I always thought he would be a priest someday. He even mentioned it once or twice, but it doesn't appear that way now," he said, winking at Sue.

Stunned for a minute at his revelation, she tried to hide her reaction. "Why? I mean, what exactly does the tradition mean?"

"Over the years, the belief was that the third child would be the ticket into heaven for the rest of the family. Guess no one wants to take any chances today either." He smiled almost mischievously, "after all there probably are more Irish priests than any other."

A choking sensation tightened Sue's throat. That had never crossed her mind. She knew he was a good Catholic, going to mass regularly, but Patrick a priest. That was a thought she had to dismiss quickly. Fortunately, the game had begun and she focused her attention on what was happening on the court. Patrick made the first two points of the game and the crowd came alive, throwing popcorn in the air and chanting, "Indians, Indians, Indians," in a pulsating mechanical drone.

It took two overtimes and four substitutes to replace most of the first string that fouled out, but the Indians won the game 72-70. Patrick was overjoyed as he rushed to hug Sue and then Father Andrew.

"Well, that was worth the flight to Dallas and the bus ride here. What a performance!"

"Thanks," let me get a quick shower and we'll all go celebrate."

"It's already late, Patrick. I'm going to let you two spend some time together," Sue offered, knowing that tonight would be the only chance they would have to visit.

"Are you sure?" Patrick questioned, looking a little surprised.

"Absolutely. I'll have you all to myself when he is gone." She turned and smiled warmly at the priest.

Patrick drew his arms around her and held her close. "Okay, if you really don't mind."

"I'm going home to sleep and you'll wish you had in the morning." She reached to take Father Andrew's hand.

"It was a pleasure to meet you. I know how much it meant to Patrick to have you here. You two be careful." Turning her gaze to Patrick, she warned gently, "See you in English class. Don't be late!"

Patrick and Father Andrew found the quietest place they could in the little bar hidden in the back of the gas station three blocks from the campus. Although many of the townspeople knew it was there, not much was said about it because the proprietor gave substantially to the Baptist Church building fund. The fact that he owned three liquor stores was virtually overlooked as well.

Squeezing into a corner seat, Patrick handed over a beer to his friend and mentor. "I guess I'll treat myself. I try not to drink too much during the season," as he took a gulp of the sudsy draft.

"I think you deserve it."

After twenty minutes of small talk and catching Patrick up on people back home, Father Andrew looked at him squarely. "Patrick, I need to know why when you are around Father Michael you change. You appear so distant. You act as if you don't even like him. You know how much your family loves him, but you just don't seem to share that feeling. I've noticed for a long time. I'm sure everyone else who knows you has."

Patrick looked like he had been hit in the face with a baseball bat. He bit his lower lip, barely daring to breathe. "What has he said?" emphasizing the *he*, unable to conceal his disfavor.

"He hasn't said anything, Patrick," Father Andrew answered gently. "I can just tell and it bothers me, hurts me to watch the way you change when he just enters the room."

Patrick's chest was tight and he felt droplets of sweat forming on his forehead, although the air conditioner was blowing a steady stream of cold air just over his head. He hadn't expected this question. If anyone else had asked him, he might have stormed out angrily, but he paused and tried to regain his composure. The silence was disarming, but the priest waited patiently. He was trained for this type of exchange and Patrick was beginning to feel like a trapped animal.

"I...," he stammered. "I just don't really like him. I question his sincerity sometimes, wondering if he's really who he purports to be. That's all."

"That's all?"

Patrick knew the priest was probing. He wondered if there were other signs with maybe other boys, but he couldn't ask, in fear it would give him away.

"Yeah," he shrugged, worrying that it was obvious he was lying.

"Patrick, there are good priests and those who are not as good. We're all just men. I've always thought you would be a good one, someone who would bring great honor to the church. I think you've allowed these feelings to pull you away from your faith."

"I go to mass," Patrick said quickly in a defensive tone.

"And so you do. Your head or your heart?" he asked benignly, not waiting for an answer. "Be careful not to base your decisions, possibly your future on what you perceive to be a foible of humankind, some personal imperfection of an individual."

"I understand," Patrick said thoughtfully as he swallowed the last taste of his second beer. "Hey, I really appreciate you coming all this way just to watch me play," grateful that he could change the subject.

"I'll tell everybody back home you're a star."

As the two friends stood to leave, Patrick slapped Father Andrew on the back. "You do that, but better than that, tell your old buddies at Notre Dame. I could use some help."

"I'll do that too. I'll tell them you not only can dunk a round ball, but you go to mass every day."

Patrick smiled, but inside he felt like needles were pressing into his gut.

Back in his dorm room, he lay in semi-darkness, glad that his roommate was still out, hopefully for the night. Father Andrew's words had stung him, leaving him in a less than celebratory mood. His thoughts went back to another night that seemed so long ago. It had been a long time, eight long years, almost nine now. In a split second, he was ten years old again. Why couldn't he forget, just put it out of his consciousness? He started to call Sue, but looking at the clock he knew it was too late. She would be asleep, but would be sweet about being awakened. He reached for the phone and then stopped. He had to deal with this alone. Just like he had done all these years. And then on what should have been one of his happiest nights, he buried his head into the middle of his pillow and cried.

౷∾ళ

The weeks raced into December and dread crept into Sue. She had found the holidays almost unbearable since her parents' deaths and now Patrick would be leaving for two weeks.

But there was no ignoring the time of year. The town was dressed for the holidays with cheerful Salvation Army volunteers at the four corners of the main shopping area tolling their bells and wishing the generous a Merry Christmas. A life-size nativity scene sprawled across the side lawn of the First Baptist Church. Bales of hay were scattered strategically along the outer edges so believers could sit and watch a brief enactment of the Christmas story every Friday and Saturday night.

The oil derricks were the big draw. Each was silhouetted in red and green lights as had been the custom since the oil boom in the 1930's. The discovery of oil in the area had once brought thriving camps and rowdy settlements, but that was all gone now. All that remained as a reminder of that era were the few pumping wells outside of town, a half dozen mansions owned by a lucky few big landowners, and the derricks now used only for decorations. People came from as far away as Dallas on the holiday weekends to see the twinkling bulbs dance across the dark East Texas skies. It was impossible not to feel the magic of Christmas.

"All we need is a little snow on the pines and we'll have a scene right out of the movies," Sue said, knowing that scenario was unlikely. It rarely snowed in Townsend and when it did, it was mostly sleet instead of puffy flakes.

"I'll bring you some from New England. How would that be?"

"You just bring yourself back."

Patrick placed a long slow kiss on her mouth before stepping out into the crisp winter air. He stuck his hands in his leather bomber jacket and started to walk down the driveway. When he reached the end, he turned to see Sue still standing at the door.

"I love you. See you in two weeks."

Had she heard him correctly? Several times during the last couple of months, he had come close to saying those words. Or, that's what she told herself, but this was the first time he had actually said "I love you." She barreled through the door and raced to him, forgetting she was in her socks and the concrete was wet from a winter shower. It didn't matter. She fell into his arms. "Oh, Patrick, I love you so much. I'll miss you, but you've just made this my best Christmas ever."

≈∞≪

Spring semester passed so quickly it was almost a blur, a hazy mixture of young love, homework and basketball. Always basketball. But, there was still time for movies and leisurely drives along the oily back roads, tangled in poison ivy and sumac, rarely traveled by even the people who owned the adjoining property. And still time for ice-cream. Sue loved ice-cream. She often thought back of the times she would go to the ice house with her dad. The iceman would take the oversized tongs, picking up what seemed like a giant block of ice and placing it on plastic in the trunk of the car. Then they would have to hurry, drive fast to get back before it started melting. Her mother would just be finishing cutting up the peaches, putting them in the creamy mixture. She would loosen her apron from her cotton plaid shirtwaist dress, hang it on a hook by the sink and join the family outside.

Sue's job was to sit on the old wooden machine, covered with a kitchen towel, while her dad cranked the wheel. Alice refused to sit, but because she wanted to hear her daddy's stories, she stayed close by and added the rock salt when it was needed. Both girls loved to hear his stories, from when he was a boy or how he helped win the war. They had certainly heard them more than once, they had lost count of the times, but they never tired. And when it was time to eat the ice-cream, they were usually joined by neighbors once they saw what was happening in the backyard.

Sue hadn't let herself think about summer. She knew Patrick would be leaving right after exams to work on the lobster boats. Her heart ached as she registered for a sophomore English class and agreed to work for a local attorney, filing briefs and typing letters. She really didn't need the money, but she wanted the diversion, anything to keep her mind busy and off of Patrick. Thinking back, there was never enough money when the girls were growing up. Her parents counted pennies and scraped together enough to send her and Alice to summer camp. But now the insurance benefits and money from the Fireman's Fund made their lives comfortable though not extravagant.

She wrote Patrick every day, long letters, telling anything she could think of that might interest him. Once a week he telephoned, telling her how much she was missed.

The dog days of summer dragged on, lingering well into August making the city pool the busiest place in town. Little kids came to play and cool off, mothers came to watch and worry and give five minute warnings; teenagers came to hang out and preen, beach towels in tow, staying just long enough to check on the latest gossip…who was going steady with whom…who had just broken up. Missing a day at the pool could mean missing a complete courtship! She remembered those days, but now she and her friends were too old to hang out there. Besides, most had summer jobs or were going to summer school. A few had married. One even had a baby. It was strange how one year of college separated youth from something close to adult responsibility.

"I even feel different, Sis," Sue told Alice one night over burgers at the Drive-Up Hamburger Joint. "I look to the future now. Tomorrow is more important than it used to be. Remember when today was all we thought about; now I think about spending the rest of my life with Patrick, wherever that takes me."

They were interrupted momentarily by a teenage server, roller skating up to their car window with fries, burgers and malts. The carhop, who couldn't have been old enough to drive, instructed Alice to roll her window down a few more inches so she could attach the metal tray of food.

"Anything else, Ma'am?"

"Oh, why doesn't she make me feel at least a hundred years old?" Alice said rhetorically as soon as the server skated off, casually weaving between the poles that held the aluminum awning.

"Okay, back to Patrick. Has he ever really said what he wants to do, what he wants to be?"

The question caught Sue off guard. She suddenly realized she didn't know, didn't even know what he planned to major in. Right now they were taking their basics. It hadn't occurred to her how he planned to earn a living for the two children she planned to have or how to pay for the two cars they planned to drive.

chapter 3

When Sue met Patrick at the airport in Dallas the last week of August, he smothered her with kisses and gave her a tiny box. His plan had been to save the gift until dinner but he was too anxious to wait. Curious, Sue nervously removed the wrapping and opened the package. Inside she found a small, gold ring with a note in Patrick's handwriting that simply read: **Promise me!** Immediately she began to cry.

"Hey, now don't do that. Don't you like it?" he asked, worriedly.

"I love it and I love you," she answered.

"Then pledge to me you'll wait for me and someday be my wife. But tell me we can get out of this godforsaken part of the world."

Sue laughed, "I promise you both."

Having spent a year in Townsend, Patrick had finally admitted that it really was a quiet and safe little town where people watched out for each other. When someone was sick, people visited; when someone died, they took food for the family and if a child needed a coat, one mysteriously appeared.

When teenagers acted mischievously, they knew there were consequences. Toilet-papering yards on Friday night automatically meant cleaning them on Saturday morning. Neighbors borrowed a cup of sugar and the local service station owner checked the oil in every car. At night during the summer older people sat in swings on their front porches while the young ones caught fireflies. Signs advertised: **Shop Townsend First** and people did.

Though not especially different from any other small town in the South, Townsend held a quaint charm and simplicity. Those with old money and those with no money coexisted, both equally proud of their homes and children. Small frame and larger two story brick homes sat alongside one another, nestled beneath tall pine, pecan and occasional sweet gum trees. Fragrant magnolias and creeping moss draped oaks dotted front yards where always the St. Augustine grass was trimmed on Saturday. In the spring, gardenias, camellias and azaleas filled the flower beds and gave a sweet scent to the air.

Now driving the two and half hours back to Townsend, Patrick found himself excited about returning. The young couple talked nonstop about what had happened during the summer, discussing what courses they were taking and time schedules for the classes. Even though they had talked about this repeatedly on the phone, they said it all again.

∂∽∾

Worried, Sue went to Alice at the end of September, "Sis, I need your help".

Surprised because it had been a long time since Sue had asked her for advice or a favor, Alice quickly asked what was wrong.

"I know you're probably not going to be happy with me, but sooner or later, most likely sooner, I am going to give in to Patrick…you know…I can't help it," she said, blushing. "I love him and I know it is just going to happen. He really tries hard not to push me, but we're both losing our resolve. Anyway, I need birth control pills, but I just can't ask Dr. Tilton. Yuk. Can you imagine what he might say? Talk about a lecture…I can hear him now," rolling her eyes and jerking her shoulders and head quickly as if to shake off the thought.

Alice laughed, visualizing the old doctor who had delivered them both giving her little sis a lengthy lecture in his slow, precise drawl. Then more seriously she said, "Sue, I'm not unhappy with you. If Dwayne and I hadn't married when we did I wouldn't have held out much longer. God knows he did everything he could to convince me to have sex. Besides, I hear most everybody over at the college is doing it.

"Listen, as bad as things are between Dwayne and me right now, I still want to get pregnant. I have about two or three months of birth control pills you can have. Then we'll go over to Planned Parenthood in Rose Hill and get you set up on your own."

"Thanks Alice, I love ya," hugging her tight, an act she performed often as they had grown extremely close and dependent on each other since their parents' deaths.

Without any written prescription or other knowledge about birth control pills, Sue didn't know much about taking the pill or when it would start being effective. That certainly wasn't something they taught at Townsend High. She popped one in her mouth and felt a sense of relief.

Still cautious, the next few weeks she held Patrick at bay, but in the last week of October she succumbed to his pressure. After sharing a meal at her house and spending a couple of hours on the couch snuggling and watching television, Patrick kissed Sue fervently, his hands sliding under her blouse. Slowly he undressed her. With his shirt off, their bare skin felt good against each other. Patrick reached for her and felt her moist warmth, "Please Sue."

"Okay Patrick, I think I'm ready."

Slightly taken back, he still lost no time in pulling her closer. "Are you sure?"

"Yes Patrick."

"Can we go to your room so we can be more comfortable?"

"Let's go to Alice's room." She had mentally prepared herself for this moment and somehow it caused her less guilt if it didn't happen in her own bed where she had slept since she was a baby. *It was bad enough that she was doing it in her parents' house.* She took his hand and led him to her sister's bed.

"Can we leave a small light on so I can see your face?"

"Sure, just leave the door to the bath open."

He stood with his bare butt to her and with his foot nudged the door open slightly. Crawling back into bed, he kissed Sue tenderly, stroking her body. She loved the way his cologne smelled and the way his skin felt against hers. He was becoming more and more aroused. Sweat beaded on his forehead although the room was cool. Kissing him, she rubbed his moist back as he awkwardly fumbled with a condom. He had been so insistent and sure of himself; now he appeared nervous and clumsy.

∂∙∕

It ended about as soon as it started but both lay there for a long time before talking, spent from the nervous anticipation of the night. *It wasn't at all like she had imagined for so long, plus it hurt—more than she had expected.*

As if reading her mind, he offered, "I'm sorry it wasn't very good for you but this damn mattress didn't help any. What is it made of?"

Managing a smile, Sue realized he had probably never slept on a feather mattress. "It's down, down feathers, don't you like it? Alice and I both have had them since we were little girls."

"Let me just say it interferes a little with the process. You sunk down so far that I...."

Kissing him she tried to convince him that it had been okay. "We'll get better." She couldn't tell if this was his first time or not, but she didn't want to ask, fearing it might spoil the moment or make him think she was unsure of him. Nothing mattered except they had been together and Sue belonged to him now.

They lay together for a long time before Sue noticed Patrick seemed distracted. "Is something wrong?"

"This canopy bed gives me the creeps. It makes me feel like I'm inside of something and can't get out." He stood up quickly, naked in the light.

She turned her face but really didn't know why. They had just had sex, yet she felt funny looking at his body. He sensed it and crawled back in the bed, pulling the covers.

"Are you sorry, Sue?"

"Sorry? Only that I waited so long. As you can see, I'm a little inexperienced in all this. It scares me that I love you so much."

He pulled her closer to him and put his arms around her, holding her tight. "I love you, Sue. Can I stay tonight?"

"I don't think that would be a good idea, but you can take my car and come over sometime tomorrow. I don't need it."

He kissed her tenderly and dressed. She lay there thinking about what had just happened. Soon after she heard him drive away, she fell into a deep sleep, only to be startled by the phone ringing.

"It's me. I forgot to tell you again before I left that I love you. Sweet dreams," sounding more confident now than a couple of hours previous. Smiling into the darkness Sue fell back asleep. She woke before dawn and for awhile lay there thinking about Patrick, knowing she would never be the same.

❧

The next night Sue told Patrick she had gone on the pill in late September.

"Why didn't you tell me?" he asked, leading her this time into her room.

"I knew you wouldn't want to wait and I still needed time" she whispered, turning to him.

Touching her gently at her waist, he looked around. Even with only the light from the hall, Patrick could tell that the pillows and spread were pink; everything was unmistakably feminine with dainty touches all around the room. Several crystal perfume bottles sat squarely in the middle of the antique mahogany dresser. As Sue tossed the extra pillows on the floor, Patrick glanced at the old fashioned painting of an English style garden above the bed. Pink roses and heather along with other flowers he didn't recognize surrounded a tiny cottage in the print. It reminded him of a picture his grandmother had in her living room.

Smiling, he asked, "Do you still need time?"

"Whenever you're ready" Sue answered.

That was all the invitation Patrick needed as he undressed her and then himself. As they settled in between the frilly white sheets, the scallops on the eyelet tickled his skin. He had never been in a bed so crisp. Suddenly he wasn't thinking about the sheets or the walls or anything but making love to Sue. She seemed to melt beneath him as he slid deeply into her body.

"This is how it's supposed to be, isn't it Patrick?" Sue murmured weakly.

For a minute, he didn't answer and she touched his forehead with her fingers, twisting his hair, whispering the question again in his ear.

"Yes, it was too good to be true. Nothing should feel so special—not to me. I don't deserve it," turning slightly and moving his head away from her hand.

"How can you say that Patrick?" reaching over to cup his face. "You deserve the best and we will get better with practice."

He laughed as if what she said surprised him. "You sound like my coach. But I agree, practice does make for perfection," as he reached for her again.

"Oh, no you don't," she whispered, pulling away. "Enough of a good thing for one night, we have the rest of our lives," rising and reaching for her robe. Noticing his frown she wondered if she had said the wrong thing or if he was just disappointed that she had put him off.

"You're going to have to take me back to the dorm you know. You'll need your car in the morning." For the first time Sue wished he had a car.

"Can I take a quick shower first?

"Sure, I'll lay here and wait for you."

When Sue returned, Patrick was sleeping. He looked content and cute to her. "Wake up sleepyhead, tomorrow's a school day."

He dressed quickly without talking. Walking with him to the car, she asked, "Wouldn't it be nice if we were married and you could just stay here?"

Patrick grimaced slightly, not responding.

"I mean, someday" she quickly added, but the look on his face was not lost on her. Sometimes he perplexed her with his reactions and mercurial moods.

When they reached the dorm he was still quiet, almost pensive.

"I love you, Patrick."

Turning to look at her, he paused and with a forced smile, said, "I love you Sue," then quickly jumped from the car, never looking back as he usually did.

chapter 4

Basketball season was once again a flurry of activity and Patrick was excited because he was playing really well. Although his grades were not faring the same, he was managing to keep them high enough for his scholarship to remain intact. Sue told him in East Texas it was called "holding on by the skin of your teeth."

"Another saying from the *foreign land*," he laughed.

Even attending his home games and some of his closer out-of-town games and rarely studying, Sue was making mostly A's with an occasional B. School had always come easy for her and she enjoyed everything about it.

Always the planner she hoped Patrick would know soon after the season ended where he would be playing next year. She realized it would be somewhere out of state and that would be a big adjustment for her. She hated leaving Alice whose marriage was so shaky. No matter, she would follow Patrick anywhere.

"Patrick, what time do you think you'll be finished with practice tomorrow?"

"Probably early since we're leaving at lunch Friday for the tournament in Ranger. Why?"

"I just thought I'd fry some chicken and make some mashed potatoes. You said you really liked my chicken when I fixed it before."

"I did. It was great. Like I told you then, I never tasted chicken like that. Hey, would you mind if I brought Marcus? I told him about it and he said he sure would like to taste it. He misses his mother's cooking. I think he's really homesick."

Sue was quiet and frowned slightly. "Isn't he black?"

"Well, yes, Sue," his voice rising slightly. "He's the little guard from the southern part of Illinois. Why? What difference does that make?"

"In Townsend, a lot. We just don't do that here."

"Do what? Have black people over for dinner?"

She hesitated, "We don't mix like that much here."

"Well, welcome to the twentieth century, Sue. It's 1971. Townsend needs to get with the program," he said, his voice rising in anger.

"For your information, Yankee Doodle, this is not the land of Lincoln or the cradle of liberty, but we have our ways here and that happens to be one of them," she said, shocked at her own words.

"It's a stupid, narrow minded way, just like half of everything else here in this place. You are so far behind, you'll never catch up."

"Maybe not. Things change slowly and eventually they'll change here, too."

"Well, I haven't got the time to wait. Fry your chicken for someone else. Marcus and I will go where we are BOTH welcome," and with that he got out of the car and slammed the door. She sat silent for a few minutes and then started the car and drove home.

She didn't hear from him that night or the next and he barely spoke the next two days after class. Knowing he was leaving and would be gone until late Saturday night she wanted to talk to him before anymore time passed. When she saw him up ahead, she called for him to wait.

"I'm sorry Patrick. Please try to understand. I don't have any problem with Marcus or any of your other black friends. It's just..." her voice trailed off.

"I'm sorry I got so mad Sue, but it is hard for me to understand. Let's just forget about it. We're from different parts of the country and different cultures, but I still love you," and then he smiled, "Even if you are wrong." He leaned down and kissed her. "Let's get some coffee."

❧

Hearing that scouts from several major universities including Notre Dame had been at the last two games, Patrick was ecstatic, knowing he had played well.

Toward the end of November, his coach received a call from a recruiter at Notre Dame explaining they wanted Patrick to visit the campus in Indiana in mid-December. Although there were several other colleges showing interest in him, his mind was only on Notre Dame. To him, playing there would be like a dream come true.

Patrick told Sue about his plans that included flying there, being shown around campus and talking to the coaches. From there he would catch a plane to Boston for Christmas.

"Sue, I'm sorry that you can't come home with me for Christmas. I had thought we might work that out this year."

"It's okay," she stammered, trying to hide her disappointment. This is more important, but I'll miss you terribly."

Unable to mask his excitement about the impending visit, Patrick talked about nothing else, making Sue feel a little left out.

"Would you help me pick out a couple of new sweaters to wear in Indiana?"

"Sure, but you don't need any help. You match colors better than any guy I know. I always like everything you wear."

"Thanks, for years I've had my pick of which hand-me-down clothing I wanted," he laughed.

"That's the beauty of having three big brothers. I'd just like to have a couple of new things for this trip."

"How about Saturday?" she asked. "I don't think the stores in Glenview will still be open when you finish practice today or tomorrow."

"Good, let's go about 3:00 p.m. and we'll eat dinner there where there are more restaurant choices."

Sue couldn't believe what a shopper he was. He looked at sweaters in every store until finally he decided on a brown one with black stripes and a solid blue angora.

Looking at the blue sweater she commented, "That one looks good with your eyes, but at this point I'd say anything would. I can't believe you shopped so long. I'm starved."

He reached for the shopping bag with one hand and took her hand in his other. "You females can't ever figure us guys out can you?"

"You can say that for sure."

"Hey, I know a neat place on the lake about six miles from here that serves great fried catfish. What does that sound like to you," Sue asked.

"Fried what?"

"Catfish, you know."

"I have never heard of that kind of fish. Where did you come up with a name like that?"

Sue laughed, "I don't know. That's just what they're called, but they do have whiskers. My dad fished and he used to bring them home to clean. Alice and I didn't like to see them. They were big and ugly."

"Well, where is this place? If I've tried chopped barbeque and fried squash, I might as well taste catfish," wrinkling his nose.

Pointing, Sue said, "Go that way. I'll tell you where to turn." They drove on the main road for a couple of miles and then turned at the fork in the road onto a narrow oil-based road.

"I never would have found this," Patrick said, looking at the thick underbrush.

"It's not hard once you've been here a couple of times. Over there. Park up there."

Patrick pulled the car onto a pea-gravel covered incline over-looking the lake. "That didn't take long."

"I told you it wasn't far."

They walked down a splintered gangplank to an old weath-ered wooden building with tiny twinkling lights lining the metal roof that had long since lost its shine. Three couples were stand-ing in the screened-in waiting area drinking beer and wine out of plastic cups. Warm for this time of year, people were enjoying being outside in just a sweater.

"You know I usually don't drink much during the regular sea-son, but cold beer sure sounds good. Or maybe it's just that they always taste better in plastic," he winked. "Want one?"

Sue thought a minute, "I think I'll have a white wine."

Grinning, Patrick came back carrying a cup in each hand. "Classy place you've brought me to," handing Sue her wine.

"Thanks, I mean for the wine," she smiled.

"Well the beer's good anyway," Patrick said after taking a swallow.

"I think you'll like the fish, that is, if you keep an open mind. Lobster it's not, though."

"I'm just giving you a bad time. You haven't seen me push away much food anyway, have you?"

"My mom and dad used to bring us here a lot in summer when I was a kid. I wish they could have met you, Patrick. They would have liked you."

"You really miss them don't you, Sue," Patrick asked softly.

Sue swallowed hard, "Yes, and the upcoming holidays make it even more so," almost in a whisper. Then to change the subject she pointed, saying, "See all those stumps? This is the fishing side of the lake; that ramp over there is where people launch their boats. On Saturday mornings this place is crowded with little metal, what we call, *john boats*. Most of them only have about a 25 horsepower motor or less."

"How big is this lake? I've never even known it was here."

"Gosh, I really don't know. This is the smallest part. There are some really nice homes around on the other side, the water skiing side. My parents once owned a little weekend house here, with a wood stove. It was primitive to say the least, certainly nothing like the fancy ones they're building now. We used to come out to swim and ski. I thought it was really cool until I saw a huge water moccasin in the water right where I was swimming. I don't think I've been back in the water since."

He stifled a grin. He had long since understood that people here had some unique ways of describing things, at least unique to him, anyway. "I take it that a water moccasin is a snake."

"Yes, and there are a lot in this lake. Did you give the man over there your name?"

"No, I was enjoying looking around, listening to you, but I guess I'd better sign up. I can't put this off forever," he said, pinching her waist and then walking over to have his name added to the list for those waiting for a table.

"The other thing this lake is famous for is *parking*."

"Huh?"

"You know, high school kids parking, making out in the car. At some point, everybody comes out here at least once on these dark roads to park. It's just a tradition, but it's kinda spooky and scary and really dark. I guess you could say it's a rite of passage for the local kids. Of course, our parents say don't you dare do it and everybody does. Probably most of the parents who grew up here did it too."

"O'Brien," the man yelled, "Your table's ready." He seated them by a window, but by now it was too dark to see the lake's surface except the serene reflection of the twinkling lights.

"This is fun, Sue. I'm glad you brought me."

She ordered the small catfish platter with fries and hushpuppies.

"Okay, here goes. I'll take the large order with coleslaw on the side. And would you bring us another beer and wine, please?"

When the waiter brought the food, it was so heaped with small, crisp filets of fish that a couple fell off on the table.

"Why didn't you tell me this was going to be so big," Patrick asked with his eyes wide with surprise.

"You're a big boy. You can eat that."

"Ummm, this is really good. Now I'm sorry I was so mean. What's the name of this lake?"

"Indian, Indian Lake," she responded.

"Any Indians around here? Everything seems to have some kind of Indian connection."

Sue laughed, "Well, I guess there were at one time, although I don't know that. I really never thought about it. I know there was never any major tribe or anything or we would have studied about it in Texas history. There was a small tribe up by Nacogdoches or Lufkin, about 75 miles southeast of here. I remember studying about it. I think there's still a reservation or something there you can tour."

"I hope I don't get so full I can't have a dish of that peach cobbler with ice cream," he said, licking his lips and grinning. "I'm becoming quite an East Texan, don't you think?"

"I don't think I'd stretch it that far, but I love you anyway," she said, reaching over to pat his hand.

When he finished the cobbler he made a double handed gesture to indicate time out. "I'm stuffed, but it was great." Looking at the reflection the moon was making on the water, they noticed the line of people congregating outside, anxious now to get a table inside, out of what had now become the cool night air.

"I guess we'd better go. It looks like these people could get vicious.

"I enjoyed that Patrick. Thanks for agreeing to try it."

"Hey, I'd do this again."

"Me, too. Would you mind if we brought Alice sometime. I know it's been a long time since she's been here and she really loved it."

"Okay, we can do that," he said with a slight frown. "I need to practice my sparring."

"Oh Patrick, you're just jealous because she can match your sarcasm. Neither of you really mean it, I don't think."

Softening, he responded, "I know. I guess she's the bossy big sister I never had. God knows I didn't need another sibling."

"It's funny, you know. She never bosses me, never really has."

"Bossing me is her way of protecting you," he offered.

"I guess you're right. I don't know what I would do without her. She's been my rock since Mom died."

"She's one tough cookie, that's for sure."

"Yeah, and life hasn't been too positive for her lately, but she'll be okay. She's a survivor. She's always said I was the strong one, but she's really the one."

Taking her hand as they were leaving, Patrick and Sue trudged up the small hill to the car. "It sure was easier going down wasn't it?"

"We were lighter," Sue smiled, moving closer to him, feeling safe and comfortable. Once in the car she said, "To get back to Townsend we go that way. It's a little further back home. I'll direct us, just don't go too fast so I can watch."

He drove with his arm around her, pulling her over toward him as close as he could.

"Turn at that next road to the left."

He did and then onto a smaller curved road.

"No, not here, you're supposed to go straight."

But Patrick eased down the narrow passage and turned off the engine and lights. "I'm not missing my chance," as he covered her mouth with his.

She responded by putting her arms around him tightly. "Just hold me, Patrick. I want to feel your heart beat."

They sat in the car talking and kissing until it began to get cold. "What do the kids do when it is really cold here?"

"They leave the engine running, then turn it off a minute and watch the windows fog up. As soon as it gets cold they run the engine again."

Starting the car, he said, "I think I know a better place for this," driving back to her house.

❧

Before he left for Indiana, Patrick apologized to Sue for not having time to pick out her Christmas gift, but he promised to bring it when he returned second semester. Hoping for an engagement ring, Sue was afraid that might be premature. Besides she reminded herself, *she had his promise ring that she never took off.*

Unlike other visits home, Patrick only called three times during the holidays causing Sue to worry.

Hoping he was busy with family, she tried to stay busy making ornaments for the Christmas trees at the nursing center and the hospital. Sue made a mental note to remember to drive to Rose Hill with Alice to pick up birth-control pills but then decided to call her sister.

"I need to go to Rose Hill this weekend," she told Alice. "I ran out of pills a couple of days ago, but Patrick won't be back for two more weeks anyway."

"Okay, just let me know when. You don't want to take any chances, little sister."

However, in the rush of Christmas, Sue forgot.

❧

When January came, Sue drove to Dallas where Patrick was waiting, holding two small packages for her and his heavy, worn suitcase.

"I missed you," he said, handing her the gifts and apologizing for not calling more often. In one was her favorite bottle of perfume, Youth Dew, with a smaller purse-sized bottle and in the other box was an eight track tape by her favorite duo, The Righteous Brothers. Hiding her disappointment about a ring, she kissed Patrick softly.

"Thank you, Patrick. I've missed you so much." She handed him his presents which he opened excitedly. The first contained a gold money clip engraved with "I love you, Sue" and the second was a dark green cardigan sweater.

"Hey, this will look great at Notre Dame," and though not sure he was being offered a scholarship, it was clear he was counting on it.

❦❧

Even before the semester started Patrick was busy with basketball practice, leaving less time for them to be together.

When Sue questioned him about seeming distant and removed, he told her he had a lot on his mind, plus he needed to spend more time studying to improve his grades.

Although they continued trying to see each other almost every night Patrick began leaving earlier than he had in previous months. When they made love, he appeared to be the same thoughtful, gentle Patrick but Sue wondered if he had the same interest and passion that he had once displayed.

In late March Patrick received the call he had been waiting for and immediately afterwards he phoned Sue. "I got the scholarship; I got it Sue," sounding out of breath.

"Oh, Patrick, I'm so happy for you, for both of us."

"Let's go celebrate tonight at Seafood Inn. Can you pick me up at 7:00?

"Sure," she said, a little surprised since they rarely went out anywhere special on a school night. Excited, but a bit nervous, she wanted to talk about her plans for joining him in Indiana and was anxious to hear his suggestions.

Over dinner Patrick talked more than he had in the last two and half months. "I still can't believe it" he kept saying.

Sue decided when he didn't mention anything about her going to college near Notre Dame that she would broach the subject. "Patrick, you know it is too late in the year for me to apply to a major university like Notre Dame for the fall semester. So I think I'll go talk to the career counselor at the college tomorrow between classes and see what the entrance requirements are at nearby small colleges.

Patrick's expression turned serious. "I've been thinking, Sue. Maybe you should go to a university near here so you are not too far from Alice. I'll be really busy the first semester at Notre Dame. You could fly up a couple of times during the fall."

Feeling heartsick, Sue quickly interrupted, "But Patrick, I want to be near you. I won't be in your way or interfere. I know you will want to concentrate all your energies to the basketball court, but at least I could see your games and maybe we could be together on weekends."

"Sue, I think you would be really lonesome, not knowing anyone. I would worry about you, and I just can't take that on and do what I need to do. This will be the best for now."

Knowing that she should stop pushing the subject, she decided instead to go talk to a counselor so she would have the information to bring up again when Patrick had time to settle down from all the excitement and news of the scholarship.

A week later, when Patrick had not brought up the subject of Sue going to school near Notre Dame, she decided to mention it again. "Patrick, I still want to go to school near you. I'll make friends and be okay. I plan to live in the dorm just so I can meet people."

"Sue, we have already discussed this. I just think it isn't a good idea—not at first. Maybe our senior year you could transfer, but it won't work next year," he said with a slight irritation in his voice. For the next hour they didn't talk much about anything and Patrick said he needed to get back to the dorm. "I'll call Jay to come pick me up tonight. I don't want you to have to get out."

Sue thought this strange, since she had been *getting out* taking him to the dorm for almost two years, but not wanting a fight, she refrained from saying what was on her mind. Already, their relationship appeared fragile; she dared not chance making things worse.

While Patrick waited for his friend, they spoke little and he looked relieved when he heard the loud muffler of the car. "See you tomorrow," he said as he kissed her lightly on the cheek.

Sue sank in the big recliner that had been her father's. Sometimes when she sat here she thought she could still smell his cologne, yet she knew it was her imagination. She longed for that connection again and times like tonight she missed her parents dreadfully. Tears came to her eyes as she thought about them, something she always did when she was worried or sad. Tonight she was both, but even more, she was scared, scared of losing Patrick. Something was bothering him and she could not figure out what.

She started to call Alice, but decided to call her best friend Jane, hoping she was in her dorm room. They had been inseparable before Patrick, but had drifted apart when Sue began spending so much time with Patrick. Since Jane was attending the University of Texas this year, their conversations were even less frequent. Now she really needed to talk and knew Jane would listen.

Just as Sue was about to hang up Jane answered a bit out of breath.

"Hi, what are you doing?"

"Sue, is that you? I can't believe it. I'm so glad you called. What's up?"

"Oh Jane, I'm so worried. Patrick and I are having trouble. I need to talk to you."

"Hang on a second while I set this pizza on my desk! Okay, now tell me what's going on."

Lately any conversations they had, had been about clothes, make-up and gossip around town. Sue had never mentioned that she and Patrick were having sex or discussed details about their relationship. Suddenly, she was telling Jane everything she and Patrick had done in the last two years. They talked like old times for more than an hour. Laughing, they gave each other a pep talk because Jane was having roommate problems. When they hung up Sue felt better.

The next day upon seeing Sue, Patrick apologized for his actions the night before. "Can you pick me up after practice today?"

"Of course, Patrick. At the dorm or in front of the gym?"

"Give me a few minutes after practice to shower and clean up. If you can be out front of the gym about 5:30 p.m., I'll watch for you."

Sue felt better after seeing him and decided she was worrying too much. After classes she rushed home to prepare his favorite meal, chicken cacciatore, as a surprise, knowing he would be starved after practice. Although the formal season was over, Patrick continued to practice on his own with some of the guys from intramurals. *He's definitely committed to being the best*, Sue had thought many times.

Patrick ate like he hadn't tasted food in months. "That was great. Thanks for the surprise." Patrick said, leaving to turn the television on in the den, while Sue continued cleaning the kitchen. When she finished she went in and snuggled up to Patrick on the couch. He kissed her and before long they both had their clothes strewn across the den and were making love on the couch. Patrick seemed like his old self again, smiling and saying tender and loving words to Sue.

When Sue returned from taking Patrick back to the dorm she called Jane again. "I think everything is okay now," as she recounted the night.

"Well, it's not here. She's a witch," Jane reiterated, referring to her roommate, "and a slob too." Both girls laughed.

"I'll never be able to pay the phone bill from last night, so I'd better go. Just wanted you to know. Good luck with the witch," Sue giggled.

"Bye."

"See ya."

Sue slept better that night than she had in a month. The next few days, Patrick was sweet and attentive, but by the weekend he was moody again, seemingly on a rollercoaster of emotions and taking Sue with him.

His dreams were nagging him, and lately they were always the same. They had been before he called Father Andrew about getting his scholarship to Notre Dame, and now they were more frequent. In them, every time he was a Cardinal Bishop in Rome, the closest confident of the Pope. He could even see his own robe, the tiny red buttons. He had only seen one Cardinal in his life and that was three years earlier. Nor had he been to Rome, yet the pictures were vivid. A line of tourists stretched around the Vatican to get in, not with the chance to see the Pope, just to be a part the Holy See.

After the third dream, he called Father Andrew to tell him about the images, to ask his counsel. They had talked for more than an hour and Patrick worried how he was going to pay the bill. And when he hung up he was more confused, further distressed than when he called. *I don't want to be a priest,* he had told Father Andrew, but his mentor was unyielding in his guidance. *We do not always have the opportunity to select our future. Remember, your fate was decided before you were ever born. Other events drive us, direct who we will be as well, and we don't even know it.*

The remainder of the month and into May they fought over things that had never been a problem before. Everything irritated or set Patrick off which was out of character for the Patrick Sue had fallen in love with and known all these months.

With only one week of school left Patrick called Sue and told her he was coming over, that he had borrowed a car from "one of the guys down the hall." For almost two years, Patrick had never used anyone's car but Sue's. *Wonder why he's doing that now,* she thought, a little exasperated. *If it's that easy, I wish he had borrowed one a lot of nights before this close to the end of the semester.* When Patrick arrived he was nervous and serious. "Sue, we have to talk."

"Okay, but don't I get a kiss?"

Ignoring her question he rushed on, "Sue, this is really difficult for me. I have been weighing this since I was home Christmas. I should have been more forthright with you earlier, but I wasn't sure. I've fought it and I thought I could get past it, but I can't."

"What in the world is wrong, Patrick?"

Beginning to cry, tears fell to his shirt. "Sue, we can't ever get married. I... I...I have decided to become a priest."

Sue was shocked. She thought their problems might be another girl or a disagreement with his family, but the idea of his becoming a priest left her completely speechless for a few minutes. "But Patrick..."

Trying hard to compose himself, Patrick said, "I'm really sorry, Sue. I know that I've hurt you, but this is something I have to do. Maybe I'm selfish, but you can't believe how many nights I've spent agonizing over this. I may be making the biggest mistake of my life, but if so, it is not without thought. I love you, but I can't marry you."

"Patrick, I know you go to Mass every morning and you've talked about being raised Catholic, and all, but I never dreamed you were that serious about it."

"It's been in the back of my mind for years. I've toyed with it. There have been times when I thought I would leave the Catholic Church completely and then I would start feeling guilty. It is my heritage, the only thing I know; so the best way I can deal with it is to just give in and be the best priest there ever was—to be everything a priest should be."

"I wish you had shared some of this before…before we had sex," Sue said, her voice shaky but growing louder. "I believed you. I thought we would spend the rest of our lives together." She stopped, now crying almost uncontrollably. She looked down, twisting the tiny promise ring on her finger.

"I know Sue. I was wrong, but I thought I could change the way I felt. I thought I could resist the pull I kept going back to. I'm truly sorry. Can you ever forgive me," he asked, gently turning her to look at him.

Sue wheeled away, "What difference does it make?" She was shouting now, "You're leaving and never coming back. You've made your choice." Then in a softer voice she asked, "Is there anything I can say that will change your mind?"

"No, Sue, nothing."

"Then just leave, Patrick, just leave me alone," she screamed. As he started for the door she yelled, "Get out of my house," slamming the door behind him so hard one of her mother's plates fell off the wall, breaking into tiny pieces. She rushed over and bent down to look at the pile of splintered porcelain. Then she sat down beside it and sobbed.

When Patrick reached the car, he was crying too. He thought he would feel relieved that he had finally told Sue; all he felt was sadness.

Sue cried herself to sleep.

Final exam classes were different than the regular schedule giving Patrick and Sue fewer chances to encounter each other and when they did it was only to exchange glances. Friday night Patrick called, but Sue's excitement of hearing his voice lasted less than a minute.

"I'm leaving tomorrow, Sue. I just wanted to tell you good-bye. I'm sorry; I'm really sorry, Sue. I know you don't believe I could do this if I love you. I do love you, I wish I didn't, but I do."

Having had some time to compose herself from the initial shock of the week before, she answered calmly, "I do find that hard to believe, Patrick. I don't regret these two years. I'm glad I had them with you. Good luck." Beginning to cry as soon as she spoke the word luck, she hung up the phone.

Patrick called right back. "Please Sue, don't hate me. Maybe we can still be friends and you could come see me some time in the fall like we talked about."

"We'll see Patrick," knowing that would not happen.

"Goodnight Sue." She thought how many times she had heard him say that and knew she would see him in the morning, but this time it was final.

"Good-bye, Patrick."

Early the next morning before the sun was up Patrick caught the Greyhound to the airport in Dallas. Confused and tormented by his recent decisions and the hurt he had caused Sue, he wiped a tear as he glanced at the illuminated letters on the sign, "**Leaving Townsend. Come Back Soon.**"

At home where she had lived her whole life, Sue wondered where he might be and why she felt so strangely different inside. Perhaps, it was because she was two months pregnant with Patrick's baby. She hadn't told him because there had been no reason. After all, he had said, "nothing would change his mind."

࿎

chapter 5

Needing Alice more than ever now, Sue asked her for help. "I'm so afraid, Alice, scared of having this baby, of raising a child in Townsend without a father."

"Sue, you know I will be by your side throughout all of this. To hell with what anybody in town thinks. They haven't walked in your shoes! Besides", she continued as she shrugged, "what else do I have but my half-assed job at the nursing home?"

Alice, who was normally fun-loving and carefree had been having a difficult time lately, especially since the divorce was almost final; she had once wrapped her life around Dwayne and that had fallen apart. For a few minutes she was quiet, allowing herself to think back.

From the moment they had started dating in high school, Alice could concentrate on nothing but Dwayne, son of the local funeral home director/owner. Dwayne was wild and one of the few guys in high school who had a new Corvette and the money to go with it. While other businesses were drying up and closing down, Dwayne's father's was obviously doing well. Around town, it was always a joke among the high school kids that Dwayne's dad was always glad when someone died and happy when a baby was born because that gave his business hope for the future. Dwayne's mom ran the town's only flower shop next door to the funeral parlor. No one thought this to be a conflict of interest since she was the first to give a homecoming or prom corsage to any boy who couldn't come up with the $6.00 to buy one for his girl, or to send a pretty bouquet to the nursing home or provide the arrangement for the pulpit at the First Methodist Church.

Alice knew her parents had been disappointed when she announced she was quitting college and marrying Dwayne. They had so hoped she would become a nurse and work at the hospital over in Glenview or maybe meet some young doctor, join the country club, volunteer at one of the schools or head up a community project. But Alice was adamant, as she had always been about anything she wanted, and refused to listen to their pleas. Dwayne was going to take over the family business in a few years and be as rich as any local physician.

Alice remembered their wedding night, an unseasonably warm November night, as if it were yesterday. Three months after her eighteenth birthday, she had married Dwayne Strickland in the First Baptist Church of Townsend which was packed with people and the flowers that Dwayne's mom had provided. Carrying a bouquet of orchids, Alice, in her lustrous white dress had felt like a bride out of a magazine standing next to the handsome rogue. Even with his reputation around town and despite the fact he wore his hair too long by most standards, most adults gave him the benefit of the doubt, believing he would settle down, make a good husband, become an asset to the family business and console the town's mourners.

At the reception, both James and Sarah cried, wishing Alice would have changed her mind. Dwayne's parents beamed with pride at the young couple. His parents had wanted the wedding to be at the Methodist Church where they belonged, with champagne and dancing at the reception. But this was one time when Alice didn't get her way with her parents.

"This wedding is going to be at our church and of course there will be no drinking or dancing, heaven forbid!" her father had stated firmly. Alice's parents had finally consented to allowing both a groom's cake and a bride's cake although they thought it was silly and said so. "No one in recent memory has had a German chocolate cake on one table and a white cake on the other side of Fellowship Hall." her mother said, relenting, but thinking this seemed pretentious. They were not people who liked to look showy. Reminiscing now, Alice could see them, smiling through tears, as she and her new husband drove away with cans clanking behind Dwayne's gold corvette. They didn't smile, however, she was told when they read **"Just Married, Hot Springs Tonight"** written in shoe polish on the rear window. They were modest people in every way.

Soon after the wedding, Alice was ecstatic when she learned she was pregnant. Not sharing her enthusiasm, Dwayne didn't mourn when she miscarried.

"Alice," Sue said, bringing her back to reality, "I am so sorry about you and Dwayne. I don't think I have been as sensitive or attentive to your problems this past year as I should have been. I've been too concerned about my own and that isn't right. You've always been here for me."

"Oh, Sue, don't even think about it. I've had enough pity parties all by myself."

"Men can sometimes be real jerks, can't they?"

"I'd say more like true assholes!" Alice exclaimed.

Sue laughed for the first time in a very long time. "You have a way with words, Alice, but I must admit we probably think alike; I just don't have your graphic vocabulary."

Alice asked, "Did I ever tell you about what Dwayne did to me on his birthday, the first year we were married?"

"No," Sue said, feeling better about her worries as she settled on the couch in Alice's den, reminiscing.

"I was so excited because I wanted to make his birthday special. I even drove over to Spring Hill and bought him a bottle of Crown Royal. I hadn't been in a liquor store since I bought Boone's Farm at RED'S when I was a sophomore in high school. I know that guy at the cash register knew I was using a fake I.D., but he just winked and said 'sure hope you feel as good tomorrow as you look tonight' and put it in a sack. I didn't."

Sue asked, "Do you remember when Mother always sent Daddy to the package store in Spring Hill right before Christmas every year so she could make rum balls? He wouldn't go to RED'S because someone might see him!"

Both girls laughed.

"Yes, God, those things were nasty. What a waste of good rum. Mother never did know when I stole that bottle from where she hid the leftover rum in the flour bin. A bunch of us girls drank it, and then I filled the bottle to the same level with a sugar concoction."

"Alice, you're terrible."

Ignoring Sue's comment, Alice remarked, "Oh, on to the birthday, well since I was a married woman I guess I had started thinking like Mom, not wanting to be seen in a liquor store in Townsend. Anyway, I then went to Sears and bought him a power saw he had been wanting. I should have used it on him, knowing what I know now! I spent hours cooking his damn favorite meal of chicken fried steak, fried potatoes and strawberry shortcake, and what did he do? He came in stumbling drunk at 10:00 p.m., smelling of alcohol and cheap perfume and promptly passed out."

"Alice, you knew Dwayne cheated on you when you two were dating, didn't you?"

"Yeah, I knew about that Tina girl. You know who I am talking about, don't you?"

"You mean the one who did it some nights with lots of boys?"

"Yeah, only one night when I was at the Dairy Queen with some of my girlfriends, I heard the boys setting up what they called a gangbang with her. I guess they figured we couldn't hear since they were playing Elvis on the radio so damn loud."

Alice continued, "I guess Dwayne's a boob guy. Seems Tina and his latest catch, if you can call her that, both have huge ones."

She stopped and laughed. "The first time we were together and he saw a girl with big boobs, he turned, looking, and said, 'Emerson's.' That's the code word the guys used to mean '*em are some big ones*' when they don't want anybody to know what they are saying. I have to admit he could be pretty funny sometimes, but right now I don't see anything very positive about him."

"Yes, I know what you mean, Alice, I wish I could hate Patrick, but I can't."

"Being pregnant with his child doesn't help any, I'm sure. I think it would be harder for me if we had had a baby together. I think the miscarriage is when I started feeling the way I do about Dwayne."

"Why then?"

"Sue, I didn't just lose the baby for some unknown reason. I was in the beauty shop and overheard Mrs. Floyd, you know the town gossip, telling Glenda and Ann that Dwayne was having an affair. She didn't know I was in the back, putting on a smock. Anyway I was so upset I ran out of the shop and right into a parking meter. I hit it hard. It was the very next day when I miscarried."

"Why didn't you tell me, Alice?"

"Oh, I don't know. I felt stupid and ashamed of the way I acted. I didn't tell anybody, but apparently somebody at the beauty shop told Dwayne's mother. She called him and chewed him up and down."

"So, why did you stay with him after that?"

"He cried and begged me, said the affair was just a stupid fling. He told me he would end it and be a good husband. I was dumb enough to fall for it until I found out he was still seeing her. Maybe he really loves her. When his daddy gave him the ultimatum to leave her or the family business, he stayed with her. Tells you something, doesn't it?"

"Yes, it tells me he's the dumb one."

"Yeah, that's what I think about Mr. Priest-to-be. Are you going to let him know once the baby is born?"

"No," Sue responded, sadly. "He made his choice. It's too late now. I love him, but... well, I don't think it would matter anyway. You should have seen his face when he said nothing would change his mind. It was weird. The whole priest deal was weird. Oh well, it doesn't really matter. I'll never figure it out, no matter how much I try to reason through it. Even in his last call he told me he loved me. I'm not sure he had it all completely figured out either."

During the next months, Sue and Alice spent many hours together talking about their futures, both pledging to move away someday, maybe to Houston or Dallas. Together they often shopped Rose Hill for maternity clothes or for baby things since Sue still didn't feel comfortable in Townsend.

"Oh, my gosh, Sue. Look at these booties and socks. Aren't they the tiniest things you've ever seen? I don't know when I have had so much fun. Look at this dress!" she squealed. She held up a tiny yellow pinafore over a white eyelet dress, with a tiny hat that matched the satin sash of the pinafore. "I'm buying this and you can't stop me."

"As sure as you do, I'll have a boy."

"I'm telling you, it's going to be a girl. I just know it!"

"And how do you just know it?" Sue quizzed her sister teasingly.

"Because I just know, now don't ask me anymore questions." Walking over to the hanging mobiles, she spotted one with butterflies, "This is perfect. We have to paint the nursery, Sue. We just can't wait much longer or you won't be able to bend over to pick up a brush!"

"I'm just not ready."

"Well, you better get ready; because this baby is coming out in two months, no matter what. November will be here before we know it." She reached and patted Sue's protruding middle, "I don't know why you are so obstinate. We should have already filled a trunk with blankets and a closet with clothes. No baby in this family is going to be seen wearing only a diaper and that's all, not if I have any say."

Stopping to draw a quick breath, she added, "We haven't even bought diapers or bottles. That's it! I'm stocking up whether you like it or not. Are you sure you are not going to let anyone give you a shower?"

"NO!" she said emphatically.

Sue sighed, "Okay. For you, I'll go along."

"Not for me, Sue, for the baby, whatever her name will be! That's the other thing, you say you haven't come up with a name you like, but I don't think you're trying. Why don't you buy one of those little baby name books. I see them on the wire rack right by the check-out counter for ninety-nine cents, every time I'm in Piggly-Wiggly. How hard would it be to pick out one little measly girl's name?" Alice pleaded.

The sales clerk had walked over and eyed the sisters three times but turned away seeing they were in an obvious discussion. "I'll come back," she whispered on the fourth time.

Tears came into Sue's eyes as she reached to squeeze Alice's hand. "I'm sorry, Sis. I haven't been a very good mother-to-be. You wanted a baby so badly and couldn't and here I am, having one when I shouldn't. I'll be better. I promise."

Hugging her, Alice said softly, "I know it hasn't been easy, but it will all be fine. This little one is going to be very loved and that's what's important. Come on, let's each pick out a dress, a couple of bibs, a sleeper and at least one bunting? Have you seen a baby bed you like?"

Almost bashfully, Sue answered, "I looked at that one the last time we were here," pointing to a white Jenny Lind crib. "It's sweet, isn't it?"

"That's my girl! Now you sound more like yourself."

☙❧

The next week they painted the nursery pale honeydew and arranged the creamy white crib against one wall and a chest of drawers to match on the opposite.

"Where do you think we should put the rocker?" Sue asked.

"By the window so you can show her the birds and squirrels while you rock her."

As Sue's due date approached, Alice thought she appeared even more nervous and moody, but shrugged it off, assuming she was afraid and sad that this very special event was not going to be shared by the man she said she "loved beyond words."

chapter 6

As Alice was leaving to help Sue with the baby, she looked at her watch. At 8:15 she knew she was running late, but she stopped to answer the ringing phone. Her mother-in-law was just calling to say hello and invite her to lunch on Thursday, something she had continued to do even when Dwayne had moved out. Often her mother-in-law had shared her feelings about the young couple's relationship and always she reminded Alice that she loved her like a daughter.

"I was just getting ready to walk out the door. I'm on my way to hold my new niece again. I'm so excited. She is beautiful. She looks a lot like Sue I think; only she has his eyes."

"He did have beautiful eyes, but it would probably be easier for Sue if the baby didn't look anything like the father," Alice's mother-in-law added. "What did she name her?"

"Faith."

"Faith what?"

"You mean a middle name?"

"Yes, I'm guessing Ann."

"No, just Faith, nothing else. It almost seems symbolic, like the baby represents that link to him. But, I think that any hope for his returning is futile. I haven't asked her anything though. I know what you're thinking, seems weird in East Texas not to give a child a middle name, doesn't it?"

"Well yes, everybody here has two names whether they use them or not," her mother-in-law answered.

"Like Sue Ann and Mary Alice," she said with a laugh. "It's just customary, but I don't think Sue thinks this whole deal is very traditional or customary. She's been really down lately."

"But strong, don't you think?"

"Yes, she did put his name on the birth certificate. She said she wants the baby to have his last name; even though he's gone, he was a part of Faith, whether he wanted to be or not," Alice added.

"I know it's not been easy in a town like this with so many hypocrites looking down their noses. Did she ever let him know she was pregnant?"

"Nope, she said she didn't want him to come back just because he felt guilty. He would always resent her for messing up his plans. That wouldn't be any better life for her or Faith and certainly not for him. But she said she doubted that it would really make any difference. That's what he had said."

"I'm happy that she has this baby. It's about time something good has come into both your lives. I can't wait to see little Faith. I'm sending the cutest yellow ceramic bootie filled with fresh flowers over later this morning."

Alice said quickly, "If you can, just bring them. We will be there all day. I'm stopping by Daylight Donuts for donut holes and pigs-in-the-blanket for our mid-morning coffee. Come join us. I know Sue would love that."

"I'll try; I'll just have to see how busy I am. I have the shop by myself today, but if it's slow, I'll put a sign up that I'll return later."

"Okay; thanks for calling and try to come."

"If I don't, give Sue my love and tell her I'll see her and the baby soon. Bye now."

Pulling up to the house where she had grown up, Alice was overcome with emotion. Her parents had put so much into this place, adding the little sunroom in back. The roses were still pretty, even if showing a little neglect. Her dad had nurtured the tiny pines he planted when they first moved in, and now they were taller than the second story. Sweet gum balls and pine cones sprinkled the lawn as squirrels scampered to find a stray acorn from the neighbors' yard. It had been years since the girls had stuck toothpicks in the sweet gum balls from the big tree in the front yard and sprayed them gold and silver for Christmas decorations. Now only the remnants of a life built together were left. The last few years were sad ones for this house, but there had been many happy times here. Today would be especially wonderful because there was new life. Alice jumped out of the car and ran into the house shouting: "Sue, where are you and my sweet bundle of Faith?"

Finding Faith lying in her cradle crying and wet, Alice began running room to room and then into the backyard, yelling and looking for Sue. Hurriedly she went to the neighbors and each time a front door opened Alice screamed "Have you seen Sue? Have you seen Sue?" but Sue was nowhere to be found.

Nothing indicated a forced entry, not that anyone in town locked their doors. Nothing seemed awry. Sue's clothes were still in her closet. Faith's morning bottle was empty in the sink.

When Alice reached to pick up Faith, a tiny gold ring that she remembered Patrick had given Sue last fall fell to the floor. Almost in hysterics, holding Faith, Alice called the police and waited.

༄ঙ৽

Alice refused to leave the house for a week, thinking any minute Sue would either come walking through the front door, or the police investigation would yield a clue. Meanwhile, she fed, bathed, changed and burped the baby girl, tending to her every need. Alice's face was the first thing the baby saw every time she opened her eyes and the last thing when she closed them. It was her touch, smell and voice that filled Faith's world, and finally, just eleven days after she was born, Alice took the child with all her belongings and moved her to Alice's home, the only home the child would ever know.

From the first hour they were settled in, friends began to stop by with cards, well-wishes, gifts, food and advice.

Alice counted seventeen sleepers, six dresses, three blankets, a crocheted afghan, two bassinette sized quilts, socks, booties, diapers, countless toys, stuffed animals and miscellaneous bottles, bibs and rattles Neighbors brought casseroles, homemade bread and all manner of desserts: two blackberry cobblers, a banana pudding, oatmeal cookies, an Angel food cake and one of Grammy B's coconut cream pies.

"What am I going to do with all of this?" a bewildered Alice asked her mother-in-law.

"As soon as everybody leaves, we'll deliver it to the nursing home," she whispered, "except we're keeping that pie!"

"Have you ever seen so many cute baby things?"

"Everyone has been so thoughtful. Did you know the bank started a college fund for the baby?"

"That's unbelievable, but what's more unbelievable is that Sue's gone and we may never know what happened. How could anybody do harm to someone like her? It's just unfathomable."

"I know, honey." She hugged Alice and drew her close. "I'll help you put all these things in the spare bedroom if you like."

"That would be great. Would you read the cards off each gift so I can make a list? I want to send thank-you notes."

"You bet." She walked over to the kitchen cabinet for a pen and tablet. "This could take a while," she said, smiling.

Two hours and two pots of coffee later, the women had finished the list and were arranging the closet of clothes according to sizes.

"I'm going to need to find a place for some of this. Did you ever decide who sent the silver spoon?"

"No. There wasn't a card inside."

"I feel bad not thanking someone. They'll think I'm rude."

"Maybe they wanted to be anonymous."

"You think? That doesn't sound like people around her," Alice said, laughing. "It's a puzzle, but I don't have time to worry about a little ole spoon. It appears I have a girl to raise!"

PART TWO
Wondering and Wandering

To miss the path, to go astray
To wander blindly in the night
But searching, praying for the light
Until at last we find the way...

chapter 7

Notre Dame, 1972

Immediately the authorities found Patrick in Indiana and questioned him about Sue's disappearance. His coaches and teammates said it wasn't possible that he had anything to do with her disappearance since he was playing in a pre-season non-conference tournament the day she was discovered missing as well as the day before and the day after.

Heartsick that something terrible had happened to Sue and feeling responsible, he was equally distraught to learn she hadn't told him about the baby.

On Friday night he borrowed money from his roommate and flew to Dallas Saturday morning. From there he took the bus, probably, he figured the same one that had taken him back and forth to Townsend the two years before. Though the landscape hadn't changed with miles and miles of trees and exits to a couple of towns off interstate 20, Patrick couldn't help but think it was different.

When he stepped off at the station, memories poured down on him like a warm summer rain. *This is really where it all started.* He thought about his first day when he was filled with anger and bitterness, when this was the last place on earth he wanted to be. Then he met Sue. She had made him comfortable here. Now he was adrift, a stranger again. He wasn't sure why he had come.

෨෴

"I'd like to meet with Chief Murray when he's available," Patrick told the receptionist at the police station.

She glanced up from filing her nails and Patrick noticed how young she looked to have bleached hair. He didn't know much about the process, but it seemed that something might have gone wrong, maybe too much orange color in the mixture, or it could be the black roots and the lighting. He wasn't sure, the lighting was definitely deficient.

"You have an appointment?" she asked, indifferently as she chewed gum and flicked the file against the metal desk. Her long, dangly earrings swayed to the rhythm of her chewing, reminding Patrick of one of those plastic bobble-heads he had seen in the back window of a Chevrolet sedan.

"No. I don't. But I don't mind waiting."

"Well, you'll have to. He's not here."

"Do you know when he might be back?"

"Nope." She turned to study her long nails and reached for a bottle of polish.

Patrick couldn't help but notice the name, Razzle Dazzle Raspberry. It didn't exactly match her personality or anything else in the drab room. He had visited the police station where his dad worked a number of times and it was nothing like this. Though it wasn't a fancy place by any measure it looked like a fine parlor compared to this room. These walls, once an olive green were now long faded and water stained from an apparent ceiling leak.

He took a seat, picked up a two year old copy of National Geographic, and flipped through the pages.

The steady drip of water from the window unit into a rusted metal pan, along with the constant smacking of the receptionist's gum, were unnerving him. He expected the air conditioner to stop at any minute and for her to blow a bubble. He was right about the bubble.

When an hour had passed, he stood up and walked the couple of steps to her desk. "Do you think you could find out how long it might be before the chief comes in?"

"Is it an emergency?" she drawled sarcastically.

"No, but it could be," he caught himself. "I mean I have to leave tomorrow."

"Shouldn't be much longer. He's probably over at the coffee shop. He usually goes there about this time, most days."

Patrick tried to hide his agitation, but knew he wasn't doing a very good job when the door opened and the chief walked in.

He strolled by Patrick without a word, tipped his hat to the receptionist and went into the first office past her desk.

She mumbled something Patrick couldn't hear but the man soon came to the door.

"You wanted to see me?"

"Yes, sir. I'm Patrick O'Brien. I…I'm…"

"I know who you are. Used to watch you play ball. Sit down," he said gruffly as he motioned to the only chair. "So, why'd you come back?"

"I'm not sure," trying to make eye contact with the officer's steely stare. "I thought maybe I could find Sue."

"We've looked everywhere," he said, softening a little. He was a giant of a man, solid for his sixty-five years, except for the slight paunch that had developed around his middle. His hair was gray and cropped short.

"We have absolutely nothing to go on, not a single clue. No fingerprints, no blood, no note, no missing jewelry or money and no body. It's like she walked off into thin air, except I've known that girl since she was a baby herself. I was a pallbearer at her father's funeral. She wouldn't have left that baby for anything."

"But there has to be something. What about her car?"

"In the garage. No money was withdrawn from her account. Nobody saw her going anywhere. We checked with the train conductor. He couldn't remember any young woman. He said a couple of older women, a soldier and a man in his early twenties bought tickets. His receipts all matched. The bus didn't run that

day. The taxi company hadn't run in two days of the disappearance."

The chief turned to face Patrick, his penetrating eyes focused
directly at him. "I wouldn't normally be telling you this, but your
coaches convinced me they could account for you every minute
of the time she disappeared."

"Sir, I would never do anything to hurt Sue."

"Son, you could have gone all day without saying that. Anything else? I'm a busy man."

Patrick looked around, knowing that there was no one else
waiting, but he knew his time was up. "One more question and
I'll leave. How's Alice holding up?"

Rising to his feet to let Patrick know he was dismissed, the
chief replied, "She's strong, like her daddy. And I understand
Dwayne's parents are helping out. Are you going by to see the
baby?"

Patrick shifted his gaze and he could feel the color drain
from his face. "I don't think that would be the best thing. I think
Sue would use her old expression and say 'Let sleeping dogs lie'.
I'd rather you keep this visit between us." A lengthy silence fell
on the room.

"Glad I'm not the man who had to make that decision.
Thanks for stopping by," as he led Patrick out of his office. He
turned without as much as a handshake.

૭ન્જ

It didn't take Patrick long to fall back into a routine at Notre
Dame. He liked the small classes and diverse population, but
most of all he enjoyed the Catholic atmosphere and of course,
basketball. He learned quickly, however, that despite his height
and talents, he was a small fish in a big pond. It was a humbling
experience for someone who had been the star for two years. If

anything, it had caused him to grow more introspective or had he matured? He wasn't sure.

One year faded into two and then the third and Patrick's days of playing college basketball came to an end. In some ways that was good because it gave him a chance to concentrate on improving his grades and taking the harder courses he had saved. He hadn't planned to extend his stay this long, but his coach had insisted that he couldn't take more than twelve hours a semester.

The best part was that he was able to move into an efficiency apartment and out of the dorm. His place on the third floor of an old brick building that had been a warehouse was only 280 square feet with a small refrigerator, a hot plate and the smallest bathroom he had ever seen. The Murphy bed enabled him to have a few feet of walking space, but he didn't have to share a single inch of anything with anybody for the first time in his life.

To fill his free time he took a job at a coffee shop two blocks from campus. He had come here often late at night over the past two years and become acquainted with Tony, the owner, a slight, balding man with dark circles under his eyes and whose pasty, translucent skin looked ghostly. He wrote poetry and most nights played the guitar and sang ballads for the local group that hung out at the Java Café. Patrick liked it because Tony provided newspapers from major cities around the world, plus a large number of magazines. None were for sale, a customer needed only to buy a cup of coffee and he could linger and read for hours. Professors stopped by for morning coffee, but students dropped in all hours of the day and well into the night. Tony usually closed up around midnight, but had been known to stay open all night if he had an audience.

Patrick noticed his friend had been slowing down lately and worried if he might be sick. He wasn't sure how old the little Italian guy was but had once heard him refer to being with his parents on Ellis Island in 1906. Whatever, it wasn't like Tony to be late opening.

Patrick was doing his morning jog and stopped at the café at 6:45 only to find the door shut tight and the lights dim. When he came back later in the morning he found Tony there, but there was no clip in his step.

"I'm okay," he told Patrick. "I overslept. Can't a guy sleep a little for God's sake?" he added in his raspy gravelly voice, enhanced by a two pack a day cigarette habit.

Smiling, Patrick said, "Guess I didn't know you ever slept or ate for that matter."

"Every now and then I do a little of both."

"I can take on a few more hours here, Tony. You don't even need to pay me." Concern filtered through his voice.

"Thanks," Tony said, patting Patrick on the shoulder. "I'll be all right, really. But, you can put those newspapers on the shelves," pointing to the bundles on the floor in a corner.

Patrick glanced at his watch and noted it was almost 8:30. These papers were always in their place by opening, but he said no more. Tony was a proud and private man. The next day he was dead from a massive heart attack.

Stunned, Patrick and many of the other patrons and employees just hung around the little shop once the maintenance man opened the door and said that's what Tony had always said he wanted if something happened to him.

A day later his son and daughter-in-law arrived from California, locked the doors and hung a FOR SALE sign on the front window. Although it sold within a week and reopened within a month, Patrick never returned; it would have been too painful without Tony's voice.

❧

With only a week remaining before graduation, Patrick called the police station in Townsend again. Ironically it had been three years to the day since he left and almost two and a half years since Sue's disappearance.

"Still nothing," the chief said quickly. "We've done all we know to do, but we haven't closed the case. Something might show up one of these days, but I doubt it. I am retiring in a couple of months, and none of the younger guys will be as interested as I was. The new chief is not from around here," he added. "I wish I could say something to make this easier for you. I wanted more than anything to solve this case, more than any case I have ever been involved with, but apparently it isn't going to be on my watch."

Patrick was silent as the chief continued, "You sure have a pretty little girl, son. They say she has your eyes. Now, if I don't talk to you again, Good luck up there."

"Thank you for all you've done, sir," Patrick said, a lump growing in his throat. He wanted to say more, but stopped short, wished the old chief his best and hung up the phone.

chapter 8

Waiting to leave for Europe and to study in Rome was difficult for Patrick. For months he had not allowed himself to think about his upcoming travel, but now he was wondering if the day would ever arrive.

Because Patrick was from a family of modest means, touring Europe and studying in Rome would have never been possible had his Uncle Robert not left him, along with his siblings and cousins almost $100,000.00 each. Robert, Patrick's paternal uncle, was not held in high regard by the other members of the family, due in part, to his reputation for womanizing and bootlegging. Known about town in the forties for his tall stature, good looks and outgoing personality, it would not be unusual to find Robert partying among Boston's rich and famous and befriending many of the young debutantes in the city.

Although he held no real or "respectable job" as Patrick's father Joseph, described it, he always managed to have a large roll of hundred dollar bills in his pocket which intrigued the young ones in the family and irritated their elders. So it came as no surprise, to anyone, when Robert married a very rich woman from one of the Brahmin families in Boston.

One night when he was young, Patrick had overheard his parents telling a friend about Robert and Kathleen. "She may have been rich, but she certainly wasn't pretty," Joseph had told the friend.

Surprised because he had never heard his father talk like that about anyone, it had become clear to Patrick very early that Joseph did not approve of Robert's activities or lifestyle. The most telling sign was when he heard the friend say, "I understand she died in childbirth because the baby's head was too big for her to deliver."

"We never really knew for sure, but if that were the case, that baby was probably just like Robert. I never saw a man acquire a *big head* quite as quickly as he did when he put his hands on money." His dad had responded.

As it had turned out, Robert's chance to enjoy her money didn't last long when he was killed inside a billiard hall one night just months after Kathleen died. When the authorities questioned the other men in the hall, no one had seen anything or anybody. According to the story, everyone present kept to the theme that since dead men don't talk, the death was ruled an accident, and Robert's assets, according to the will, were divided among the nieces and nephews to be awarded as each turned twenty.

His dad had said that although Kathleen's family was not at all pleased that all that Brahmin money was going to educate fourteen Catholic children, what disturbed them the very most was the amount of money left. No one ever knew what happened to the bulk of what Kathleen left Robert, but the guess was that his gambling debts exceeded his monthly dividends.

Patrick felt badly that his dad did not inherit any money from his own brother and upon receiving his allotment, he asked his dad to take half. He still remembered his dad's reply.

"Son, your mother and I have everything we need. You have a life before you. Tainted as that money is, it will allow you to do something that you otherwise would never have experienced, opportunities your mother and I never had. So enjoy it."

chapter 9

Italy, 1975

Two days after graduation, Patrick boarded the plane. When he took his seat he found himself next to an attractive well-dressed, middle aged woman, with upswept black hair, who immediately introduced herself and began talking.

"Hello, my name is Carmella Mordini." Before the plane left the ground he learned she lived about half-way between Rome and Florence in Tuscany. "We are close to the cusp of the Lazio, Umbria and Tuscany regions." Her English was flawless but her Italian accent beautiful. "And you?" she asked.

He had wanted to introduce himself earlier, if nothing else to be polite, but she had not given him the chance in her enthusiasm. "O'Brien, Patrick O'Brien. I am from Boston, or just outside of Boston, really," as he reached to connect his seat belt.

"What brings you to Rome? Or is this just a layover?"

"Well, both I guess. I'm going to study in Rome beginning in three months, but first I'm going to travel around, just go wherever the rails or my feet take me. For once in my life I'm going to be impulsive, unencumbered," Patrick stated, hoping his nervousness of flying internationally did not show.

"That is wonderful. So where will you go first?"

"I think Florence, or maybe Assisi."

"Then it is settled. You will come with me. I will call my husband from the airport and tell him I am bringing another man home," she said laughing.

Stunned by the swiftness of her offer, Patrick countered, "We have a ten hour flight. You should perhaps wait until the ninth hour and see if you still like me before you invite me. And, what if your husband asks why you are dragging this American stranger home?"

She laughed again, "He is accustomed to my eccentricities and my big heart. You should see how many homeless cats and dogs I have taken in," she teased Patrick.

"Tell me about your home?"

"It is fabulous, or it is to me. We have a 260 hectare estate and country manor, 16 kilometers outside the little town of Farina. I think that is about 640 acres as you figure it in the States. We grow olives and sell olive oil to many markets throughout Italy. We also have a small vineyard, but we make and keep the wine for ourselves or give it to friends. And Stefano, my husband, grows just enough tobacco to make his nasty cigars."

Patrick was intrigued, "It must be beautiful."

"So very beautiful, it is like an oil painting in progress. Some days my view from the villa is a vast emerald panorama; other days it has an amber cast, but when the rains have come it almost has a tinge of turquoise. The landscape changes, depending on the direction of the sun or the thickness of the dew. Tuscany is a kaleidoscope, one of the most beautiful places in the world, a jewel no less!" she said, sounding like a young woman in love.

Thinking he might read or even sleep a few hours, Patrick had brought a book, but it looked as though neither would be possible. However, he found himself enjoying listening to this interesting, unconventional, exuberant woman. He began to relax, listening as she continued talking about Italy. *At last I am going to a real foreign land. Sue would have smiled at that.*

Carmella finally took a breath and a break, "So, tall Irishman, tell me who you are?"

Smiling, Patrick began explaining his background, his basketball scholarships, life at Notre Dame and more about his study plans. He didn't remember talking this much at one sitting in his entire life, but Carmella, who herself was intriguing, seemed sincerely interested. She, he knew, was old enough to be his mother so when she patted his knee as she talked, which she often did, he didn't take offense or think she was being flirtatious. She was absolutely one of the most endearing persons he had met. Generally anyone this forceful or pushy would have been a total turnoff to Patrick causing him to turn inward, but he found himself laughing at her stories and answering her array of questions.

"Let's have a cocktail, Patrico," she said as the flight attendant approached them. "At home, it is vino, vino, vino. Let's be naughty and have a Scotch and water. The Scots—they were your neighbors, right?"

Patrick smiled, although he had not been to Ireland or Scotland, he understood and said, "Why not? When going to Rome, do as the Romans do!"

"Just bring us each two please and you will not have to check on us so often," she told the attendant.

"Tell me about Stefano."

"Patrico, I am the luckiest woman in the world, and he is the most handsome, generous man anywhere in Italy.

Patrick was a bit amused because no one in his twenty-two years had ever changed his name, but surprisingly he liked the way it sounded.

"Stefano was a friend of my uncle Gianni whom I came to visit as a young girl."

"What do you mean; are you not from Italy?"

"I was born there, but my father left Italy when I was two, thinking he would find his fortune in America. He and my mother moved to the San Francisco area where he shifted from job to job. But he would not give up, or he wanted to save face and not go back to Italy broke and jobless, so he just stayed.

"My mother was very unhappy; when I was fourteen she brought me back for a visit, and we stayed with her baby brother Gianni. We lived with him for awhile and my mother finally wrote a letter to my father telling him she was not leaving; that she loved him very much but America held no hopes for her, and she begged him to come home to Italy. About six months later he did come back, but he was a defeated man. He had failed in America and missed his chances in Italy. He had a heart attack and died at thirty-five."

Stopping just long enough to sip her drink, Carmella continued, "My mother's family took care of us after that. Her parents had a great deal of land and my uncles worked very hard. I think that is why they never understood my father. He was too much the dreamer for them."

"Anyway, Uncle Gianni was ten years younger than my mother, but they were very close. My mother was a wonderful cook so always he had his sidekick Stefano coming to dinner. I fell madly in love with him and as they say, the rest is history. At eighteen, I married him. He was twenty-four and already beginning to acquire land and grow anything he could think to plant."

"Do you have children?" Patrick asked in a quieter tone, noticing than many of the other passengers had placed their eyeshades on in preparation to nap.

"In eight years I miscarried six times and then finally I had the most beautiful baby girl, Elisabette. She is a fashion designer in Milan, the apple of her father's eye and the darling of her mother's heart. We tried many times, but she was the only one God gave us. She is very special," Carmella said finishing her second scotch and water.

"Were you in the States for vacation or business?" Patrick asked, astonished at himself that he was asking so many questions.

"Business, my dear, we are expanding our line of olive oils to the States so I was in California for three days and then in New York. I have a wonderful friend who spends time at the Cape so we met in Boston. It seemed to make sense to fly out of there and I am so glad I did or I would have not met Mr. Patrico."

Three hours had passed and as many Scotches had been con-
sumed by both travelers. By the time dinner was served, Patrick
felt a little dizzy. Never remembering drinking three Scotch and
waters in such quick succession, he was glad to see food, even
airline food.

After dinner, the captain lowered the cabin lights and Carmella dozed off. Patrick saw this as his one opportunity as well.
They both woke to breakfast being served.

"I just ate dinner," Carmella laughed. "How can this be?"
They had each slept almost five hours and were only about two
hours from Rome.

"I am more thirsty than hungry," Patrick said, arranging his
napkin for a bite of breakfast.

"Do not eat too much, love. We will have lunch, and tonight
Carmen will prepare the most glorious meal you will ever have
eaten."

"It sounds as though you really are taking me to your villa."

"Patrico, you are young, you know no one. We will introduce
you to Italy the right way. You are our guest as long as you like."

"But why?" Patrick could not resist asking.

Carmella paused, one of the only pauses, he thought, since he
boarded the plane. "When you sat down you just looked somewhere between lost and excited. Your mannerisms told me you
are a good boy who is striving to be a good man, but you're still
a clean cut shaggy, red headed kid with the most gorgeous blue
eyes. You look in search of discovery. I guess it is a mother's in-
stinct, but it appeared that you could use a little gentle prodding
to find yourself. I am just the Italian mama to lead the way. And,
you are going to love Stefano. He will show you his vineyard, his
olive trees, his cattle and his nasty tobacco and give you a map
that you can trust. When you have seen Italy, you must come back
and tell us your thoughts."

After the plane landed, they both picked up their luggage and sailed through customs. Like a small child, Patrick followed Carmella to the parking area that housed her Mercedes.

"Let's go Patrico; it will be your own *Roman Holiday*, just a few hours away."

Those who knew Patrick would never have believed he was going home, with an almost stranger. Patrick could not believe it himself, but in a way it seemed like he had known her for years.

"Oh, I almost forgot. Come with me to the phone. I must call Stefano!"

Standing off to one side of the pay phone, Patrick heard her say "Buon giorno, Carmen," although he didn't understand any of the conversation after 'Good Morning." For a moment he was lost in thought, watching a swarm of people pulling luggage, boarding buses, hailing cabs and hugging loved ones. Suddenly Carmella's voice brought him back as he took a long step to catch up with her and open her door.

"Stefano was already outside so I just told Carmen to tell him. Also, she will have a small lunch for us. We should be there by 12:00 or 12:30 p.m. depending on the traffic from here around Rome, but we will miss the worst of it," she said as she pulled out onto the airport exit. "Now we are finally on our way."

"Those are the smallest cars I have ever seen. They look like they came out of Cracker Jack boxes."

"Yes, but they are quite good for Rome, if you can say that about any car for Rome. Rome is a terrible city to drive in; terrible traffic, no places to park, pedestrians everywhere. Everyone is manic. If you are going to be in Rome as long as you think, then you should buy a scooter and sell it when you leave. But walk when you can. That is the easiest," she said as she swerved past a car that had taken to the shoulder.

"You certainly drive fast," grabbing the handle on the door.

"That is why they build roads, my dear, and cars," as she flashed her lights and passed another car.

Patrick looked back at the stream of cars, "Do you always drive like this?"

"Oh no! Sometimes it is much worse," she said, laughing loudly. "Let us pull in here and buy a cappuccino for our drive."

"That sounds good. I'll get them. At the rate you are driving, we will have to drink fast," he grinned at her.

"Extra espresso in mine."

Back on the road Patrick said: "I'm a little nervous that Stefano will be upset that I am coming with you."

"Darling, do not worry your Irish brain another minute. Stefano will be delighted. You will see. Do you not think I know this man to whom I have been married almost all my life?" she asked, and it was obvious to Patrick that she loved him as much or more now than as a girl of eighteen. "You will like Carmen as well, although you will understand her very little. Oh, but do you speak French?"

"No, I know a few words, but very few. It is like my Italian and Spanish. I took Latin in high school. I wish I knew Italian, but I plan to study it in Rome with my other courses. Does Carmen speak French?"

"Yes, it is her first language; Italian is her second. Her mother is French and her father Italian. Her parents worked for us before Carmen was even born. They are still with us. Enrico and Claudia are part of our family."

"What do they do?"

"Enrico is Stefano's right hand. He does everything. Claudia was our housekeeper for many years, but when Carmen turned seventeen, Claudia turned those duties over to her. She is a marvelous cook and she is teaching Carmen. Together they cook our meals three nights a week. Because Stefano and I both love to cook, we do the remaining nights. Carmen has a little sister Gigi, so we believe they need to be home together some. Family, that is very important in our culture. Look at the vineyards, Patrico. They are just beginning. The closer we get to our place, the more you will see. When you leave us you will see even more."

"Does Stefano make red or white wine?"

"Both, but much more red; most of our wine is a blend of Sangiovese and Merlot. He makes some Chianti with a blend of our Sangiovese and Canaiolo which he buys from growers in various parts of the Chianti region. Our white is usually a Chardonnay/Pinot Grigio blend, much more Chardonnay than Pinot, probably about 70/30. I have not even asked you. You do like wine, do you not?"

"Yes, but I am really just learning. In college, during off season, we drank a lot of beer, but now I'm trying different kinds of wine and I find I like them all. I'm sure after a few months in Italy I will know much more."

"I forget you are from the States. Our children start drinking wine quite young, and we think nothing of it."

"I forgot to mention that the cappuccino was excellent," Patrick said.

"Yes, we have the best. We are almost home, Patrico," as they turned off the main highway down a much smaller road. This is all our land, but the villa is still over a kilometer from here."

"It is truly beautiful, Carmella."

"It gets even better," she said, blushing with pride.

Pulling up to the villa, Patrick was awestruck. In front of him was a magnificent structure of muted brick and stucco. Six oval arches graced the front at the ground level with twelve matching, but smaller ones on the second level. From each flowed the most beautiful mixture of red, white and pink flowers Patrick had ever seen. The backdrop was a combination of rolling hills, olive trees, grape vines in perfect rows and a small lake. Beyond the main house were smaller bungalows with matching architecture.

Carmella began honking as soon as the manor came into view. Immediately, two women, who Patrick assumed were Carmen and Claudia, came running out. Soon everyone was hugging and kissing and talking at once. When Carmella introduced Patrick, they each hugged him without hesitation. Then from around the side of the house came a large, balding man with a barrel chest and a voice to match.

"Carmella, I have missed you terribly," he said, his eyes sparkling as he whispered something in Italian, and she sank into his bear hug like a little girl.

Surely this is not Stefano, Patrick thought; this is certainly not what he had pictured from her description.

Bursting into his thoughts, Carmella called, "Patrico, meet my darling Stefano. I told you he was the most handsome man in the world, now did I not?" she said, kissing the burly man again.

Stefano smiled broadly and offered his hand to Patrick.

"You did, indeed, Carmella," Patrick said, grinning.

Stefano laughed, heartedly and knowingly.

"My beautiful Carmella, she does it every time. She describes me and then brings people home and they do not know what to say, but their face says it all."

"But you are handsome, my love."

Patrick could tell she truly thought he was. He had not known this woman but twenty-four hours and he already knew that beauty to her was everywhere. She saw everything and everybody as a special creation, except maybe Stefano's cigars.

"Sir, I apologize for intruding like this."

"Nonsense, if Carmella likes you so will I, although there was that one cat I was not too fond of," he teased. "It is Patrico, right?"

"Sure," not knowing what else to say.

"Then you make yourself at home and stay as long as you like. I will show you to your quarters," putting one arm around Patrick and picking up a suitcase with the other.

"I'll take that," Patrick said, reaching to take the suitcase.

"You have one, I have one," Stefano answered, pointing to the other duffle.

Already Patrick liked this giant of a Teddy Bear man.

Upon entering the guest house Patrick found that it was as neat and lavishly appointed as he had guessed it would be.

"You get comfortable and do whatever you need. Then join us in the main house. Just come on in, no need knocking," and Stefano was gone.

Patrick looked around at the terrazzo floor, the ornate mirrors, a small marble fireplace and fresh lavender flowers on the dresser and in the bathroom. The bathroom was huge. *This is bigger than the room Joe Jr. and I slept in the whole time we were growing up* he thought. Unsure of how long he would stay he took only a few clothing articles out of his suitcase. Carmella and Stefano had both assured him he was welcome for an extended stay, but he was not accustomed to such hospitality and generosity and wasn't sure how to react.

After taking a quick shower, he hurriedly changed into fresh clothes, not wanting to keep anyone waiting for lunch. The flight had left him feeling worn and grimy, but he suddenly felt better, as he headed for the main house.

He spoke a loud, "Hello," entering the house. Not knocking was strange to him, but after his upbringing and sports involvement he followed directions well.

"We are in the kitchen, Patrico," he heard Carmella say. "Come through the entry and to your left."

Patrick quickly noticed that she had changed into an obviously expensive multi-colored floral silk pant suit. "I am just helping Carmen and Claudia a minute, then we will go in the dining room."

Stefano came through the door with a handful of basil. "Your request, my dear," he said, handing the herbs to Carmella. "She has me trained well, do you agree?" he asked, smiling at Patrick. "Many of the Italian men would be horrified to see me respond to her every whim. But she is my wife, my life."

Patrick hardly knew how to respond. This man was so out of character of what he expected a rich Italian estate owner to be, but he said, "She is quite a woman; I knew that in a very brief time. She is so full of energy, obviously in love with life".

"That is why I love her so much. Now, young man, come sit in the dining room and tell me about basketball. Carmella tells me you were on scholarship at Notre Dame. She also says you are going to study in Rome to be a priest."

Patrick followed Stefano into the large dining area. He felt small looking at the table that could easily seat two dozen people.

"Over here, we will eat lunch at the smaller table," Stefano said, signaling him to a nook that overlooked the lake. "This is one of my favorite rooms in the house."

"I can understand why," Patrick answered.

When the women came in with lunch, the two men were discussing the view just outside the window.

"I wanted you two to have time to talk. That is why I helped Carmen with lunch," she offered.

Her explanation indicated to Patrick what he had sensed. Although exuberant and outgoing, she was aware of giving her Italian husband his space, a role Patrick would see again, especially in those areas where Stefano was in charge.

"We'll have a light lunch, but tonight a feast," she said.

After setting three small salads of puntarelle, radishes and endive with anchovy dressing, at their places, Carmen put a large platter filled with fried artichokes in the center of the table.

"May I pour you some of Italy's finest?" Stefano asked proudly, but not waiting for a reply, he began filling first his wife's glass and then Patrick's. "You did say, yes, I believe," he said laughing.

This is a happy home, Patrick thought, as he waited for Carmella to take the first bite.

"Please, Patrico, you must eat. Stefano has much work for you," she teased. "You did not think I brought you here for nothing. Now you are captured."

"I can't think of a more pleasant place to be a captive."

In a few minutes Carmen brought the vignarola, a stew of fava beans, peas and artichoke, seasoned with guaniciale, Patrick learned.

"This is so good. I don't think I have ever tasted fava beans and I have never heard of guanca...," he struggled with the pronunciation.

"The fava season is coming to a close. Earlier in May you could eat them raw, right out of the pod. But as they grow they begin to assert themselves and are better cooked. As for gwan CHA leh," she pronounced slowly for Patrick, "it is similar to pancetta which you have probably eaten. This has a little more fat content which just makes the dish richer."

"Much of this, the sweet peas, and the artichoke in the salad—they will be gone soon. It is a pity you were not here in early May. These artichokes are at their best then, Stefano explained.

Patrick could see that this was definitely a man who enjoyed his food. "Is there a market near here?"

Stefano laughed, "Yes, about ten feet from the house. We grow our own vegetables."

"You didn't tell me that," Patrick exclaimed, looking at Carmella.

"There was so much to tell I forgot about that and the herb garden."

"After a gelato, you will have to indulge me, Patrico. I would like to show you around. That is, if you are not too tired."

"Oh no, I'm fine. I am anxious for the tour."

"Good, while you two gentlemen do that I think I will lie down for a short nap."

"The lady needs her beauty rest," Stefano said, standing and then kissing her on the top of her head.

"Poor Patrico, you will pay for your keep. The tour is very lengthy," she said, rolling her eyes. "Stefano, he does not have to see it all in one day. We have to have reasons to keep him here."

"Okay, first the tobacco," Stefano said, leading Patrick outside. He could faintly hear Carmella saying, "I should have known," but he knew she was being playful.

"How did you learn to speak such good English, Stefano?"

"My parents sent me to boarding school in Naples. They wanted me to learn English and manners. The former was easier than the latter," he smiled. "Anyway, I try to use it as much as I can, so I will not forget it. But most of the help speak only Italian. It is good that you are here. I can practice my English."

They turned the corner and were in the courtyard. Flowers were growing everywhere, some hanging, others in pots and urns. Fresh flowers adorned vases on each table of the courtyard.

"We will take a look at the vegetables and herbs, and then jump in the Land Rover for a look around the larger grounds."

Everything was impeccable, not a weed in sight. "Cesar takes good care of this don't you think? But it is Carmella who adds the love. She comes out here every morning and checks the garden. I sometimes hear her talking to the vegetables and herbs as though they are her children. Sometimes she sits for hours on that bench and just looks at everything."

"She is very proud of this place and very proud of you, Stefano." Stefano blushed slightly, "The only thing I could not give her was more children. She wanted a houseful, but that was not to be. I guess we could have adopted, but once Elisabette was born, she seemed more content. Maybe Elisabette will be here this weekend. She usually tries to come once a month. We are very fond of her new husband, Guliano. Since he owns a wonderful old hotel in Milan it makes it difficult for him to get away, but he accompanies her when he can."

The two men rode around for another hour. "More tomorrow?"

"Great."

"I will take you back to your bungalow so you can rest awhile. Carmella will expect you at six o'clock for drinks on the terrace. It is the perfect place to watch the sunset."

Tired, Patrick was glad to be back to the bungalow for awhile. It was almost four o'clock. Setting an alarm for five o'clock, he fell onto the bed. When he heard the alarm, he was startled, not remembering where he was. After looking around, he thought he must be dreaming until he remembered Carmella and Stefano. "What a nice couple," he said aloud.

When he walked out back, he was amazed to see that there was a small patio with blooming flowers growing around the perimeter. Two lounge chairs faced a grove of olive trees, framed by hills in the far background. *This is like a Renaissance painting. It almost looks as though time has stopped over this landscape,* he thought. After showering, he dressed for dinner or the feast, as Carmella had said. Not sure what to wear he hoped his khaki trousers and tieless shirt would be appropriate. This way of life was so new to him, it made him feel a little uneasy not knowing quite how to act.

When he arrived at exactly six o'clock, Carmella strolled onto the terrace, putting his uneasiness to rest with a big hug, followed by a kiss on both cheeks.

"It is so wonderful to have you in our home."

"You look stunning, Carmella," he offered shyly.

"How debonair you look, Patrico."

Although he knew this was not exactly true, he was relieved that his attire was acceptable and that he had brought his razor. Before the trip he had determined he wanted to let his hair grow and not shave, to satisfy his curiosity of what he would look like scruffy. Those plans would wait, he decided

"First, we must have a Bellini cocktail," Carmella said, "and then Stefano can boast about his latest wines."

"I don't think I have tasted a Bellini."

"Oh, they are so good on these warm nights. They are a refreshing mixture of peach juice and Prosecco, a sparkling wine," she explained. "We buy Prosecco because it comes from the Veneto region."

Embarrassed that he drank the cocktail so fast, Patrick said, "That was indeed refreshing. I was thirsty after my short nap."

"So, you did rest?"

"I set my alarm for one hour and that brief time certainly gave me new energy."

"Red, or white?" Stefano asked, as he held up two bottles. He was like a little boy wanting to open packages at Christmas.

"Stef, he may want another Bellini."

"No, this is fine," Patrick said, seeing how eager Stefano was for him to sample his wine.

"I think red, tonight."

"Good choice." He poured a tiny amount and waited on Patrick to taste. Fortunately, Patrick had seen this in the movies or he would not have known to slowly bring the glass under his nose and then sip gingerly.

"This is outstanding, Stefano. My compliments to the wine master."

Stefano chuckled, obviously proud. "It is better than it should be in these Riedel glasses. Some years, the grapes need help and this was one of those vintages, but it is good, just not as good as some. At dinner we will have some of the older, fuller bodied reds. And tomorrow you have to see my wine cellar."

"And the entire house," added Carmella. "Tomorrow, tomorrow," she said softly, "but tonight we drink to our new friend, Patrico, and enjoy some of the most delicious foods in the world."

Carmella was true to her word. For hors d' oeuvres, Carmen brought to the terrace, baccalá fritto, which Carmella explained to Patrick to be fried salt cod, a Roman classic.

"Shall we move to the dining room?"

"Let us again sit in the smaller room. It just feels so much more intimate than the big room when there are just the three of us. The table was set to perfection with more gold ware, china and stemware than Patrick had ever seen in one setting. He knew he would have to watch closely to be certain he was using the correct utensils and crystal to match the food courses.

"The first course is gnocchetti alla 'amatriciana, Patrico. I am giving you your first lesson in Italian food tonight so you can impress the locals when you dine."

He was glad for her information because he knew very little about Italian cuisine, except for spaghetti and pizza, which he admitted to himself, was not exactly fine cuisine.

"This is quite delicious. Let me guess before you tell me. I taste potato, tomato, onion and maybe bacon."

"You are very close. Actually those are potato dumplings and the sauce has finely chopped pancetta."

As Stefano poured more wine, Patrick began to feel warm inside. Wondering if it was the wine, his thoughts turned inward for just a brief moment, reminding him of the same feeling a young child gains when he crawls into his grandmother's soft lap on a warm summer night. *That is the way these two people make one feel*, Patrick thought, *safe, wanted and comfortable.* Because he had not experienced such happiness in a long time, he hoped this would be the beginning of a long and caring friendship.

A large plate set before him interrupted his thoughts. "I will not be able to wear the clothes I brought if I eat here much longer."

"This mortadella stuffed pork loin is ever so light as is the Tuscan kale and leek flan," Carmella stated.

"What about these rosemary roasted potatoes?" he asked, glad he recognized them.

"Oh, do not be silly; you are thin as a rail."

"Yes, that is what she told me once and look at me now," Stefano laughed, touching his protruding stomach.

After the main course, they slowly ate their radicchio, frillee and artichoke salad.

"At lunch today you noticed we had the salad first like you Americans are accustomed. It is customarily not that way here. We have the salad after the main portion. When you go to a restaurant and choose to have a salad you will have to ask if you want it served first."

"I wouldn't have known that. This is very good, but it does seem odd having it last."

"It will not be last because Claudia has made a delectable dessert called millefoglie, the Italian version of the French pastry meaning thousand leaves, layered with rhubarb and grappa cream. But let's go into the courtyard and let our meal settle first."

"Would you like some coffee, Patrico?"

"Yes, that would be good. I'm afraid I might fall asleep in my chair otherwise."

"Have a nip of Amaretto liqueur, on the side," Stefano said as he handed both Carmella and Patrick each a glass just slightly larger than a shot.

"Thank you, I do believe this is the finest meal and warmest treatment I have ever experienced. May I toast my new friends?"

The three clicked their glasses before sipping the warm liqueur.

"We hope this introduction to Italy will be the first of many wonderful times for you," Carmella said softly.

After dessert, Patrick said, "I don't know exactly how to say this, but growing up my parents always taught us to help clean up after a meal. I don't want to sound like I have no manners but..."

"Patrico, you have impeccable manners, but Claudia will definitely not let you in her kitchen."

"Okay," he grinned, "Then I think I will crash. I'm very full and very sleepy."

"I am too, Patrico. Don't worry about waking up early. Carmen will have your breakfast whenever you show up in the main house."

"I will check back about 10:00 a.m. or so to finish our tour," Stefano said, his large hand covering a yawn.

"Goodnight," Patrick said, rising from his chair.

"Goodnight, Patrico," they said almost in unison.

The next morning Patrick slept until 9:30 a.m. When he saw the clock, he jumped out of bed and hurried to the bath for a shower. Although he remembered that Carmella had said it didn't matter when he arrived for breakfast, he did not want them to think him lazy. By ten o'clock, he was dressed and walking briskly to the main house, when he saw Stefano pulling up and waving. Stefano waited and slapped Patrick on the back as he arrived.

"Good morning, life too difficult for you here in the Tuscan hills?"

Patrick smiled, feeling a flush on his cheeks.

"Don't feel bad. I have been out since 5:00 a.m., but my lovely wife is still in the bubble bath, I am sure. When I came by about thirty minutes ago, she was just getting in so I know if today is true to form, the bubbles are still bubbling. The woman does love her lavender salts, beads and milk baths. Provence has nothing compared to this woman. Her collection of lavender rivals the south of France," he laughed, thinking about this beautiful woman covered with gleaming white, frothy bubbles up to her soft black hair that she let down for her bath.

"This is one time that she admits to enjoying the lap of luxury," he said, winking at Patrick.

Patrick laughed. Here was this big bear of a man, with the loud, gruff voice, who worked daily in the heat of the Tuscan sun, side by side with his men, talking softly about his wife's bubble bath. *I am sure my college English professors could make something poetic or symbolic about all this*, Patrick thought.

"Let me grab a cup of coffee and we can go," Patrick offered.

"Absolutely not, you enjoy your breakfast. We have plenty of time. Those grapes and olives are not going anywhere, anytime soon."

"After last night, I didn't think I would ever be hungry again, but I must admit that looks good, eyeing the huge platter of fresh fruit and pastries."

Carmen spoke to Stefano in Italian.

"Carmen wants to know if you would like some prosciutto and cheese as well."

"No. This is more than enough."

Each man filled his plate and drank espresso. When they finished Stefano filled a thermos and grabbed two cups. He talked to Carmen in Italian and then asked Patrick if he was ready.

"Ready. But, will you thank Carmen for my breakfast and ask her to tell Carmella good morning?"

Stefano gave Carmen the messages in Italian, and they were off to view the olives and grapes.

"It is warm this morning. Did you not bring short pants, Patrico?"

"Yes, but I didn't know for sure if they would be appropriate."

"Certainly, let's stop and you can change. It is especially hot under the trees and in the vineyards so you need to be comfortable. In the summer months I wear shorts most of the time. Only yesterday I did not, so I suppose you wondered."

Patrick ran into the bungalow and quickly changed into shorts and a tee-shirt, immediately feeling more comfortable.

Looking first to one side of the road and then the other, Patrick said, "The vineyards are beautiful, Stefano."

"Thank you; I never get tired of coming out here. I have a certain peaceful feeling when I walk down these rows. You must come back in October for Crush."

"Is that harvest?"

"Yes. Crush is the time during harvest season when grapes are picked and crushed, which means the grapes are quickly broken open so yeasts can get into the grapes and begin fermenting the sweet juice."

"Do you pick by hand or use machinery?"

"Since this is a labor of love, we pick by hand, a lot of hands. When I started, Enrico and I did most of the picking, but as you can see, I have added many vines. I always get the word out if I need extra assistance, but I have four or five men who have helped for years. They cut off individual bunches of grapes with a hooked-tip knife and put them in containers. They know to look for the ripest bunches. An experienced picker can harvest over a ton of fruit in a day so it really does not take that long. We make it a fun time, too. We have lunch out here both days and when we finish we have a big party for the pickers and their families on the second night. Usually a lot of friends show up for the picking and the party."

"That does sound like fun. I would love to be a part."

"Then you must come."

"After you pick then what?"

"That is when the machines come in. We will drive to the building where the crusher-stemmers are kept. Don't worry, you will not have to roll up your cuffs and stomp. That is all mechanized now," he laughed. "Plus, I like to get the grapes to the crushers as soon as possible after they are picked, so none will rot."

"How many tons does this area usually yield?"

"It varies from year to year, of course, but lately about five or six tons, much too much for a hobby. Either I am going to have to begin selling some or acquire a lot more friends."

"If you harvest five tons of grapes, about how many bottles of wine would that make?"

"Around 3,500," Stefano grinned. "See what I mean? But, I pay the pickers in wine, not money so that generally takes care of about 1,000 bottles and then what we do not keep for ourselves, we give away. I also barter some with the wine if I need new equipment or help working on a machine, plus the bottlers get paid the same way."

"I am very generous with my wine because it is my passion." He looked at his watch. It is past time for lunch. I begin talking about my grapes and lose all focus of time."

"This is the building where we crush and bottle. You'll see it better when you come back in October," Stefano said, pointing.

When they arrived at the house, Carmella was waiting on the veranda, a huge smile on her face. "Elisabette and Guliano are coming Friday. He must return on the night train Saturday, but she is staying a week," she said excitedly.

"That is wonderful, you two together will weaken my wallet, I am afraid, in that amount of time," he teased.

"Patrico, you are going to love Elisabette and Guliano. I told her about you and she is anxious to meet you."

"Carmella, I really should leave here tomorrow," Patrick said, not wanting to wear out his welcome."

"No! Patrico," she said, looking downcast. "You must stay, at least until Saturday. I know you want to get on with your travels, but you really must stay to meet our children."

Stefano turned and smiled at Patrick. "The woman is quite persuasive. Don't disappoint her or she will never forgive you."

"I would like very much to stay, but I just don't want to be a bother."

Carmella reached over and put her fingers to Patrick's mouth. "Shhh… It is settled. If you want to leave Saturday, we will check the train schedule to Florence, and Stefano, Enrico, or someone, will take you to the train. Besides, Guliano will need to go also. On Friday morning, bring your laundry to Carmen and she will have it ready for you to pack on Friday evening."

"You are very good to me."

"Then you will come back soon?"

"He is coming to Crush!"

"Oh, Patrico, you will love that. We have so much fun."

The three sat down to a light lunch of crusty bread and pappa al pomodoro, a thick soup made from tomatoes and drizzled with olive oil. A platter of cheeses, pears, olives, prosciutto and mushrooms sat untouched until Carmella noticed. "We've been talking so much I almost forgot," as she passed the plate to Patrick.

"Here I go again," Patrick said as he began to fill up on the lunch. Putting his hand on his stomach he said, "Stefano, maybe we should walk through the olive groves," knowing they went for miles and miles.

"You see, I was once as thin as you. I told you before, time and Carmella made me like this," he said, grinning.

"Since you are staying until Saturday, why don't we see the groves tomorrow and you can have the afternoon free. There is a scooter in the back which I will get for you if you would like to look around some on your own."

"That sounds great, plus that would give you some time to do things you need to do."

"I am fine and everything that I need to be doing you can do with me. I thought you might like exploring some by yourself."

"Yes, that sounds like fun."

"I will pull the scooter around," Stefano said, excusing himself from the table. He stopped to kiss Carmella on the cheek. "Nice bubble bath? You do smell wonderful."

"Isn't he terrible?" she said, obviously loving the attention.

"Patrico, if you take the same road we came in on, you will see a great many lesser roads. If you take any of those, you will be able to see much of the countryside. If you get lost, just stop and ask anyone and they will be able to tell you how to get back. Have fun but be back for cocktails at 6:00 p.m."

"Thank you, Carmella. I am having such a good time," as he excused himself from lunch and met Stefano outside.

"I am sure Carmella has already given you your instructions."

"Yes. I'm to stop if I get lost and be back by six o'clock."

"Be careful and enjoy the afternoon," Stefano called and waved as Patrick stepped on the gas pedal and took off.

Patrick drove up and down dusty roads through the hills, looking at the wonders of this beautiful region. The old farm houses were fascinating, many looking as though they had been there more than a hundred years. After awhile he stopped the bike and sat under an olive tree for more than an hour, just studying the twisted and gnarled old tree and thinking about the life ahead of him.

He could not help but think of Sue and how he wished she could see this. Then he stopped himself. He had made his decision and it did not include her. It was times like this that he questioned his choice. He knew he had to stop thinking like this, but he had loved her, his first real love.

Closing his eyes, he dozed for a short time. When he awoke, he quickly looked at his watch. It was almost five o'clock. *I must get back and freshen up*, he thought as he jumped on the scooter. Although he had tried to study the roads, he quickly realized he might be lost. He paused to think about a few mental markers he had made and then using the sun as his guide, he found the right road, arriving back with plenty of time for a shower and change of clothing.

At exactly six o'clock, he knocked on the front door. "Come in, Patrico," Stefano called. "I see you did not get lost."

"No, but I thought I might be for a few minutes."

"Come with me; I promised to show you my cellar."

The two descended a long stairway down to a basement. Patrick was expecting it to be a little musty and stale, with a furnace and the other practical items stored in it as some of the basements in New England. When they opened the door they were in a giant space with walls of beautifully carved wood. A large table and eight chairs sat in the center. Hundreds of bottles of wine lined the room.

"These are my collectibles," he said, selecting one; a great Bordeaux with a 1948 vintage. "We will have one of these wines tomorrow night at dinner when the children arrive."

"Now, over here are the whites from last year and the reds from the last several years are here. This is my Vin Santo, or holy wine, that we will use to bless the harvest this year."

"I meant to ask you today, while we were in the vineyard, how do you know when the grapes are ripe?"

"I walk through and taste the grapes. Sometimes Enrico will taste and also Carmella. I like to get another opinion, but when the grapes are ripe, they taste ripe; your mouth will not pucker. It is romance, but it is also science. The sugar, acid and tannin all have to be in balance. The tannins must not be green or tough; the sugars need to have climbed and the acids cannot have fallen.

If I pick too soon, before the sugar rises, the wine will be weaker and have too much acid, but if I wait too long it is just as bad, no structure to balance the fruit."

"It sounds awfully complicated."

"It can be since the weather plays a big role, but generally I can get close to when they will be ripe by counting the days from the time of flowering. Each variety ripens a little differently, but I look back at my records from the year before and predict it to within a few days."

"You are truly an interesting man, Stefano."

"I am a blessed man; I have many things to make me happy; everyone does not have that good fortune. I am thankful and so is Carmella. That is why we like to share this place with people like you. It is too much for just us."

As they ascended the steps, the men could hear Carmella saying loudly, "My turn, my turn. I want to show you the entire house Patrico," now taking him by the hand and leading him into the great room. He had been able to get a glimpse of it a couple of times, but he had never gone inside.

"This is magnificent!" he exclaimed. Like the wine cellar, the room was paneled in dark mahogany with extensive carvings. A thick, rich border of wood molding encircled the chandelier which looked to be of real gold. Light shone through crystal pendants as if they were diamonds. But it was the fireplace that really caught Patrick's attention. It was big enough for a person to walk in, with the enormous black andirons that held oversized split logs, ready to be lighted with the first chill of autumn.

"I don't have words for all this, Carmella; it is like nothing I have ever seen in a house before," remembering his own boyhood home, with the multi-colored afghan his mother had crocheted to cover the worn spots on the couch, the curtains ordered from a Sears catalog and the swing set that rusted in the backyard. He could almost see his mother sitting at her sewing machine in the corner of his parent's bedroom, stitching the dresses she made for his sisters because there wasn't money for store bought ones.

"We will go quickly through the remainder," as she took him from room to room filled with lavish tapestries and murals on the walls, satin drapes that reached and spilled over onto the terrazzo floors.

"This was once the nursery. I have not changed it much because, hopefully, Elisabette and Guliano will fill it up for me with lots of noisy little bambinos," she said, happily. "This entire wing is Elisabette's."

"So, this is where the famous baths are taken," Patrick teased, as he looked at the round marble tub. Actually, there was marble everywhere he looked.

"That is Stefano's," she remarked, pointing to an enormous marble and glass walk-in shower. The mirrors looked centuries old, true renaissance marvels. The canopy over the bed matched the drapes and the stacks of pillows that lined the velvet duvet. Frescoed ceilings added more mystery to the setting.

"I love this room," Carmella gushed. "This is where I read," pointing to a chaise in the corner by another, yet smaller fireplace.

"You are getting the grand tour," Stefano said, handing each of them a glass of champagne. "Just a little something bubbly, as if Carmella is not enough," Stefano teased as he kissed her gently. "Now you two had better finish this fairly soon if you are going to have time to relax before I cook the steaks."

"Just a few more rooms and we will be finished, Darling, tilting her glass to him as if to toast his request.

When Patrick and Carmella walked through one of the brick arches onto the terrace, the sun was beginning to set.

"Hurry, Patrico, the sun is going to melt right over those hills and you will see the reflection on our lake."

Patrick stood looking to the west as the light from the golden ball oozed into the glistening water surrounded by the dark green landscape. Within minutes the sky had turned to crimson with just a few streaks of turquoise.

"This is, indeed, heaven on earth," he smiled, looking directly at Carmella. "It is going to be difficult to leave."

"Then stay."

"I can't, but I do hope you will have me back."

"Patrico, you are welcome here anytime. When the studies are weighing you down or you are lonesome, whatever the case may be, you jump on a train. You know it is quite inexpensive and even after your classes on Friday you can probably arrive in time to watch the sunset with us."

"You have to promise to come at least once every month. There is always something special. In September, we hunt for the wild mushrooms, and then of course we harvest the grapes in October. November is when the olives are picked; December is then a time when we slow down after the busy fall and enjoy the sights and smells of the holidays. Carmen and Claudia make the most wonderful sweets. The whole house smells of gingerbread and juniper. Enrico and Stefano find the biggest tree available, and we decorate it in the great room. We have twinkling lights and candles everywhere. You cannot miss that."

"There is a true rhythm to life here," Patrick mused.

"Yes, and it is rewarding and fulfilling because we do so much of it ourselves," Stefano added. "In the winter months, Claudia spins wool and makes some beautiful accessories, which she often sells at the markets in Florence. Now she is teaching Carmen. Enrico and I cure our own prosciutto in January and in the spring we pick the vegetables and fruits right here. The women make the most tasty pecorino cheese during a rare, slow time in March. Life is busy here, so we never get bored. Speaking of busy, I must start the steaks if you two will go with me to the courtyard."

"I will follow you anywhere for a steak," said Patrick.

As Stefano readied the grill he said, smiling, "You thought only Americans grilled, huh?"

"Honestly, yes, I never thought about that in Italy."

"Tonight is my night to cook, so this is what I do best."

He left for a moment and returned with antipasta of bruschetta al pomodoro. He poured the three of them a glass of red wine.

"This is one of the more robust wines to go with our bistecca al fiorentina. Everything tonight is from our land, Patrico."

"That has to give you a great deal of satisfaction. But, I haven't seen any cattle."

"But tomorrow you will see my pride and joys, my Chianina."

"Is that a breed of cattle just in Italy? I have never heard of them."

"Correct. They are probably the oldest breed in the world. They have even been the models for Roman sculptures. Just since World War II, has the United States known about them, although some have been in Canada. The U.S. government will only allow the semen to be imported, and it was only this year that a half-blood Chianina and Angus/Holstein bull calf was born in California. There is speculation that this year or next, Italian full-bloods will be exported from Canada into the U.S."

"Why can't you export them?"

"We have had a few documented cases of foot and mouth disease here in Italy, so we are prohibited from exporting cattle to the U.S. I think that will change soon, however."

"I am anxious to see what they look like."

"They are bigger here than most parts of Italy, even bigger up toward Arezzo and Siena."

"Can you two think of something else to talk about before dinner?" Carmella asked, smiling.

"You mean like bubble baths," Patrick grinned.

Carmella hit him with her paschima and laughed.

"We will eat in the courtyard if that is all right. I had Carmen set it up for us before she left work today."

"That is cheating," Carmella said.

"Yes, dear, but that is the only cheating I do!"

"Well then, I will overlook this tonight, besides the steaks smell good," she added.

After dinner, Carmella said, "Tomorrow my baby girl will be here. I am so very excited."

"Yes, I am also, but first I have to show Patrick the olives and the cattle and then he will have seen most of everything."

"I will be earlier tomorrow," Patrick promised, "So now I must get some sleep. The dinner was fantastic; my compliments to the chef."

"Thank you. Did you tell Patrico that tomorrow night is his night to cook?" he teased.

"I need to make friends quickly with Carmen, but it is not going to be easy with my English and her Italian."

"Goodnight, Patrico."

"Goodnight all."

As planned, Patrick was up early and waiting for Stefano when he came in singing, his deep rich voice reverberating off the richly appointed walls of the dining room.

"I must have my coffee and then we will see the olives. I don't guess there is a big hurry; many of the trees have been here over a hundred years, and they will most assuredly be here another."

"Enrico and some of the other workers are pruning many of the trees today. I usually supervise, but he knows how as well as I. We cannot let the trees get too tall so we prune annually. It is a long process since we have more than 200 trees."

Pausing to fill his cup with more coffee, Stefano asked, "Are you ready? Do you want to take some with you?"

"No, I'm finished. Carmen made me a cappuccino, actually."

"She is spoiling you, huh?"

They drove slowly, looking at the trees, planted up and down terraced hillsides.

"It looks as though it would be hard to work on slopes so steep."

"Yes, the terrain here is harsh, so harsh that all of Tuscany is responsible for only about four per cent of the olive oil production. The climate is also difficult because the trees are particularly vulnerable to frost. Olive trees in other regions yield twenty times as many olives, but the good news is our olives are a concentrate of flavor and aroma which makes the oil more pronounced than anywhere else in Italy."

"Do you pick these by hand?"

"Well, yes and no. We don't use machines if that is what you mean. We hand pick what we can from the ground and then set up scaffolding. If all else fails we use bamboo canes and tap the branches, but I don't like to resort to that because the olives can get bruised. But, one way or another, every olive is caught in the nets we use to carpet the grove. I doubt that anyone thinks this is as much fun as the grape crush. This is hard work. That is why it is the 'cash crop' as you say in the States. But after all the hard work, the men and I head for the woods to hunt wild boar, so we look forward to that."

After they had driven along the hillside for what seemed like miles Stefano said, with pride, "I am very proud of our oil. I think it is the best in all of Italy. There they are," he said, stopping the vehicle. Cattle roamed everywhere. "They have a very distinctive look, don't they?"

"Yes, the shoulders, back and rear quarters are especially well formed," Patrick noted.

"Now you have seen the farm. Oh, there are a few chickens over by Enrico's. He takes care of them. Carmen gathers the eggs every morning. No need to see them. I'm sure you have seen chickens," he laughed. "After lunch, you are on your own again. Elisabette and Guliano will be here around five o'clock, so drinks will be ready at six."

"I'm looking forward to meeting them. I think I'll read and enjoy the patio of my bungalow until then."

After a lunch on the terrace, Stefano said, "See you at six".

❧⳥

When Patrick reached the terrace, he saw that Elisabette and Guliano were already there, each drinking a glass of wine."

"Hurry, Patrico, I want you to meet our children," Carmella called.

Guliano stood. Almost as tall as Patrick, the dark Italian had smooth black hair and a straight mustache. Patrick thought he would pass for a movie star. Unfortunately, Elisabette, he decided, took more of her father's looks than her mother's. Not unattractive, she just didn't have the same striking facial characteristics or smooth lines as her mother. But her personality was a reflection of both and she stood and hugged Patrick immediately as her mother introduced them.

Guliano smiled, "Hmm, Patrico. I have not known an Irishman with that name. Carmella has a way of making everyone Italian," he stated as he grinned at his mother-in-law, obviously with love and admiration.

As soon as Patrick sat down and took a glass of wine Guliano stood again, "I propose a toast," holding up his glass, "A toast to the new grandparents-to-be."

Looking faint, Carmella cried, "Oh Elisabette, Guliano, is it true? Are you sure?"

"Yes, mother," Elisabette said, beaming. "That is why Guliano wanted to come, too. He really needed to stay in Milan, but we wanted to be together to tell you."

Beside herself with joy, Carmella asked, "Did you hear that Stefano? We are going to be grandparents!" fanning herself with her napkin.

"Yes," he said his voice cracking. "I am a happy man. Congratulations Guliano!" he grabbed him and gave him a bear hug. "My darling daughter, you give me great joy," kissing her on both cheeks. "This calls for a celebration! Remember that bottle of wine I showed you Patrico? I have one even better." Before Patrick could nod yes, Stefano took off for the wine cellar.

"This is great news," Patrick said, "Congratulations to both of you."

Carmella was still spinning around. "Elisabette, we have to go into Florence this week. We must pick out some things for the baby."

"Okay mother, but I think we have quite some time before the baby will be born."

"Elisabette, please indulge me."

"You know I will mother; that is why I planned a week here," she said, smiling.

Dinner was high-pitched with the excitement evident in every word spoken. When they were all finished, Patrick excused himself so they could spend some time alone as a family.

"I must pack. I need to catch the 10:00 a.m. train if that's okay, Stefano."

"We hate to see you go, Patrico, but we will get you to the station."

"I'll see you all in the morning. Goodnight."

"Goodnight, Patrico," they said in perfect unison.

Back at his bungalow, Patrick laid awake, thinking about Elisabette and Guliano, how excited they were and how they had come together to share their news. He remembered Carmella saying how she had so wanted a houseful of children and Stefano telling him about not being able to give her the one thing she wanted most.

His thoughts then strayed again to Sue, how lonely she must have felt when she found out she was carrying his baby. If he had known, he wondered what he would have done. He doubted he would have left her like that, no matter what his plans for the priesthood, but she had saved him that decision. She had loved him too much to make him choose. How different things might have been. He certainly would not be here, halfway around the world.

The next morning, Stefano and Guliano drove him to the train, but not before Carmella hugged him again and again, telling him to be careful, to write, and to come back soon. She had packed him snacks, enough he guessed, for several days. Glancing back one last time, he saw Carmella standing on the terrace, one arm around Elisabette's waist, the other waving to him. Pablo, the fat, orange cat, lay on top of her Mercedes, yawning, with his tail thumping up and down.

"Thanks for everything, Stefano. You have been so kind, so generous with your time. I can never thank you enough."

"You just did," he said, slapping Patrick on the back. "Now go see the sights so you can come back to see us."

"Okay, you take care, Guliano, and congratulations. I am sure you will make a good father, that is if Carmella ever lets you or anyone else hold the baby." Both men smiled.

"Thanks. For sure this baby will be loved, Guliano said, smiling.

Patrick waved from the train, knowing he would be in Florence in an hour.

ॐ∞ॐ

chapter 10

It took Patrick only ten minutes to walk from the train to the Duomo. Stefano had suggested an inexpensive place to stay nearby and knowing the hotels fill quickly in peak season, he had called ahead for Patrick. Looking at the prices, Patrick thought it cost more than it should have, but the location was excellent. His room was small and clean though somewhat tired from the countless other tourists who had obviously selected this no-frills place for a number of years. Dropping off his two bags, he realized he was hungry. From his research, he had learned that Florence was the perfect city for walking, with the centro storico practically car-free. Finding a place to eat lunch took only minutes because small food stands were everywhere. He selected one that had a vacant place to stand and ordered Chianti and Panini, deciding a quick sandwich would be an easy and cheap lunch. Tonight he could splurge and sit down for a nice quiet meal. His plan was to see inside the Duomo. Noticing that an English speaking tour was about to begin, he rushed to join the group.

After climbing more than four hundred spiraling steps to the summit, he realized that although he jogged some, he had let himself get out of shape after basketball. He must walk more, he reminded himself. Stepping out from the dark cathedral into the sun, he squinted as he looked up at the red-tiled Duomo. He marveled at the architecture of this magnificent structure, built five centuries prior. Admiring the Baptistery in front of the Duomo, dedicated to John the Baptist, the patron saint of Florence, he followed several others inside the vault of the Baptistery to see the magnificent gilded mosaics from the 1200s. He decided to pass on climbing another four hundred plus steps to the campanile, thinking the view from the bell tower would be similar to that from the Duomo.

For a full week Patrick walked around the city, taking in the museums, churches and markets. He spent two full days at the Uffizi, looking at centuries of art by Leonardo da Vinci, Rembrandt, Raphael, Michelangelo and numerous Florentine, Flemish and Venetian masters.

In the Mercato San Lorenzo, Patrick found a box of Florentine stationary for Carmella and a leather wallet for Stefano. Even though he knew they had everything they wanted, he wanted to be polite and send something for their hospitality and kindness.

On his last day in Florence Patrick took the train to the medieval walled city of Lucca and then on to Pisa. Upon his returned to the hotel, he packed and prepared for the continuation of his journey to Venice.

The next morning according to Stefano's recommendations, Patrick caught the early train. In order to secure a budget room, Stefano had said it was important to arrive before lunch. After locating a small, dark single room with a shared bath near the Rialto Bridge, he was surprised by the cost. He knew it would be expensive, but had not counted on paying double what he had paid in Florence. Later, while walking around the city, Patrick quickly understood the lofty price and why Lord Byron had described Venice as "a fairy city of the heart." Normally his first stop would have been the Basilica di San Marco, but his whole life he had read and heard about the Grand Canal. So he hopped on the number 1 vaporetto for a leisurely cruise from Piazza San Marco to the Ferrovia. Along this two mile ribbon of water he saw the palazzi, churches and buildings dating back from the fourteenth to the eighteenth century, their facades faded to muted reds and greens.

He thought to himself how strange not to see cars and asked an older Italian gentleman on the water bus if he spoke English. "A little," he answered with some difficulty.

"What does a policeman drive?"

The old gentleman smiled broadly and Patrick wondered if he understood. Then, just as Patrick began to ask in another way, the man pointed to a small boat, with the word "Policio," passing the vaporetto on the side opposite where Patrick had been looking.

"No cars?" Patrick asked.

The man shook his head to say no.

As the day heated up, he stopped at a gelato stand around San Marco Square, already dreading going back to the small room he had taken, knowing that it had no air-conditioning and only one small window.

It hadn't taken long for Patrick to understand that Venice is indeed, a city of canals and narrow alleyways, a city built for water travel. After getting lost three times, he gave up and decided not to worry about seeing sites on a schedule, but rather to roam about discovering what he stumbled upon.

For the next three days he marveled at the statuaries, the marble columns, the art, the elaborate ceilings and furnishing of the churches and studied the weathered decadence of a city fighting against the elements.

He found the islands of Murano, Burano and Torcello, though small, to be more beautiful in some ways than Venice. On his last night he found his way to the Campo Santa Margherita, to watch the people and stop in a little trattoria along a canal that the hotel desk clerk had recommended. It was dark and musty inside and the walls smelled of aged wood and stale wine. But it was also full of what appeared to be locals and international groups of students. Two girls, who looked to be college-age, sat at a small round table in one corner drinking cappuccinos and writing postcards. A rowdy group of seven boys stood around the bar drinking beer and a mixed group of boys and girls were talking quietly over wine. Several middle-aged couples were playing chess while still others were engaged in animated conversation, hands waving in the air.

Patrick thought it looked like a fun place and sat down near the group of boys and girls and ordered a Campari. Before long, one of the girls asked if he would like to join them at their table. They were all from the American Midwest, backpacking their way across, "as much of Europe as we can in two months," one of the boys said.

Four of them were students at Iowa State and one attended classes at a small university in Kansas. When Patrick told them he had just graduated from Notre Dame, they all did a cheer.

"I'm Jenny. Where are you going from here?"

"I'm not really sure, but I need to move on. It's quite expensive to stay here, plus I think I have about done the city."

"We're going to Lucerne on the train tomorrow night if you'd like to come along," a guy named Kenny said.

Patrick had not given any thought to that direction, but he was tempted.

"It is much cooler there and we're tired of sweating in our sleeping bags," the student from Kansas said.

"I didn't get your name."

"Oh, I'm Mike."

"I want to see the lakes and the mountains. The pictures in the brochure are so pretty. I'm Kathy," she added.

"What time is the train?" Patrick asked.

"It leaves at 9:00 p.m. and we arrive, I think, at 5:30 or 6:00 in the morning. That gives us a break from the sleeping bags although I haven't found train sleeping to be all it is cracked up to be, either," said Kenny.

"Yes, but the bathrooms are sure better than we are used to," Zeke offered, and they all laughed.

Then without thinking about it further, Patrick said, "Then I guess I'll go, too. Where shall I meet you?"

"What do you think?" Kathy asked.

Kenny, obviously the accepted spokesperson and leader of the group said, "Why don't we meet about 6:30, at that little café, you know the Bueno Vino, I think it's called; the one by Piazza San Marco. It is on the Rialto Bridge side. We can eat a pizza or something before we board."

"Sounds great; I'm going to stop at the market and get a few items for the train on my way," Patrick said. "I'll have to check out of my room before noon, but I think they'll allow me to leave my bags. The hotel, if you can call it that, is close to the Rialto Bridge."

"At least you have a place here. We're all the way out in Padua. We couldn't find a hostel or anything cheap so we are riding the train back and forth," Jenny commented.

"How long does it take you?"

"About thirty minutes. Hey, I guess we had better be going, too. I need to wash a couple of T-shirts tonight so they will dry before I pack," Kenny said.

"I wouldn't call what you do as packing," Zeke said with a big grin.

"Well, you don't see that many wrinkles do you?" Kenny remarked, hitting Zeke with a fisted hand on the upper arm.

"No, you're one big wrinkle so it is difficult to count them individually," Jenny teased.

Patrick had to admit Kenny looked a little rumpled, but clean, nonetheless.

"Okay, lay off," Kenny said, unfazed by his friends' remarks. "Pay up and we're gone!"

"We'll see you tomorrow, Patrick," as they left laughing.

It was obvious to Patrick that they enjoyed each other and he was glad he had made the quick decision to accompany them at least as far as Lucerne.

Kenny's mention of washing t-shirts reminded Patrick he needed to do the same. *They should dry fast in this heat but the humidity is another matter.*

The next morning he went back to the Basilica, this time paying to go up to the open balcony area on the front of the structure that overlooks the San Marco basin.

Afterwards, he bought a couple of paperback books for the train and an inexpensive backpack from a vender on the bridge. He had grown tired of rummaging through his duffle whenever he needed something quickly so he thought this might help and also give him more room if he saw something he wanted.

Excited about having some people his age to converse with and anxious to see Switzerland, he met his new companions at the designated time and ordered pizza and house red wine.

When they had finished they walked to Venice Station, Santa Lucia, arriving thirty minutes before departure time, and bought their tickets. Deciding to pay for a sleeping couchette in hopes of getting a better night's sleep, the girls counted out extra money leaving the guys to rough it in a regular seat. By midnight all were asleep until they were startled awake around 1:00 a.m. at the Swiss border by a guard, who requested to check their passports. Shortly after this stop, Patrick fell back to sleep and when he rubbed his eyes open, they were nearing Lucerne. Though dark, there was enough light from the moon that he could see a glimpse of the lake against the backdrop of the Alps. Feeling a chill for a minute he considered pulling out his windbreaker, but guessed the sun would be up shortly after they reached the train station.

Jenny and Kathy came through the doors to the section where the other boys were still sleeping.

"Hello. How were your beds?" Patrick inquired glad to see them.

"Hard," Jenny replied. "I think you guys were smarter than we were."

"Maybe you should ask my neck," Patrick suggested, smiling.

"The books all talk about the comfortable night trains. They even make it all sound so romantic," Kathy said, frowning. "The dorm bed will actually feel pretty good in the fall," she laughed.

"Shhh. That's a stretch," Jenny whispered, trying not to wake Kenny, Zeke and Mike.

"I'm awake," Zeke mumbled from under his pillow which was cupped around his head. "Are we there yet?"

"The good news is it is nicer weather," Patrick told him.

"As soon as we arrive I'm buying myself one of those cool Swiss Army knives that has about twenty different blades and stuff on it," Mike said, yawning.

"Then what will you do with it?" Kenney asked, sitting up slowly.

"You never know, so you need to watch out!" he grinned.

At the station in Lucerne Patrick agreed to meet them at five o'clock at the famous old wooden bridge. Although none of them really knew where it was, they determined that it would be a place they could find. Walking in the dim morning light, Patrick found an open coffee shop and bought a pastry and coffee. *This is nice*, he thought as he sat down in a small booth.

When the stores opened, he decided he liked Mike's idea of a Swiss knife as a gift for each brother. Sometime in the night he had also thought about looking for watches for his mom and dad. Going from store to store, he found knives and watches. Although the prices were about the same at all the stores, one owner offered to box and ship them to the States. Before paying, Patrick asked, "Could you give me a few minutes to write a quick letter, before you pack it for mailing?"

Nodding yes, the woman handed Patrick a pen and single sheet of paper.

Patrick wrote:

July 1,

I'm in Lucerne, Switzerland. I met up with some students in Venice from the Midwest and traveled by train with them. I'll probably only stay here another day and be on my way to who knows where! I thought you might like Swiss watches. I think the watch you gave me when I was ten was one of my best gifts ever, second only to my blue bike. I don't have John, Robert or Andrew's addresses, so will you please give them these knives when you see them? Also, please tell Mary Margaret and Rose Marie I didn't forget them. I'm getting them rosaries blessed by the Pope when I return to Rome. Don't tell them what they will be receiving though. Mom, you're getting one also.

Gotta go; the woman is waiting on me so she can pack the box.

Love,
Patrick

Following his shopping and a lunch of cheese fondue, Patrick took a boat ride on Lake Lucerne. As he looked up at the snow capped mountains, he marveled how the scene looked like a postcard.

After overhearing tourists on the boat discussing the Lion Monument, he figured he had just enough time to see it before meeting his friends. Rushing to the wooden bridge he met first Kenny, who reported, "We are going on to a little town that is by the lake where we can camp. Want to come?"

"I already paid for a room tonight, plus I don't have camping gear. I think I'll take the train to Innsbruck tomorrow. But thanks," Patrick said, a little regretful that he was going to be alone again.

"We're going on before it gets dark. Sorry about dinner."

"No problem. You guys have fun. Maybe we'll meet up again."

They waved good-bye as Patrick walked to a small café on the banks of the River Reuss to read and eat a light dinner.

⊱❦⊰

After the next two days in Innsbruck Patrick headed south to the walled city of Assisi, birthplace of St. Francis, and then on to southern Italy. He didn't detrain in Rome, but rather continued on to Monte Cassino to view the monastery and abbey, perched high above the valley. Then it was on to Pompeii.

For the next two weeks, Patrick took in the sights of Capri and Sorrento, impressed with the rocky rose-tinted coastline of Capri and the charm of Sorrento, situated on a plateau high above the waters of the Bay of Naples.

He could see Vesuvius again although this time from much further away. The trendy shops and boutiques were of no interest to him, but he found the museums interesting and the cafes fun. Again, his hotel room was much more expensive than he had expected, but the view of the harbor was worth it. He spent the next few days reading and planning the remainder of his trip.

On his last night in Capri, Patrick decided to treat himself to a nice restaurant. The host seated him at a table by a window near two ladies, he guessed to be in their early seventies who were speaking English. Knowing he would soon be sitting in a windowless classroom instead of enjoying views like this, he lingered, looking out the window at the setting sun and turquoise water below, thinking of the many beautiful vistas on his trip. When he turned around he noticed the two women were looking at him, smiling. Since their plates had already been taken away, and he knew he would not disturb their dinner, he smiled back and asked, "Where are you ladies from, if I may ask? I have heard your accent and it sounded American."

"We thought you might be from America," one of the women said slowly.

The other lady quickly added, "Tulsa. Tulsa, Oklahoma. And you?"

Patrick replied, "Boston, by way of a few other short stops."

"Why don't you join us for dessert, young man?"

"I don't care for dessert, but I would like to join you for a cup of coffee, maybe."

"I'll have the local peaches and a scoop of yogurt sorbet," the first woman told the server, and then said, "I'm Rose, and this is Grace."

"I'll have the same," Grace said, nodding and smiling at Patrick.

"Have you been here before?" Patrick asked.

"Oh my yes, we come every year. Isn't it a serene paradise?" one of the women asked.

"Yes. I was surprised it is so small."

"Only four miles long and less than two miles at its widest point," Rose said, sounding like a school teacher from his junior high school.

"Have you seen the Blue Grotto?"

"Yes, it is the deepest blue I believe I have ever seen. I guess the hole in the cave's roof gives it that color," Patrick replied.

The school teacher, as Patrick thought of her, said, "I remember that some English writer, his name escapes me now, once wrote that the grotto belongs 'to the immense categories of things that cannot be described, because their beauty cannot be appreciated only by the eyes.' I find that so very true."

Grace, the smaller lady, who Patrick decided had probably never worked outside the home said, "We have been coming here since two years after my husband died, for ten years now, I guess. Her husband died first, nodding toward her friend, then mine. They were both in the oil business in Tulsa. Have you ever been to Tulsa?"

"No."

"Nice and clean city; not much crime and nice people."

"Would you ladies like to walk around, to the central square?"

They looked at each for less than a second and responded, "yes," at the same time.

"We don't usually go out of the hotel much at night alone, but a tall American can surely protect us from any harm."

Rose added, "We have never heard of any problems, but one never knows."

Patrick paid his check and they signed their dinner to their room. When they stood, each lady took one of Patrick's arms and they went venturing out into the night.

After they had walked awhile, Rose offered, "Why don't we go in this little bar for a nightcap? My treat."

After another hour of talking, Patrick learned that, indeed, Rose Holland had been a teacher, seventh grade, but only for a few years.

"I am just bossy. I know that is why you guessed it," she laughed. "I guess we need to call it a night, do you think, Grace?"

"I suppose, but I have so enjoyed this nice young man."

Walking them back to their room, Patrick stopped, "Thank you for a great evening. It was nice to talk to Americans. I've been alone for much of my journey," he said, feeling a little nostalgic, if not homesick.

"Come see us if you are ever in Tulsa."

He smiled, realizing that he didn't even know Grace's last name.

The next morning he traveled by bus through the mountainous scenery to the ferry that took him to Sicily, stopping for the night in Taormina. After reading so many fictional accounts, he thought how fun it was to see Sicilian life in reality. Bustling and beautiful with almond and orange blossoms adding scent to the scenery, the landscape made him wonder why the movies only showed the Mafioso and never mentioned the spectacular views and rich heritages.

Patrick found Palermo, the capital, with interesting squares and market places, churches and palazzos in every style from

Moorish to Baroque, to be his favorite, but time was running short. Admitting to himself that he hated to leave the panoramic views he knew he must and was somber as he caught the boat to Naples. At first he tried reading, but soon he found himself staring out to sea.

chapter 11

Arriving back in Rome during the second week of August, Patrick was surprised that it seemed deserted.

"Where is everyone?" he asked the manager of the small apartment building where he would be staying. The gentleman smiled and spoke in broken English, "Holiday Ferragosto—people go from heat."

Patrick was not sure what the man meant but he had enough information now to ask other questions of someone who spoke better English.

"My name is Patrick O'Brien. I'm in your book," pointing to his name on the register for rooms.

"Ricardo," the old man said slowly, lightly pointing a finger to his chest and then pounding it with his hand. "Come," he said to Patrick pulling a key marked 208 down from a board mounted to the wall. Patrick followed the older man up the stairs to a small efficiency apartment. After setting his bags on the floor, he began looking around when the manager again said, "Come." Patrick obediently followed him to an old iron circular staircase that led to a roof terrace where he was pleasantly amazed and pleased. Obviously proud, the old gentleman grinned and began pointing out the four newly repainted iron chairs around a small table and the flower boxes lining the sides of the terrace. Though most of the flowers had turned brown from lack of water, the effort displayed told Patrick that he had chosen the right apartment. Noting that the iron rail around the roof needed a coat of paint, Patrick figured the old gentleman had either run out of paint or energy, or both.

"Very nice, Ricardo, Sir."

Quickly the man said, "Come."

Patrick smiled to himself. They were beginning to look amusing, the young, tall Irish-American, walking one step behind this bent-over little Italian man. They walked all the way back down to the first floor and out a side entrance.

"Look."

Patrick did not understand what Ricardo expected. In front of the man was a new blue scooter with a letter attached.

"Look," he repeated, handing the letter to Patrick. Patrick opened the envelope and a set of keys fell out. He unfolded the sheet of paper and read the message: *"You will need this in Rome. Be careful and come to see us soon. Love, Stefano and Carmella"*

He was so moved and caught up in his thoughts that he almost forgot the old man, who was still standing there. Patrick looked up. Ricardo was smiling broadly as proud for Patrick it seemed as if he had given it to him. Then Ricardo took one of the keys from him and showed him the lock and where he should chain it to an old cypress tree that took up much of the small lot beside the apartment.

"Thieves bad!"

Patrick understood. "Thank you."

He rushed in to call Carmella and Stefano to thank them.

❧❦

Anxious to see the Vatican and St. Peter's Basilica, Patrick was up early the next morning and off on an adventure. After taking one look inside the Basilica he determined it had to be the holiest Basilica and definitely the largest of the Catholic faith. In spite of the many churches and other basilicas he had seen throughout Italy, he knew this had to be one of the grandest creations of Rome's Renaissance. Just seeing Michelangelo's Pieta, Patrick decided, was worth a person's journey. As he stopped to admire the thirteenth century bronze statue of St. Peter, he noticed the foot was worn from the touch of the faithful masses.

It soon became apparent that there were too many museums for him to even begin to see until he could take a day for each, but that didn't stop him from rushing to see Michelangelo's work in the Sistine Chapel. Leaning his neck back downward to his shoulder, he stared up in awe. From his studies he knew these were the scenes depicting the Creation and that of Noah, along with Old Testament prophets, ancient Sibyls, the ancestors of Christ and old scenes of salvation. Dizzy from standing, looking upward for so long, he walked over to a bench to sit and change the level of his view. Marveling at the magnitude of the frescoed ceiling as well as the wall painting of the Last Judgment, Patrick began to plan more visits to the chapel to absorb the full effect. There was so much to see and he caught himself wanting to take it all in immediately.

The next day he was off to explore the Roman Forum and Colosseum. Stopping on his way at an outdoor market he bought fruit, bread, salami and a bottled drink for lunch. Walking among the dusty, crumbling arches and shakily re-erected columns of the Forum, he began to imagine what it was all like two thousand years before.

While he was exploring the Arch of Septimius Severus, the Umbilicus Urbus and Imperial Rostra, he passed the curving wall that marks the site of the Temple of Vesta. There he spotted a young girl jumping up on an empty pedestal to pose as a Vestal Virgin while her friend quickly snapped a picture. At the same minute a guard stepped from behind a statue of one of the remaining Vestals and shouted, but the giggling girls ran out of sight. Patrick laughed, but straightened his face as he approached the guard to ask where he could eat his picnic lunch.

"Palatine Hill is away from the crowds and comfortable enough," the Italian said in perfect English, pointing in its direction.

"Thanks, I'm starved." After climbing to the top, he found a shaded, grassy area and stood briefly looking down at the old gated alleyways where Rome's rich and famous had once lived. Sitting on the warm grass, eating his lunch, he began processing the events of the morning.

Peaceful and a little tired, he dozed. When he awoke, he wasn't sure how long he had slept. It was growing late, but he was anxious to see the Colosseum and decided it was, perhaps worth the five thousand lire, which he figured to be about two dollars, to rent an audio guide. He was right because it explained, in English, much of the famous sports arena's history as he wandered through the maze of walls and crumbling bricks. Because it was growing dark, he trudged back to his parked scooter. Hopping on, he took one last look back at the ancient structure and thought how impressive the Colosseum really was, a silhouette and symbol of the city itself. It had been described to him in that way by friends at Notre Dame who had been to Rome, but seeing it himself made it real and lasting.

❧

By the end of September, Patrick was thoroughly immersed in his studies. When the phone rang, he jumped. It rarely rang and he had considered not even having it connected, but decided it was a good idea in case someone from his family needed to get in touch with him quickly.

"Patrico, how are you?"

He recognized Stefano's voice immediately. "Very well, studying hard."

"Can you take a break and come to the opening of crush this weekend? I would like for you to do the 'Blessing of the Harvest.' It would mean a great deal to Carmella and me."

That was all Stefano had to say to Patrick who felt a keen sense of respect and love for the couple.

"I would be honored. My last class ends at 3:00 p.m. on Thursday. I need to check the train schedule, but I'm sure I could get the first one after four o'clock."

"I will look at the schedule here and assume that is your train and be at the station to pick you up."

"I'm looking forward to seeing you."

"Carmella sends her love."

"And I, mine," Patrick offered.

"See you Thursday."

"Thanks, Stefano."

After he hung up the phone, Patrick began to worry, realizing he had never been to a harvest. He made a note to ask someone at the seminary how he needed to prepare.

Both Stefano and Carmella were at the station to pick him up.

"It is so good to see you, my love," as she kissed him on both cheeks. Stefano shook his hand hard and then pulled him into his usual bear hug.

"How is Elisabette?

"Patrico, she is doing wonderfully. Only two and a half more months and we will have a grandbaby. I am so excited. I am going to Milan as soon as the first labor pain hits. Guliano promises that he will call. It is going to be a marvelous Christmas this year with the new little blessing. I know that you want to be with your family, but we are glad you agreed in your letters to share the holidays with us. I might let you hold the baby a minute," she teased.

"With a grandbaby, the house will never be the same again," Stefano managed to get in.

"You must see the nursery. Elisabette and I painted and decorated it on her last visit. I really liked it as it was, but I admit it was dated. Elisabette wanted to use some brighter colors. I rather liked the soft, subtle ones, but this is a new generation." Elisabette told me, "I must get with the program!"

The crush was even more enjoyable than Patrick expected. For two days, he ate and drank and visited with the locals. When it came time to do the final blessing of the harvest, he looked down at his hands, stained red, smiled and began:

"*God watereth the hills from above; the earth is filled with the fruit of thy works. He bringeth forth grass for the cattle, and green herb for the service of man; that he may bring food out of the earth; and wine that maketh glad the heart of man,*" — *Psalms 104:13-15.*

On Sunday morning when it was time to leave, Stefano handed him a large envelope.

"What is this?"

"It is an early Christmas present."

Fumbling with the envelope, he finally managed to see what was inside: two round-trip plane tickets from Boston to Rome.

"I'm sorry, but I guess I don't understand."

"They are for you to bring your parents here. If you cannot be there for the holidays, they can be here. They may already have family plans for the twenty-fifth, but they can come here whenever is best for them. We will be here during the entire holidays."

Stunned, Patrick said, "No, this is too much."

"Patrico, it is a gift. You must take it or our feelings will be hurt."

He paused, thinking about his parents. "It would truly be a wonderful opportunity for them. My mother is in the beginning stages of multiple sclerosis. If she is ever going to see the Vatican, it must be soon. I hope they will accept. Seeing Rome is a dream for all Catholics, but they would never allow themselves to spend that kind of money. There has just not been much money left over ever for anything that they would deem unnecessary." He stopped, overcome with emotion, "They've never treated them-selves to life's extras. I'll call them in the morning and let you know as soon as I know what they decide. You are such wonderful friends and much too good to me," he said, turning to hug both Carmella and Stefano.

"You are a special gift to us. Now we must go if you are not to miss your train," Carmella added, wiping tears from her eyes.

☞☜

After much persuasion, Patrick's parents agreed to Christmas in Italy, although Patrick knew the decision had not come easy for them. At first they told Patrick they needed to stay until the 26th so the other children could be at the family home for Christmas Eve and Christmas Day, but his brothers and sisters convinced them that they needed to be in Rome for the Pope's blessing on the 25th and enjoy the sights during the most holy of holidays. Once the decision was made, Patrick's mother, in her excitement telephoned every few days, with questions.

"Mom, if you keep spending all your money on long distance calls, you won't be able to buy a pizza here," Patrick teased, obviously pleased that they were thrilled about this once in a lifetime trip.

He called Stefano and Carmella again to confirm the plans and then sat down at his desk.

Dear Mom,

Here are the tickets, as you can see. I have made your plane reservations for the evening of the 23rd. You'll arrive in Rome early the morning of the 24th. You'll probably want to rest some and then we will go to dinner on Christmas Eve and back to my apartment. There is a vacant apartment here which I have rented for you on the 24th, 25th, and 26th. I want to show you around the Vatican, including St. Peters, the museums and the Sistine Chapel. Also you'll want to see the Colosseum and the best of Ancient Rome. We'll go to the annual December 25 Urbi et Orbi Blessing from the Pope at his window, overlooking St. Peter's. I have to take you to the Christmas Fair on Piazza Navona. It's a holiday market that you just need to experience. On the 27th we'll take the train to Stefano and Carmella's. So you do not have to ride the train any more than necessary, Carmella said she'll drive you all around Tuscany on the 28th and then to Florence to see the Duomo on the 29th. The 30th will be a nice day to just relax or see whatever you have missed. We'll ride the train back the next day for some light sightseeing and then you'll fly out the next day.

Hope this sounds good to you. I can't wait!

Love,
Patrick

His mother called as soon as she received the mail. "Patrick, we are so excited. Please tell Carmella and Stefano we can't wait. This will be the best trip of our lives. Your dad's beside himself. Everybody at the station is going to be sick of hearing about this," she laughed.

ॐ—ॐ

Seeing his parents' faces made the hectic week worth every minute. The excitement in their voices filled Patrick with gladness. His dad seemed more relaxed than he had seen him in years, smoking cigars with Stefano and swapping stories. Although it was physically difficult for his mother to keep pace, she was a trooper and pushed herself to see everything Patrick had planned, snapping pictures as fast as the shutter allowed.

It gave him an odd feeling to see his parents in Italy. He tried to understand why. Maybe because as a kid he never saw them stray far from Boston satisfied to center their whole world in a few square miles. Now, he was showing them places they had only read about and that pleased him.

At the airport, he felt incredible loneliness as he waved goodbye to them. Slinging his jacket over his shoulder, he walked away aimlessly.

ॐ—ॐ

chapter 12

Spring came and so did new doubts. Patrick's studies were not going as he had thought. The more he learned, the more he questioned. One night over dinner while Father Shaun was telling him a story, the inner battle took full control.

"Patrick, I know that it is the obligation of the priest to keep complete confidence about confessions. I won't reveal names, but I must talk about this to someone because it is heavy on my mind."

The two men had had many spirited conversations, and although they had disagreed on several issues, they had always remained close. In spite of their friendship, Father Shaun had never confided in Patrick.

"You are going to be a priest, Patrick, and you will more than likely have the same dilemma, so tell me what you would do. Today, I had a parishioner from another church, a boy about fourteen come to me with a story. He said he wanted to talk with me, for me to listen, but that he expected no answers. He just had to talk; he did not know what he was going to do, if anything. His priest has been molesting him. It has been going on for awhile. Apparently, it started when the boy was quite young. The boy wants it to stop, but he does not know how to do that. He said his parents would never allow him to quit going to church. Patrick, I am afraid he will come back, but the next time he will want me to do more than listen. He is going to want advice and although I have been at this a long time, I do not know what to tell him. If I suggest he tell his parents and they confront the priest I am afraid they will say I told the boy to tell. That would be terrible for me. I do not think the church would look kindly on me. But on the other hand, I feel so badly for this boy. I am really surprised he came to me. I think he came in an effort to be cleansed, but I did not help him. I would think he would have lost faith in any priest if that were happening, but he did come and he will be back; it is too troubling for him. I know he will."

Sitting there in silence, Patrick could feel his face turning red from the anger raging deep inside of him.

"What would you do, Patrick?"

For a long time Patrick didn't speak. Hesitantly, he said, "I would have to offer to help the boy, to go with him to his parents, whatever it took to stop the sickness."

"But Patrick," Father Shaun said, obviously flustered and not really wanting that to be Patrick's answer. "Think about the consequences. The church is not going to want to hear that or accept that. The officials would think I was bringing great harm to the church. They would want me to be quiet."

"What about the boy, Father Shaun?" Patrick demanded his voice louder than he meant it to be.

"I know, I know, but he is just one. This could be explosive over one boy."

"If there is one, there are others."

"Maybe not."

"But maybe so."

"Patrick, the stakes are so high. I know this priest. He has major ties with the Vatican. He has received the Pope's blessing many times. There are rumors he is in line to become a cardinal one day. I wish the boy had never come to me," the priest said, sighing.

Suddenly wanting to be alone, Patrick interrupted, "I need to study. I wish I could say what you want to hear, but I can't." He stood and gathered his belongings.

"Thanks for listening to me, Patrick. You will not say anything, will you?"

"I don't know this boy, the parish or the priest. He didn't come to me," he said in a constrained voice.

The restaurant was closing as the two men walked out into the night. Although it was almost April, there was still a chill in the air and the sweat on Patrick's chest made it seem even colder when the wind blew against him. At the corner when they parted, Patrick suddenly felt cold, alone and more confused than ever. He lie awake into the night thinking, contemplating his life.

May brought the semester to a close, but no closure for Patrick as he continued to struggle with his thoughts. He needed to get away from Rome for a few days so he did what he always did when he felt this way; he took refuge at Stefano and Carmella's.

Upon returning to Rome, he felt better, following rest, good food and lengthy conversations with his two Tuscan friends. He began to look forward to his job at St. Peter's as a docent and tour leader. Because he loved going to the Basilica and thought it was one of the most beautiful structures anywhere, he was excited to be able to share it with people from all over the world.

A week later he saw Father Shaun who Patrick had not had an opportunity to talk with since their visit in April.

"Why don't we have dinner tonight, Patrick? Are you free?" the priest asked.

"Yes, that would be nice."

"I'll meet you at the Lorenzo Trattoria at 6:00 p.m. if that's agreeable with you."

Because he had gone directly from St. Peter's, Patrick was early to the trattoria so he ordered a glass of vino della casa and waited.

Seeing his friend, the priest, he stood to greet him.

"How was your first day at the Basilica?"

"It was good. I'm still learning some of the history, especially about the Papal Crypt and the sub crypt. I do several different tours so it might take a few days to get used to the timing and schedules."

"Patrick, I don't think even those of us who have been here many years know everything about the Basilica and museums. It is a fascinating place. Don't you agree?"

"Yes, and probably the greatest creation of Rome's Renaissance."

"You have completed your first year of schooling," Father Shaun said, more as a statement than a question.

"Yes. Is the first the most difficult?"

"I found them all to be about the same, different courses, but similar pressures," the priest stated.

"Would you like to order?" the waiter asked.

"I'll have the spaghetti alla carbonara and an espresso."

"I'll have the same but no espresso," Patrick said.

The two men sat for awhile watching the tourists and locals walk by the small restaurant. Located near the Spanish Steps, the area was always crowded with street performers, artists, kids playing soccer and young couples hand in hand.

"The azaleas are about over I see," Patrick said wistfully.

"Yes, but I believe during this April and May, they were the prettiest I have seen them in years."

"It is definitely heating up. I wasn't here much of the last summer, so June is new to me."

"Just wait until August. You know almost every shop closes the last two weeks of August because it is so hot. Everyone goes off to the beach. If you are going to be here, it is a good thing you have your scooter; the buses run only on a limited basis."

"I did arrive here last August, and I agree, this is not the place one wants to be in that heat." Pausing, to change the subject, he continued, "I must ask, did the young boy who you mentioned at our last dinner come back?"

"No, I never saw him again. I really worried that I would," the priest said, looking relieved.

"I had hoped he would, because he must have been hurting," Patrick said quickly.

The priest frowned and looked squarely at Patrick, "You are young and have much to learn about the church, Patrick. It is powerful. I told you—it is all encompassing, absolute power."

"Yes, and as the saying goes…. 'Absolute power corrupts absolutely!'

The waiter brought their food and the two men ate without talking. When he brought the check, Father Shaun took it and said, "I'll get this, and I really must be going. I'll see you at mass, Patrick."

"Yes, and thank you for dinner. I didn't mean to offend you, I just feel strongly," his voice trailing off.

"Every man has to follow his own course, Patrick."

And live with himself, Patrick thought, but he didn't reply.

"Goodnight Father Shaun."

"Goodnight Patrick."

Patrick ordered another wine and watched the throngs of people heading to a free concert. He could not clear his mind from thinking about the young boy. "The demons he will fight," Patrick said, under his breath.

രൈം

As the summer and fall semesters drew on, Patrick knew his days of pursuing the priesthood were numbered. The only time he was happy was while he worked at St. Peter's. The visitors were friendly and humble asking questions whether they were Protestant or Catholic. When he worked in the Vatican museums and the Sistine Chapel, he found himself continuing to be awestruck by the beauty of the art and grandeur of the Renaissance, but his heart was heavy and no matter how hard he prayed or how many questions he asked, he could find no peace. He was on an endless and useless journey that had taken him to a dead end. For all these years, he had wanted to believe that this is where he belonged, that this was his calling. Now he realized he had misinterpreted the signs. He had given it his heart and mind, and it had eaten at his soul; he had been robbed, again. He could never be enough to change the Church. He could never loosen the clutches of the Vatican. He would never be strong enough to right the wrongs of this powerful force. His only choice was to completely divorce himself of its hold and to play no role in its webbed effect. He would be the Church's spider no more. He had to flee. He had to get peace.

chapter 13

In November, Patrick called Stefano and Carmella.

"Oh, Patrico, it is so good to hear your voice," Carmella said excitedly.

"Carmella, I know it's the busiest time of the year for Stefano, but I was wondering if I could come up tomorrow and talk with you for a short while."

"Patrico, is something wrong? Are you all right?"

"I'm fine," he said. "I just need to talk. Will you please ask Stefano just to be sure it's all right before I come?"

"You know it is. We are never too busy for you, but I will ask just the same and call you if there is a problem. If you do not hear from me tonight, what time can we expect you?"

"I'll take the afternoon train. I believe it arrives there at 4:58 p.m."

"Good, in time for cocktails. I am looking forward to seeing you, Patrico. Are you absolutely sure you are okay?"

Patrick mustered a light laugh to convince Carmella he was all right. "I'm really fine. I'm anxious to see you both."

Carmella was waiting when his train arrived. She thought he appeared nervous and worried.

"Stefano was in the shower so I told him I would come on. He said he would be on the terrace waiting."

Knowing he must be tense, Patrick was struggling to cover his apprehension.

Stefano was on the terrace, as promised, when they drove up.

"Patrico, it is so good to see you, but what brings you up here in the middle of the week?" he asked, handing a drink to Carmella and then one to Patrick.

They all sat down, but Patrick suddenly stood, rushing into his sentence, said, "I am going to Boston for Christmas, and I am not coming back to Rome. I am leaving the Church."

"Leaving, what do you mean?" Stefano said, looking stunned.

"I'm giving up my training for the priesthood. I'm no longer going to be a Catholic."

"But Patrico, you will always be a Catholic!" Stefano countered.

"Maybe on a sheet of paper somewhere or maybe in some peoples' minds, but not in my heart," Patrick countered.

"Why? Why this change of heart," Carmella asked, tears running down her cheeks.

Patrick paused, he wanted to tell them the truth, everything, but he cut himself off.

"I have studied and I have prayed, both more than you will ever know, but there are just some parts of the Church that I can no longer accept. I thought being a priest would bring me happiness; that I could be a champion for the people who no one else would listen to, but I cannot. The church is too big, too powerful, too singular and so is the priest—he *is* the Church; he *is* the power. It is not power I want, it is peace."

"Patrico, I am a Catholic; I was born a Catholic and I will die as one; it is all I know, but I am not a scholar. I will support whatever you decide. Nothing changes."

Carmella was weeping now. She stood and walked over to Patrick and put her arms around him.

"Patrico, we love you, and we know you did not make this decision without a struggle. I am selfish. I do not want you to leave Italy."

"I'll return here someday to visit, and you must come to the States to see me. Thank you for listening. I know it's difficult for you to understand and I honor that. Please know that I am not walking away from God. My quarrel is not with him and my faith is strong. I will serve in some capacity, but not as a Catholic."

"What will you do, Patrico?"

"I'm not sure. In the last year I've read many books about other doctrines. I will continue doing that. I have found that my basic tenets are no different from many of those beliefs. In most, the governance of the Church is not in one man. In some churches it is shared by all the faithful. There's a very small seminary in eastern Maine that I may explore. I hear it's remote and beautiful there.

"I'll miss this part of the world, here where you are, and I'll desperately miss you," he said with tears welling up in his eyes. "You have been so good to me. I love you both." Standing, he continued, "It's late, and I know what a busy time this is for you, Stefano. I'll take the night train back."

"You will not, young man," Carmella said sternly. "We are going to have some dinner and wine, and you will stay in your bungalow as always."

"I didn't bring clothes," Patrick said.

"I will find some clothes around here. I'm sure Enrico has some that will fit you. Tomorrow you can help us pick olives. You cannot leave Italy without that experience," Stefano said softly, still obviously shaken by the news.

Patrick smiled; he wanted to stay, needed to stay. This place was like a cocoon for him. He wished his parents would be as understanding, but he knew that would not be the case.

"About the scooter, what should I do with it?"

"Patrick, we have three here. Sell it or give it away. It is nothing," Stefano urged.

"Then if it's all right with you, I think it would mean a great deal to Ricardo, the old, Italian gentleman who works at the apartment building."

"Do what you wish; it is yours."

"I think I'll offer it to him; maybe I can leave Italy feeling good about something," his voice tight with emotion.

"Then you two find him some clothes so he can freshen up and get back here to help me with dinner. This is a working trip," Carmella teased, but Patrick could tell, her heart was heavy.

"Just do me one favor, will you Patrico?"

"Certainly; what is that?"

"Throw a coin over your shoulder into the Trevi Fountain."

Patrick looked at her with a confused expression.

"Then you will come back to Rome and to us some day," she smiled warmly.

PART THREE
Conquering Fears

And looking back along the past
We know we needed all the strain
Of fear and doubt and strife and pain
To make us value peace, at last...

chapter 14

Like the title of Eugene O'Neill's book, Patrick's flight home was a long day's journey into night, both literally and figuratively. He didn't know how he was going to break it to his parents, the quintessential Catholics, the unquestioning, undoubting followers of this doctrine. How could he explain without explaining? He would just have to do his best and leave the rest unanswered.

The week before Christmas, Patrick played the good seminarian, still acting like a student searching for knowledge in the Eternal City, just home on a holiday break.

The day after Christmas he broke the news to his parents and it didn't go over any better than Patrick had expected. His mother cried and his father shouted. Knowing his parents thought they had failed him somehow, Patrick tried to make them understand that none of this was their fault; it was a decision he made after years of struggle.

"You have disgraced the family. What will Father Michael say?" his dad shouted. His mother wept, walking around the living room, wringing her hands. After three hours, he packed a few items of clothing and headed to his brother John's apartment.

"Whether you agree or not, I just need a place to stay for the night," Patrick told him, after riding the "T" to his place.

"You're welcome here as long as you want to stay, Patrick. You're the strong one, the knowledgeable one. I'm just a blind Catholic follower. If you tell me you quit, I respect that without question. You have obviously fought the good fight."

"I couldn't say it better, big brother. May I sleep on the couch?"

"You can sleep in the bed; this good Catholic boy is spending the night at his girlfriend's house, the girlfriend who is on the pill," he said, grinning sheepishly. "So help yourself to the beer in the fridge and watch television or whatever. If you are here tomorrow, I'll see you about five o'clock."

"Thanks John. I'll not forget your help."

"Please don't. I may need a place someday."

Three days later Patrick went home.

"Mom, Dad, I have to talk, so please try to listen. I'm truly sorry about all of this. I would never hurt you for anything, but I am a grown man and I've made a decision I can live with. I only ask you to accept it, not agree with it. I still pray to the same God as you. I would like to stay here until the end of summer when hopefully I can start my life over somewhere else. In the meantime, I need to work enough to help pay the bills.

"Oh Patrick," his mother said, "I'm so glad you're home. Your dad and I have talked many hours since you left. You're right. You're grown. You have to decide. We can't do it for you."

"Patrick, I apologize for the things I said. We were just shocked; your mother is right. You stay here as long as you want. We are who we are and we can't change that, but neither can you. We will just have to accept each other's choices."

Hugging them both, he said, "I'm tired. I'm going to bed. I'll go to the marina tomorrow and see if Mac has any work for me. I'll pay my way, I assure you."

In January Patrick wrote to the Maine Seminary for Theological Studies asking for admissions information. He had done his research and knew the teachings there were non-denominational, Protestant, with a leaning toward the Presbyterian, Congregational and Methodist churches.

In the introductory letter that he returned with his application and transcripts, he explained his background and waited.

The next two months were especially cold as he helped his old friend Mac, the lobsterman, repair traps and sand and paint the boat he had been using in the waters off Boston Harbor for well over forty years. He had missed Mac, their talks and easy banter.

"How many more years you think this boat can take the waters?" Patrick asked; glad to have on his heaviest coat as the wind whipped against him.

Not looking up, Mac answered slowly, "Eh, we'll leave together, me and MicMac. I can't imagine me in any other boat or anybody else with the Mic. We both have a few more good years. I guess one of us will let the other know when it's time."

"You think you'll ever put a GPS in her?"

"I know these waters better than any damned electronic equipment could ever possibly know 'em! Hell, no! When I can't find the lobsters, I'll quit!"

Patrick smiled. He had known Mac since he was a toddler when his dad had brought him to the docks to see the traps. That had been more than twenty years ago when Mac was in his early fifties. The crusty old salt was now even more set in his ways, weather-beaten, impatient, a no nonsense kind of guy.

Patrick was drawn to him immediately and begged his dad to take him to the docks on the weekend where he knew Mac would be. He had fished out of Gloucester for a few months and then Rockport, but he always came back. "This harbor is my home," he would say. When Patrick was old enough, he pressed his dad to let him work for Mac in the summers and on weekends, rather than at the grocery store where his older brothers had sacked groceries. At first his dad had been unwilling, worried about the dangers, but Mac convinced him that the sea would teach the young boy to appreciate the sunrises and sunsets and the responsibilities in between. His father had liked that.

Mac was right about the sea. Patrick loved the openness and quickly gained an appreciation for it and the hard life that came with it. He couldn't imagine working it all his life, but knew it was Mac's whole world. As a nine year old boy Mac had worked in the processing room of the lobster cannery to help out at home. With his mother and a host of other women he picked the meat from the shells, washed it and put it in cans. When he was thirteen he joined his dad and other men in the factories where they boiled the lobsters, but he knew he couldn't stay inside so he took the first chance he could to work on the docks.

It took him years, but he saved enough to make a down payment on a boat and christened it the MicMac after the Mikmaq Canadian Indians who had been fishing the seas before the Europeans settled in The New World. Of course, when he told the story he added that it went well with his own name. Patrick had heard his stories countless times but he never reminded his old friend of that. Besides, they somehow changed a little each time he told them. Mac wasn't always keen on the details.

Patrick had stirred him up with his questions and now he was going to have to listen.

"I can't imagine not going out in this boat," Mac said with a pained look.

"I don't see that happening ever."

"Ayyup, you're right. I want to be buried at sea, so I might as well make it easy on everybody and just keel over out there someday. Don't let them look for my body; that would be a waste. I'll be right where I want to be. Just don't let anybody else take ole MicMac out, 'ear?" he added, nostalgically.

"I hear you, Mac, but I figure you have another twenty years or so. Don't be getting sentimental on me now."

"Well, hell, I'm seventy-four years old. I can't live forever, but I have outlived two wives, a daughter and six dogs. Not bad, 'eh," he said with a twinkle in his eyes. It was becoming increasingly harder to even see the exact eye color.

"You need to have your cataracts operated on if you're going to keep going out there," Patrick cautioned.

"Screw the cataracts. No doctor is going to take a knife to my eyeballs!"

Laughing, Patrick said, "I don't think that's exactly how they do it."

By this time, the two friends were inside the shop and Mac had popped the top of a Schlitz beer. "Here, have some of what made Milwaukee famous."

"Believe I will. Thanks." Patrick took a gulp, "Not exactly Guinness."

"Beggars can't be choosers. How's your old man taking you not going to mass?"

"He doesn't like it, but we've agreed to disagree."

"Hmm, don't sound like a comfortable situation. He should just be glad you believe in something. Lotta men don't. I didn't used to, but as I get older, I do a lot more thinking. That damn old man sun don't just come up on its own."

"You're right, Mac."

"What have you heard from that fancy college up in Maine?"

Patrick grinned. "Nothing yet. I don't think it's very fancy."

"Anything past sixth grade sounds fancy to me."

That very day, his letter of acceptance to begin his master's degree came in the mail with the extra good news that they were giving him credit for eighteen hours he had taken in Rome.

PART FOUR
Finding Himself

Who fails finds later triumph sweet
Who stumbles once walks then with care,
And who knows the place to cry "Beware"
To other unaccustomed feet. . .

chapter 15

Maine, September, 1977

Patrick's search for a new beginning took him to the far reaches of Maine. Remote and beautiful, it reminded him in some ways of East Texas, though it was not as hot. The trees were just as predominant and he loved the lush landscape. Throwing himself into his studies, he went to classes, studied and worked in the campus library to help with expenses. Although he made few friends, he impressed his professors. With the credits accepted from Rome, his taking heavy course loads, and writing his thesis in the spring, he was able to graduate in August with his master's degree. A week before graduation, his favorite professor, an older gentleman who had taught for almost forty years, called him to his office.

"Patrick, I have recommended you for a Congregational Church over at Hidden Harbor. It is very small, but I think you, with your youth and enthusiasm can make it grow. The building is historical; it has been there for years, but in those years, no one has really tried to reach out to the people. These people, as you know by now, are rugged individualists; it is a hard life. The population is made up of fishermen, artists, nature lovers and survivalists, but they need God as much as anyone. The right person can succeed there, and I think you are the right person."

Patrick was elated. "This was just what I was looking for. The Maine seashore brings me serenity."

"Good, then I'll set it up."

He called Stefano and Carmella to tell him he was being ordained on Sunday and then he called his parents.

Not many people from the outside came to live near Hidden Harbor, although there were plenty of tourists heading up to the Harbor, especially in the summer months when the whale

watching boats went out. It was also a departure destination for
boats to Nova Scotia, and a stopping off place for those going to
Acadia National Park and West Quoddy Headlight at Lubec, at
the very edge of the Eastern Time zone. But in the winter months
he knew almost everything closed down because of the extreme
cold. Most restaurants and hotels closed by the end of October
and many didn't open back until Memorial Day weekend and
Patrick wondered how he would adjust. It could be a lonely area,
but the locals who stayed told him they found ways of entertain-
ing themselves. He laughed to himself, another *foreign land*.

∂∽∽

The first person Patrick met at the Seaside Diner, one of the
few places that remained open, was Carol. She had summered
in Hidden Harbor with her parents when she was growing up
and when things turned sour in New York City, it just seemed
natural to make her way to Maine to continue her painting and
photography. Although she still occasionally went back to the
City to show her work at the gallery and to see her parents in
Connecticut, she had lived here permanently for three years. A
tall brunette with long thin legs but an ample bust, Carol had a
fresh look, probably as a result of wearing very little makeup and
pulling her long hair back in a simple pony tail. No matter how
casual she dressed or how much she tried otherwise, her sophis-
tication was evident. In some circles she had been described as
having good bones and carrying herself well. Her eyes were the
color of strong coffee, definitely too dark to twinkle or to give
the slightest hint of emotion.

Because of her family's financial circumstances, her father
was a physician in Connecticut, she had been able to wear designer clothes, attend the best schools and travel extensively, allowing her opportunities and experiences she easily referenced in

conversation. Yet in many ways, she was quite regular, a paradox of sorts.

Patrick found himself intrigued by her, and they talked over coffee for more than an hour. During the next several months they saw each other occasionally in town, generally finding their way to the Seaside for hot cocoa or coffee.

Their conversation always led to questions about her art and his assignment as the new congregational minister. He told her it was more difficult than what he expected because so few people remained in the coldest part of the winter and even fewer braved the weather to hear a sermon.

"I can't say I blame them."

"But you will visit sometime, won't you?"

"Are you inviting me?"

"Sure. I thought you already knew that you were welcome."

"Around here Patrick, people don't assume anything. I suggest you get out and go door to door, create some winter activities and before long you might have a full house at that little white church."

"I'll do that, but you didn't answer my question."

"Sorry, but I've forgotten the question."

"Will you visit the church?"

"Certainly Patrick, but it's been awhile since I've been in a church. I hope I remember what I'm supposed to do," she said, laughing.

Grinning, he teasingly instructed, "Just bow your head when everybody else does. Try to close your eyes and not look around during that time. It's really easy. What stopped you from going?"

"I never really started. Oh, as a young girl I went some with my mother to the Presbyterian Church. My dad is an agnostic. It's not that I'm not interested. I am. Traditional religion has not ever been my thing, although I've studied Eastern beliefs, different doctrines. As a philosophy minor, I've had my share of discussions."

"I'd like to hear more sometime."

"Well, I'm usually here about eleven on Tuesday mornings after I give my art lesson at the community center."

On Tuesday Patrick was at the café long before 11:00, hoping that Carol would really show up. When she did, he immediately felt a little self-conscious. After all, she was from a wealthy family, one that not only admired fine art, but obviously owned a great deal of it, from what Carol had said. Patrick had tried to remember any art in his parents' house and decided the best he could come up with was the free 8" x 10" calendar of Norman Rockwall pictures his mother brought home from the local pharmacy in December each year and hung on the kitchen wall.

When he finally got the courage to ask her for a real date, she said, "It's about time, talk about a slow learner." He laughed his deep laugh and let out a sigh of relief. At almost 28 years old, he knew it was silly to be nervous, but he couldn't help himself. After all, it had been a long time since he had had a date.

They went to dinner at one of the marina restaurants and then afterwards back to Carol's small house, a yellow clapboard cottage high on a hill overlooking the water. Colorful buoys hung on one side of the house and lobster boats bobbed in the bay below. The yard was a sea of flowers. They were greeted by the largest Maine Coon cat Patrick had ever seen, and immediately, the cat wrapped himself around Patrick's leg, as if to check him out and decide on giving his approval.

Carol reached down and picked him up, "Peri, meet Patrick."

"What's his name?"

"His real name is Dom Pérignon, but I call him Peri. He was a gift from my friends, Fredrico and Marc, when I left New York."

Looking around, he was charmed by the entire surroundings. Her art work was fabulous, the detail unbelievable. But it was her photography that really took him in. The faces were alive and told so many stories. He noticed a mystery in some where there seemed to be something purposely missing, not because of a lack of clarity on her part, but rather because of the angle from which they were taken. Many were reflective silhouettes, eerie in their mysticism.

As they shared a bottle of wine and talked until almost three o'clock in the morning, Patrick found himself wanting to hold her and stay the night. When she asked him not to go, he almost stayed but forced himself to return to his small apartment.

The next day after he called and asked if he could see her again, he stopped to buy bread and wine along with a hanging basket of fuchsia. As she met him at the door, he kissed her and followed her in.

"I love the basket of flowers. Let me show you why," taking his hand and leading him out back to see her lavender, rosemary and other herbs. He had noticed she had some flowers the night before, but as he looked closely again he could not believe how many there were. Her backyard was aglow with flowers, rhododendron shrubs, beach roses, crocus scattered among what seemed like hundreds of ferns and other greenery. Staring at the beauty, he was amazed and convinced that she was obviously an artist in many ways. Already he knew he was falling in love with her and hoped she felt something close to that for him. Pulling her toward him, he kissed her. She looked at him straightforward and smiled, knowing he would not leave her house this night.

Over dinner, they discussed their lives. She told him about her two year affair with a magazine editor who was married and about her work at the art gallery. "I thought he loved me and would leave his wife. I was so stupid. For two years I dated no one but waited for him to come over when he could, to squeeze me into his life," she said with a tinge of bitterness still in her voice. "Sometimes he stayed all night. I don't know what he told her. She must have known. I met her twice and she was friendly enough, but I think she knew."

Carol paused and then pushed herself to go on. "Anyway, I got tired of waiting and after going on one of my photography trips and being away from him for a couple of months, I knew I could survive without him. When I told him I was tired of having him part time, the left-over part, he simply left. I never saw him again. Shortly after that I left the gallery and came here." She smiled, seeming to be relieved to have told him.

Patrick told her about his family and how close he and his older brothers were, of his basketball days, and of life in Indiana and then Rome. She knew he had been raised Catholic from previous conversations and asked him what happened. "I became disillusioned," not quite telling the whole truth. "There were just a lot of things I could no longer accept. The Catholic Church is just not changing with the world. I couldn't live a life I didn't believe in anymore," Patrick offered, but he didn't elaborate.

Carol pressed, but he sidestepped her direct questions, "I guess I just got older and realized that some things were just not congruent with who I am now; I'm not bitter that I spent all that time believing in some things and some people, but I'm glad I'm where I am now."

And Carol was glad, too. Carol urged him along, "But why the Congregational Church, why not Presbyterian, Episcopalian, Baptist or some other?"

"Well, growing up in New England, I had heard a lot about the Congregational Church, as I'm sure you had too, especially since you're from Connecticut. There are quite a few Congregational Churches there. They share many similarities with these other religions, especially Presbyterians in New England. There are many reformed churches that are a result of a series of unions between other groups like the United Church of Christ and the Congregational Christian Churches, but you don't want to hear a lesson," he laughed. "Did you know that Harvard, Yale, Dartmouth, William Bowdoin and Amherst were all founded by Congregationalists?"

"No, but I hadn't really thought about it," she teased Patrick. "But please keep explaining," Carol replied.

"I guess the thing that appealed to me most is the democracy of the Congregational Church and the independence. The theory of it forbids the minister from ruling by himself or any single body of people being in complete control. Freedoms are guaranteed to every person; every person has a say. There are checks and balances that keep any one group like the lay officers or the minister or one or two members from having special authority."

"In the Catholic Church, the priest has all the control, and that's not good. No one person should have that much power, but enough about that."

"Well, the word in town is that your church is really growing. People are driving some distance to hear you—the red headed Irish Preacher with the deep voice and funny lilt."

Patrick blushed. "Now, where are you hearing this?"

Smiling, she loved to banter with him and watch his reactions. "Seriously, I heard a woman at the community center saying you really know the Bible well. And then another said she liked the way you used parables and contemporary comparisons and that you weave quite a story. People like that. It makes them feel comfortable in an atmosphere that might otherwise be stuffy and stiff."

"I'm Irish, don't forget. We take great pride in our storytelling," he replied, a twinkle in his eyes, showing great pleasure in what she had just related.

"I tell you that, but I want you for my very own, and those women better not get any other ideas…"

He gazed directly into her eyes to be sure she was not still teasing him.

"What else should I know about you Irishmen?"

"Well, we tend to be somewhat unpredictable, practical, independent thinkers. And, of course, we're romantic poets, lovers of song and dance" he winked.

"And quite humble I can tell"

After helping her with the dishes, he followed her to the couch. Before long they found themselves in her bed. When she awoke at 5:00 a.m., Patrick had been gone at least an hour, at first light, but had left a note on the breakfast table: **"I love you. Can I see you tonight?"**

Carol picked up her coffee cup and drifting to the window she watched the sun dance on the dew-covered flowers outside the kitchen. Winter had released its grip and spring had finally caught on, though the early morning chill lingered possessively. The warmth of the room and her old gray sweats made her feel snug and tended to. It was quiet, save Peri's contented purring. She had planned to paint today, go down to the water with her canvas and launch herself into another art project, think about nothing but the reflection of the light on the cobalt sea. But now all she could think about blue were Patrick's eyes.

She had not expected to feel this way about him. She hadn't wanted to fall in love again, not with him. Not really with anyone. It hurt too much if it didn't work. But last night had changed her mind. Patrick had been so gentle, taking her to a place no man had ever taken her before. She stared out at the ocean. Maybe she would tend to her herbs today and take a long bath, use the new salts she had bought at the little boutique that had just opened in town.

Patrick arrived at her doorstep in Levis and a navy blue lightweight sweater at exactly six o'clock, a wine bottle in one hand and bouquet of calla lilies and lavender freesia in the other.

"You're spoiling me, Patrick."

"I hope so." He leaned to kiss her. "You smell good."

"That's because I spent most of my afternoon in a perfumed bath with soft music and a trashy novel."

"Are you trying to seduce me?"

"Do I need to," she smiled wickedly. "But first let me put the flowers in a vase and get the corkscrew for you."

She went to the kitchen and came back with two wine glasses and a tray of cheeses. While Patrick opened the Bordeaux, she busied herself arranging the flowers in an antique vase. He poured each of them a glass of the rich red wine that immediately emitted the aroma of toasted oak and ripe fruit.

"Mmm. This is excellent. I'm surprised you can find this here."

Laughing, he said, "I didn't. I brought several cases with me from Boston. It is good, isn't it?"

Carol watched Patrick take another sip. She thought it sensuous the way he let the wine linger in his mouth. Curling up beside him, she whispered, "I read your note."

"And?" he answered nervously touching her arm.

"And I love you." Her voice was soft, but strong.

He pulled her close in a tight hug, ran his hands through her long hair and touched her face. "This could be the start of something good."

ॐॐ

Patrick loved this time of year in the northeast. It was like the whole world had wakened up from the winter's blast and was now lazily enjoying the warmer days and cool crisps evenings. Besides in May the humidity was low and the mosquitoes hadn't yet grown to be the size of moths.

"What do you say about a short trip down the coastline? Drive up to Portland and then work our way through the little fishing villages and maybe see a few lighthouses?"

"I would love that Patrick. It's been years since I've seen most of those places."

"Good. I'll be here at seven o'clock in the morning. Is that too early?"

"Not for you and the fishermen," she laughed. "You're certainly not gaining any points with Peri, taking me away," she added.

"Tell him we will bring him a toy rat," he teased. He knew how much she loved the huge, bundle of fur and whiskers.

When Patrick arrived at her house a few minutes before seven o'clock the next morning, Carol met him in her robe.

"Here's my bag, Patrick. I just need to dress."

He put his hands inside her robe, feeling her soft naked skin. "I guess we could just stay here," he smiled, running his fingers over her body.

"Oh, no you don't! We're going on a trip."

"Well, it was worth a try," he grinned, while bending over to rub Peri's neck. "You be a good boy and watch the house."

As they were driving out of her driveway, Patrick said, "We will probably be in Portland by 10:30 or 11:00 a.m. Have you been to the Windsor Museum of Art?"

"No, I haven't. I understand it has some nice impressionist and post-impressionist works there. One of Renoir's portraits is there."

"I need to run a quick errand when I get to Portland, so could I drop you at the museum? I'll only be a couple of hours."

"Certainly, but what kind of errand?"

"Oh, the church has an account at the Portland First Trust Bank and I've needed to close it out. This would be a good time," he said, needing an excuse for his real errand.

"On the way back, can we stop at Damariscotta on the river?" Carol asked.

"Sure, whatever is fine."

"First let's stop at some of the antique shops in Wiscasset."

"That sounds fun," Patrick said. "Then I'd like to see Pemaquid Light. Maybe we could spend the night at New Harbor. I guess it depends on how much time we spend looking and shopping. Wherever we are when it gets late will be fine with me. Nothing will be really crowded for another three weeks."

Patrick drove to the square in Portland where the art museum was located. "I'll be back shortly. Enjoy!" he told Carol.

When he arrived at the jewelry store, he introduced himself to the man who greeted him at the door.

"Hello, my name is Patrick O'Brien. Are you Mr. Frost?"

"Yes, you called, right?"

"You're holding some engagement rings for me. I need to select one and have it wrapped."

"Yes, yes, here they are Mr. O'Brien. I have this one carat marquise, in a cathedral solitaire setting; a very elegant ring. Then, I have this pear shape with a six prong V-tip setting, adding it to the velvet tray.

"I don't like that one. It's not feminine enough."

"Look at this emerald cut. It is near colorless and the clarity is excellent. It is, however, closer to 1.5 carats, but its simplicity is intriguing."

"Would you show me a wedding band that goes nicely with that?"

"Surely." He returned with a small band that included ten emerald cut diamonds, channel set.

"I like this set very much."

"Let me show you one more—an oval shape. This is an outstanding diamond with an elliptically shaped bezel. It is 1.5 carats also."

"I still like the emerald shape the best."

After they discussed price, Patrick said, "I'd like to give her the engagement ring tonight as a surprise. If she would rather have another design, can we exchange it in the morning?"

"Certainly. Are you nervous?" the jeweler said, noticing the beads of perspiration on Patrick's forehead.

"A little," Patrick replied, smiling. "Should I take the band now or wait?"

"Your choice, but you may exchange either or both or whatever in the morning."

"Okay. Please wrap the engagement ring and I'll just take the wedding band with me."

"Done."

Handing the small package to Patrick, the jeweler smiled and said, "Good luck and best wishes."

The purchase had not taken as much time as Patrick thought it might so when he arrived at the museum; Carol was still strolling along, looking at the paintings.

"Hey, are you having fun?"

She turned, "Oh, you scared me. I wasn't expecting you back so soon, but I'm almost finished."

"Do you want to have a bowl of clam chowder?"

Carol nodded her head, "That sounds good. I'm hungry."

"Let's drive to the waterfront. We could take a boat ride after that," Patrick said, feeling relieved that the ring purchase was over.

"I made a reservation for 6:30 at Michael's Dockside Restaurant; I hope that's okay."

"Patrick, you are so thoughtful and fun. I'm happy with whatever you choose."

"You make my life so rich, so much bigger, Carol," pulling her close to him as they walked by the numerous souvenir shops that lined the street by the waterfront.

"Look Patrick, over there," pointing to a group of street vendors. "Let's look at the paintings."

Carol bent down to better inspect a small canvas lined with tiny seagulls and long stretches of blue sea. "Isn't that good?"

"Not as good as yours," he whispered, careful not to let the artist overhear.

"But look at the detail."

"If you want the painting, let's get it."

"We can look around some more. I just thought it was especially eye catching. Maybe because it was small, but effectual."

He took her hand and they strolled through the maze of vendors, each trying to persuade tourists to stop and take a look.

"Are you ready for dinner?"

"Yes, I'm famished. You wouldn't let me have anything but chowder."

His eyes lit up. "I didn't want you to ruin your dinner."

Michael's Dockside featured elegant dining, but it also attracted many of the locals to its friendly bar overlooking the water. The crowd was eclectic with people of all ages, dressed in every manner of clothing.

Patrick chose the formal dining room. The maître d' checked his notes and seated them in a small, romantic alcove overlooking the water. Patrick had been very insistent when he made the reservation, reiterating that this was a special occasion, requiring a romantic, quiet setting. Patrick discretely handed him a substantial tip.

"This is perfect," he said, pulling out the chair for Carol.

"What a pretty view. You picked a nice time of the year, before the crowds start growing, Patrick."

"I've only been here a few times, but it's always nice it seems this time of year. Do you want seafood?"

"Yes. Any seafood."

"I'm having the lazy man lobster, I think."

"That sounds good to me. I really like it, but I hate all the messy work when the lobster is in the shell. I like the thought of the work being done for me."

"Let's have a drink first." He signaled for the server.

"Don't you wonder about all these people, where they go in these boats, what their lives are like?"

"You are a people watcher, aren't you, Carol?"

"Yes, I suppose I am. I find it all so interesting." Her look was almost plaintive as her eyes scanned the water.

"I find you, oh so interesting," he said, unable to wait any longer. "I have a small gift for you," handing her the wrapped box.

"Why, for me now?"

"You'll see," he said, with a hint of nervousness in his voice.

Carol opened the wrapping carefully and then lifted the lid.

Taking her hand, he squeezed tightly and said, "Will you spend the rest of your life with me, Carol? Will you marry me?"

"Oh, Patrick, it is so beautiful. Yes, yes, and yes!" she said as tears ran down her cheeks. He felt tears welling up in his eyes as well.

"I never expected this. When did you do this?"

"When I ran my so-called bank errand this morning, I had to tell you something. I had called the jeweler two weeks ago and I've been trying to work out all the logistics of this," as he pulled her closer and kissed her softly.

"I love the design of the ring. I can't believe you did this by yourself."

"The jeweler said you could exchange it in the morning if you would like to look at others."

"I wouldn't consider that. This is so special. I love you so very much."

Patrick pulled the matching wedding band from his pocket. "Do you like this for the band?"

"It is beautiful, too. I'm so excited; Patrick, I'm not sure I can eat."

"You'll settle down in a few minutes, but I must admit I'm pretty keyed-up, myself." A shy smile flickered on his face.

"Can we go back in the morning and pick out a band for you?"

"Sure, I'd like that. When would you like the wedding?"

"Soon, as soon as possible, but it will take some planning. Do you think August would be good?"

"You're the bride, you get to pick. I just have to show up," he teased.

"I can't wait to call Nancy. I would like for her to be my matron of honor. Oh, I am so excited."

"I need to call John, my oldest brother, to be my best man. But first, I must call to talk to your parents. I want to ask for their permission. What do you think they will say?"

"Hallelujah, our old maid daughter is finally getting married," she said, laughing. "Seriously, they will be happy for us both. I've told them quite a bit about you on the phone. My father would like you better if you played golf, though."

"I'll learn," he said, chuckling. In a serious voice he said, "I hope my mother can come to the wedding. Her MS seems to get worse by the day. The trip may be too much for her, but I hope not."

の〜め

The drive home Patrick had planned was to be a slow, leisurely one through the backroads and out of the way places, exploring antique shops and hidden harbors not discovered by tourists. But it quickly became obvious to him that Carol's heart was no longer into lighthouses, heirlooms or fishing villages. She talked nonstop about the wedding, rarely glancing at the scenery or taking the opportunity to stop at a roadside flea market.

Finally, Patrick laughed and said, "Let's find a bed and breakfast in Camden tonight and then we'll head home.

の〜め

It would have been an absolutely beautiful and bright summer day had Carol not awakened in a foul mood. Patrick's enigmatic moods after they made love were driving her crazy. They had fought about it again last night and he had stormed out of the house without saying goodnight.

She didn't know what she had done wrong. In the height of passion she had called him Paddy and he had stopped their love making and moved away from her, cold and reticent. When she looked in his eyes, she was almost afraid of him until she saw what she thought was a tear. Why was it that she always loved someone who couldn't give himself completely to her? She had been through this before and she didn't need to get hurt again.

She was still in bed when Patrick knocked at the back door. She could see him from her room, *those damn eyes,* she thought. She started not to respond, but he continued to knock.

"Please, Carol, I'm sorry. Just let me in so we can talk."

Naked, she climbed out of bed, slipped into her robe and slowly walked through the tiny porch to the door.

Contrite, he asked, "Can I come in?"

Without answering, Carol opened the door, shrugging her shoulders.

"I'm sorry, Carol. I rarely lose my temper. I was wrong. It won't happen again. I love you." His voice sounding as pained as the look in his eyes.

"Do you, Patrick? Sometimes I'm not sure."

Her robe was slightly askew and Patrick couldn't take his eyes off her sensuous curves. He pulled her to him, crushing her against him, and lifting her chin, he forced her to look in his eyes.

"Please believe me when I tell you." Pausing, he asked, "Can we go into the bedroom and talk?"

"Talk, that's all, Patrick," moving his hand away from her skin.

Wanting him, she willed herself to pull away and sit on the edge of the bed. For an awkward moment Patrick stood before her and then he did something so out of character that it caught Carol off guard. He stripped off his clothes and stood in front of her. Reaching down, he took her hand and lifted her up to meet his eyes again. In half protest and half acceptance, she let him remove her robe.

"I'll show you how much I love you," he said, gently pushing her down on the covers.

Blushing slightly, she said, "It's not the sex, Patrick," touching his hair and outlining his face with her fingers. "It's afterwards. It's what you become…"

He pulled her closer, savoring her softness…"Just love me, Carol. Teach me how you want me to love."

"We have to talk."

"There is nothing to say. I acted badly and I'm sorry." He buried his head against her breasts and began kissing her skin.

She wanted to turn away until she felt his hard, warm body. The distance between them melted away. She knew she should stop him, but as always she could not resist him.

chapter 16

The minute Patrick heard his father's voice on the phone he knew something was wrong.

"It's your mother, Patrick. You need to get here."

"Dad, slow down. What's wrong?" He could hear his father's sobs in the background.

"She's dying. Can you hurry?"

Patrick looked at his watch. It was 4:00 a.m. "I'll leave here by six o'clock. Dad, are you sure?"

His voice cracked. "The doctor says she might pull through, but he isn't hopeful. Just come."

"I will Dad. Will you tell her I'll be there by noon?"

"Yes," he answered softly, his voice breaking again and then the phone clicked.

He needed to call Carol to tell her, but first he needed to clear his head. For the longest time, he lay there not wanting to move. His mother had always been there. He couldn't imagine her not. He wished the last few years hadn't been strained. Even though they said they forgave him for leaving the Catholic Church, there was tenseness when they were together. They didn't understand nor would they ever because they would never know the truth.

His parents' relationship with Father Michael had continued for all these years, and they often mentioned how much they appreciated the way he talked so proudly of their children, but especially of Patrick. "He's a fine lad" he would tell them. "I knew he would be a priest," he often said to Joseph. After Patrick left the priesthood, Father Michael went to console them. "He'll come back someday; I know he will in some capacity or the other. He's a strong lad." They told Patrick of their many conversations

with their priest and how he prayed for Patrick. Patrick thought
to himself, *yeah, I'll bet he does. I'll bet he prays I'm forever silent.*

Now he tried to focus on the good times with his family. His
dad had worked long hours to make enough money to support
his large and seemingly always growing family. A police officer
in Boston, he also worked overtime as a security officer in one
of the financial centers downtown and still had to drive thirty
minutes to their small home, outside Boston. His mom had taken
a nursing course and worked for a local doctor until John was
born, a year and a half after they were married. He would soon
be thirty-four. Andrew was born next, followed by Robert and
then Patrick. Finally, after three more boys, his parents had the
girl they had longed for, Mary Margaret, and then another girl,
Rose Marie, and then of course, Joey. For twelve years there was
always someone in diapers.

After Joey had started to school, his mother, Margaret, went
back to work for Dr. Bennett, and finally his parents were able
to have a few things that they wanted and often needed, like an
electric dishwasher. His mother laughed and said, "I really don't
need one; I have seven." Knowing the oldest children were going
to be off in college soon, his father had insisted.

Though these years brought their share of struggles, they had
been happy ones for the family with Joseph Sr. always finding time
to play ball with the boys. He loved football and even played on the
police association team a few years, but when he took his second
job, that had to be put aside. His boys loved basketball and excelled
at St. Xavier High, so their dad put a goal up in the back driveway
where at almost any time after school or when they weren't at their
part-time jobs he could find at least one wanting to play a game of
H-O-R-S-E. Together, the family always went to mass regularly.

Wiping a tear, Patrick thought about how happy his parents
had been before his mom began to be dizzy, drop objects without
a warning and stumble for no apparent reason.

It was 4:30, he needed to get moving. He dialed Carol's number and she answered sleepily.

"I'm sorry to call so early."

"Patrick, what's wrong?"

"My mother is very ill. My dad doesn't think she'll make it. I need to leave quickly."

"I can be ready in less than an hour."

"No, Carol. That's not necessary. You haven't met any of my family. It would be too much."

"But Patrick, I want to go with you."

"You've been saying you needed to go to the gallery. Why don't you ride with me to Boston and then take the train into the city. You could stay with Nancy and spend some time doing the things you need to do with your art and photography. Didn't you say you wanted to shop there for a wedding dress?"

"Yes, but I feel bad not going with you."

"It's fine. Really. Can you be ready by six?"

"Sure. It's too early to call Nance, but if she's not home, I'm sure Marc and Fredrico will be. I'll call her from the train station.

"I'll be there by six o'clock."

৵৽৵

As Carol boarded the train, she waved good-bye to Patrick, knowing he was worried about his mother and feeling badly that he was alone. Secretly she was excited to see Nancy. She liked Nancy's husband David, too, and was crazy about Hannah, her godchild. Hannah would be three in two weeks and Carol had not seen her in nearly six months. *I must get her birthday present while in the city*, Carol thought. *Maybe she would even give it to her while she was there. Who cares if it was early?* The toy selection in New York City would be much better than in Maine.

Carol and Nancy had been best friends since she could re-member, all through school and at Columbia University where they were roommates. It would have been difficult if they had not liked each other because their parents were best friends, also. Their fathers had met in Medical School and still shared a medi-cal practice. Nancy's father was a specialist in obstetrics and gy-necology, Carol's father, a pediatrician. The fathers often laughed and said, "Once Herb caught 'em, they couldn't get away. A baby might go straight from his hands into Sam's." The girls, who had heard this so often, just rolled their eyes. They knew the next thing would be the slap on the back which one father would give the other. The fathers tried to play golf every Saturday morn-ing unless there was a baby to deliver or another medical emer-gency. Carol's father, Dr. Sam, as he was affectionately called by his patients, would have liked to have played on Sunday morning instead, but Dr. Herb was an elder in the Presbyterian Church, one activity they did not share. The topic of religion was rarely discussed out of mutual respect for each other's beliefs or posi-tion. The girls' mothers visited often too, sometimes over coffee, but always they worked together on charity projects.

Carol always enjoyed riding the train because it gave her time to think and look at the landscape, something important she thought for an artist to do. Although she liked painting land-scapes, her preferences were photography and portrait painting and often she used one of her photos as a basis for a portrait.

She was deep in thought when the older gentleman sitting next to her asked where she was going. "I'm staying in the city with friends," she told him. "I have a little work to do at one of the galleries and would like to shop some," she said, smiling at him. "You know women!" "What about you?"

"I used to live in the city and my doctors are still there. Lots of good doctors in Boston, but I know these, so I go back. I've got the time, got nothing but time," he said. Because he didn't offer why he was going to the doctor, Carol didn't think she should pry.

"I worked a little in the film business when I was younger," he offered. Before she could say anything, he added smiling, "and I know what you are thinking, but it wasn't silent films." His mood had lifted since he began the conversation.

She laughed, "My friends, whom I am going to visit… he and his brother, own a company that produces documentaries. His wife, my oldest friend, met him when she was a journalism intern there. She fell desperately in love with this nice Jewish boy from Brooklyn. That was what she told her parents," Carol smiled, adding, "Nancy knowingly failed to tell her parents he was fifteen years her senior and divorced. She said she wanted them to meet him first so they'd be charmed." Carol continued, "They weren't, but they did come to love and accept David."

The old man fell silent for a few minutes. Carol really hadn't planned to talk on the trip, but for some reason she felt sorry for him. He looked lonely, and if not sad, at least worried. She asked him, "So do you have children?"

"One son, about your age, the younger of two boys. My oldest died in Vietnam. Not wanting to become involved in a depressing discussion, she simply said, "I'm sorry." "I'll bet you have grandchildren," she added, trying to lighten the topic. "Not yet," he said. "My boy lives out in California so I wouldn't get to see a grandchild much anyway. He's not married, says he works too much."

They were about an hour away from the city. "If you'll forgive me a few minutes, I need to finish up some plans I should discuss with the art gallery director tomorrow." Taking out her pen and notebook, she began to write.

"You an artist?" he asked, interrupting her thoughts.

"I try, I do some photography and watercolor, a little oil," she offered. Her attempt at ending the conversation was seemingly foiled.

Silent for a few minutes as she wrote, he then muttered, "My wife was an artist."

Carol picked up on the "was." Again not wanting to tread there, she added, "I'll bet she was good," and left it.

"She was."

Before long they were at Union Station. "It was nice talking with you, Mr..." stopping, "I am sorry; I didn't get your name."

"James Gentry."

"I am Carol Neilson. I hope your stay in the city is nice."

"Yes, thank you and the same to you," struggling slightly with his small carry-on, arranging his hat and nodding as he departed the train.

When Carol saw Nancy and Hannah waiting in the main terminal, she stepped up her pace. Hannah ran, as Nancy tried to keep up. The two women hugged. "It is so wonderful to see you," Nancy said excitedly. "I'm sorry about Patrick's mother, but I will take any excuse to get you to the city."

"Oh, I'm so glad to be here. How is my little Hannah," asked Carol as she reached down to take her hand. Squirming to get closer, Hannah looked up and asked "Pwesents Arol?"

Carol laughed, "Not yet, but maybe tomorrow," feeling badly that she had not brought something for either Nancy or Hannah.

Interrupting her thoughts, Nancy said, "Oh, I have got so much to tell you, but first I must see your ring. Carol it is beautiful."

"Thank you. Patrick picked it out all by himself."

"Let's get a taxi home and put your things away."

Riding to Nancy and David's apartment Carol felt truly back home. Having lived in New York City off and on for more than seven years, she had not forgotten how much she loved the excitement, the constant activity.

☙❧

When Patrick arrived in Boston, he went straight to the hospital. Stopping at the visitors' desk for directions, he hurried to his mother's room. When he turned the corner, Father Michael was walking out of the room. Patrick looked straight at the priest but said nothing, rushing past him. Immediately his worst fears were confirmed, Father Michael had been there to give last rites; his mother had passed away with his dad and Dr. Bennett at her bedside.

Patrick's dad was crying, uncontrollably. Patrick had never seen his father like this. A kind man, but never very demonstrative, his career as a street cop hadn't allowed for many emotions. Putting his arm around his dad, Patrick cried alongside him for a full five minutes. As he tried to choke back more tears, Joseph Sr. began rambling, "She seemed to be getting better. I sent the other kids home to get some rest. Andrew won't be in until tonight. She took a turn for the worse. I called Father Michael and he came right over. She smiled at me and was gone so fast. Patrick, what am I going to do without her?"

Patrick wondered himself. They had been married thirty-five years, shared seven children and a life together. All he could see now was this big, tough, Irish man, hurting so much, looking small and much older than his sixty years. Seeing his dad like this broke Patrick's heart as he cried for his dad's loss, and for his own.

Patrick knew his mother had suffered so much in the last two years when the multiple sclerosis had taken its powerful grip. Although many people live with the disease for years his mother, who was only fifty-five, had not been so lucky.

Patrick walked outside the room into the hall. There, near the chapel, stood Father Michael. "Oh my Paddy, I'm so sorry my lad."

Patrick's face flushed red. "Don't you ever call me that, again. I am not your Paddy or your lad. I never was! Let me tell you something else. Just because I've kept your secret, doesn't mean I've forgotten." Patrick heard his voice getting louder. He paused and gained some measure of control. "Now, leave before I say more than you can take."

᭑᭙

When the phone rang in Nancy's apartment at nine, David answered, "Oh, hello, Patrick. I've heard so much about you, I feel I know you. Let me get Carol for you. Good to talk with you."

Taking the receiver, she whispered, "Hi, Darling."

"Hi, I wanted to wait as late as I could so as not to disturb your visit and meal, but I needed to tell you, Mom died earlier today."

"Oh, Patrick, I'm so sorry. I will rent a car and drive there tomorrow."

"No, Carol. I want you to stay there. My brothers and sisters are here plus lots of aunts and uncles and friends. I'll be okay. You stay there. The service will be Thursday and I'll stay with Dad until Saturday morning. Can you find things to do until then?"

"Certainly, but are you sure you don't want me to join you?"

"Carol, I really appreciate your caring, but I'll be fine. You just have a good time with Nancy."

"Okay love, if Nancy won't kick me out, I'll stay. Besides, Hannah has already shown me the room where I will be sleeping at least four times."

Nancy laughed in the background.

Patrick asked, "So, how was the train ride? Long?"

"No, it was actually quite nice, a little more conversation than I wanted, but rather pleasant, all in all."

"Good. Give my love to Nancy and I'll call you sometime tomorrow. But don't stay waiting. Go and do what you want. I'll catch you sometime."

"I love you, Patrick."

"I love you, too. Sleep well." The phone clicked and Carol was alone with her thoughts, if only for a minute.

"Night, Arol. I go to bed now."

"Goodnight sweetheart. I'll see you in my dreams," as she reached down to kiss Hannah on the top of her head.

❧◆❧

Carol took a taxi to the gallery early the next morning, promising to meet Nancy at Tavern on the Green at 1:00 p.m. for lunch. The restaurant choice was a little fancier than she would have planned, but Nancy had made the reservation as soon as she learned Carol was coming to the City.

Walking into the gallery, she saw Fredrico waiting for her. "Oh, Darling, I have missed you so much," as he gave her a kiss on either cheek.

"Good, you're supposed to miss me," she smiled as she kissed him back lightly on the lips.

She often, laughingly, told people that Fredrico was the sister she never had, a dear friend who had always been there for Carol. Alone so often during her affair, he and his partner Marc, a gourmet cook, often invited her over for dinner or drinks. Together, they would sip Dom Perignon or good Bordeaux until the wee hours of the morning.

Because Fredrico would never hear to her going home alone at those times she stayed over in their spare bedroom where they had reserved a couple of drawers just for her.

"Let me see the ring, Darling. Oooh, I love the emerald cut. It is gorgeous and sooo big!"

"Are you coming to the wedding?" she asked while twisting the ring with her thumb.

"I would not miss it for the world. Do you think your new hubby will be ready for your gay friends?"

"Oh, Fredrico, Patrick is very open-minded, as is his church. Besides, he has heard so many wonderful things about you and Marc he could not help but like you both. Anybody so dear to me will be the same to him. He's just that kind of guy." Carol said.

"What did you bring for the gallery?"

"Only a few of my smaller pieces. I rode the train, you know, from Boston so only what was easy to carry," Carol said, pulling out the eight photographs she had recently taken, matted and framed, plus two watercolors of the Hidden Harbor area.

"The colors are brilliant," Fredrico noted. He loved Carol's work and was anxious to do another showing for her. "When will you be ready for another event Darling?"

"Lately, I have not done as much as usual."

"Why? Are you depressed?"

"Depressed? Don't be silly. I am in love, remember? I have other priorities like cooking and other such domestic endeavors. I must not let Patrick find out I'm a lousy cook, huh?"

"Well, how have you fooled him this long?" He laughed, his eyes lighting up. He loved to tease Carol, especially about her cooking.

"There you have all those luscious herbs you sent me photos of, and you haven't a clue what to do with them."

"But FREDDY," she knew he hated that name so she stressed it. They are so pretty and smell so good."

"But herbs are grown to be used. I walk fifteen blocks to the market just to buy a little rosemary and oregano, and pay a fortune and you just look at yours and ask, 'Aren't they pretty,' Silly woman!"

"But I know what to do with basil now. Patrick taught me how to make caprese salad. Although I have been to Rome a few times, I'm afraid my interests weren't in gaining cooking secrets. When he was there, he fell in love with the simplicity of the tomato, baby mozzarella and basil salad. So see I'm a gourmet."

"That will be the day. How does he feel about your boxed macaroni and cheese?"

"He rather likes it, Mr. Smarty Pants."

"Well, as much as I hate to, I guess we had better get to work. Oh, can you have dinner with Marc and me tomorrow night? He's planning a wonderful meal."

"Yes, but I can't drink too much wine and stay the night. I have to meet Patrick in Boston the next day."

"Okay, Darling, we'll tape your mouth at 10:00 p.m. But first you must tell us how a nice, rich girl from Connecticut fell in love with a poor Irish-American minister."

"If I knew Freddy, I would tell you now." Shaking her head, "That's a mystery even to me." As Carol was leaving the gallery, Fredrico asked, "Darling, would you like to take your portfolio with your photo essay back with you."

"Oh yes, Fredrico, I'm so glad you reminded me. I think it's time. I'm emotionally ready now."

"Why don't I take it home with me and you can get it tomorrow night. You'll be going straight back to Nancy's. If you take it now you'll have to drag it with you all day. Besides, this way you can't change your mind about coming to dinner."

"You know I wouldn't do that. I'm anxious to see Marc as well. Give him my love until I can myself."

He hailed a taxi for her to the Tavern where it was nice to have time alone with Nancy. In spite of Carol's love for David and Hannah, it was difficult to really visit, especially with Hannah vying for attention. The lunch, rack of lamb and salad, was a real treat for Carol since she never ate lamb in Maine.

"Let's go to Macy's. I want to get Hannah's flower girl dress if we can find something, and also I must not forget her birthday!" Carol offered.

"Sounds great to me, but I'm buying the dress."

Carol frowned, "No, you're not. I will not even go if that's the case."

"Okay, you win if you're going to play that way," Nancy said asking for the check, "but this is my treat, and don't even move your hand toward the check or your purse."

"Thanks Nance, it was lovely." Carol straightened her napkin, "By the way, I almost forgot. I'm taking my photo essay portfolio home finally. Fredrico is taking it to his place and I'm going to pick it up when I have dinner with them tomorrow night. You'll have me out of your hair for awhile."

"Carol, I wish you would stay a month. I miss you."

"I miss you also, but I'm really anxious to get back to Maine if you can believe that. I truly love my life there. I loved the city but it is so serene and unpretentious in the country. No one even locks a door, much less a gate."

"Well sure, there's no hustle-bustle and no traffic. But don't you miss the theater, the ethnic foods and all the cultures coming together?"

"I suppose at times, but not enough to ever want to move back." She looked around at the sparkling glasses and hand paint-ed china, "Oh, I almost forgot, Fredrico and Marc are coming to the wedding. Will Patrick be surprised?" Carol laughed. "I don't know how much to warn him or just let him take in the full effect all at once."

"I think you had better warn him," Nancy giggled. "Some-times Freddy's a little over the top, Darling," Nancy said mock-ingly. "But I do love those guys, too."

"I'm anxious to show Patrick my photo essay now that I'm over Richard and getting on with my life."

"He'll be impressed. Who wouldn't be?"

"I hope so. I think it is probably my best work."

After paying the check, Nancy said, "Okay, let's do Macy's."

"I'm ready." Carol reached for her purse and pushed back her chair to stand up.

After two hours of shopping, Carol left with a mustard colored silk tie for Patrick and a pale rose watermark taffeta dress with pearls and matching shoes for Hannah. Holding up the tie, she said, "This will look nice with Patrick's hair."

"I still can't believe you're marrying a red-headed man. In college you would have never dated a redhead," Nancy said, teasingly.

"I know," Carol admitted, "but I'm not doing much of anything these days like I used to do. Who would have guessed I'd marry a minister?"

"Not me, that's for sure," Nancy said, not hiding her astonishment.

"Oh, Nance, I'm so excited about Hannah's dress. She's going to look so sweet!"

"I hope she acts the same," Nancy moaned.

"She will. She's an angel and you know it."

"You're not with her all the time," Nancy laughed and rolled her eyes.

Carol stopped, "That's it, that's what I'm getting her for her birthday!" Sitting between two stuffed bears was the biggest stuffed giraffe Carol had ever seen with a huge orange ribbon wrapped around his long neck.

"How would we ever get it home? It's at least four feet tall. Do you realize, you would be giving my three year old the world's largest, most expensive giraffe short of the San Diego Zoo?"

"She'll love it. What are godmothers for if not to spoil? I'll tip the cab driver well if he'll help me put it in the car."

"Well, you are obviously good at spoiling her," Nancy said, throwing up her hands.

Nancy held the sacks, looking exasperated, as Carol maneuvered the giraffe into the largest shopping bag she could find.

Still two feet of the long neck stuck out. By the time they were outside, both women were laughing so hard they had tears in their eyes. "I'll try to get a taxi," Nancy said, waving to a yellow cab heading her way but the driver took one look and drove right by. As the second one drove by shaking his head, they looked at each other more subdued; a little surprised they had been snubbed.

"Damn New York cabbies. They are so independent!" Carol announced, frowning.

"Carol, you may have to hide in the store and then come running out so I can get one to stop," Nancy said laughingly.

"Thank goodness," Carol said, under her breath as a cab swerved to miss a car and jerked to a screeching halt at the curb.

In a foreign accent, the cabby asked, "Ladies, have you lost your minds?"

"Probably so. We need to go to 300 East 75th Street on the Upper East Side?"

Putting the small packages in the trunk, he said, "You want long-neck to sit up front with me?"

"That would be great," Nancy said, giggling again.

When they arrived at the apartment, Hannah was waiting. "She would not even take a nap," the housekeeper said. "She is so excited that she is getting a 'birfday pwesent!" Marie, who had worked for Nancy since before Hannah was born, was a short, round Puerto Rican woman about fifty years old who talked fast with a strong accent. It was obvious that she loved Hannah.

It will be a miracle if Hannah ever learns correct pronunciation, Carol thought.

Because Marie was so dependable, Nancy never worried about going places and leaving Hannah with her.

Wrinkling her nose, she said, "It sure smells good in here, Marie. What are you cooking?"

Marie answered, referring to her boss as she always did, "Ms. Nancy, it's your favorite: Roasted New York Strip loin with adobe rub, roasted potatoes with rosemary, green beans with julienne carrots and ham. I told Mr. David what I was cooking and he said he would pick up the wine."

"Arol, Arol, is that mine?"

"Yes, sweetie." There was no time to wrap the stuffed animal, and Carol was not sure how she would have disguised it anyway so she was actually relieved Hannah had seen its head sticking out of the huge sack. Pushing it toward her, she said, "Happy birthday, little angel."

"I wove it!" Hannah fell onto it on the floor and gave it a big hug.

"We'll show her the dress and shoes later. I'm not sure she'd be impressed right now," Nancy said, making her way over to the wet bar and asking, "How about a martini?"

"That sounds wonderful. I don't remember the last one."

"Straight up and dirty?"

"You have a good memory." Carol sat on the long white tapestry couch and took off her shoes, wriggling her tired toes.

"That's not something I could forget. Remember when we first learned to drink them?" Nancy laughed.

"Yes, but I would rather not," Carol said. "I wasn't a pretty sight that next day."

"We are a little more mature now, I hope."

"So do I. That would kill me now."

Hannah had fallen asleep on "Mr. Wong Neck" as she had already named him, a name Nancy was sure would change at least twenty times.

"That is what I was afraid of, Ms. Nancy. I tried to get her to take a nap."

"That's all right Marie; we can have our drinks quietly."

"Everything is ready and the table is set. Would you like for me to stay and serve?"

"No, no Marie. Carol is family. I will handle it from here."
Nancy knew Marie had her daughter, grandson and mother-in-law at her house, plus a less than energetic husband, so she always tried to let her leave as early as possible. Though Marie never complained except to say there were a lot of people in a small, cramped space, Nancy knew she probably had to clean and cook when she arrived home. Some days she would suggest to Marie to make extra food and take it home, especially if it were something she could carry easily on the subway. Marie, who had worked hard all her life, reminded Nancy often that no matter how difficult her life, she was glad to be in the United States. Often she would say, "My family happy here. Good people. Muy bueno, Senora."

By the time they had their second martini, their conversation had drifted to the wedding and Patrick.

"So, tell me more about this hubby to be."

"Oh Nancy, he's wonderful, though I admit a little complex."

"Explain."

"I'm not sure I can. He's the most thoughtful, loving man I have ever known, but sometimes he acts…I don't know…removed, distant, and perhaps absorbed in another life that I'm not in."

"Well, that's not good. Have you talked about it?"

"I tried, but it just seems to make things worse. He goes further into a shell. It's always…" She paused, a little embarrassed. "He gets that way sometimes after we have had the most passionate love making."

"That's strange. I didn't think men even thought after sex!"

Carol laughed, feeling a little guilty for bringing up the subject. "Anyway, that's one minor, tiny flaw," she said, trying not to let her apprehension show.

"Speaking of, I think I'd better try to call him before I drink any more martinis."

Patrick answered on the first ring, surprised to hear Carol's voice.

"How are you dear?" Carol asked.

"I'm better. It's good to see everyone though I dread tomorrow. I'll be glad when the funeral is over. We are having the mass at 10:00 in the morning and a small service at the graveside. The wake is tonight. There will be a lot of people, I'm sure."

"How is your dad?"

"He's better, but not great. He is really taking this hard. I think it was just so quick. He knew Mom was really sick, but I just don't think he ever dreamed that she would die this soon. My sister Margaret is having a difficult time, too. Well, everyone is, but she was probably Mom's favorite because she was her namesake, the oldest girl, and they have always been close. There are little kids everywhere. I don't even remember all their names. I told my brothers that these Irish Catholics need to slow down or we're going to have another population explosion. I thought most professional people, even Catholics, used contraceptives now, but apparently not in this family."

Carol laughed, glad that he was able to have a sense of humor during a time she knew was difficult for him.

"Carol, I hope you are having a good time."

"Yes, Patrick, I am but I miss you. I even told Nancy that I was ready to get back to Maine. I wanted to hear your voice, but I won't keep you on the phone."

"I'm glad, Carol. I miss you. I'll call you tomorrow. Bye, I love you."

"I love you, Patrick."

After sharing two bottles of wine over dinner, Carol yawned. "I think I'll excuse myself."

"I think I am ready, too. Shopping is hard on us. See you in the morning," Nancy added.

Turning to David, Carol said, "Your wine choices were splendid."

"Thanks. They are some of the new Super Tuscans. I think they paired well, don't you?"

"I think they were wonderful," Carol said sleepily. "I have not had this much to drink in awhile. Goodnight all."

The next morning, Carol woke at 9:00 to the smell of cranberry muffins and coffee. She pulled on her robe and hastily went into the kitchen, regretting she had slept so late.

"Good Morning, Ms. Carol. You must have slept well."

"I did, Marie," Carol responded, "I'm usually up by 6:30. I guess the wine did the trick. Your dinner was delicious and I don't remember sleeping as well in years."

"Thank you. I have had a time keeping Hannah from waking you."

About that time Hannah came bounding into the kitchen dragging the giraffe that was a foot taller than the little girl. "Hi Arol, wanna pway?"

"Sure, just let me have a little coffee, first."

"What are your plans today?" Nancy asked, as she walked into the breakfast room dressed in a beautiful cherry silk suit, with her make-up on and every hair in place.

Carol, still in her satin robe, looked up. "I feel terrible for being so lazy."

"I'm just glad you rested. Now quit worrying." She reached to squeeze Carol's hand.

Carol sighed, "I wish I had called Sergio before I came. I would love to get my hair cut, but I know he's been booked for months. Do you think I dare call?"

"Carol, he will be so glad to see you, he'll miss his tofu lunch for you."

Carol laughed and reached for the phone.

Nancy grabbed the receiver, "I'll call for you. If there is a choice, what time will be good for you?"

"It doesn't really matter. I want to order wedding invitations at Bloomberg's. If I could find a dress for the wedding, I would be delighted. If not, I'll have to go to Portland soon. I'm just not sure I have enough time today to really shop since I am getting such a late start so I'll take an appointment anytime."

"I can't believe you aren't having something made at Goldstein's."

"I know Nance, but I really want something simple, since the wedding is going to be small and the reception will be outside. Plus, most of the people there are frugal, simple, and hardworking. I don't want to come across as a snob from the city. And, Patrick would not be comfortable with my being too fancy."

"Okay it's your wedding, but I can probably get Sophia to measure you, and you could select the fabric today."

"Thanks Nance, but I'll find something."

Just as Nancy had predicted, Sergio was indeed, delighted, making an appointment for Carol at noon.

"Carol, unless you need me, I think I'll stay here. Is that okay?"

"Sure, I think I'm going to be scurrying from one place to the next. If I'm running late I'll just go straight to Fredrico and Marc's. Otherwise, I'll be back to freshen up. I'll call you. If Patrick calls, tell him I'm sorry I forgot to tell him where I was going. Ask him what time I am supposed to be in Boston, in case I miss him tonight. And don't wait up tonight."

Nancy smiled. She had heard that for four years at college and although they always told each other that, one waited up for the other anyway.

An hour later, Carol was on her way. The city was bustling, teeming with cars, buses and people scrambling for their place, moving at top speed in the crowded maze. It took her almost thirty minutes to get to the sprawling department store where people were lined up at every register to pay for their purchases. Carol felt oddly out of place. Feeling the pressure of the fast pace, she hurriedly narrowed her invitation selection down to two and completed the information form while the sales clerk impatiently waited.

"I want to show these samples to my fiancé, and I'll call next week with the one we choose. Will that be okay?"

"Certainly," the woman nodded. She appeared to be either bored or distracted, Carol wasn't sure which, but she didn't have time to contemplate. Placing the ivory-colored textured paper in her purse, she rushed through the crush of shoppers and headed the two blocks to Sergio's. *Whatever made me crazy enough to think I could do all this in one day, she thought.*

Carol stepped into the salon and immediately felt calmer. Sergio met her with a glass of champagne and a kiss.

"I've missed you Darling," he said softly.

Carol had forgotten how good she always felt when she had her hair cut. She wasn't sure if it was the serene atmosphere of the salon, peppered with vanilla candles, a Mozart symphony playing softly and Sergio's individual attention or the down time. Maybe it was the champagne. Whatever, it didn't matter, she felt renewed, ready to face the ugly crowds again to look for a wedding dress.

It was almost six o'clock when Carol arrived at Fredrico and Marc's, exhausted but pleased that she had been able to find the perfect dress.

One ring of the doorbell and the door sprang open.

"Carol, my dear Carol. Come in. The drinks are chilling," Marc half shrieked, hugging her. Fredrico instantly joined them.

"Patrick just called. He got our number from Nancy. He said he would try again in half an hour. I assured him you would be along soon."

"I forgot last night to tell him where I'd be. Did he sound all right?"

"I don't know how he usually sounds," Fredrico said quite animatedly, "but he didn't appear suicidal or anything, Darling."

"Freddy, you're awful. He just lost his mother."

"I was merely answering your question, love. Now, go sit down and I'll bring you a chilled glass of the usual. I need to help Marc in the kitchen a few minutes."

Carol sat down in the tufted Queen Anne chair and waited for what she knew would be Dom Perignon. She felt comfortable as always in their apartment. It had been a refuge when she lived in the city. A cocoon she could crawl into when life wasn't exactly what she wanted it to be. She looked around at the familiar setting and began to relax.

The phone startled her.

"Would you get that for me darling girl?" Marc called.

Carol reached for the white antique telephone, "Hello."

"Carol?"

"Oh, Patrick, I'm so sorry I forgot to tell you that I was coming here tonight."

"That's okay. I would have just left a message with Nancy as to what time to meet me in Boston, but I wanted to ask you something. Scott called and said he would do the services Sunday for me so I have that covered. I don't want to leave here very early tomorrow, but if I don't, it will be really late when we get back. I thought maybe you would rather not have to catch the train really early either. So why don't I pick you up at about 3:00 p.m. at the station. I checked the train schedule. I think it actually arrives at 3:06 p.m. We'll have a nice dinner in Boston and I know a quaint little Bed and Breakfast just outside the city on our way home where we can spend the night or if you prefer we can stay in a hotel on the harbor, if there's a room available."

"Patrick, that sounds great, either way. But, first, how are you?"

"I'm better now than any time since I arrived. I'm anxious to see you and get back to Maine. I hate to leave Dad, but that has to happen. Joey and Rose Marie will be close, so that helps."

Another reason Patrick didn't want to leave early was so he would have time to stop at a travel agency in Boston before going to the train station. His plan was to surprise Carol with a trip to Vienna, Austria, for their honeymoon. Although she had traveled to many European cities, she had somehow missed Vienna and she had mentioned wanting to go there, to see the opera and the Schoenbrunn Castle.

"This will work out well. It will give me time to get my things together in the morning and not have to rush so much. I'm excited to see you, Patrick. I have missed you so much. This is the first time we have been apart like this, you know."

"I know, and I worry about you in the City."

"Patrick! I lived here, remember?"

"Yes, but anything can happen. So be careful going back to Nancy's tonight. Have fun though with your friends Fredrico and Marc. What are you having for dinner?"

"I'm not sure, but it'll be special I know."

"See you tomorrow."

"Goodnight, Patrick."

Fredrico walked in with hors d'oeuvres. Marc followed closely behind with another plate.

"Okay, Darling, I have peppered tuna skewers with wasabi mayonnaise on watercress," Fredrico answered.

"And, I, my dear," Marc fluttered, "have southwest tomatillo duck triangles and these are just some roasted almonds with rosemary and fleur de sel to snack on."

"As always you two out did yourselves. This alone could be dinner." She tasted a tuna skewer, "mmmm," as she mouthed the word "perfect."

As they talked and laughed, catching up on missed times, Marc poured her more champagne and then another glass for himself.

"What are you drinking, Freddy?"

"A gin rickey, my latest obsession."

Carol laughed, knowing Fredrico was forever changing his drinks and trying something new.

"Would you like one of these?"

"No Freddy," she said quite emphatically, "are you trying to kill me? I think I will just drink my champagne for now. This tuna is delicious and the duck, yummy."

"Darling, we have a proposition for you."

"Uh…oh, this could be scary," she said, laughing.

"Marc and I want to come early to Maine and do all the decorations for the wedding and the food and decorations for the reception as our present to you and Patrick."

Stunned, but not really surprised, because these guys had always been so good to her, Carol listened to their plan, knowing they would do a wonderful job although many of the guests might not know what they were eating. "That is so sweet of you two, but that is too much to ask."

"You are not asking, we are telling you." Before she could say more he continued, "Good, then it's decided. We will be there two days early. Is there a good place to buy flowers close? Oooh, this is going to be so much fun." He clapped his hands together.

"I think I know just the place for flowers in Hidden Harbor, but I'll go over next week to be sure. If you insist, we will be honored and forever grateful to you, but that is a big undertaking."

"We are up to it, Darling."

"Okay then. You can stay with me. I'm so excited. You two are such good friends. I love you," she said, tearing up.

"Now stop that and have some more champagne while I get dinner on the table."

Carol looked at the dinner and thought it looked truly delightful: baked snapper with potatoes, oregano with white wine, green beans with Dijon mustard and caramelized shallots, and an apple, onion and walnut salad with cider dressing.

Marc poured a Pouilly-Fuisse'.

When they had finished, he said, "Let's go on the veranda and visit a bit before we have the Black Forrest Boule-de-Neige."

"Marc, I am stuffed. I don't know where I would put cake. I won't be able to get in my wedding dress, if I keep eating like this."

"Let's have a little coffee. You must taste a small piece. It is a new recipe with kirsch in the cake and also in the whipping cream; I made it yesterday because the cake part has to sit overnight."

"Tell us about your dress," Fredrico pressed.

"I bought it today."

"Let's see. You have it with you?"

"That's bad luck, but I'll tell you about it. It is really quite simple, an antique white, silk jersey, strapless, mermaid sheath. There are hundreds of the same fabric gardenias appliquéd down the back and a chapel length train. I also selected the matching short jacket beaded with mother of pearl. It has leg o'mutton sleeves."

"It sounds splendid. You will be the stunning one. I am already getting giddy about this wedding," added Marc. "May we have carte blanche with our choices of food for the reception or do you want to choose?"

Smiling, Carol said, "Of course, you can do as you like. I trust you completely. Just remember these are not New Yorkers or very fancy people."

"They will be when we finish," Marc giggled.

Thinking it first to herself, she then said, "This could be interesting."

"Now, let's eat cake!" Marc brought out a snowball of a cake decorated with candied violet petals.

"You two amaze me. Where do you get these ideas?"

"We are just naturals, Darling. At least he is," Fredrico said smiling at Marc. "And he is handsome as well as talented; what more could a man want?"

"Mmmm, this cake is sinful," Carol gushed.

"Good, I am pleased you like it," replied Marc.

Carol asked, "Marc how is Renaissance?" Carol loved to walk around in his antique store, always amazed at the unique selections, items from all over the world, usually very, very expensive, but one of a kind.

"It is wonderful. I just received the most ornate and elegant armoire from Nice. I have a client in mind. She only wants the best and she is supposed to come to the city from her weekend home in the Hamptons later this week."

"If you have time, on the way to the wedding, you should stop at some of the small shops along the way. You might be surprised with some of the finds. I bought an Eastlake chair recently when I visited Camden. I thought it was a steal, especially since I rarely see them anymore. The shop itself was charming."

"That trip we'll only be thinking of one thing...wedding bells."

"My turn, Markie," Fredrico said, cutting in. "Your hair is stunning, Carol Darling. You've had it cut since yesterday. Did you see Sergio?"

"Yes, and he sent his love to you two."

"We have not seen him in a while, but he always makes it to the showings at the gallery. He is quite talented with the scissors and a great fan of all the arts."

Picking up her empty glass, Carol said, "I absolutely hate to say goodnight. This has been so much fun, but I have to get up early and get everything packed to leave. Marc, may I help clean up?"

"Don't be silly."

"Then I must get my things." She stood and walked over to hug each friend.

"We understand. We're just so glad we had this chance to see you. We'll keep in touch about the wedding plans."

"If I can do anything in advance to make it easier for you, please let me know."

"We'll take care of everything, but do check on the availability of what flowers you want."

"Markie, I will go down with Carol and hail a cab while you pick up the dishes."

"Goodnight, dear," Marc said, kissing her.

"Carol, don't forget your portfolio. I'll carry it. I can't wait to hear what the lucky groom thinks about your photographs."

"I'm anxious to show him too," she mused, as they stepped out of the elevator.

"Goodnight my darling friend," Fredrico said, giving her his traditional kiss on both cheeks, while the taxi driver waited impatiently.

"Goodnight love, and thanks for everything." When she got into the taxi; she realized just how tired and full she was. *Those guys exhaust me, they are so energetic.* "I need to go to 300 East 75th Street. If I fall asleep, please wake me," she told the driver, and immediately she dozed off.

It was after 10:30 p.m. when she opened the door and thinking everyone was asleep, she tiptoed down the hall to the room where she was sleeping.

"Well, what did they serve?" Nancy's voice startled her. "Come on, you didn't think I could wait until morning to hear about dinner, did you?"

Putting her packages and portfolio down, she squeezed in close to her friend on the couch. "It was quintessential Marc and Fredrico. You'll feel stuffed just hearing about it!"

❧❧

The next morning there was just time enough time for Nancy and Carol to visit over a cup of coffee before Nancy and Hannah left for a birthday party and Carol for the train.

"Nest time, I'm sweeping wif you, Arol."

"Okay sweetie, next time you can sleep with me. I will even read you a bedtime story. How about that?"

"Yippee, when?"

"I am not sure, but hopefully it will not be too long," though Carol could not even imagine when she would get to do this kind of trip again. In two months she would be married and settled in again to life in rural Maine.

"Thank you for a wonderful time, Nance. I'll keep in touch about the wedding. Tell Sophia to do your dress superbly."

"I feel bad having mine made when you're not, but you know she does such a good job for me. I promise not to look better than the bride though," she said, teasing Carol.

The truth was that Nancy, who wore more make-up and had her hair styled often, was more attractive than Carol. She liked elegant, stylish clothes while Carol was content with slacks and sweaters. Though different in many of their preferences, the two women were comfortable with their individuality and showed complete understanding of each others' likes and dislikes.

"I doubt that, but it's okay because Hannah is going to up-stage both of us!"

"You're probably right."

As the time approached for each woman to get in a taxi and go their separate directions, they hugged and then Carol hugged Hannah. "You be a sweet girl and mind Mommy about you know what. Remember, real panties for a flower girl," she prodded,

trying to help Nancy who was having a terrible time potty training Hannah and feared Marie was a being a little lax with her.
When she complained, Marie casually answered, "She will do it
when she gets tired of a wet bottom, Ms. Nancy."

"Otay Arol, Bye."

૭✦ળ

chapter 17

The train was less crowded and quieter on Saturday and Carol was glad of that. The commuters were taking a well deserved respite in the suburbs. Taking a seat by the window, she sat by herself, glancing out at the skyscrapers, the steam rising from the tops of buildings and the lines of traffic as they flew by her sight. Her thoughts turned to Patrick and the tranquility that life in Maine brought.

Patrick was waiting at the station and saw the train come to a stop and he rushed to the exit, noticing immediately that Carol had much more than she could easily carry. She quickly handed her packages and portfolio to the porter who passed them to Patrick. Then grabbing her suitcase and an extra shopping bag, she descended the steps into Patrick's outstretched arms. He kissed her softly and said, "I missed you so much."

"Patrick, I don't want to be without you again," she said, reaching for one shopping bag and then taking his arm, "I have so much to tell you."

"Yes, like what is all of this?" he asked, grinning, as he held up the packages and portfolio.

"I can't wait to show you my dress and also my portfolio, which I picked up at the gallery."

"Your hair looks nice."

"I wasn't sure you would notice."

"I like it like that, but it also looks nice pulled back. You know what? I just like everything about you!"

"How was everyone when you left?"

"Oh, not too bad. My family has a lot of faith, but that of course won't keep them from missing Mom. It will, however, sustain all of us until time eases some of the grief. I really don't know what will happen to Dad. Mary Margaret wants him to go live with her, but I think he is too young for that. Whatever he decides I'll support. I think her three kids will drive him crazy, but her husband is a nice guy, and he and Dad get along great. They can both watch sports for hours. After a few years of that, Mary Margaret might divorce Ted and leave him with Dad," Patrick laughed. "If, of course, Catholics in our family ever divorced."

Patrick hugged Carol and asked, "What kind of restaurant sounds good to you tonight? Would you rather stay downtown or out on the way back home?"

"You know what I would really like, Patrick?"

"What?"

"I would like to go to Quincy Market and walk around, and then have a burger or something really simple."

"Too much gourmet the last couple of nights, huh?" he teased.

"Yes, I loved it, but that's enough for awhile. I thought after last night, I might never eat again, but I'm really quite famished now. I didn't eat breakfast or lunch. But if I eat now, it might ruin our plans for later."

"Who cares? I'd like to go to Quincy. I haven't been in years. Let's grab a snack now and then again right before we head to the room."

"I would like that, and if it is all the same to you, why don't we stay the night somewhere close to Quincy. It will probably be dark when we leave."

"Sounds good to me," Patrick agreed.

After walking around the market for a few minutes, Carol saw a Chinese fast food place. "I think I'll have an egg roll to hold me 'til dinner. You want one?"

"Yeah, I'm a little hungry. Maybe we can find a nice sit down burger place later."

After the snack they began walking through the little shops. "There is nothing I need, but I love looking at these places," Carol said.

"You are trying to make a shopper out of me, aren't you?" Patrick teased. "It won't work, you know."

"But I'll never stop trying," laughed Carol.

Strolling hand in hand, enjoying the late afternoon, they passed a flower stand, where Patrick bought a bundle of fresh mixed blooms for Carol. "For you, my fair lady."

"They're beautiful. I'll put them in water when we get to the hotel, and hopefully, they will last a couple of days when we get back. I'll get a packet or two of sugar when we eat. I understand sugar preserves them for a little longer, but I've never known for sure."

Two hours later Patrick said, "If you're ready to check in, let's try the Harbor-Ritz Hotel. I think it is the most terrific location for having a glass of wine and watching the boats come and go. We might want a burger in their restaurant or even call up room service. What do you say?"

"That's great, either way. I know you must be tired from the stress, if nothing else."

"Seeing you gave me a rush of adrenalin, although tonight I'll probably crash."

∂∞∞

Arriving back at the room after a glass of wine in the bar, Patrick called room service. Like two kids, they sat on the bed eating and watching television. While Patrick was putting the tray outside the door, he laughed loudly, remembering an incident from many years previous.

"What is so funny?" Carol called as she stepped from the shower.

"One time I was at a fancy hotel in France, the only fancy one I ever stayed in, and I called up breakfast room service. I was only in my undershorts, and I stepped out to put the tray by the door. Before I realized it, the door shut and locked. There I was, standing in the hall in my shorts, no key and speaking very little French."

Holding her robe around her, Carol was shaking with laughter, picturing the scene, "So what did you do?"

"I just stood there looking stupid for what seemed like hours although I know it probably was not more than ten minutes. I thought I might have to go down the steps three floors but I didn't know what I was going to do when I got to the lobby. Finally, this robust woman, who looked at least eighty years old, came out of her room down the hall. When she turned and saw me she immediately looked frightened. I guess she thought I was a serial rapist who had lost his pants. I was more horrified than she was, but fortunately she knew enough English to know what I said. She laughed until I was afraid she was going to have a heart attack, and then I thought if that happened I certainly wouldn't be able to explain. She told me she would send a bellman to rescue me. In about five minutes, this very reserved old gentleman came up with a pass key. He was not laughing."

Carol continued to laugh. "No wonder they call us crazy Americans," as she crawled into bed and cuddled up next to him. Kissing her, Patrick held her tightly in his arms, until Carol realized that he was fast asleep. Smiling, she turned off the television, still seeing Patrick the priest-in-training standing half naked in the hall of a fancy hotel.

The next morning, Patrick said, "Why did you let me go to sleep?"

"You needed the rest, dear. I know what you were thinking, but there are plenty of nights for that."

"Now, how did you know what I was thinking?"

"You're a man."

Loading the car, Patrick was careful to put the portfolio in the back seat where nothing would be bent or damaged. "Let's get back to the sticks," he told Carol.

"I have never heard that expression. I am not sure what that means."

"That is a hold-over from my two years in East Texas. People who live outside town always say they live *in the sticks*."

"Then, I guess it fits," Carol agreed.

Driving out of Boston, Patrick said, "Now tell me about this portfolio."

"It is a long story. Are you sure you are interested?"

"I am interested in anything involving you."

Carol paused, and then began, "Well, a little more than a year before I left New York, Richard had a friend who was editor of People and Places Magazine, and this friend wanted to do a series on *Women and Religion*. So Richard told him about me, and the editor called and asked if I were interested. He told me he wanted a variety of photos of women from different religions and the role they played. I was really interested, although it meant extensive travel for about two months which would take me away from the city. Looking back, I think that was Richard's plan, a way to gradually wean me away so he could break it off when I returned, and that is exactly what happened.

"Anyway, I met with Henry and he told me he wanted a photo essay that would include two Baptist missionary women working in a remote area of Mexico, not too far from Guanajuato. He wanted some cloistered Catholic nuns from the God's Blessing Convent in Laurel, Wisconsin, and a middle-aged Latter Day Saints woman who served a calling as the Relief Society President in Salt Lake City. She was the younger daughter of a polygamist in an off-shoot revised LDS group who had escaped from his clutches when she realized he was going to marry her off at fourteen.

"Henry had the story planned out and said he would send a writer with me or I could take the photos and let him know if I had enough information from talking with the subjects myself to write a short piece about each woman. He wanted to use the two Baptists, at least three nuns and the Mormon lady, and he had already made these contacts. The story was to be titled *Women of God*. It turned out to be one of the most interesting eye-opening experiences of my life and I wouldn't trade it for anything."

"So, continue," Patrick prodded.

"My first subjects were two middle-class Baptist school teachers who decided to help the poor in Mexico. They had gone to several remote places on their summer vacations for six years, using their own money and taking children books and clothes and toiletry items. Basically they taught the children about sanitation and hygiene at first and then began teaching some of the children about God, salvation and so forth. After asking their church if they would provide tracts, it wasn't long before the church was sending money and other donations. The women talked about how much more progress they could make if they could stay throughout the year, instead of just summers, because in terms of much of their work, the missionaries felt as though they were starting over every summer, seeing how much the people regressed when they were gone. Linda, the oldest, was a widow and her one daughter was grown, and Gayle was a divorced mother of a boy in college. They decided to approach their pastor for help in sponsoring them full-time. Very positive and supportive, he gave them a list of other churches and ministers that they could contact. Soon, they had enough pledges to quit their teaching jobs. That was ten years ago. Now they have a school and a small church in this poorest of poorest places you will ever see, no electricity, no running water. These women are happier, they say, than they have ever been. They feel they have a purpose and are changing lives. One of the boys in their school is actually going to go to college on a scholarship provided by the sponsoring churches. I cannot remember which university, but it's somewhere in Arizona, I think.

"I stayed with them for about a week. I was supposed to stay longer but the conditions were dire at best. I never was much of one who thought I would like to camp out, and although it was not exactly like that, their house was quite primitive. Remember, there was no electricity, no sewer system, and no running water. But I got great photos and a story I was not soon to forget. I often wished for a command of the Spanish language. My French did not exactly come in handy," Carol laughed.

"My Spanish wasn't very good, but the women interpreted my conversations with many of the people. Some of the younger ones even spoke some English, compliments of the missionaries, especially Jorge, the young boy going to college. I called Henry and told him I thought I was finished unless he needed to send me back after he saw my work. The women were very interested in my art background and suggested I visit San Miguel de Allende which was only about an hour and a half away. I asked Henry about that, too. He agreed I was ahead of schedule so I could take two to three days. I'm glad I did.

"San Miguel was full of international artists and Americans; some of whom were retired, some just wanting to get away from everything. Of course, they could live there for less money than in the States. The town was a really pretty place, a Spanish colonial type city with a beautiful plaza. The architecture of the old buildings and churches reminded me of Europe. It seemed that almost everyone spoke English. The town itself may be an artist's haven, but it is surrounded by poverty. Anyway, the artist part was an extra perk that had nothing to do with my assignment.

"After that I flew out of León to Dallas and then on to Salt Lake City, making it quite a long trip. My photo subject, Emily had offered to pick me up and had described the car she would be in and what she would be wearing. It was late when I arrived, but she was waiting right out front of the terminal. An attractive woman, about forty years old, her clothes and new Volvo spoke of money. She dropped me at Hotel Utah, close to Temple Square, with a promise to pick me up at 10:30 the next morning. Have you been to Salt Lake City, Patrick?"

"No, I haven't. I really don't know much about it, either. Believe it or not, I haven't even studied much about the Mormon doctrine."

Continuing, Carol said, "Am I rambling too much?"

"No, no, this is great," Patrick said, encouraging her.

"Although I had studied about the Mormons, I certainly gained knowledge from Emily. When she picked me up she explained that she thought it important that I quickly see some of the landmarks of the Latter Day Saints and meet other Mormon women to gain their thoughts, insights and backgrounds. She had the next several days planned for the two of us. We headed straight to the Visitors' Center at Temple Square, where the life-size murals depicting the story of the church were absolutely beautiful. They lined the walls of a spiral ramp. I wanted to spend more time looking at the art alone, but that first day was an overview, and I knew there would be time later for me to return.

"It was mid-afternoon when we left the Visitors' Center. I don't think Emily thought we would be there that long, but there was so much to see and a video on the history of the church. She knew everyone and seemed to enjoy talking with them and introducing me, explaining my photo mission."

"Emily's plans for the second day included a walk through ZCMI Mall, which by the way Patrick, is church owned. Actually the church owns a great deal."

"That's what I have heard. This is really interesting. Did Henry ever tell you why he chose these three particular religions?"

"I asked him that because I thought it was strange: Baptist, Catholic and Mormon. He said he wanted religions where it was tradition for the woman to be in the background, on the sidelines, in other words, in a submissive role. These religions, he figured, would never allow a woman to be a minister, deacon, etc."

"Well, he chose well," Patrick said, laughing.

"Yes, but in the settings where I found them, it didn't matter. They were simply women serving God, and their role was not an issue. Gender was a moot point. And that is obvious in the story and the photographs. Henry wanted to include some Middle Eastern women but none responded to his inquiries."

"Okay, that's interesting. So keep going. I'm intrigued."

"Remember, we started late because Emily wanted to take me to a special rehearsal of the Mormon Tabernacle Choir which didn't start until 7:00 p.m. It would have been a really long day for her if we started early in the morning. Did I tell you she has five children?"

"No, but that would be a long day in and of itself!"

"Yes, I agree, but they were really nice kids, perfectly behaved. Her husband is a cardiac surgeon at the LDS Hospital so his schedule is extremely intense, and he's not able to give her much help with the children. He does, however, set aside as much time as possible to be with each child during the week. She's probably the only loser of his time, but she handles it well. Remember, it is part of her role.

"Anyway, after the mall, we went to *Mormon Handicrafts*. I've never seen so many beautiful fabrics. Emily wanted me to see the women quilting. It was fascinating. They do very nice work with tiny, tiny stitches. It appears to be a labor of love. Each quilt is sold and the money given to a worthwhile cause. I was very impressed because I saw it as their form of art. Then choir rehearsal was marvelous. The voices were mesmerizing, but more than that, you would not believe the acoustics in the tabernacle. You could, indeed, hear a pin drop. That's not an exaggeration. I had read that but always thought it to be propaganda. It's not.

"Every day we saw something new, something that was a part of Emily's life and her religion. She invited me to one of the Relief Society meetings at her ward, but she's actually the president over all the Mormon Relief Society groups in the world. In the last year, she has been to fifteen countries to train other women for the Relief Society. She does have help, two women they call counselors. You should see her office. It looks like a plush living room, overlooking Temple Square and the Joseph Smith Memorial Building."

"What does a Relief Society do?"

"They have weekly meetings dedicated to the improvement of women. Meetings focus on such areas as the cultural arts, literacy, homemaking skills, spiritual development and so on—those kinds of things.

"Finally we took off and drove back to Emily's childhood area. That was part of the deal with Henry. So for almost a week we looked back in her life. I know it was not easy for her. She said it was cathartic. I got some of my best pictures of her there against that sepia backdrop. That is when I really got the essence of the woman. What an abnormal childhood she had. Can you imagine having a father as a polygamist? She is really grounded, which to me is amazing. Although she says she harbors no real resentment against him and says she has forgiven him, she added that regrettably there is absolutely no love there either. By the way, he is still a polygamist. Her feelings for her mother are more mixed: sympathy, but a total lack of understanding of her mother. She told me she just could not fathom how a woman can do what she has done, but she said she guessed it was ignorance, or gullibility. Her mother was brought up by a polygamist also. It was a cyclical journey, one from which she could not break away. Emily said her mother was not strong enough or smart enough or perhaps she was just content. She never really knew.

"Emily's life now is 180 degrees different from her childhood. Although there was very little contact with the outside world in the town where she lived as a child, she always thought something was wrong. When she gained an iota of a clue that life was a bit off center, she did everything to find out why. Fortunately a few books portraying different ways of life had somehow found their way to the local library without anyone's suspicion, and Emily poured over them. She began asking a few questions to whomever she could. She was rebuked more than once, but she finally found a sensitive ear, an old, old, woman who worked at the local post office. Emily asked the right question one day and the old woman saw the look in her eye. She told her, 'Child, it's too late for me, but you are young and wise. Be here Thursday afternoon at four o'clock. Can you do that? Are you seriously prepared to leave, never to return?' Emily told the old woman she was, and apparently the old woman read her well. Another woman, who had left ten years previously and whose mission was to rescue these girls did just that for Emily."

"Now, Emily is deeply involved in genealogy. Of course, this is what that all Mormons are encouraged to do. The church has probably the best genealogy libraries in the world. Anyway, Emily believes this is especially important to her because of her past. She wants to trace her heritage, to maybe get a glimpse, of why her father was the way he was. She was quick to point out, however, that this would never be an excuse for him because every person is responsible for his or her own actions. She keeps a journal which is one of the church's recommendations to its members so that her research and collected knowledge can be passed down to her children.

"Patrick, I'm talking way too much. You don't want to hear about this in such detail. I'll make the rest of this quick."

"No, no. I am really enjoying this and learning a lot. Let's stop though, get a cup of coffee and stretch."

"That was nice," Carol said after the two had taken a short break. "Now I can talk for two more hours," she laughed.

"Good, this is making the trip go faster. Okay, what is next?"

"Remember I told you that each woman was interesting and I learned so much at all the places, but the convent had to be the most memorable, the most touching and the photographs almost a little haunting. The missionaries in Mexico were so generous and selfless and the people so sweet, but the language gap made it so much more difficult and I felt a lot was lost in translation. And of course the conditions were so bad. But all of the women were so strong. I realized I could never have their strength."

"Sure you could, if you had to be or wanted to be."

"No, if you had met those women, they would have made the same impression on you, but the one who made the deepest impression on me was at the cloistered Carmelite convent in Wisconsin."

"Why?"

"Well, first the Reverend Mother would not allow me to take any close up facial shots of the nuns. Every photo had to be almost a silhouette. The results were wonderful, but it made me really nervous going in because I was worried that I would not be able to fulfill my assignment for the magazine. Once I finished with the photos, I was so glad that had been a requirement. I would never have done that on my own, and I think it was the turning point of the entire work.

"The convent has a simple, but comfortable building for guests. The surroundings are beautiful and even the main meal provided. But it was so... I don't know how to explain it."

She paused, "Empty, is the word, maybe. All of those women certainly didn't feel that way. Many have been there thirty and some up to forty years and will be there until they die. But to me, the silence was deafening. The stillness and starkness of the place just filled me with utter loneliness. I felt so much for those women. Again, they didn't complain. It was I who had these feelings, but seeing them rise at five o'clock every morning and meditating, praying and doing manual labor alternately until 8:15 at night just seemed so lonely, so unfulfilling."

"Many of the women have college degrees and some have held positions of authority, but have given it up to go there. It is their choice; I suppose, their calling, but it is so removed from everything we grow up thinking we will do in our adulthood, unless, I guess, one grows up Catholic. You know more about that, so maybe it is not unusual at all?"

After thinking a minute, Patrick responded, "The tunnel is so narrow that you don't allow yourself to think about the outside world and traditional expectations, if you grow up thinking that is your calling in life. You block it out, thinking you are being so unselfish and so right about your decision that sometimes you end up hurting yourself or someone else sometimes."

"Did that happen to you, Patrick?"

"Oh, I thought about it more than you will ever know, but I thought about it as I said with no added dimension. You've probably read about the guilt trips the nuns give kids in Catholic school. Well, I think we live with that guilt so much, we sometimes guilt ourselves into choices. But, I guess it is different for everyone. Go ahead; you were talking about the schedule and so forth."

"I don't really know, Patrick, I just felt sorry for some of the women, especially one of them, a woman named Ann. They just seemed to be missing so much, the touch of a hand, the warmth of a hug, the pleasure of a tickle, or the peacefulness of knowing you share a special bond with another human being. Maybe, all women don't need these things, maybe they have so much more and I am the loser, but I just know I couldn't live that way. If they feel a yearning for more, they didn't express it to me, except Ann. I think admitting it would have been a sin for many of them, a sin some would have trouble living with.

"Actually, the Reverend Mother didn't want to participate in this project at all, but she wants to build a school, and Henry promised her a major donation from the magazine if she agreed. I never knew how much, but it must have been substantial.

"I spent the first week there watching the women in their routines and reflecting on these experiences. I watched their body language, their eyes and movements. In the second week, I began to talk with many of them. A few didn't wish to engage in conversation but three seemed hungry to talk. Remember Patrick, these women are normally not allowed to talk except for forty-five minutes a day during recreation time. You would think they would all be eager for conversation; however, as I said before, I don't understand their way of life. By the way, there are eighteen nuns living there. They raise their own vegetables and milk a couple of cows from which they make their own cheese. They have a greenhouse and sell their flowers to a local florist to bring in an income for the maintenance of the buildings.

"The nuns, who were willing to talk, taught me so much, especially about sacrifice. One of the women told me that as a little girl she changed her name to Ginger because she wanted to grow up to be a dancer just like Ginger Rogers. She must be terribly unhappy," Carol laughed, but not in a cheerful tone. "I cannot think of a worse place for her. That would be like an alcoholic working in a distillery. She never told me what changed her mind although I pressed her time and time again. In the middle of the third week I commented to the three women individually, we never talked as a group, that she must have a strong faith to live like this, to give up all worldly and material goods and thoughts. Their responses were as different as each of them. Ginger said certainly it was true that she did have a strong faith, but she also approached it as her service here on earth. She rather danced around the remainder of my questions; the only dancing she does, I might add. Isabella told me that she believed she was destined to live this life, this prayerful existence made her feel whole and totally connected to God.

"It was what Ann told me that I was completely and utterly unprepared for. When I asked her the question, she didn't say anything for the longest time. It was beginning to make me nervous because I was afraid I had said the wrong thing. Finally, she lifted her gaze, her eyes looked straight at me and then she called me by name. That was the first time I had heard my name, I think, in three weeks." She said, "Carol, I have told no one, but for some reason I truly believe I can trust you. You cannot use this in your story so you may not even want to hear what I am about to tell you.

"I told her to continue and she reminded me that the Reverend Mother could never know. I asked her why she was telling me and she looked me right in the eyes and said she needed to say it, to share it; she had carried the secret so long, and she said she had thought about it so much and that, for some reason she felt a particular bond with me, an unexplainable, almost friendship, if that were possible, in that setting."

"Well, hurry up," Patrick laughed. "This is driving me crazy. It's like a movie."

Carol continued. "Here sat a woman in a cloistered convent dressed in a habit, but even with her head covered, I could tell she was beautiful. She had the most defining eyes, an almost lavender color and her skin had a glow that I didn't see in the other nuns. She said she always tried to work in the vegetable garden so she could at least get some sun on her face, so as not to look pale.

Then she looked at me again, and I remember her exact words. She said, 'You asked me about a strong faith? Perhaps, I see it differently from the other sisters. I do understand faith as the Bible says, as the substance of things hoped for, the evidence of things not seen, but sometimes I think I confuse faith with love, because Carol, I didn't come here because I was a strong Catholic girl who wanted to live a godly life. I was not even reared Catholic, I came here because I loved a man who no longer loved me. I came here to run away, not to run to something. I came here because I had his baby and was not strong enough to look at her everyday and see him in her. I came here because he chose to be a priest and if I could be a nun, I would be closer to him in a strange way. I knew that was the only way. I came here because the outside world no longer held anything I wanted. So, if you can say that faith is one's capacity to love no matter what happens, to give up everything to keep that love alive then Carol, I have faith.

"Then she told me her daughter's name and that she left her with her sister when she was four days old. Everybody thinks Ann is dead. She said that in many ways she was. That's it, Patrick. End of story. Now you have to see the best part, the photographs."

Patrick suddenly felt like he had been slapped by a huge wave and was drowning. Driving, he looked straight ahead so he would not give away his emotions. He thought, *"It can't be. No, it is a coincidence. There is no way Sue would have done that."*

"Well, here is our turn off. We're almost back," he said, making small talk and trying to still his racing heart.

"Are you too tired to come in, Patrick?"

"If it's okay, I think I will go home to unpack and clean up. Then I'll pick you up. We're going out to Vincent's on the Bay tonight, my dear. I have a bit of a surprise." He was beginning to feel calmer, but his mind was still trying to comprehend what he had just heard.

"I'm glad you told me where we're going Patrick. I'll dress differently than planned. That is an elegant place. What is the occasion?"

"You'll see. I'll be back in about an hour and a half," he said as he kissed her cheek.

Driving away he let his memory drift back: *Sue if that is you, why didn't you just stay in Townsend and marry some nice guy. . . Why did you have to do this to yourself. . .just because I ran away, you didn't have to.* He hit the steering wheel hard with his fist. "Why?"

As quickly as he asked himself, he stopped. Always the master at suppression, he willed himself to do what he had been doing since he was ten years old, trying to forget and convince himself that that *Life has a way of dealing cards that one plays or discards, and once that game is over, it can't be replayed.* "We both made our choices years ago and now we have to go on," he said out loud, as if to fool himself into believing it.

There was no question that he loved Carol. She had captured his heart, but it wasn't the first time his heart had been stolen, and the first time is always special. It's not something a person forgets easily, that time of innocence when one believes there will never be another one as perfect as the first. He knew he wasn't the only person who had ever felt that way and it made him a little sad.

chapter 18

The phone was ringing when Patrick ran into the house. It was Carmella.

"Patrico, I have been trying to call you since Friday. We have two new grandbabies," Carmella gushed.

"Two?"

"Yes, can you believe it? Elisabette had twins again, a boy and a girl. And this was just as big a surprise as Alex and Alexia."

"Congratulations, to you all. Are mother and babies doing well?"

"Yes, they are coming home tomorrow."

"What did they name them?"

"Penelope and Paulo."

"I like both names. You are getting the house full of grand-children, just like you wanted."

"Yes, Patrico, it is quite noisy when they arrive," she laughed.

"Carmella, I was just about to call you. I was just getting in from Boston."

"How is everyone?" she asked.

"Mom passed away on Wednesday. Although she had not been well, this was somewhat unexpected."

"Patrico, I am so sorry. Why did you not call me? I would have come for the funeral."

"That is exactly why I didn't call, Carmella. I knew Elisabette was due any day. You needed to be there, and I knew you would feel like you should fly here. It would have been too much to ask."

"How is your father?"

"He's not handling this very well. It was hard to leave him, but I had to get back here. One of my sisters is with him. I'm not sure whether he will go home with her or what. We'll just have to wait to see. He's still a young man, only sixty, so I hope he will keep the house and try to stay busy. How's Stefano?"

"He is fine, handing out cigars, wouldn't you know?"

"Carmella, tonight I'm surprising Carol with a special honeymoon package to Vienna."

"How exciting, love. Will she really be surprised or do you think she knows?"

"I don't think she has any idea. We've talked about several places in the Caribbean, but never Europe. She has mentioned wanting to see Vienna any number of times so this is the perfect opportunity."

"Then Patrico, you two must fly to Florence or Rome and spend time at the manor!"

"I know Carol would love that, but I'll have to see if I could change our return flight and also if I can be away several more days. I'll work on that, but are you sure? I know you're really busy."

"I am never too busy for you, my love."

"But you and Stefano are still coming to the wedding, aren't you?"

"We would not think of missing it."

"I would like for the two of you to sit up front with my dad."

"That would be an honor, Patrico."

When he hung up the phone, Patrick knew he would have to hurry to get ready in order to pick Carol up on time. Besides, he didn't want any spare time to think. He arrived at her door with a minute to spare.

"You look beautiful! I've never seen that dress."

"I bought this in New York to surprise you sometime. I just didn't know it would be this soon. You don't look too shabby either."

They were seated promptly at a corner table, overlooking the water.

"This is nice, Patrick. I never dreamed we would be doing this tonight."

Although he had planned to wait until after dinner to surprise her, as usual, his excitement wouldn't hold. He pulled out an embossed white and gold envelope and handed it to her.

"After he brings our champagne, you can open it," he said, smiling.

"What is it? You hand it to me and then make me wait. How mean!" she teased.

The waiter brought the drinks in special fluted glasses which Patrick had requested when he called for the reservation.

"To us," he said as he lightly touched her glass. "To a long life, together."

As soon as they sipped the first taste of the sparkling wine, Carol carefully, but quickly opened the envelope and inside the card read: *Vienna for Two*. Slowly she read the highlights for their honeymoon.

"I can't believe you did this. When did you have time?"

"Just a little side stop in Boston, that's all."

"So that's why you needed extra time. Oh! I am so excited. I have wanted to see Vienna for so long."

"Michelle at the Travel Service said she would try to reserve terrific seats for us at the opera. She said that since you speak French you might understand some of it. Me? Well, I'll be lost, but I will enjoy it, nevertheless. Afterwards you will finally get your Sacher Torte at the Hotel Sacher next door."

"This is going to be so wonderful."

"My only disappointment is that the Vienna Boys Choir doesn't perform in August, nor does the Spanish Riding School, but I do have a day trip arranged to Baden, and we'll actually get to see some of the Vienna Woods as well. Then if you like, we can go down the Danube to Krems," he added enthusiastically.

Finally noticing a pause, the waiter interrupted. "Would you like to order sir, perhaps an appetizer?"

"Give us a few more minutes." Turning back to Carol, he asked, "Are we having lobster or would you rather have something else?"

She knew Patrick never tired of lobster and would eat it every day if he thought he could afford it.

"I think I'll have the filet of sole."

"The two pound lobster for me, Sir. And, could I see your wine list, please?"

"My pleasure. I will get the sommelier."

"Patrick, have I told you today how much I love you?"

"No, but if you don't, then tell me quickly so I can get a refund on this honeymoon," he teased.

"I don't think I told you that Fredrico and Marc want to do all the decorating and food for the reception as a wedding gift to us."

"That's great, a little scary, but great," he said, smiling. "If I don't recognize the food you will tell me what I am eating, right?"

"I tried to impress upon them the need for toning it down a little."

"Then no rainbow flags or banners, I hope."

"Patrick, you're terrible," but she laughed. "They are over the top sometimes, but I love them dearly."

"You don't need to worry. I'll like them because you do. I'm really rather anxious to meet them. Oh, I almost forgot; Carmella called. She and Stefano are grandparents twice over again."

"Twins, again?"

"Yes. A boy and a girl, again."

"And no one even expected it?"

"No one. Carmella said the doctor was just as surprised as anyone and a little embarrassed. Needless to say she is on cloud nine, talking a mile a minute. She and Stefano are still coming to the wedding, though."

"That is wonderful news on both counts. I know I'm going to love them. They have been so sweet to you."

"I told Carmella what I was about tonight and she immediately invited us there after Vienna," he said with a little hesitation, "but I told her I didn't know if that was possible."

"Oh Patrick, can you work that out?"

"You mean you would want to do that?" he asked, feeling a sense of relief.

"Certainly. You have talked so much about their place. I really haven't seen as much of Tuscany and Umbria as I would like. Do you really think we can?"

"I can call the travel agent in the morning to see if our tickets home can be rescheduled. I'm sure she can change it, especially if I add a flight between Vienna and Florence. Would you like to fly to Venice instead and spend a couple of nights there and then take the train to their place?"

"Patrick, this gets better by the minute."

"And longer; I hope I don't get fired."

"If you do, we can just stay at Carmella and Stefano's. It sounds like a dream world anyway." Pausing, she gushed, "The dinner was delicious."

"Yes, I rather enjoyed my lobster."

"I noticed," she smiled.

"It's messy, there's no way to eat a whole lobster gracefully, is there?"

"If there is I have never quite been able to master it."

"Would you like dessert?"

"Would you share something with me?"

"Only if it is chocolate," he said with a wink. Patrick signaled the waiter and asked about dessert.

"You choose, Carol.

"The *Chocolate Eruption* will be just fine, knowing that is what he would prefer."

Riding home, Patrick put the top down on his Karmann Ghia. "I might have to trade this in when we have a baby."

Carol tried to hide her excitement since this was the first time Patrick had ever brought up children. Once she had mentioned it, but when she hadn't heard a response, she was hesitant to push the issue.

"Patrick, do you want children soon?"

"Fine with me."

"I do love you, Patrick."

When he killed the car motor at Carol's house, he leaned over and kissed her gently. Both sat looking at each other and the stars.

"What a nice night," as he traced her lips and face. They were like two teenagers gazing into each other's eyes, kissing and exploring each other's body, almost timidly. For a split second his thoughts went back to another car, but just as quickly he brought himself back to the moment. He pulled Carol as close as he could to feel her warmth.

"Let's go inside. You are driving me crazy," he said, breathlessly.

He was peeling off her clothes before they could even get to the bedroom. Her dress settled somewhere on the floor as he hurriedly shed his shirt and pants. It was at least an hour before they caught their breath again. They said nothing for a long time, just laying there in each others' arms.

"I love you so much, Carol," he whispered.

"I love you Patrick," as she snuggled to him.

Within minutes they were both in a deep, peaceful sleep. As always, when Carol awoke, he was gone. She knew that he liked to be back in his house before the sun was up or anyone was out for the morning, which in this part of Maine, at certain times of the year, first light could be 3:00 a.m. She doubted, however, that the lobstermen cared who was sleeping where as they started another day of throwing traps. When she called him at his office at the church, he told her he had been there since six o'clock trying to catch up on the work he missed while he was in Boston.

"How are you this morning, sleepyhead?"

"I'm great. Last night was so special, Patrick."

"Yes, it was for me also."

What he hadn't told her was that he hadn't slept at all. He had paced and thought and hit the wall, literally. Then finally he had showered, dressed and driven to the church.

"I know you're busy, but I just wanted to say good morning. I'll be so glad when we can wake up together every morning."

"I'll still probably be long gone before you open your sleepy eyes."

"No Patrick, I want to get up with you to have coffee before you leave. I like to paint early anyway. But nights like the last one make me really sleep well, so if that continues, you may be right."

"I don't plan for nights like that to stop just because we get married."

"Good, but then you had best plan on making your own coffee."

"It'll be well worth it. I need to run by the hospital about four this afternoon to see Mrs. Winters. I just talked to her daughter and told her I would visit. I'll see you soon after that."

For most of the morning Carol worked on the wedding list and organized the activities she needed to accomplish over the next few weeks. She showered and dressed for a quick trip to the grocery store so she could start dinner before Patrick arrived. Around five o'clock she heard his car and then saw him at the door. "Hi. I was about to put these upstairs in the studio; do you want to see them first?"

"Are those the pictures with the story?"

Carol began gently pulling the photos out of the portfolio one at a time. This is Emily. She's very attractive, don't you think?"

They looked at several of her and then the missionaries from Mexico.

"Bless their hearts. They haven't seen make-up in years."

"I believe you," Patrick smiled.

"This is Ann. She is beautiful without make-up. I found her to have inward beauty as well. I think I told you the Reverend Mother wouldn't allow me to take a direct shot.

He knew immediately that the photo was of Sue. He tried not to let his eyes linger on the photo. "What a waste," he commented.

When he kept looking at the next photos of her, Carol teased: "Do you miss looking at nuns?"

Patrick managed a smile; "Do you think she is ever happy?"

"I asked her that myself."

"She said she had grown peaceful there and that if peacefulness and happiness were related, then yes. She told me she only gets sad when she thinks about not watching her daughter grow up."

When he had seen all of the photographs, Patrick said, "This is truly remarkable work. You have captured the essence of each of these women so beautifully."

"I hope so. I sent each of them two photos and they all wrote me back. I have saved the letters. They are as touching as the women themselves. I'll be right back; I'm just going to run these up to my studio. Will you pour each of us a glass of wine, please Patrick?"

Upon her return he handed her a glass and kissed her lightly. "What did you do today?"

After describing her morning, she added, "I talked to the contractor today and the carpenters are coming tomorrow. He assures me that all the renovations will be complete no later than August 10. That will only give us ten days until the wedding. I think we are cutting it close, but it would be so nice to have it all finished before you move in. Besides if we wait until after the honeymoon, he said he would be really busy, getting several projects dried in before winter."

"That should give them and us enough time, hopefully," as he opened the back door leading out onto the yard.

"I'm just worried about them making a mess and hurting my flowers. They are so beautiful, and Fredrico and Marc would never forgive me if I let the flowers get crushed."

"You will need to remind them because you know those carpenters won't be thinking about that when they start hauling wood. Did you pick up the final plans from the architect?"

"Yes. They're right here."

Patrick studied them. He knew the house was perfect for her right now and that she was doing the expansion to make him feel like it was his house too. He really needed the study and by extending the sunroom, he would have a place to put his exercise equipment. Even so, he had stressed to the architect that care must given to keeping the character of a sea cottage.

"I'm so happy that we will be able to add the deck over the sunroom. We'll enjoy that. It gives us a much better view of the water," Carol said, sipping her wine, "this is good wine, don't you think? I'm getting better about making selections."

"Yes, I noticed it is Italian."

"For you, Patrico," she teased.

"I wonder what Carmella will do to your name," he laughed.

"I guess I will be Carolita or something along that order." They both chuckled.

"That roast smells good."

"I've never been much of a cook; I've contacted every woman in the church, neighborhood and my past for their recipes and help. I'm really trying. Do you want to sit out here for awhile and look at the yard before the demolition derby starts?"

"Yes, the weather is wonderful. I hope it doesn't rain for awhile."

"Oh, Patrick, I hadn't even thought about that. Now that gives me something else to worry about."

"Don't fret. Everything will be just fine."

"Okay. I trust you."

The thunder woke her and then she heard rain hitting the window. She picked up the phone to call Patrick. It was midnight, but she didn't care. When he answered he was laughing.

"I knew that was going to be you."

"You told me not to worry, and I told you I trusted you."

"Just a minor glitch; I haven't said my prayers tonight."

"Did I wake you?"

"No. I was reading. Are you disappointed?" he asked laughingly.

"Yes, I was hoping to wake you. Now say your prayers and go to sleep."

☙❧

chapter 19

Fredrico and Marc arrived two days prior to the wedding, their car filled with boxes and boxes.

"What is all of this?" Carol asked after she hugged and kissed each of her friends.

"You cannot look at anything, Darling," Fredrico said.

"First, I must see Peri before I lift anything," Marc told Fredrico, as he scurried into the house.

"Before either of you unpack, please come in and have something cold to drink and unwind."

"Okay sweetie," Fredrico said, putting his arm around her waist and walking with her.

They all sat on the veranda overlooking the water below, drinking lemonade, while Peri took turns curling around first Marc's and then Fredrico's legs as they took turns stroking his back.

"Peri the purrer!"

"It is more like Peri the chirper. Do you not just love that little noise he makes?"

"Oh, I just noticed your solarium. You did add a great deal of space. It's charming, except of course, for that dreadful treadmill," he teased.

Carol knew that Fredrico had never exercised anything but his mouth in his thirty-something years, although she decided to forego putting that into words. Fredrico could always come up with a better line.

"I know dear, but it had to go somewhere and the sunroom is certainly better than the living room."

"That's what happens when you fall in love, suddenly you are sharing something that you would never believe, right Marc?"

Marc blushed.

"Tell Carol what that is."

"When I first began learning to cook, my mother returned from London and brought me the most charming little tea set and table. I cherish it, but Fredrico thinks it is rubbage. I admit it is a little childish looking, but I love it."

"I've never seen it. Why is that?"

"I just could not part with it, so now it is in a closet."

"Maybe someday it can come out too," Fredrico laughed. He was obviously proud of his play on words.

"Fredrico, I wish we could have a cat," Marc said as he put Peri in his lap.

"I know, so do I, but I just cannot abide those disgusting litter boxes."

Carol added, "I agree. I'm fortunate that the only time I have to leave one out is when I am gone overnight. Otherwise, Peri is a man of the yard. Bless his heart; lately he has been so confused, since I have been gone so much. And of course he has lost his place on my bed. The worst has yet to come I am afraid. Now this is a secret! Patrick doesn't know about it yet, but I am getting him an Irish setter puppy as a wedding present!"

"Carol! Have you lost your mind?" Fredrico shrilled, wildly waving his arms. "Your beautiful flowers; the flora and the fauna will never be the same."

"Believe me I have thought about that. Peri was so easy to train. I am a little worried, but Patrick will have to teach him quickly."

"As they say, a man's best friend…I'll keep my fingers crossed," Fredrico said, intertwining his index and center finger and holding them in the air.

"Where is the big guy?"

Carol smiled and thought to herself, *wait until I tell Patrick that line.*

"He has gone to Bangor to pick up Carmella and Stefano. They were going to rent a car but Patrick insisted on going for them. They have been so wonderful to him. He's going to let them use his car while they are here and then they'll ride with us to Portland, when we leave for our honeymoon. Their flight leaves a couple of hours after ours."

"Where are they staying?"

"At the Hilton Harbor. Actually just about everyone who is coming for the wedding is staying there. We reserved a block of rooms. Nancy, David and little Hannah will be in later today and two of Patrick's brothers and his dad will be here tomorrow as will my mother and dad. It is going to get very busy around here. Tonight we are taking you and everyone else to dinner at Harbor Docks. Now, make yourselves at home; you know where your room is."

"Marc, we must take the coolers out of the car. Carol, we prepared some before we came and froze what we could. We have it all on dry ice. We didn't want to be in the kitchen the entire time. This is too nice," he said, looking out at the lobster boats.

"I'll help."

"You will not move as much as a little finger. You might chip a nail before the wedding."

Carol looked at her hands and said, "That reminds me. I should get a manicure. My herb garden takes a toll on my nails. I'll call now. It may already be too late."

While the two men unloaded the car, Carol called the salon.

"Right now? Okay, I am on my way."

"Freddy, Marc, Roxie can do my nails if I go now. I'll be back shortly. The house is yours. I'll make sandwiches when I return. Bye."

When Carol returned Fredrico and Marc had put everything away and had a chicken and avocado salad waiting for her.

"You two are too much. I was going to make lunch."

"And we didn't want you to harm your nails, plus we were afraid it would be boxed macaroni and cheese."

"Shush, I told you I am much better now that I'm getting married."

"I'll ask Patrick about that," Marc said, smiling.

They took their lunch outside and visited until Carol saw Patrick drive up in her car.

"That must be Carmella and Stefano. I am so ready to meet them."

Carmella stepped out of the car talking.

"This must be the lovely Carol," Carmella said, as she reached to give Carol a hug.

"I am so happy to finally meet you. I feel as though I know you both," Carol gushed.

Before Patrick could introduce Stefano, he too rushed forward with a hug for Carol.

"How was your flight?" she asked when he had released her from his giant arms.

"Very pleasant."

Carol quickly continued, "Please let me introduce everyone else. Patrick, these are my wonderful friends, Fredrico and Marc."

"Hello, it's my pleasure," he said, shaking hands then, "Please meet Carmella and Stefano, my Roman parents."

Within minutes, Carol, Carmella, Fredrico and Marc were talking so fast Patrick said, "Come on Stefano; I'll show you around."

"Wait love, have you had lunch?" Carol asked.

"Yes, we stopped," his voice trailing off as he and Stefano headed down the hill.

After about thirty minutes Patrick said, "Do you think it is safe to go back? We won't be able to get a word in, do you think?"

Stefano smiled, "Doubtful, but we can try."

The others were still sitting and chatting when Patrick and Stefano walked up. Patrick smiled and put his hands up to call for a time-out.

"We want in on this conversation," as he reached down to kiss Carol on the cheek.

"Then you better talk fast," Carmella offered. "Patrico, she is as delightful as you promised and these two are so much fun," turning to Fredrico and Marc. "We are planning the reception except Carol gets no say."

"Wait until Nancy gets here. She'll help me with these three."

"Is it time for wine yet?" Patrick asked.

"It is always time for wine," Stefano volunteered.

"I'll drink to that," said Fredrico.

"You'll drink to anything," added Marc.

"Guess what Stefano brought?" as Patrick returned with a large case, wrapped and packed for travel. "Wine from the wine master himself," Patrick continued, pointing to Stefano.

"I have heard how delicious it is. I'll get the glasses," Carol said.

"Wait, there is something else," Carmella said. "Will you get the other package Stef?"

He placed a large wrapped box in front of Carol, as Carmella said, "this is just something to go with the wine. Patrico, are you watching?"

"Yes, go ahead."

Carol carefully removed the wrapping and began taking out glasses.

"Oh, Riedels," Fredrico exclaimed, clapping his hands together, "People after my own heart."

"These are so nice," Carol said.

"I am a true believer that all wines do taste better in those," Stefano offered.

"Patrick, look!"

"I see. Thank you both so much."

"There is more," Carol said as she continued to take out glasses.

"These are different love," Carmella explained. "These are champagne flutes from Murano. I doubt seriously if Patrico bought any while he was in Venice," she teased. "They probably would not have fared too well in his duffle bag," she said, remembering his bags from his trip when she had first met him.

"You're correct, Carmella. The only person who benefited from that trip was Alexia because it was easy to put a lace bonnet in my duffle. Then what happens? Elisabette has twins and I had nothing for Alex."

"Thank you both so much," Carol said as she stood up to hug both Carmella and Stefano. "And speaking of grandbabies, do you have photos?"

"I thought you would never ask," Carmella murmured.

Stefano cut in, "But first I must make a toast because we will have finished this case of wine before Carmella finishes talking about the grandchildren. To Patrico and Carol, may they have a wonderful life together."

They clinked their glasses as they sipped the wine.

"Excellent!"

"Outstanding."

"This is wonderful, Stefano."

"Yes, Yes."

"Thank you. Now you can bring out the pictures," he said, beaming with pride about both the wine and the grandchildren.

After two glasses of wine and several rounds of photographs, Stefano said, "We had better go to the hotel and unpack."

"I'll take you and then tonight we'll pick you up for dinner and leave my car for you to use tomorrow," Patrick offered.

Carol cut in, "We'll see you at dinner, and thank you again for the glasses."

"Our pleasure, Carmella replied.

Patrick had no sooner left for the hotel when Nancy, David and Hannah drove up.

Everyone embraced as Hannah began tugging at Carol's leg. "When are you getting mayweed, Arol?"

"In two days, my special little one. How was your trip?"

"Otay." At that minute Hannah spotted Peri and was off to play.

"I expected you sooner."

"I know, we had planned to leave earlier, but you know how that goes."

"Wine?"

"Yes, please. That sounds delicious, but then we must go to the hotel to refresh."

Fredrico, Marc and Carol had another glass while David and Nancy drank their first taste of Stefano's wine.

"This is nice," David said.

"You'll meet Carmella and Stefano tonight. He brought the wine from Italy. The grapes are from his vineyard, and he makes the wine himself."

"It's very good," Nancy added.

"Hannah, do you want some lemonade?"

"Pwease, Arol."

"We really must go to the hotel," David said, finishing his glass.

"Do you know how to get there?"

"I think so. I was there some years ago."

"Then we'll meet you at Harbor Docks for dinner at 7:00 p.m. Is that time all right?"

"Perfect."

"Bye, Hannah."

"Bye, Peri. Bye, Arol."

After a lengthy dinner and more wine, everyone began complaining of being tired and sleepy.

"Tomorrow is a long day. Patrick, you still have time to get out of this," David teased.

"I'll let you know tomorrow if I need a getaway car," Patrick said, winking.

Walking to their car, hand in hand, Patrick squeezed Carol's hand and said, "Only two more days to be Ms. Neilson."

"I'm ready, so ready to be Carol O'Brien. I think everyone got along famously, don't you Patrick?"

"Yes, but I knew they would."

"I see why you love Carmella and Stefano."

"Yes, they're a great couple, but I really liked your friends, too. That Hannah is so sweet!"

"She is a handful," Carol said, laughing at memories of some of her antics.

"Are you staying tonight, Patrick?"

"No. I think I will let you rest tonight and tomorrow night because after that, you'll never be rid of me."

When Carol went into the house, Fredrico and Marc had already gone to bed. We must have exhausted everyone, she thought as she readied herself for bed.

The next day was busy with the remainder of the guests arriving. Patrick had been concerned about his dad being alone, a little nervous about meeting his new father-in-law and generally worried about everyone getting along. He need not have given it much thought because Nancy's parents came with Carol's as a surprise to both daughters and with his two brothers and the other guests in the mixture, there was never a lull in the conversation. He was relieved that the rehearsal and rehearsal dinner went smoothly and that everyone was back at the hotel or at Carol's for the night.

As he walked around the apartment the last time as a single man, he thought about the last two years and the direction his life had taken. He felt happy and content, but as always there was something deep, deep inside that never allowed him to find complete peace.

He lay on his bed, remembering the cast of characters at dinner and became amused. He decided that if he woke in the morning and this were all a big fairy tale, how different it would be. He figured Carol's father would have chosen David for her; Nancy's father would have gladly switched him for David; and Carmella would have opted for Nancy over Carol as Patrick's wife. Fredrico and Marc would kidnap John and give him to Nancy and Carol's hairdresser friend, Sergio. Stefano and Carmella would claim Hannah as another granddaughter and his poor dad would be out looking for some, very homely Catholic girl to marry Patrick. He was still smiling as he drifted off to sleep.

☙❧

The wedding was small, simple and beautiful, with the little church filled with well-wishers, friends and family. Carol was a stunning bride, but it was just as she had predicted; Hannah up-staged everyone. Every few steps, she stopped to curtsy to the wedding guests, blowing kisses. She almost dropped the basket of petals. After the ceremony, Nancy said, "I promise Carol; I don't know where she got the idea. I feel so bad."

"Nance, I loved it. How could I not? She is precious. I told you she would take everyone's heart. Besides you now have her potty trained, do you not?" Carol said laughing. "Now let's get dressed for the reception. Patrick is waiting, and I'm curious be-yond hope about what Marc and Freddy have done. You know they would not let me see anything after ten o'clock this morning," she said, rolling her eyes.

Carol met Patrick in his office. "We're finally married, Mrs. O'Brien," as he smothered her in kisses.

"I almost can't believe it. Shall we go see what Freddy and Marc have done to our place?"

"I'm not sure," Patrick said with a wink. "This could be dangerous."

As they drove up to the house, they saw twinkling lights and candles illuminating the entire back yard.

"Is it on fire or are those decorations?" Patrick teased.

"I'm not sure, but be ready to call the fire department just in case."

"It really is gorgeous, Patrick," as they walked through an elaborate twig arch, with fuchsia, tear drops and Baby's Breath spilling over. "The fragrance is heavenly, isn't it?"

"Yes, I'm amazed, Carol," he said, as he ducked slightly to miss hitting his head on a branch.

The crowd cheered and clapped as the couple entered the back yard. Hannah ran to Carol, hugging her as Carol bent down to greet her.

"Did I do dood? I haf on pantwees."

"I know Hannah. You were precious and I'm so proud of you. Have you found the cake?" But Hannah was gone, looking for the cake as soon as the question had been asked, Carol supposed.

Patrick found Fredrico and Marc; "You guys did a terrific job. This is unbelievable. Thank you so much."

"We loved every minute of it. Have you tasted any of the refreshments?"

"No, but I am on my way."

"Carol, can you believe these decorations?" Nancy asked.

"No this is even more beautiful than I ever imagined. And the food is just as pretty, but I am too excited to eat. Look at those tables!" she exclaimed.

The first table was completely filled with hot hors d'oeuvres: crispy shrimp wontons with sweet and sour dipping sauce, crab cakes with a plum tomato salsa, tiny spinach and artichoke pizzas, fried mozzarella, cheese scones and smoked salmon rolls, fish fritters, and roasted red peppers with garlic.

The second table held any number of cheeses, spicy Mexican shrimp cocktails with avocado, cold meats and a pasta salad.

Serving as the centerpiece for the next table, a traditional wedding cake was surrounded by dishes of lavender ice cream, a spiced molten chocolate cake, lemon crème brulée tart, a chocolate mascarpone cheesecake and a spiced walnut cake with lemon sorbet, honey and mint.

The final table held two elaborate punch bowls on either side, one with champagne, another with harbor breeze punch made of grapefruit and cranberry juices and vodka. In the center was a carved ice sculpture with pear martinis flowing through two entwined wedding bands.

"Dad, have you ever seen anything like this food in your life?" Patrick asked, putting his arm on his dad's shoulder.

"No son, your mother would be so proud for you."

"I know Dad. I miss her so much. Are you having an okay time though?"

"Yes, these are all nice people. There is a mixture here for certain," he said with a smile.

Patrick smiled back. "You noticed, huh?"

Patrick made every effort to involve everyone as he went among the crowd greeting people from his church and thanking them for attending. He made his way to Carol's parents to thank them again for sharing their daughter. Her mother hugged him with tears in her eyes and her father stiffly shook Patrick's hand.

"We are happy for both of you. I understand you are leaving late tomorrow for Vienna. Nice choice! Bring Carol to see us when you can. She has not been as good about that as we would like," his new father-in-law commented.

"I'll do my best, sir. He looked around to be sure everyone was having a good time.

At 10:00 p.m. only a few people had left and most of the guests were lingering and enjoying the food and view. Although it was long past time for Patrick and Carol to make their exit for the hotel, they agreed that they were having too much fun to leave.

"It may be awhile before we see some of these friends again," Patrick said. "If you want to stay later that's fine," he said, handing her another glass of champagne.

"I really would like that. We can certainly sleep on the plane tomorrow night, but I'm afraid Hannah may finally pass out, and I would like to toss my bouquet to her, so I'll go ahead with that."

The crowd came together when Patrick's brother John asked for their attention. "We need to have a few toasts before the bride and groom escape." Carol's father was next to toast, and finally Patrick said a formal thank you to everyone, toasted Marc and Fredrico and then the crowd. "Normally we are supposed to leave, and I know you are ready for us to go, but we are having too much fun with you. So Carol is going to toss her bouquet," he said, winking, "and we are staying a bit longer. So enjoy! Marc and Fredrico assure me they do not mind cleaning up late tomorrow!"

Hannah was ecstatic. She ran around showing her bouquet to anyone who would look, but it was not long until Nancy found her curled up in a chair asleep with Peri.

At midnight, Patrick and Carol finally departed for the hotel.

"Patrick, I have something special for you when we get to the room."

"Oh," he said with a smile, "I didn't know you had been holding back. This should be a really wild night. Why didn't you tell me? I would have left before the reception," he joked.

"Not that," slapping him lightly, "A present."

"You really are going to jump nude out of a cake, aren't you?"

"Patrick!"

When they arrived at the door of the honeymoon suite, Patrick leaned down to lift Carol. "Here we go," he said, carrying her to the bed. Kissing her, he whispered, "I have a present for you also, but it can wait."

He began undressing her as soon as he laid her on the bed, smothering her in kisses. As he bent over her, she reached for the clasp on his pants and then slid her hand inside.

"You're driving me crazy, Mrs. O'Brien."

Soon their nude bodies melted into each other. It was almost two o'clock when Patrick turned to look at the clock. "Time flies when you're having fun!"

"I want to just lie here beside you forever," Carol whispered, curling her fingers in the hair on his chest.

Patrick kissed the curve of her neck and began running his fingers down the small of her back.

"I said lie beside you," catching his hands and holding them. "I want you to open your present."

"I just did," he said, stealing a chance for another kiss.

"Patrick!"

"Okay, but you are so sexy, I can't help myself," he whispered, trying one more time to rekindle her passion.

She stood up, naked, the light from the lamp illuminating her tall, slender body. He watched as she slowly put on her robe. When she went to find his gift, he pulled on his briefs and took a small package from his suitcase. She came back and he was sitting on the bed, waiting, looking like a little boy at Christmas. Then he handed her a box.

"You first," he said. Inside was a tiny frame with a note: "Any art or photo of your choice from Vienna, Venice or Florence. I couldn't think of anything else. It's not very creative."

"It will be fun for us to look together; this will be our first art together. I can't wait to look for just the right piece." She paused, "Your turn!"

When he opened the box a tiny porcelain object and silver disk fell onto the sheets. He picked them up and looked closely. It was a tiny porcelain Irish setter with a tag that read, "Pat's Irish Shamrock," and when it hit him, his face lit up. "Could this possibly be what I think it is?" he asked, hopefully.

"Yes, when we get home from the honeymoon, he'll be six weeks old and we can take him from his mother. I decided to name him so they could have his papers ready. I hope that's okay."

"Sure, I'm going to call him, 'Rocky.' This is terrific; I haven't had a dog since I was a teenager. She was a mutt, but I truly loved her. She was killed by a car and my parents never let us have another one. My mother said she had too many kids to take care of anyway, without a dog. I guess we weren't too good about feeding and cleaning up." A familiar longing filled his thought. "Her name was Boots. I remember I was ten," he said brusquely, and Carol saw the look in his eyes that she had seen before. The look that told her he was alone in his world.

The next morning Patrick woke before the alarm and eased out of bed, gently closing the bathroom door before turning on the shower. As he came out of the bathroom and started for the door, she said softly, "You running out on me already?"

Turning, he smiled, "I was trying not to make any noise. I'm going to get coffee."

"I've been awake since you went to shower, just lying here thinking about yesterday and last night."

He leaned down and kissed her gently, "Yesterday, last night, why? What happened?" he teased as he sat down on the bed.

"What time is it, Patrick?"

"Seven o'clock. I'm going to see if anyone is in the coffee shop. I told Stefano we needed to leave at 11:00 a.m. I'm going to try to tell Dad good-bye before he, John and Joey leave."

"I'm getting up now and I'll be ready anytime after 8:30. I'd like to go by the house to see if Marc and Fredrico are still there and say good-bye to Peri."

"I'll be back in about thirty or forty minutes. Would you like a Danish or something?"

"Yes, anything, a muffin would be fine, but don't make a special trip back, just bring it when you're finished seeing everyone."

When Carol was dressed, she decided not to wait for Patrick and headed for the restaurant where she found him talking with his dad and brothers and her dad and David.

"Is Nance awake yet?"

"Yes. I think she's just helping Hannah, and then they'll be down."

"I'll go check."

Hannah and Nancy were just coming out of the room when Carol turned the corner.

"Wook Arol, your fowers," Hannah exclaimed, holding up the bouquet.

Carol smiled down and lightly patted her on the head. "That means you are next to be married."

"Ugh!" Hannah frowned.

Carol looped an arm around Nancy's. "Thanks for being my matron of honor. I'm going to miss you. I don't know when I'll get back to the city."

Nancy looked around at the harbor that was the backdrop for so much of the little town. It was serene, filled with boats begging to be released for the day. Some people were already making their way down to the docks and it wouldn't be long until it was a frenzy of activity.

"I guess this is really home for you now," she said, a touch of sadness in her voice.

Although it was only 10:00 a.m. Carol was surprised that Marc and Fredrico were already gone. She walked in the kitchen to find the cabinets and table covered with gifts that guests had left.

A note was taped to the refrigerator: *"We decided to work after everyone was gone. Finished up about 6:00 a.m. Full of caffeine, so heading back to NYC. Have a wonderful honeymoon. Love to you both! Freddy and Marc"*

"They are such dears. I couldn't ask for better friends." Looking around, she added, "Can you believe all these presents? We don't have time to open them all. We'll have to wait until we return. Here is something else from Carmella and Stefano. I thought the wine and glasses were our wedding gift."

"I did, too. Go ahead and open it. It looks like a painting."

Tearing off the paper, Carol unveiled a landscape painting of the Tuscan countryside, framed in antique gold. The card said: *"So you will not forget us. Love, Stefano and Carmella"*

"As if we could ever forget them; the colors in this are so soft, yet crisp and detailed. It is beautiful, Patrick. I know just the place for it."

"I don't want to rush you, but we need to go."

"Okay, just let me kiss Peri," she said, stroking the cat's long hair. "You be a sweetie. Jean will check on you."

chapter 20

The flight to Vienna was uneventful. Patrick read brochures about museums and landmarks and slept little while Carol was rarely awake.

"I guess I was more tired than I thought," she said when he woke her for breakfast.

"Weddings are hard for you, huh?" he asked her.

It was still early morning when they arrived at their hotel, an elegant old pensione centrally located inside the ring between Stephansplatz and the Staatsoper. Tall, vaulted and frescoed ceilings and floors of beautiful dark wood adorned the room that was furnished in Old Vienna Biedermeier style.

Carol unpacked while Patrick went to the desk for a map.

"Are you ready for a walk?"

After they had gone a few blocks, Patrick stopped a taxi and asked to go to the Museum of Fine Arts. "You want to see Rubens, and a few Rembrandts, don't you?"

"Yes, and they have the world's largest collection of Brueghel's."

"Our next stop will be the Belvedere."

The Austrian Gallery, home to works by Renoir, Monet, Van Gogh, Pissarro, and Max Liebermann, and a walk through the gardens was more than Carol had even imagined.

"Patrick, this is even better than I dreamed."

"I'm starved," he said, taking her hand. "Let's get something to eat. I think I remember reading about this place," peering through the ironworks into a covered courtyard of a vine-covered building. Daily specials were posted on a chalkboard by the front door. "What do you think?"

"Looks good to me," Carol said, suddenly realizing she too was hungry.

After wiener schnitzel and apfelstrudel, Patrick leaned back in the booth and let out a sigh. She read his thoughts perfectly.

"You're tired, aren't you?"

"A little, I didn't notice until I sat here for awhile. Then after that meal, I feel drained, but happy."

With her foot she rubbed his long leg under the table and then put her hands over his. "We have a whole week, Patrick; we don't have to do it all today!"

He grinned at her for a minute and then just gazed directly at her enjoying the silence and the comfort of their relationship.

"You know what I would like to do, Patrick?"

"What?" forcing himself to sit straighter.

"I would like to go back to the hotel and have a nice, long, relaxing bath with tons of bubbles and maybe a glass of wine."

"I don't think the Europeans have those big round tubs for two," he whispered, mischievously.

"I think I used the word relaxing. You would never allow that. There is a nice balcony outside our room, I noticed. Perhaps you would enjoy that."

He smiled longingly at her. "Then a bath it is and a nap for me."

Carol sank into a cushion of pearlescent bubbles, enriched by the fragrant luxury of almond oil, jasmine and musk. The hotel had left a bowl of rose petals and she sprinkled them on the creamy foam.

"Are you sure you don't want me to join you?" Patrick mischievously grinned, handing her a glass of cool Pinot Grigio.

She closed her eyes, pretending to ignore him.

"I guess that means no…" He stripped to his briefs and stretched out on the duvet and immediately fell into rapt slumber.

Carol had no idea how long she had been in tub when she forced herself out. Standing, she felt replenished and warm inside. She drew a pale green knit sweater over her head, found a pair of low-rise jeans in the drawer and tied her hair up with a ribbon that matched her pullover and went to check on Patrick who was sitting on the balcony.

She put her arms over him, forming a V on his chest and leaned to kiss his ear.

"You smell delicious," he said, turning to look up at her.

"I certainly feel better."

"Yes, you do," as he stood and put his hands on her narrow waist."

She gave him a long, lingering kiss.

"My turn, but my shower won't take long," he winked, pinching her gently.

He had to admit, the hot, sudsy water felt good hitting his skin. He stood there longer than he planned, letting it pepper him on the back. The mirror was fogged and the warmth of the small room covered his nude body as he stepped out of the shower. He didn't deserve to feel so good, he thought to himself as he wrapped the thick towel around his waist.

"If the rest of the trip is anything like the first day and night, I don't know if I will ever take you back to Maine," he said, lightly pulling the cover over her long, sleek body. "You have made me a very happy man, Mrs. O'Brien."

"Did you say horny or happy?"

The moon cast its glow through the curtains, revealing a broad smile on his face.

"Well, both, and it's your fault," he admitted freely. He kissed her cheek, "I hope you sleep well," adjusting his pillow to her level.

Her eyelids were heavy, the word, "goodnight" barely left her lips before she was asleep.

After breakfast the next morning, the couple walked to the Schönbrunn Palace. Standing in the gardens that encapsulated it, Patrick said, "I know you are disappointed about the opera, but I noticed on a flyer that there is an operetta both tonight and tomorrow night."

"That's perfect, Patrick. It was not so much the opera itself that I wanted to see, but the opera house, besides I saw in the palace that during the Rainbow of Music this month there will be waltzes there every night."

As the week took shape, the couple took in as many sights as time allowed, seeing the homes where Mozart, Schubert, Strauss, Haydn and Beethoven had lived and their statues that adorned the city. At high noon on Wednesday they gathered in the city's oldest square to watch the twelve historical figures and pairs of figures of the Anchor Clock parade across the bridge of the Anker Insurance Company building, accompanied by music from various eras. They ordered special tortes and carafes of coffee in some of the famous Vienna coffeehouses, and walked along the same cobblestone streets and medieval alleys as the Hapsburg royalty had, more than six centuries prior.

At the Prater, Patrick won Carol a small stuffed animal and they rode the famous giant Ferris wheel in spite of Carol's objections, but over a glass of wine at a small tavern, she admitted she was glad he had cajoled and coerced her into the ride.

"I'll keep the teddy bear for our first child and tell him or her how mean Daddy was to make Mommy get on that big, scary ride."

"Are you still taking the pill?"

"No, and after this week, you might worry."

"I told you, the sooner the better," he smiled.

"The desk clerk told me that we should go to a Heurige in the wine growing district of Grinzing. They have about twenty of these wine taverns. They're actually outdoor wine gardens and he said the wine tastes better under the sky. Each door that has a sprig of pine or fir and small plaque with the word 'Eigenbau' written on it means it is open and the grower serves his own wine. They call it new wine because it can only be served the year it's made." He added, "It probably will not be the best wine we will ever drink, but it is worth the experience."

"I'm game; do you know how to get there?"

"The clerk said to take tram #38. It is about a twenty minute ride."

Along the route there were vineyards scattering the fertile landscape. Many of the grapes, had already been picked and were piled two and three feet high, filling and spilling over the edges of open trailers, parked haphazardly along the sides of the roads leading to the outdoor wine gardens. Like translucent purple marbles, the grapes sparkled in the fading light.

Pointing, Patrick said, "Look! The clerk told me we might see some grapes, although he said it will be about three weeks or so when most of the harvest takes place."

"The houses are so quaint. They look like scenes from a child's fairy tale," Carol said.

In Grinzing, they walked hand-in-hand, absorbing the sweet smells of summer blossoms that filled the moss containers hanging over the terraces. At wooden tables and benches people of all ages lingered, talking and laughing, sipping wine from quarter liters.

"This looks like a fun place," Carol said, watching a group of tourists toasting.

"You want to try this it?"

"Yes, let's do."

Patrick took Carol by the arm as she led him through the vine covered trellis to a sign that read, "Built in 1527."

In a wine garden, they quickly learned, everybody is jovial and friendly. Within minutes they found themselves sharing a

table with five Canadians and three students from Munich who
appeared to be vying for the wine drinking championship. First
they drank and then they sang and drank again.

Looking at his watch, Patrick noticed it was after ten. "If
we're going to feel like seeing the Vienna Woods tomorrow, I
think this should be my last wine."

He gazed up through the leaves of the grape arbor to see the
skies twinkling in the ebony sky.

"I think I should have stopped an hour ago, but the cold
cuts, cheeses and Schweinebraten were so delicious that I thought
I needed a little more wine," Carol added, giggling, with a slight
slurring in her words.

"Mrs. O'Brien, I believe you are becoming drunk," he teased,
"but be assured you are in good hands."

She grinned, "That I don't doubt." Falling asleep on Patrick's
shoulder during the train ride, she didn't know when he put her
to bed.

When she awoke the next morning she said, frowning, "Oh
Patrick, do I ever have a headache! I think I should have had more
mineral water and less wine. Would you get me two aspirin and a
large glass of water, please?"

"Sure," he said, smiling as he handed them to her.

She drank the whole glass in one gulp; "More please. I'm
really thirsty."

"Do you feel like going anywhere?"

"I'll be fine as soon as these take effect. Why don't you shower
and I'll nap a few minutes."

Within thirty minutes she felt better and dressed quickly for
the thirty minute train trip to Baden.

"Do you feel like walking to the village? I think it's just about
a ten minute walk."

"I really am feeling fine now, Patrick. My head is okay and
that toast settled my stomach. I had a great time last night. That

kid from Munich was funny, wasn't he? I hardly remember going to the hotel though."

"The reason you don't remember is that you were asleep. I'm just glad you're fine now," he said, pulling her closer to him.

"Can you smell the sulfurous baths?"

"Yes. We should have brought our bathing suits. Look. There's a thermal pool, just right over there!"

"I read they have several, and this was once a popular destination for Napoleon, Beethoven, Mozart and others."

As they entered the pedestrian-zoned small downtown they saw boutiques, beautiful gardens and sidewalk cafes lining the square.

"I might like to do some shopping."

"I was afraid of that," he smiled, "Would you like to meet me back here in an hour or so?"

"What will you do?"

"I think I'll go over to that café, pointing to an open air seating area, have a cappuccino or something and just watch the people stroll around the square."

"Are you sure? I really haven't done any shopping and these look like wonderful shops."

"Take as much time as you like. I'll be right there. Do you want a glass of wine before you go?" he asked, teasing her.

"Patrick, you're cruel."

Smiling, he dodged to keep from being hit.

"Don't leave," she said, as she walked away, looking like a woman on a shopping mission. Two hours later Carol came back to the café, arms loaded with shopping bags.

"Look Patrick."

Turning his head to see, he quizzed, "What did you find?"

She began pulling a sweater out of one bag, "Isn't this beautiful. It is pure Austrian wool."

"That's perfect for Maine. What else?"

Actually, I found three sweaters," showing one to him. "This is for you, holding up a brown wool sweater with just a hint of orange blended through the wool, around the collar, wrist and waist bands.

"I like that."

"I thought it would look good with your hair. What have you done while I shopped?"

"I've talked to several people. I particularly enjoyed one older Austrian gentleman who came here today with his wife so she could take a thermal bath. She has arthritis so they make the trip from Vienna three times a week. He was very helpful with information. He suggested we take a boat down the Danube to Krems and then take the train back. You'll like this. He said they usually have some kind of art show in an old converted tobacco factory. He also told me it was too bad we're not going to be here at Baden over the weekend because they have musical events celebrating the grapes. They do that each year for a month."

"There is so much to do and see; tomorrow is our last day, Patrick," her shoulders drooping as she finished her sentence, "I have had such a wonderful time."

"But then we are off to Venice for two nights. This time I am riding the gondola!"

"You didn't when you were there?"

"No. It looked too romantic, those guys serenading couples..." He paused and glanced down at her, "Now it will be good to be romantic."

❧◦❧

Their last day there, they found seats on the upper deck of the boat for a three hour ride down the Danube.

"Look, there must be hundreds of castles along this river. It seems as if they are around every curve in the waterway. Every time I look up there is another one on the top of a hill. Is this not gorgeous?" Carol added.

Terraced vineyards lined the hills of the Wachau region; Baroque buildings jutted out among the tall trees as the boat slow waltzed down the waterway.

When they disembarked they discovered why Krems is a must see; one of the oldest towns in Austria with buildings from the twelfth century, its arched gateways framed the entries to the cobble stoned streets where vendors were selling local wines from kiosks.

"Should we taste?" Patrick asked.

"Today I believe I can face wine again. Yesterday, I wasn't so sure," Carol laughed.

∽∾

They had been in Venice for less than an hour, when Carol exclaimed "There it is, Patrick!"

"What?" He looked startled.

"The painting I want!"

Under a sunburned umbrella, that looked as old as the Rialto Bridge, sat a young man in his late twenties, his brush dancing across a fabric of vibrant hues. He didn't look up as they approached, but concentrated on the canvas stretched in front of him.

"Excuse us," Patrick said softly, hating to disturb his intensity.

He stopped, placing the brush gingerly in the wooden groove of the easel and looked up.

Without as much as asking the price, Carol said, "I want that one," pointing. It was oil, a single gondola on a deserted canal against a backdrop of slumbering, crumbling, brick structures. "Look at the way his shadows caught the light. It's magic. Oh, I love it, Patrick."

"I'm glad you found what you wanted. "Will you, can you pack it for travel?" he asked, turning to the artist who obviously spoke little English, but was accustomed to the request.

They waited patiently as he wrapped it as if it were a baby in a fleece blanket. Then they walked, up and down the narrow alleyways, pretending to know where they were in this city of palaces and canals.

"In some ways Venice looks out of place and out of time with the rest of the world, don't you think?" Patrick asked, not waiting for an answer. "I think I identified with that when I came the first time. Its faded glory lures you. It's too bad the future isn't as promising as the past."

"You're not getting sentimental are you?"

"No. I still think it is one of the most beautiful places I've ever been," he answered, glad to be back on a crowded street.

"Hungry?"

"Starved!"

"Let's try that trattoria. Pizza and wine okay with you?"

"Perfecto, Patrico," Carol giggled.

By train the trip to Florence took three hours. Carmella met them at the station and immediately swallowed them up, talking nonstop to the villa.

"Patrico tells me you want to take a cooking class."

"I do?" Carol looked surprised.

"You told me a long time ago if we ever went to Italy, you'd like that."

"Yes. I guess I did."

"It's okay if you'd rather not," Carmella said, carefully. "But if you decide, I have one arranged for tomorrow. You can decide when you've had time to think about it."

"What do you know about it?" Carol quizzed.

"The owner is a dear friend of mine, Ilaria. She takes you to the neighborhood market where you select your own fresh ingredients. That alone will inspire you. Then she teaches you about oils. Finally you cook, of course while sipping a glass of nice wine."

"Patrico, her husband does a wine class at the same time."

Patrick looked at Carol hopefully. It's up to you."

She was quiet for a minute. "Okay," she said, though not extremely convincingly and the mood seemed to change from upbeat to slightly strained until Stefano suggested the couple check out their bungalow.

It was as if nothing had been moved since Patrick had last stayed there. The air, however, was strangely cool and he knew it wasn't due to the air conditioning.

"I'm sorry, Carol. I...I thought you would enjoy a cooking lesson. I would never have said anything, otherwise."

Carol looked away. It was hard to stay angry in this remarkably romantic setting.

"I'm sorry too. I overreacted and took it that you hate my cooking. But I'm the very one who has admitted I'm a lousy cook."

"You're not lousy." He brushed her hair back and kissed her. "You couldn't be lousy at anything."

ॐ∞

The next three days were a frenzy of events, first the classes, followed by shopping, wine tastings and beautiful side trips through the snaking sandy roads, flanked by cypress trees on rolling hillsides that cast long shadows over the lush valleys.

When it was time to leave, Patrick was a mixed bag of emotions; this place was so much of his past, comfortable, soothing, somewhere to take your soul when it longed for solace and strength. But Maine was home and a new chapter was beginning.

ॐ∞

chapter 21

Back from the honeymoon, life took on an easy cadence. The most difficult task for Patrick was training Rocky, mainly because he was not very good with the word "no." When Patrick tried scolding the puppy, Rocky would cock his head, and with big brown eyes look pleadingly at his master, who immediately melted under the animal's charm.

"Okay Patrick, if you can't do this, we have to take him to obedience school," Carol said finally, after Rocky rolled and tumbled over a bed of impatiens."

"I'll do it, I'll be more forceful with him," Patrick promised, but Carol was doubtful.

"I'm not yet convinced," she told him, smiling faintly.

"I'll try a leash. He understands about going out, so I'll take him out on a leash and see if that helps."

"Well, if that doesn't work, you both may be on one leash," she said teasingly, but firmly.

After three weeks and many more flowers, Rocky began to get the message about where he was allowed. But, if he couldn't conquer the yard he wasn't giving up so easily on Peri, who was neither impressed nor amused with Rocky's exuberance. Stubbornly, the puppy nudged and playfully raked Peri's fur with his front paws as if to say "Come on, be a sport." Peri tried ignoring him, acting indifferent to his spirited antics, but Rocky persisted until the cat either gave up on ever returning to his former life or decided a furry friend wasn't so bad. Late one afternoon Patrick found them curled up together, a single act that quickly became a pattern.

Patrick's church was growing as were his responsibilities. There was always someone to see at the hospital, or to visit at home, a counseling session for a confused teenager, a couple planning to get married, a funeral or a wedding. In between, there were sermons to plan, business to take care of and general daily duties. But he loved his work. He felt that he had finally found his niche.

Carol slid back easily into her routine of painting and photography.

She sent some of her work to the gallery in New York and held three private showings in the area. She was looking forward to winter's release so she could get outside more with her camera. February was always the most difficult month for her and this year it had been particularly brutal. Thankfully it was almost over.

"Patrick, I've been thinking," she said, putting the remaining dinner dishes in the cabinet. "I'd like to put together a book of landscape photographs, a coffee table book, if you will."

"Really? Maine landscapes?"

"I don't really know yet. Maybe more places. Perhaps, landscapes of New England. What do you think?"

"Well, wouldn't that mean some travel?"

"Yes, but I'd generally only be away one night, two at the most. I talked to Fredrico and he said with his connections and some of mine from years ago, we don't think publishing would be a problem. He said he has several deep pocket donors from the gallery whom he believes would help."

"So, you've already talked to Fredrico? Wouldn't it have been nice if we could have had this conversation first?"

"Oh, Patrick, don't be so cavalier! You know I talk to Freddy often and one topic just led to another, that's all. It wasn't like I was keeping something from you for God's sake," her voice rising.

"I wasn't suggesting that," he said defensively. "I am simply surprised I guess. Besides, I thought WE wanted a baby now. You wouldn't want to travel that much if you were pregnant would you?"

"That's another reason I wanted us to talk. Maybe we could postpone the pregnancy for a year. I think I can have the book ready in that length of time."

Patrick looked stunned, like someone had hit him hard from behind. The silence for the next few minutes was penetrating. "Let me be sure I understand." His face was red, his voice quivering slightly. "You want to publish a book of pictures instead of having our child?"

"You oversimplify, Patrick. What is the big damn deal of waiting a year? You have your work. I certainly don't interfere with it. And God knows you tend to everybody's needs and wishes any time of the day or night!"

"Carol, be reasonable. It's a little different, don't you think, when someone is dying in the middle of the night and their relative calls the minister to come? You want me to say 'sorry, I can't be there until morning, it's not convenient?" His face flushed a brilliant red.

"Forget it! It's always like this. We can't talk without getting into a shouting match."

Patrick lowered his voice. "Look, I'm sorry. I just don't understand. I thought we agreed we wanted a baby…now. If you don't, then I guess I'll adjust. End of conversation."

Tension filled the bedroom as Patrick clicked off the reading light and turned over without kissing Carol goodnight.

During the next three weeks, the deep freeze appeared to be thawing outside, but not within the walls of the O'Brien home. The couple talked civilly enough and went about their daily responsibilities without arguing, but the air was cool and strained. They had never stayed angry with each other this long and it was beginning to wear on them both. Patrick was tired all of the time from his inability to sleep. He also felt like a fraud when he was asked to counsel a young couple with marital problems and he couldn't solve his own. Carol felt generally run down. Her head hurt and her stomach was queasy.

Finally, Patrick broke the chill, bringing home a bottle of wine and a dozen roses. Meekly, he handed them to her, "I'm really sorry. I have been a major pain in the ass. I didn't realize your work was that important to you and I should have. Let's forget about our quarrel. You deserve the same consideration for your work as I do mine."

Hugging him, she said, "I'm sorry too, Patrick. I have acted badly, like the spoiled brat I can sometimes be. Just give me six months for my photographs. I think, now, I can have them done by then and with the other part, it won't matter if I'm pregnant."

"You're the boss. Now let's have some wine and catch up on the last few weeks." He poured them both a glass and leaned to kiss her.

❧

This was one time, however, that Carol was not going to have her way, not if Mother Nature had hers. The seed had already been planted, literally, and Dr Taylor delivered the news to Carol on the first day of spring. The heated conversation in February had been for naught. She was already pregnant then.

On her way to Patrick's office Carol felt a sense of relief. In some ways she wanted to be pregnant now and she knew how much it meant to him. Arriving at his office her mind was on a million things and she didn't think to knock.

Startled, Patrick looked up, "Carol, what's wrong?"

"Wrong? Nothing's wrong. I simply thought you should be the first to know. I'm pregnant."

A mixture of emotions crossed his face, excitement, confusion, and happiness. "But, what about your book?"

"It just wasn't supposed to happen. My book can wait. Apparently, there are some things we don't control."

"Hmmm. I'll bet that's not easy for you to accept," he grinned and said, only half teasingly.

Smiling, she said, "I really am happy, honey. We need this baby in our lives."

"When are you due?"

"End of October or first of November."

"Well, this calls for a celebration," Patrick said, pulling on his coat. Let's go shopping."

"Shopping?" Carol looked genuinely surprised. "Patrick, you never like to shop. What are we going shopping for?"

"Baby things!"

"Patrick, we don't even know what colors we want or anything," Carol said, calmly.

"Let's do something! I can't just sit in this office and try to concentrate now. Why don't we stop by the market, pick up a few easy hors d'oeuvres for a light cocktail hour. You call a few friends to join us and tonight we'll make the announcement."

"It's three o'clock already."

"I know, but tell them to come at 6:00 p.m. and apologize for such short notice. They're going to think I'm crazy, but that is okay, too. I'm going to be a daddy!"

"Tell you what; I'll run over to the supermarket, you stay here and make the calls. I'll be back to pick you up in about thirty minutes."

Patrick took his coat off and sat back down, smiling. He looked at his watch quickly and calculated, in his mind, the time difference for Italy. "Mind if I call Carmella and Stefano? If I wait until you come back it will be too late to call."

"You can call anyone your heart desires, Patrick," she said, smiling, shaking her head and rolling her eyes though she was obviously pleased that he was so excited. "Just be sure they're

someone you know," she said with a grin as she closed the door
behind her. He was already on the phone.

Stefano answered, a rather weak "Hello." Patrick hoped he
had not awakened them.

"Stefano?"

"Patrico, hello," his now voice stronger and cheerful.

"Did I wake you?"

"No, but Carmella was reading and dozed off, so I was trying
to lower my voice. She will want to talk to you, you know. She is
awake now, looking at me, smiling, knowing it is you. Hang on."

"Wait, Stefano. Just tell her to put her ear to the phone. I
want you both to hear. We're pregnant."

Patrick could hear Carmella shriek in the background and
then Stefano lost the phone.

"Patrico, Patrico, congratulations! Stefano! We are going to
have a *God baby* or whatever it is called."

Patrick's face was beginning to hurt from smiling so much,
and he knew he could feel their excitement through the phone.

"When is the baby to be born?"

"End of October or first of November. I'll call you soon
with more news. Sorry to call so late, but I just found out. Carol
has gone to the market to buy a few things so we can have friends
over for a small celebration."

"Patrico, you know you can call anytime. We are so happy
for you."

When he hung up, he sat looking around for a few minutes
before he picked up the phone again to call his dad and within
fifteen minutes he had completed his invitations.

Everyone who was invited came for cocktails, no one knowing the reason for the last minute event. Tears came to his eyes as
he lifted his glass and said, "To my loving wife and child."

It didn't sink in for a minute. Friends looked around, confused.

Finally, Tom cheered, "Congratulations Buddy. Now I get it! I propose a toast...To the soon to be expanded family."

჻

From the start it was not an easy pregnancy and Carol was sick every morning. Worried and hovering over her, Patrick hated to leave to go to work, but she assured him she would be better as the morning passed.

Within a month, their friends Tom and Jean announced that they were going to have a baby. Patrick and Carol had met the couple at a supper club party six months earlier after Patrick convinced Carol it would be fun to have a regular group of friends to have dinner with once a month. Tom, a local attorney and Patrick hit it off immediately and began a weekly handball competition. Jean, the city librarian with a passion for art and literature quickly became Carol's friend and confidante. They agreed it would be perfect to have children the same age.

At the beginning of Carol's eighth month of pregnancy, the doctor finally gave her orders to stay in bed. "If we are going to term with this one, you're going to have to rest," he said.

Carol was not happy to give in, but she knew it was important for her health and the baby's. Patrick complied with her every whim, pacing and returning every few minutes each morning until finally Carol could stand it no longer.

"Patrick, would you please go to work? You're driving me crazy," but she smiled and winked at him as she said it. At noon he was back for an hour.

"Look at me; I'm getting huge. I lie here and read and then you bring me food, and I just get bigger and bigger."

"And more beautiful every day," he said.

"Right, a beached whale is a beautiful creature," she said mockingly.

❧❧

On the last day of the month, Carol said, "I guess we are not going to have an October baby. I simply knew when the doctor put me to bed, it meant this baby would come early, but it appears he is determined to tell us when he is ready."

"He? You think it's going to be a boy?"

"You don't think a female would be so obstinate, do you?"

"I'm not about to touch that. A pregnant woman is always right."

The next morning shortly after Carol banished Patrick to his office, she called, "I think it is time.

"I am on my way!" he exclaimed, fumbling for his keys.

Hurrying into the maternity suite, Patrick heard Carol's moans. She called out to him as he rushed to her side, pushing her damp hair away from her face.

"Breathe, Carol, Push, Harder!"

Within moments, he heard the first cries of a pink bundle of softness.

"It's a girl!" the doctor said, snipping and tying the cord and placing her into the outstretched arms of the father.

"She's beautiful. Perfect," Patrick beamed, but there were tears in his eyes. He laid the baby in the crease of Carol's arms. "Are you okay?"

"Tired." She drew in a deep breath and gazed upward.

"You look beautiful too."

"She looks like you, Patrick."

Patrick grinned sheepishly, "Maybe, a little." But no one could miss the connection, the blue eyes and wispy auburn curls.

Moving to sit beside the bed, he couldn't take his eyes off of her as she cooed softly. He stared in awe.

"I promise to bring her back," the nurse said, as she carefully took her from her mother. We're going to put you in your room, Mrs. O'Brien, and I'll bring her then."

"Will you be all right while I go make some calls?" Patrick asked, touching Carol's face gently.

"I'll be fine. I'm sleepy now."

"We have a girl, Carmella! A six pound, nine ounce, beautiful little girl!" Patrick said excitedly into the payphone.

"Oh, oh...What is her name?"

"Olivia, Olivia, in honor of the olives, the sweet memories of Tuscany in November."

"Are you serious, Patrico?"

"Yes, Olivia Ann. Ann is Carol's middle name." He started laughing, "Carol said to tell you she is so glad the baby came in November and not October! She was afraid I would have wanted to name her Crush!"

chapter 22

Patrick was the same pushover with Olivia that he had been with Rocky. If she cried, he picked her up, if she refused to open her mouth for spinach, he tried tapioca pudding. When she slept he stood over her crib, watching.

"Patrick, you are going to spoil her," Carol warned.

"So?" he grinned mischievously.

When she took her first steps and fell, he almost cried, but when her first complete sentence was "I wove Da-Da," he did. He was doting as a father could be.

"Do you think Olivia needs another dress?" he would ask whenever they were close to a children's store.

"Patrick, she cannot possibly wear everything she has before she outgrows them!"

"Okay, I just wanted to be sure," he said, looking disappointed.

He loved packing up lunch and heading out with the family on their boat every Saturday that the weather cooperated. Rocky, once Patrick's sidekick, now never left Olivia's side. "I wove de puppy," she would say, as she rubbed her cheeks against his fur.

Many of their friends now had children also, so entertainment took on a different twist. Instead of dinner parties, they had picnics in the park with other families, took camping trips in Acadia National Park or bicycle rides around Hidden Harbor. Olivia especially liked her own special place on Patrick's bike, and almost every summer and early fall afternoon while she was still small, he loaded her up and pedaled around the neighborhood. When she was three, Patrick announced that it was time for her to learn to ice skate.

"Don't you think she's a little young?" Carol asked, looking doubtful.

"I was younger than she is when I first skated."

"Okay, I'll watch, but you'll have to be the one to teach her," she said, unfazed, knowing that if Olivia fell a few times and cried, he would sweep her up in his arms and carry her around the rink. But she took to the ice like a pro. Soon father and daughter were a common sight as he held her tiny hand and they skated slowly.

"Next year we'll take her skiing," Patrick announced after being at the rink. "She has a great deal of coordination, good balance," he bragged, taking off her scarf and coat and then his.

"How about my selecting something, like ballet?"

"Oh, she would be good at that as well. Wouldn't she look cute in that little," pausing, "What do you call it?"

"A tutu?"

"Yes. I can just see her at her first recital. Carol you must find her a class!"

Carol winked. "I already have. Jean and I have signed up both girls. I was going to surprise you."

"Patrick, I went to the doctor today. He can find no reason why I am not getting pregnant again. He said to just keep trying."

"That's good news. I mean that you are okay. Well, I don't have any quarrel with his suggestion either," he winked. "Did he prescribe two times a day or three?"

"Patrick, you're bad!"

"I just wanted you to know I was interested in what the doctor had to say," he said, kissing her on the cheek as he followed her into the kitchen.

"Hmmm, something certainly smells good. What's cooking?"

"New Brunswick stew."

કે∞ક

On a weekend in early spring, Marc and Fredrico drove up from Camden where they had been scouring the flea markets. Fredrico had called ahead to tell them, "We will not be there until around six or seven o'clock on Friday and we're staying at the hotel so we would like for you to meet us at the restaurant for dinner." Not waiting for a reply, he continued, "We'll leave early the next morning to shop a little more along the return trip home. Be sure to bring Olivia. Marc has a surprise for her."

"Come by the house first; we'll have one glass of champagne before going to dinner. But be prepared; it won't be the good stuff," Patrick laughed.

They were forever sending gifts to Olivia in the mail, so Carol could not imagine what Fredrico could be referring to.

When they walked in Marc was carrying a box, wrapped in pink paper and ribbon, in one hand and bouquet of flowers in the other. "For our favorite women," he said, handing the bouquet to Carol and then showing Olivia the box. "Your mommy will have to help you with this, Olivia."

Fredrico handed Patrick an insulated sack. "For you, I could not think of wasting my lips on that other dreadful champagne!"

Grinning, Patrick carefully opened the sack. It was a chilled bottle of Dom Pérignon. "You guys are crazy," he said, slapping Freddy on the back.

Carol sat on the floor next to Olivia and helped her open the box.

"Careful you two," Marc cautioned. Carol gently took the wrapping off the first item she lifted from the box, as Olivia waited less than patiently, "My box, Mommy!"

"Just a minute, Olivia."

Carol lifted out a tiny porcelain cup and saucer. "This is beautiful," she said, noticing more. She reached in and brought out all the pieces to a small English tea set.

"It is the one we told you about," Fredrico said. "You know, the one Marc's mother brought him from London, twenty-five years ago."

"Oh Marc, this is so special. We'll put it on a shelf high in her room for now. This is a gift to cherish," she exclaimed, as she stood to give him a hug and a kiss.

"Olivia, you and Mommy can have tea parties."

Olivia clapped her hands together and went to kiss Marc just as her mother had.

"Well, are you going to open the bubbly or not?"

"Sorry Freddy, I got caught up in the tea set," Patrick said.

"Thank God it is out of our place," Fredrico remarked, as a toast.

"How were the flea markets?" Carol asked.

"Wonderful, we found some great iron lamps and an old hand carved boat," Marc replied.

"The best find though was the carved wooden statuette of a woman who obviously must have adorned some boat at least fifty years ago. It is in perfect condition, meticulously detailed. It won't last two days at Renaissance. Someone will grab it up," Fredrico added.

"We were going all the way back to the city late tomorrow night, but we saw a sign that Rockport is having a fair and market tomorrow, so we must stop. If we don't get home until Sunday late, we'll be no worse for the wear," said Marc.

"I wish you guys could have been here last weekend. It was Olivia's ballet recital," Patrick said with a broad, proud smile.

"I know she was the cutest one," Fredrico said, his hands in the air.

"Well, sure," answered Patrick.

"It was so fun watching all those little girls, no two doing the same step at the same time," Carol added.

"The teacher had them grouped according to age, and Olivia was with the youngest group. One little girl just stopped and watched the other girls; another walked off the stage in the middle of the dance. We laughed so hard, I think we missed part of the recital," Carol said, laughing again.

"We'll be at the next one, if Olivia will call to invite us," Marc offered.

"Oh, for certain. I want to see those sweet little feet dance like moonbeams," Fredrico said animatedly.

Patrick looked at Carol grinning, "Fredrico, you are an artist with words."

"I don't run an art gallery for nothing," he bantered, obviously pleased with the compliment.

After dinner as they said goodnight Patrick said, "Don't wait so long to visit."

"We are definitely coming back this year in August for the blueberries. Don't let us forget. Goodnight Darling," Fredrico said, giving his traditional kiss to Carol. "Tell Olivia we said bye-bye," he whispered as Patrick carried the sleeping princess to the car.

Because Olivia showed early signs of artistic talent, Carol worked with her regularly. Even at four, her pictures were much more advanced than most children her age. At five, Carol began to let her experiment with oils.

"I know it's messy, but she's really quite good," she told Patrick as she helped Olivia take off her little smock.

"Look Daddy, I did this for you."

It was good, Patrick thought. He kissed her on the forehead and said, "When you start kindergarten, you are going to be the best artist in your class."

"That is what Mommy said, too! Can I send this one to Nana and Poppy?" she asked, holding up a water scene.

"Sure, we'll mail it tomorrow."

"I want this one for Papa," referring to Patrick's dad.

"Maybe Susan can come over this week and you two can do some finger paints. Would you like that?"

"Yes, Yes, Yes!"

"I'll call Jean later to see if she would like for Susan to spend the day here instead of day care."

"*Goodie*, and will you make us sugar cookies and lemonade?"

"Yes, Olivia, I will."

ॐ॰ॐ

chapter 23

Carol was weeding the flower beds that framed the front of the house when Patrick drove up, two kayaks perched on the top of his car.

"Hi," he said, smiling as Olivia ran to the car.

"Daddy, Daddy, why do you have those on your car?"

"Because I'm taking you and Mommy on a trip."

"Hip, Hip, Hooray! Did you hear that Mommy?"

Carol smiled, shaking her head, as she tossed a faded hydrangea bloom into the metal bucket she had found at a yard sale outside Rockland. She let herself fall back from her kneeling position to sit firmly on the pebbled steps. She was accustomed to Patrick's surprises so she waited for the announcement, guessing that he been secretly planning this for days. His excitement was obvious as he revealed the upcoming event.

He picked Olivia up and lifted her high above his head. "How would you like to go to Moosehead Lake and see a moose, my special little one?"

"A real moose, Daddy?"

"Yes, a real moose." He looked at Carol, searching her eyes for approval. "What do you think?"

"I think you're a little crazy, but then it didn't take a pending moose adventure to convince me of that."

"Well, I thought you might think that so I talked to Tom, who was game to go. He's supposed to tell Jean today. I just thought since you are going to your folks next weekend and then school starts, this might be our last chance to take a short trip to the lake before it begins to get too cold."

"So, when is this backwoods excursion taking place, just in case I need to pack a few things?"

Sheepishly, he asked, "Is tomorrow too soon? I mean, I can help you get things together."

Laughing and not surprised, Carol said, "Thank goodness I have a few hours. I was expecting you to say this afternoon."

Standing, she removed her gloves and wiped the dirt off the back of her jeans. "I suppose I'd better stop this and get some items together. Just please tell me we are not camping out."

"No," he assured her. "I reserved two cabins within twenty feet of the water. They told me that they have a little pier for fishing, a couple of hammocks, a grill, and picnic table. "See, we're going in style."

He reached over and gave Carol a kiss on the cheek. "You're a good sport. You and Jean can each have a hammock and read until your heart's content. Tom and I will take care of the kids and cook. He's bringing a canoe and bicycles. I need to attach my bike rack so I can take mine and Olivia's. What do you think about that?" he asked, turning to his daughter.

She clapped her hands together. "Can Susan ride with us, please, please?"

"We'll see. I'll bet we can work that out," Patrick said. "Now, come help me get our bikes and fishing gear."

In the garage, he handed Olivia her Mickey Mouse fishing rod and tiny tackle box.

"Can you take that and set it by the car? Come back and get your life jacket when you finish that."

Her little feet pattering on the steps, Olivia took her assignment seriously, elated at being her daddy's best assistant. She loved the outdoors and was his perfect sidekick for any adventure. "Can Rocky go with us, Daddy?"

"We'll have to ask your mommy, but I don't see why not."

Carol spent the remainder of the afternoon packing the suitcases while Patrick loaded the car with other necessities. Olivia and Rocky played within earshot. Often Patrick overheard the little girl whispering plans to the dog, assuring him he was not going to be left behind.

 festively

By the time the sun was coming into view both vehicles, packed with clothes, and loaded with outdoor toys, were being maneuvered along the winding back roads of rural Maine. Long before noon, the little girls and their daddies were wading in the cool water of Moosehead Lake while their mothers were comfortably ensconced in Adirondack chairs, enjoying their solitude, reading. Occasionally they looked up in answer to the never-ending "Watch us, Mom!"

When the men left with their daughters for a moose safari, Carol giggled and said, "I think they think we're going to be so lonesome here all by ourselves."

Jean laughed, "I know. Did you see how they looked at us so pitifully, like we had made such a mistake not accepting their invitation?"

"I hope they see a moose, otherwise Patrick will be more disappointed than Olivia."

festively

The sky was changing to a deep orange when Carol and Jean heard the loud voices of their daughters, "We saw four. We saw four mooses," Olivia yelled.

"Four moose," Carol corrected.

But Olivia was oblivious to her mother's clarification.

"They look just like Bullwinkle," Susan added, excitedly.

The men stood grinning as the little girls gave details of the boat ride, enthusiastically describing the moose, ducks and one beaver they had seen.

"One moose shook his head and sprayed water everywhere. He was so funny. You should have seen his face," Olivia said, still out of breath from running and talking so fast.

"I've got to go to the bathroom," Susan said, running off to the cabin.

"Me, too," Olivia yelled, following at Susan's heels.

Patrick laughed, "They drank a root-beer on the boat before we realized there was no restroom. They've both been about to pop for the last thirty minutes, but then they got so excited, I guess they forgot."

"Did you have a good time?" Jean asked, looking at Tom.

"It was great. As you can see they were two excited little girls. They should sleep well tonight."

"You missed a gorgeous sunset," Carol said.

"I can tell. The sky is still beautiful. Look over there," Patrick said, pointing to Mt. Kineo, silhouetted against the fading oranges and reds.

Tom came from his cabin holding a bottle of cabernet and four glasses. "Shall we toast to the moose?" he asked.

"Sounds good," Patrick said.

"Let me check on Olivia to be sure she's in the tub and I'll be right back," Carol added.

"I guess I'd better do the same. I'm afraid this won't be a very thorough bath if I don't insist that Susan settle down for a few minutes."

When the two women went inside their cabins, the men sat silent, watching a pair of herons fly over the blackness of the gentle water. A loon's cry in the distance broke the hush.

"I think I'll start a fire. The night air has a chill," Tom offered.

"Good idea. It would be nice to sit out here for awhile. Maybe we can hold the wives off wanting supper if we keep pouring wine and stoking the fire."

As Patrick was finishing his sentence, Olivia came rushing out, with Carol several feet behind, holding two plates of sandwiches.

"Well, look at you all dressed in your pajamas," Patrick exclaimed.

She climbed onto his lap, cuddling close. "Look, Daddy, look at the stars."

"Did you make a wish?"

She smiled, "Yes, Daddy. I wished we could stay here forever."

"I made the girls sandwiches. I know they're hungry and wouldn't be able to wait until we eat." Carol explained, setting the plates on the wooden table.

"Good, we were just saying we hoped we could postpone dinner awhile so we can enjoy our wine."

Carrying chips and drinks for the girls, Jean joined the others. Susan and Olivia climbed into the chairs at the old, wooden picnic table.

"I wonder what the moose are doing," Susan asked her friend. They giggled and each took a bite of peanut butter and jelly sandwich.

Within minutes after they finished eating, both girls were asleep in their daddy's laps.

"I'll put her to bed and start the steaks," Patrick said.

৵৵

Early the next morning, after breakfast, Patrick and Tom loaded their fly-fishing gear and headed for the Kennebec River while Carol and Jean prepared to go antiquing.

Five shops and six hours later they came back to the camp dragging their treasures out of the back of the car. "Look at this vintage electric fan. The woman said it was probably made in the 1920's, hence the lack of adornment and, of course, because it's black," Carol explained. "Don't you think it will be cute in the sunroom?"

"Sure," Patrick answered, without fanfare.

"Look what else we bought. I got this silver spoon set for our next little one."

He looked quickly, smiling faintly, anxious to get back to cleaning fish.

"Don't you think they are sweet?"

"Yes, that used to be a tradition in our family. It means the baby will have good fortune. I should have remembered that for Olivia," he said, frowning. His mind raced back to a time when he did remember.

"I bought this for you, Tom," Jean said, handing him a bronze lantern, "and these Nantucket lightship baskets for me."

"You girls did well."

"We're having fish for dinner…our fish!" Patrick announced. "We need to get a few vegetables. You girls want to ride?"

Olivia and Susan jumped into Tom's station wagon, ready for any adventure.

"See our new moccasins?" Olivia said, as both girls held their feet high in the air.

"Those are pretty. Where did you get them?" Patrick quizzed.

"Mommy bought them this morning."

At the grocery store, the girls immediately spotted stuffed moose toys in a variety of sizes.

"Daddy, can we please have one? Please, pretty please," Olivia begged.

Looking over at Tom, Patrick rolled his eyes while he reached for his wallet. "Can't let the mothers get ahead of us, can we?"

Later after several hours of canoeing and a short ride on a seaplane, Patrick announced to the girls, "Quiet time. Grab your crayons. We're going to sit outside and visit with your moms."

The two couples talked as the sun slowly set over the mountain, the pristine waters glistening from the afterglow.

"What a great idea you had," Carol said, patting Patrick gently on the arm.

He smiled, remembering how she had told him she thought him a little crazy when he had broken the news to her about the trip.

☙❧

chapter 24

The weekend before school was to start seemed an unlikely time for a teacher and her lobsterman boyfriend to choose for marrying, but the young educator was three months pregnant and showing, a fact that the Board of Education did not look upon favorably. So they had come to Patrick asking for his blessings and a rushed up ceremony. The honeymoon would definitely have to be cut short. At first Patrick was hesitant because of the circumstances of the union and of his promise to Carol that he would go with her and Olivia to see her parents in Connecticut. The choices were actually a coin toss of which he preferred less. Weekends with Carol's father were anything but pleasant, but not going was generally not an option. Only once in their marriage had he stayed behind which hadn't set well with Carol, and she had let him know exactly how she had felt.

He had put off the inevitable until after the camping trip. Now he braced himself for the negative reaction when he approached Carol with the dilemma. It was no more cheerful than he expected.

"Patrick, they are not even members of the church."

"I know, Carol, but perhaps they will be."

"You had the perfect answer...you don't perform ceremonies for pregnant women or non-members. That's all you had to say."

"If I said no to every couple expecting a child, my weddings would be cut in half. At least they are going to marry."

"Because they have to if she wants to teach here."

"We could go to Connecticut. I don't know why it has to be this particular weekend."

"Because it's Labor Day and you know my parents always have their end of the season party for their friends at the club. Besides, Daddy wants to show off Olivia."

Feeling powerless, Patrick slumped. "I need to perform this wedding, Carol. They don't want a civil ceremony and I'm glad for that."

"Why can't Reverend Markum do it?"

"The bride's father said he wouldn't attend if it were at the Baptist Church."

Exasperated, she continued in her tirade. "Then I guess you have made your decision."

"I could drive up early Saturday morning and still make the party. The wedding is Friday."

"That's not necessary. I'll tell Daddy you stayed home to sanctify the bonds of holy matrimony."

The sarcasm hung in the air like dense fog. She stormed out of the room, leaving him standing at the window, looking out at what would normally be his favorite view in the world.

❧❦

For the remainder of the week neither brought up the impending trip or wedding. Patrick busied himself at work and Carol took Olivia shopping for school clothes and supplies.

"Daddy, Daddy, Look at my lunch kit," Olivia squealed. She was holding a yellow and white rectangular metal box with Cinderella front and center.

"Let me see it better," he said, reaching for the handle.

"I'll show you." She climbed into his lap, opened the box and pulled out a tiny thermos. "See, it matches!"

"What is Mommy going to put in here for you?" he asked, pretending to study the newest possession.

"A peanut butter and jelly sandwich, an apple and a sugar cookie. We've already talked about it."

"What about the thermos?"

"Juice. Do you want to hear me say my ABCs?"

"Of course, but sing them for me."

"Okay…ABCDEFG… Now I've said my ABCs, tell me what you think of me."

"I think you are the smartest, most beautiful, soon to be kindergarten girl in the whole wide world." He kissed her on the forehead and added, "I'm going to miss you this weekend, sweetheart."

"I'll miss you Daddy. Mommy says you have to marry some people. Ugh! I'm never getting married."

"But I thought Kenny was your boyfriend."

Olivia giggled, "Oh, Daddy, you are so silly."

◥⋅⋖

Patrick noticed the shiny pink bike the minute he pulled up at the hardware store. Glistening in the sunlight, tiny strips of multi-colored plastic dangled from the handle bar covers and swayed with each passing breeze. It might as well have had Olivia's name on it, because it was perfect.

No matter how many times he went into this store he was always amazed. He had never seen a place with so many things, so much stuff. Snow shoes hung from the ceiling and canoes and kayaks leaned against one full wall. There were pot-bellied stoves, rakes, shovels, big implements and every size of small tool. Screws and nails and bolts filled bin after bin to almost overflowing. Brooms of various shapes and lengths were can-tilevered from a makeshift wooden structure. Looking around one might see every gadget, contraption and any other device known to man.

An oversized dusty metal sign over the cash register read "Any Day, Any Season, We Have What You Need." There was no doubt in Patrick's mind about that. If Wilson's didn't have it, it hadn't been invented. The difficult task was finding it. Getting to it was harder. But it was there…somewhere.

Patrick had stopped for a package of light bulbs and a gallon of paint and left with that plus a bike, a basket for it and horn; one of those with the soft round black rubber ball that makes a deafening high-pitched squeal when it's squeezed. *Was he crazy? Olivia would love it.*

The paint he bought was for the bedroom. He wanted to surprise Carol who had talked for months about wanting to change the walls to mauve from starchy white. Patrick had argued that it would make the room too dark. She had said it would add character and warmth. So today he was going to paint and if he had time, he would tend to the other chores he had put off earlier in the summer, like hammering loose nails in the shutters and cleaning the gutters. And he wanted to buy the deep plum bedspread at Berry Cottage she had been eyeing.

With school starting next week, Patrick knew winter would be upon them in no time, bringing with it all the bluster and rawness it did each year in these northeastern hamlets. The evenings were already cooling down and Patrick had noticed last night that at seven o'clock the temperature was 54°. Lately the weather experts had started predicting an unusually cold and wet winter. Anything that required attention outside, Patrick knew needed to be tackled soon.

Patrick was painting the crown molding when the phone rang at nine o'clock.

"Hi, Daddy. I miss you," Olivia said excitedly.

"I miss you angel. What are you doing?"

"I'm at a party, but Mommy says I have to go to bed now."

"Have you had fun?"

"Oh, yes. Nana bought me a new dress for the party. It is pink with little white kittens on it. What are you doing, Daddy," she asked without taking a breath.

"Oh, just a few repairs around the house. I have a surprise for you when you get home tomorrow."

"What? What is it?"

"I can't tell you, silly girl. That's why it is called a surprise. Where is Mommy?"

"She's right here. She wants to talk."

"Okay. Goodnight. Sleep tight. I'll see you tomorrow."

"I love you, Daddy."

"I love you, Olivia, more than life itself." He could hear Carol whispering for Olivia to go to bed.

"Patrick?"

"Hello, honey. How's the party?"

Carol laughed, "Like always. Same people, same stories. Be glad you didn't come. I'm sorry I made such a big deal about it."

"I'm sorry I didn't go with you. I miss you."

"How was the wedding?"

"Plain, simple. Surprisingly, there were quite a few who attended. Of course, both of them have lived here all their lives and know practically everyone in the area."

"I guess I had better get back outside and mix. Dad will be looking for me. He is in his element right now, you know."

"I have the picture," Patrick said, laughing. "What time do you think you will leave?"

"Early. By six-thirty."

"Be careful. I love you."

"And I you, love."

When he heard the phone click he felt suddenly lonely in the quietness of the bedroom.

It was after midnight when he finished painting. His T-shirt and work jeans were paint splattered and his muscles were already beginning to ache, but he took a look around the room and was pleased. Carol was right. It did look warmer, softer.

Pulling the old bedspread off, he folded it and put it on the top shelf of the closet. Taking the new one from its package, featherlike in its softness, he tossed it across their bed and carefully straightened the corners. For a minute he was tempted to crash on it, but the faint smell of paint fumes lingered in his nostrils. He grabbed a pillow and blanket and headed to the sunroom and was asleep in less than five minutes.

chapter 25

Patrick looked at the clock. It was 4:10 p.m. on Sunday and he was expecting Carol to call any minute to let him know she and Olivia were home. Thinking she would be back by now, he was worried about them driving, especially today when it was drizzling rain. He heard a knock at his office door and looked up.

"Come in."

Stan Harmon and Roland Wilson, two men from his church, and friends as well, walked in, both wearing somber faces.

"Hey, what brings you two here looking so serious?" Patrick asked as he stood to greet the men.

"Patrick, you need to sit down. The news we have is not good."

"What do you mean?"

"There has been an accident; Olivia has been killed and Carol…Carol is injured. She's in critical condition."

Patrick looked at the men in shock, his face the color of the white walls surrounding him, crashing in on him. His chest felt like a weight had been dropped in its center.

"Where? Where is Carol? How bad is she? What happened? Stan, Are you sure about Olivia? Tell me quickly," he begged, as he began to pace.

"Patrick, the state patrolman, Jim Taylor, a friend of mine, you know Jim; he came to my house because he knows we're friends. He thought it would be best if you heard it from me. I called Roland and he met me here. Apparently, they were almost home, only about twelve miles out. Carol must have lost control; it was probably slick, we don't really know yet. No one else was involved though. Olivia was thrown from the car. She was dead when the officers found her. There was nothing they could do. Carol is at Harbor Memorial in surgery. Come on. I'll take you."

Dazed and lost, Patrick looked around his office. His world was spinning out of control with him standing still in the middle.

"Here Patrick, I have your jacket," Stan said, putting his arm around him. "Let's go to the car."

As the two men got in Stan's car, Roland said, "I'll follow you." He was having a difficult time talking as he watched Patrick, the tall, strong individual who was always helping others in times of crises, looking suddenly small and weak and vulnerable.

When they arrived at the emergency room, Patrick tried to put his emotions in check, briefly. Bolting from the car he ran in, but an orderly stopped him.

"Sir, may I help you?"

"My wife… my wife is in there," he said, as tears streamed down his face.

At that moment two doctors walked through the double doors where Patrick assumed they were working on Carol. He recognized one who came toward him because they had served on a town committee together.

"Reverend O'Brien, we are doing everything we can, but it doesn't look good. She is badly broken up; there is a great deal of internal bleeding, but I'm afraid the worst injury is to her head. We don't know the extent of the damage; there is too much swelling and bleeding. The next twelve to twenty-four hours will be critical, if we even have that much time. She's in a coma."

"Can I see her?" By now, Patrick was sobbing. His daughter, his baby, was gone and his wife was dying. "Please, let me see her."

"It will be a few more minutes and you can go in. Let me check and I'll be right back."

Several members of Patrick's church had arrived as well as friends of Carol's from the Art League. Tom and Jean rushed into the waiting area holding their daughter, Susan's hand. She and Olivia were to have started kindergarten together on Monday.

The doctor motioned for Patrick. "I am afraid you need to be prepared. Her appearance is not good," he said with a compassionate tone, knowing that she was dying, but trying to give Patrick time to absorb it all.

One look and Patrick knew there was very little chance of survival. He reached to kiss her on the only part of her face and head that was not bandaged.

"Carol, can you hear me?" he asked, but he knew she couldn't. "Carol, I love you with all my heart. Please try, please hang on. I need you. We all need you."

Patrick sat there for a long time, his head down, thinking through the fog in his own head. He kept talking to her, hoping to see some twitch of her hand, even a moan, but the only noise he heard, or movement he saw, were on the monitors and machines that crowded the space. Finally, one of the nurses came to him. Reverend O'Brien, we need to move her to ICU; she needs to rest now. You can see her again in an hour. Patrick wondered if she would even be alive in one hour.

"Please God," he prayed, "Please give me one more chance to see her alive."

When he went to the waiting area, he was immediately surrounded by friends, hugging him, trying to console him, crying for and with him.

"I have to call Carol's parents," he told Tom. Standing there thinking out loud, he said, "I'll call Nancy first. Maybe she or her parents can break the news. They're going to need to be with them."

When he went to the pay phone in the corner of the room, he sat down, but couldn't remember the number. Carol would know it; he forgot himself for a minute. He called the New York City information operator and then, dialing Nancy, he waited for what seemed like hours. Marie answered.

"Please let Nancy be home," he thought aloud.

When she said, "Hello," he broke down crying again. His voice cracking, he said, "Nancy, Carol is hurt really bad; Olivia is dead."

"Oh, Patrick, how? What happened? How bad is Carol?" Her speech was rapid and her voice pleading.

Patrick related what he knew and then said, "Nancy, I need to call Carol's parents, but I think it would be best if your parents were with them when I break the news. What do you think?"

"I'll call my father; he'll take care of them. They'll want to go to you immediately. As soon as I call them I'll take the next flight for myself." Nancy was crying now, her voice choking. "Oh Patrick, what do you think? Can she pull out of this?"

"Nancy, I think it would take a miracle, but that's what I am praying for."

The nurse came in an hour just like she had promised, "Reverend O'Brien, I'll take you to ICU."

Nothing had changed. Patrick took Carol's hand. It felt good to touch her; her skin was cool. He wondered if she needed another blanket. When he rang for the nurse, she appeared almost immediately, but it was to tell Patrick he would have to leave again.

"Would you please see if she is cold?"

"Yes, Reverend O'Brien, I will. You can come back at seven o'clock."

When the phone rang in the waiting area, Jean answered.

"Jean, I am so glad you answered. Do you know anymore? Is there any improvement?" Nancy asked, glad that she had met Jean earlier under better circumstances.

"Not that we have heard. Patrick is up in ICU now."

Nancy continued, "Would you please tell Patrick that my mother and father are with Carol's parents? They're making plans to leave. We're all having trouble getting flights this late. Marc said he would drive me so we'll leave tonight. David will fly tomorrow while Marie stays with Hannah and Heath. Jean, I hate to ask this, but has anything been done about Olivia?"

"No, Patrick hasn't wanted to leave the hospital. They are only letting him go in ICU once or twice an hour so he doesn't want to miss a chance to see Carol. We hesitate to bring it up. What do you think we should do?"

"I guess nothing. We can deal with that tomorrow. I'm sure the funeral home is doing what they need to do. This is all too much," she murmured, crying again. "Please tell Patrick I called and the message."

"I will Nancy. We'll see you when you arrive. We'll not leave Patrick's side."

At 10:00 p.m. one of the doctors walked into ICU where Patrick was sitting. Patrick looked up, hopeful though it was obvious the doctor was not. "We need to talk, Patrick."

As they walked down the long hospital corridor, Patrick suddenly felt sick to his stomach and leaned against the wall to brace.

"I was going to wait until morning when you had some rest, but it doesn't appear you are planning to do that. Patrick, there is no brain activity. Nothing. She might live a few days, but it is doubtful, because her major organs have been so compromised. She is completely on life support. If we turn that off, she'll be gone."

"Are you telling me there is no chance? No hope?" Patrick asked his voice breaking.

The doctor noticed he was shaking and pale; "Let's go sit down," and he gave him a minute to regain composure and then said, "Yes, that is what I am telling you. There is nothing more we can do. Her brain is . . .not showing any activity."

"My father-in-law is a physician. He will be here in the morning, if not before. I'd like for him to see her first. Maybe you could talk to him?"

"Certainly, if I am not here when he arrives, the other doctors helping me will know. I understand." Lightly touching Patrick on the back, he said, "I'm sorry."

When Tom found Patrick, he was sitting, holding his head. "The doctor told me. He came to the waiting room. Without saying more, he put his arm around Patrick's shoulder and the two men cried together.

When Nancy and Marc arrived at 5:00 a.m., Patrick had not slept and he looked like it. Nancy had obviously cried most of the drive, her eyes red and swollen, make-up long washed away. She hugged Patrick tightly.

"Nancy, there's no hope."

"How can this be, Patrick? Tell me it's not true."

Meeting her eyes, he continued, "Nancy, I have been so worried about Carol. I didn't want to leave. It's so hard to think of my little Olivia all by herself." He paused, "I haven't done anything. I don't even know where to start. I'm a minister. I'm supposed to know how to handle these times, but I can't believe Olivia is gone. I haven't even seen her. All I can think of when I look around this hospital is the day she was born here."

"Patrick, you are a man first. No one expects more. When my mother and father arrive with Carol's parents, we'll all think this over and plan what to do next," she said through tears.

"I'm glad you're here. I need to thank Marc for coming too."

"He knows."

"Oh Nancy, you know how much she wanted another baby. It just never happened."

When Carol's parents arrived with Nancy's, Patrick was brought to tears again. Together they stood for a few minutes with heads down, not knowing what to do or say next. Finally, Patrick said, "I'm so glad you had a nice visit with Carol before this happened. Olivia was so excited to see you before she started school. I just wish I had gone with her." He hit the wall hard with his clenched fist.

"Patrick, you can't blame yourself. We have done the same. If only we had come here, instead of her coming to our house. If, if, if…" his mother-in-law said.

"Dr. Neilson," Patrick said, never able to allow himself to call his father-in-law anything else, "I need to talk with you for a minute."

The two men walked outside. Squinting because the light hurt his already burning eyes, Patrick explained what the doctor had told him about Carol's condition. "I'd like for you to talk to the doctor."

"I will Patrick. We can go together." Lowering his head for a moment he stopped and looked up. "But it will change nothing. The reason I know that, Patrick," his voice faltering, "I know because I have looked into the eyes of mothers and fathers and told them their child was dying from leukemia or cystic fibrosis or any number of diseases.

"I have watched their expressions, seen their lips quiver, their shoulders droop and their tears fall. At times I have even believed I could hear their hearts racing and or breaking. And I couldn't do a damn thing about it, nothing, but just stand there and give them that terrible news and wait for their responses."

By now his voice was louder, his hands pounding the stone column next to where he stood. He began to cry, his chest heaving and his breath labored as Patrick went to him, putting his arm around his normally stoic and distant father-in-law. For a long time there was silence, interrupted only by their muffled sobs.

"I couldn't do a damn thing for them, and now I can't for my own daughter."

"Dr. Neilson," Patrick said, but his father-in-law stopped him.

"No Patrick, please, before we go in, I have a question for you." His demeanor had changed and he had gathered some semblance of control. "You well know I don't have the same convictions as you. I don't share your beliefs. To me they are folly, useless, mindless folly. But today, I need something. I need to believe in something. But what God would do this? Tell me, what God would let this happen to an innocent five year old child and her mother?"

Patrick was stunned. He had not expected this outburst or these questions. He stood silent for several minutes, thinking, pondering, and searching his heart.

"I know you are hurting, Dr. Neilson and I know how helpless you feel. I have those same feelings. But I don't believe God did this or necessarily let it happen. I think there is a plan, however, and somehow our actions figured into that design. I don't have all the answers, sir, but I do believe I was given your daughter and our Olivia for these few years for a reason and so were you. We didn't question it during those good years, did we? The scriptures say *'through faith we understand that the worlds were framed by the word of God, so that things which are seen were not made of things which do appear.... that faith is the substance of things hoped for, the evidence of things not seen.'* I realize to a man like you that may not be enough, but it is enough for me."

Dr. Neilson stared at Patrick and shook his head as if to show resolve, but not understanding. Then in a voice that seemed more kind and mellow than Patrick had heard before he said, "Let's go in Patrick. We'll talk to the doctor and do what we have to do."

Patrick put his arm around his father-in-law as they walked back inside the hospital. When they arrived in the waiting area the doctor, looking directly at Patrick, said quietly, "I'm sorry, but Carol is gone."

Patrick lowered his head and cried softly.

Although the news was no easier than it would have been hours before, Patrick had worked on his emotions, trying to prepare himself for the inevitable. He was also filled with a strange sense of relief, knowing he would not have to make the terrible decision to remove the life support. Carol had saved him that choice.

Turning to his in-laws, Patrick said, "I guess I'll go home and shower. I need to go to the funeral home. There are a lot of plans to be made. I'd appreciate your help if you think you can."

"We'll need to go to the hotel for a short time. Could we meet you at the funeral home at 9:30?" asked Dr. Neilson.

"Fine."

Patrick went to tell Nancy and his other friends, but they knew from the doctor's low tone and the look on Patrick's face that the end had come.

"Patrick, can I help in any way?" Nancy inquired.

"Yes, I'm sure, but give me a little time to know what. I'm meeting Carol's parents at the funeral home in about an hour. They're going to the hotel now."

When he arrived at the house, he had never felt so alone. Though Tom had volunteered to go with him, Patrick had said no. This was something he had to do alone. When he opened the door it was apparent that Tom and Jean had sent someone with their key to turn the lights on. Even with the artificial illumination and daylight, he could feel the darkness.

There was a note that friends had taken Rocky home. Groceries already lined the bar. A small vase of flowers sat on the breakfast table. Everything else was as he left it the morning before, the morning that he had looked so forward to his family's return in the afternoon. Peri was curled, sleeping on their bed.

Patrick went from room to room... Carol was everywhere. This was her house; even when it was their house, it was still hers. This was who she was before him, with him. This is where they first made love, where they laughed and cried and planned. And now, she was gone.

When he walked into Olivia's room, he noticed her *blankie* was on the bed. Someone must have taken it from the car and placed it there because he knew Olivia had taken it with her; she would never go off for even a night without it. Now it lay as lifeless as he knew she had been when they found her. Looking around, he saw the teddy bear that he had won for Carol at the Prater in Vienna; Olivia's toys were scattered in a corner, but her art work, like her mother's, was neatly tacked to a small board on an easel, so much unfinished playing, and so many lost dreams.

In her closet, her small dresses hung side by side, but the one she was planning to wear to her first day of kindergarten hung on the door. She had shown it to him at least six times before she left to visit her grandparents. Her lunch kit and tiny satchel were next to the dress.

Rushing to the shower and then hurrying to dress, Patrick knew he had to get out of this house. How was he ever going to live here again?

The remainder of the week was a blur and later Patrick could recall very little. He remembered calling his dad and John and then talking to Carmella, but little else.

At Nancy's suggestion, the memorial services were moved to the larger Presbyterian Church. Giving Patrick the excuse that his sanctuary was much too small for the crowd of mourners who would be attending, the real issue was the memory–the harsh reality that every time he walked into his church he would see the two caskets, would have to deal with the goodbyes all over again. It would be hard to face, harder to forget.

Patrick made certain when he planned the services with his Presbyterian colleague that they were simple, what he knew Carol would want. In compliance to a request Carol had made one night when she and Patrick had discussed what should happen if either died, she was cremated. In some ways it didn't feel right to Patrick to cremate Olivia. He didn't know exactly why cremating an adult seemed different than cremating a child, but burying her wouldn't have been any easier—it was really her dying that didn't make sense, but he wouldn't consider cremating Carol and burying Olivia. He would not separate them. They were connected, an extension of each other.

After the services, friends and family went back to the house to provide comfort and support, to hold Patrick's hand, to touch his shoulder or to merely share his grief in a moment of inexplicable silence. He paced for a while, alternately sitting and standing. When he thought he might implode, he walked outside where the world was larger, the air less heavy. When finally the sun slipped behind the trees and darkness spread like the wings of an eagle, Tom said, "Patrick we must go in."

"I'm not sure I can. It's so hard to stay in that house."

"Would you like to go home with us?"

"No, Tom. I have to do this. I just don't have to do it well."

One by one the friends left and Patrick was alone. Quiet replaced the steady hum of voices, whispers, and sounds. Emptiness swallowed him like a hawk might an ant. There was nothing left but what was and what might have been. The ringing of the phone brought Patrick back to the present. Carmella and Stefano were calling from across the vastness of an ocean. And while they talked and cried there were giant pauses in a conversation thousands of miles apart.

"Patrico, it hurts so much to not be with you. We will come to you, but perhaps it would be good for you to get away. Would you come here for a stay?"

"There is so much I need to do, but I want to think about it. I know I need to get away from here, but on the other hand, I need to stay. Here, at least, I feel close to them. But it is that closeness that is hurting so bad. I don't know; I don't seem to know anything right now except nothing will ever be the same. I want to scream and throw things. I want to just go out in our boat and never come back. But I know myself. I won't do any of those. I'll survive, but it will be the most difficult task I have ever had. God has tested me on several occasions. He raised the stakes this time, and he's almost broken me."

He paused as if he had just made a decision. "I'm going back to work tomorrow!"

"Patrico, do you not need some time?" Stefano pleaded.

"Time is what I don't need. I need work. I need to focus on everything but what life was here in this house. Winter is coming soon. Carol's flowers will die too and I hate to watch that. It will happen slowly, and then there will just be brown leaves and life-less, muted blossoms on the ground. Some will blow out to the sea where I'll put their ashes. Maybe I'll go to you then. I remember telling you once there was a rhythm to life there in Tuscany, a peaceful, busy, contented rhythm. We had that here too, but the flow has changed... the music has stopped."

"Patrico, we would give anything to be there with you. We would do anything to ease your pain," Carmella said, her voice breaking.

"I know, but no one can do that. It'll just have to come in time. It'll get better I know. It won't ever be the same, but it will get easier."

For the next month, Patrick poured himself into his work and taking care of all the details related to the accident and deaths of Carol and Olivia.

ॐ∽ॐ

chapter 26

In October, Patrick flew to Rome where he walked many of the same streets he had strolled more than twelve years before. He went by the old apartment where he had lived and found Ricardo, looking much older, his back bent further, his step awkward and unsteady, but the same sweet smile came to his face when he looked up and saw Patrick. Tears bathed both men's eyes.

"Ciao!" Ricardo said excitedly.

"Ciao!" Patrick said, hugging him. The two men sat talking for more than an hour, Patrick in his limited Italian, Ricardo in his broken, struggling English.

"Come," he finally said to Patrick.

Remembering this scene from a past life, he smiled to himself. Ricardo took him to the big tree and chained there was the blue scooter, shining as it was the day Patrick left. Ricardo put his hand to his heart and smiled broadly. When Patrick said good-bye the men wept, aware that this might be their last encounter.

The next day, Patrick went back to St. Peter's Basilica, more for closure than retrospect. Once a symbol of strength to him, a place of spiritual renewal and prayerful solitude, the Basilica now only signified beauty and enduring tenacity to preserve a heritage. Looking around he tried to imagine the millions of people in five centuries who had walked in this historical and artistic treasure searching for answers, asking for peace. He remembered doing that once, but all that was left now was silence, a repressed calmness.

He took the afternoon train to Tuscany and in the warmth of its shell, Patrick began to feel better.

"When I was in Rome, I began to miss academia," he told Stefano the next morning on the way to check the grapes.

"So, what does that mean, Patrico?"

"Stefano, I have to find something to fill the void of Carol and Olivia. Nothing will ever replace them, but perhaps something could make the hole in my heart smaller. The forecasters are predicting one of the worst winters in recent history. The winters in Maine are so long and harsh and lonely if you're by yourself. The darkness, dampness and cold are overpowering. I have hated darkness since I was ten years old. I have to find some light."

He continued, "I love being a student. I know that Harvard has a renowned divinity school. I think I'd like to get a doctorate there. The best scenario would be to live with my dad in Boston during the week and go home to Hidden Harbor for the weekend. I don't know if I can qualify at Harvard, but if I can, I dare think what the congregation would do with my request. If they would accept a divinity student from Bangor several days a week to help out, I would forgo my salary just to keep the church and deliver the sermons on Sundays."

"It seems all so logical and well planned to me," Stefano said, "But when would you do all this?"

"That's the problem. I may be too late for the spring semester, but it would help if I could get in then, so I could get started. Stefano, I need a diversion. It's so difficult to be in that house."

"Can you call someone at Harvard from here?"

"I suppose I could try."

The call to Harvard was transferred to Dr. Jaime Mata, a professor in the School of Divinity, who listened intently as Patrick related his desire to apply to the doctoral program.

"Mr. O'Brien, what a coincidence. I have a nephew; actually he is married to my niece, who belongs to your church. Roland Wilson. He says you're the best. My entire family is from Maine. I'll do what I can on short notice. It generally takes much longer to get acceptance for admission here, but let me see what I can do. I've been here more than thirty years; surely that accounts for something. Give me your telephone number and address there in Italy. I'll be touch."

"Dr. Mata, I have not discussed this with my church."

"I understand. I'll not mention this to Roland or Ruth or anyone else, for that matter, until you tell me it is the appropriate time."

"Thank you, Dr. Mata. I can't thank you enough."

"Well, it's not a done deal yet, my boy, but this old prof will go into action."

A week later Dr. Mata called with a swift reply. "If you can send a transcript from Bangor and one from Rome, I believe I can expedite acceptance. Your diverse credentials are a plus. I trust we can work this out."

"I'll call both seminaries and have them forward my transcripts."

"I'll send you an admissions application. Please complete it and send it back to my attention immediately. Be sure to tell the seminaries to send the transcripts to my attention, also."

"Dr. Mata, I owe you a great deal of gratitude."

"Save your thanks. If you get in, just don't disappoint me. Make me proud. I have a history here you know."

"Yes sir, I understand. I'll give it my best."

The month in Tuscany passed swiftly. Carmella and Stefano were like medicine to an open wound. They knew when to talk, when to be silent, when to push and when to use restraint.

"I can't tell you how much better I feel. You always have a way of lifting me out of my doldrums. I'll be in touch."

"You are the son we never had," Stefano said, hugging him. "Don't wait so long to visit."

࿏

chapter 27

It was apparent when Dr. Mata telephoned Patrick the first week of December; he had pulled the necessary strings for admission. "You will receive an official letter soon, but I thought you might want to know you have been accepted to the Harvard Divinity School so you can talk to your congregation and make plans there. You'll start here January 12."

"Dr. Mata, thank you so much. I'll not disappoint you."

On Sunday, Patrick shared his plans with his congregation asking that they allow him to remain as the senior pastor, without pay, and secure an assistant from the Bangor seminary to fill in during his two year residency. Immediately the response was that he could retain his position at three-quarters pay, with help from a seminary student three days a week who would receive the other one-quarter of his salary.

"You are more than generous to me," he told them at the next service on Sunday. "I can't bear the thought of leaving here. There are days when I think I can't stay another day in my house but on the other hand I can't leave."

Immediately friends agreed to share duties, volunteering in a myriad of ways to ease Patrick's transition.

"We'll take Rocky for the week days," Tom offered.

A neighbor promised to feed and check on Peri. Patrick hired a gardener.

☙❧

On January first, Patrick moved in with his father, planning to stay from Monday until Friday of each week.

"This is great news to me, son," his dad said. "It is so nice to have another person in the house."

"So are you going to cook?" Patrick asked, teasing his dad.

"It's not that good," his father said, responding with a smile.

During the week Patrick attended classes and studied, deciding quickly on a specialization in religion and society. He spent hours in the library, pouring over research, literature and abstract theories. When there was free time, he took his dad to dinner and an occasional Red Sox game. Though it was not the life that he wanted, it was the life he had, and he threw himself into it with all his strength.

It was difficult to arrive home on Friday night to an empty house but Tom saw to it that Rocky was there and the lights were on. The setter never failed to meet him at the door, eyes shining and tail wagging. There were worse things than this, he knew. Sundays were a boost to his morale and then his week began anew.

❧

By the fall of 1990, he had completed most of his course work and all of his residency requirements so he needed only to stay with his dad for two nights a week. By this time Dr. Mata had been serving as his mentor and dissertation chairman in an unprecedented way. He had taken an immediate liking to the younger man, admiring his perseverance and fortitude.

"Patrick, the Conference of Ministers in London wants you to be their keynote speaker."

"Why me, Dr. Mata?"

"Because you have a reputation as a great scholar. You are becoming known as an expert on religion as well as its role in society and culture."

"That is only because you have recommended me."

"Nonsense, Patrick, seize the opportunity."

The next month Patrick received an invitation from Ireland Nondenominational Divinity to speak at the general convocation at Trinity College.

"Ireland, can you believe it? My ancestors fled from there because they were starving. Now, I'm being paid to return. God does work in mysterious ways," he said incredulously to his mentor.

"Yes, indeed he does, Patrick. Do you still have relatives there?"

"My sister, Margaret, has worked on our family tree for years, and yes we have distant cousins still living there. My father's side was from County Kildare, my mother's from County Waterford. The O'Brien's were much easier to trace because when they came to America the name was apparently easier to spell from the Gaelic form than most, therefore, it wasn't modified. My mother's was O'Donoghue, O'Donnchadha in Gaelic so you can imagine how it could have been written by any number of people taking down immigration information."

"Will you be in touch with them?"

"The only one I have communicated with, Tom O'Brien is my great-grandfather's brother's son. He lives close to Dublin. We've exchanged Christmas cards and several letters over the last few years. I'd like very much to meet him."

"I think you should. Stay an extra week or so. It will be good for you. Is Tom Catholic?"

"Without a doubt, but he knows I'm not. Think of the fun it might be to sink a pint of Guinness with him and hear his stories of the land."

"You might not come back," Dr. Mata frowned.

"I'll be back. Want me to bring you one of the little people" he asked, grinning.

"Get out of here. I haven't time for your foolishness," he teased. "I'll be anxious to hear of your trip. I was at Trinity College once. You'll be in awe of the architecture. And the Book of Kells, the amazing gospels," his voice trailing as he remembered the visit.

"Yes, I never thought I would see them or Ireland for that matter," Patrick said, rising from the comfort of the worn, tufted leather chair.

Dr. Mata stood and walked around to the front of his massive wooden desk. "While in Dublin have a pint for me," tapping Patrick's shoulder.

"But you don't drink."

"If I were in Ireland's fair city I'd make an exception and have a stout with you, my dear friend and colleague."

"Then I'll toast to you, Professor." Patrick said, reaching to shake his hand.

࿐

Night was turning into day when Patrick got his first glimpse of Dublin Bay. A heavy mist gave the morning a bleak, grey cast, broken only by the jagged, rocky shore and sandy beaches. Clouds swallowed the sun, hiding both its warmth and light. Yet Patrick wasn't surprised or daunted by the scenery he saw unfolding below. He was, after all, going for the first time to the country his ancestors had called home before the great famine of the 1840's took away their hopes and led them to America.

He had heard the stories again and again from his grandfather. Although the elder O'Brien had been born in Boston and never visited Ireland, he passed down the stories his father had told him of growing up on the Emerald Isle. They were accounts of hardships and poverty, of starvation and greedy landlords, mixed with dreamy literary passages and poetry, descriptions of beautifully played harp music and the traditional bodhran drums. All this along with the tales of far flung castles and folklore of leprechauns and fairies, and always depictions of the rolling green hills, wild flowers and of course, the sea.

Tom was waiting for Patrick outside customs, and although the two had never met, they recognized one another immediately.

Tom was slightly shorter, but had the same angular face, brilliant blue eyes and chestnut hair, albeit it longer and a bit shaggy.

Patrick threw his arms around his relative. "The O'Brien's must look the same all over the world," he said, grinning.

Returning his smile, he exclaimed, "Indeed, we do. But we can't help that, can we? Let me help you with your bags and I'll show you Dublin. It's a beautiful city, full of the past with its ancient culture and historic pubs, but you'll see it is fast becoming one of the vibrant capitols of the world."

Driving along the River Liffey, Tom pointed out how the river divides the city into north and south before it quietly eases into the sea at Ringsend. "You'll want to spend at least a day walking around O'Connell Street and Bridge. At night the color from the buildings on the bank is splendidly reflected on the water, creating a kaleidoscope."

"I'm going to run out of time. I know I must see the National Gallery, Christ Church Cathedral as well as St. Patrick's Cathedral, but I must spend two days at Trinity College."

"Just so you save a night with Mollie and me at our house for dinner and two days for me to drive you to Galway, then over to Shannon and Killarney, around the Ring of Kerry to see the mountains and lakes. We'll for certain see Counties Cork and Waterford, stopping at the relatives I've contacted for you to meet." Most are turf diggers or raise sheep so they think you are some kind of celebrity with that big degree attached to your name."

"Well, they are in for a big surprise!"

"I've given you a preview of Dublin, but I'm peckish, how about you?"

"Peckish?"

Tom laughed. "Thought you were Irish, but I forget you're from the States. Means slightly hungry. So now it's time for some pub food and drink."

"I tried to read and prepare myself for the variations in culture, but I must admit it's odd hearing most people pronounce just the 't' when I'm expecting the 'th' and I'm having a little trouble with a few terms like good craic. Keep trying to teach me and before long I'll even sound Irish!"

"You're hopeless, I'm afraid. That Boston accent is too strong, but never you mind. If you can drink like us and think like us, we'll let you claim us."

"Deal."

"I'll show you the best pub in Ireland. Well, one of the best. There are too many good ones to single out just one. At this pub you'll figure out what it is really like to be Irish, and you'll learn that pulling a good pint is an art and telling a good story is a gift from above."

க்ண

Mollie met the two men at the front door of their cottage.

"This is for you, Patrick," she said before they were even introduced. She handed him a beautifully hand knitted fisherman's sweater. "I started it the minute Tom told me you were coming to Ireland."

"You mean you made this yourself?" Patrick asked, obviously touched by her sincere warmth and generosity.

"Every stitch," she responded proudly.

"It is beautiful," he said, pulling it over his head. "How did you know what size?"

"Good guess, but every O'Brien man over here is the same. I figured I couldn't be too far off. I wanted it to be a surprise so I took my chances. Perfect fit it is," she said smiling, sizing him up.

"Yes, it is perfect," he smiled back and thought how lucky Tom was to have her as his wife She was not an especially pretty woman and a little on the heavy side, but she had a genuine face and clear eyes that seemed to give way to her soul. Her accent was stronger than Tom's and he found himself watching her closely as she spoke, which she did often.

"I've about got supper on the table. Are you hungry, Patrick?"

"Always."

"Let's sit in the kitchen while I finish a few things and then we'll move to the dining room."

The warmth and fragrant smells of the kitchen swallowed him. Looking around at the modest but cozy surroundings, Patrick watched Tom motion for him to select a chair at the small wooden table.

"This feels like a home."

"You may want to shed that sweater, Pat," Mollie offered. "I keep the chill off the room with my cooking."

"I'm fine right now. It smells delightful in here."

"I'm making Irish stew. I hope you like lamb."

Patrick didn't tell her that it wasn't his favorite. "I'm sure it will be delicious. So, tell me about your interests. I've heard Tom's." Suddenly it was like an opened door as she began to talk about the grown children and the two grandchildren.

"Just let me get their pictures."

"Now, you've asked for it, Patrick," Tom said, a smile breaking across his face, as Mollie rushed by him and out of the kitchen to another room.

Within minutes she was back with three framed photos and a small album. "This will only take a bit. You look and Tom will explain who is who while I put this on the table." And with that she was gone again, carrying a heavy dish and ladle into the dining area.

"This stew is excellent. My mother made it on special occasions, but it never tasted like this."

"It's probably the herbs. I grow them myself," Mollie said, her smile growing.

"Whatever it is, it is wonderful. Perhaps, it's the company."

"We need to find you a wife and keep you here," Tom said.

Patrick grimaced slightly, "I'm afraid that won't happen. I've loved and lost enough females for a life time."

"But this place is magic."

"It would take more than magic, I'm afraid," his voice trailing off.

"But," Tom started to go on until his eyes met Mollie's and they told him he had said enough.

"We just hope you come back," Mollie added quickly to change the atmosphere back to its previous upbeat tone.

"Do you think you two will ever come to America? I'd love for you to visit, to see Boston and New York, at least."

"I doubt that will ever take place. Mollie has never even been out of Ireland. I've only seen some of the British Isles."

"I've never had a longing to cross the Irish Sea, much less the Atlantic Ocean! The water's claimed too many of my family over the years. I don't intend to be another of its victims," she said with a tinge of sadness in her voice.

Patrick knew Mollie's father and his father and most of the males in her family had been fishermen and that the waters in these parts could be cruel and harsh. The wars had also taken their share of the men. He started to say that a simple ferry crossing would be different, but stopped short. Tom and Mollie were comfortable and happy and didn't need a lot of material things or travel. Their world was Ireland and that was enough for them.

The conversation shifted again to more pleasant topics such as music and sports.

"I'll clean up this table while you two gentlemen have a whisky in the living room."

"We'll help you first," Patrick offered.

"Oh, no you won't. Now, away with you both," she said, shoving them through the door. "Tom, pour Patrick some Jameson's, or perhaps, he'd rather have an Irish coffee."

❧

The days raced as Patrick explored his heritage, both the people and places that formed who they were, a simple, friendly bunch, tied to their traditions and buoyed by the splendid scenery of their land. He had worried that the stories passed down had been embellished by the emigrants who loved their country, but he found them matching his current revelations, confirming history and filling in the missing pieces of a family puzzle.

When the week drew to a close and he said good-bye to board the plane, he found himself in a reflective mood, savoring the memories of the last seven busy days. He had embraced the land and the people, and in turn they had wrapped their arms around him and captured his heart. He had never felt more Irish or so proud of his roots, knowing that he was leaving a small part of himself behind and taking a vast portion of his family's past back with him...like his forefathers had done more than a hundred years before.

❧

Over the next year, the calls kept coming and Patrick's reputation as a scholar and lecturer grew. By the time he received his Doctorate in May of 1991, he was a requested speaker at conferences in the United States and internationally. His church had continued to grow, keeping him busy as well. Life was filled with friends, work and interesting places but void of love.

Every time he boarded a plane for a conference, which he often did, Patrick's thoughts took him back to another flight, one he had made many years ago from Indiana to Texas. Then he wasn't sure why he had flown to Dallas and taken a bus to Townsend after he had learned Sue was missing. It seemed the rational thing to do, the honorable thing to do, though it yielded nothing. Now he knew it was more than a plane trip. It was a guilt trip. Nearly twenty years later, he was continuing on the same endless journey.

Why couldn't he erase this memory, his ever present thoughts of Sue? It was as if her image hung from a puffy white summer cloud that touched the ocean and enveloped his soul. And the daughter he left behind, he thought of her every time he looked into the eyes of a child. He realized there had been nothing honorable about his visit to Townsend. Honor would have meant doing more than talking with the chief of police and sending a silver spoon.

He had wondered more times than he could remember what his life would have been like if he had stayed and married Sue. But that would have meant no precious sweet Olivia, the light of his life. He still smelled her soft innocence, saw her crooked smile, felt her tiny hand in his. Even in her brief existence she had taught him so much about love. And Carol had given him this gift, shared the child and other beautiful moments with him, filling the voids of his own creation, his own making. He knew he hadn't deserved a second chance anyway. Not the way he had handled the first.

Some days when his tormented thoughts centered on the what-ifs, he wasn't sure his heart wouldn't collapse, his mind explode. There were too many, too much to comprehend, to sort out. No way to right the wrongs because the what-ifs had started so very long ago...when he was ten.

❧⊱

PART FIVE
Admitting Mistakes

Through strife the slumbering soul awakes
We learn on errors troubled route
The truths we could not prize without
The sorrow of our sad mistakes.

Ella Wheeler Wilcox

chapter 28

The moment he opened the door he knew the young woman standing in front of him was his daughter. Her eyes were the mirror image of his.

"Are you Patrick O'Brien?" she stammered nervously.

"I am," he replied softly.

She stood there, her weight on one leg and then the other for a few awkward minutes as if bracing herself for what she was going to say next.

"I am Faith, Faith O'Brien," and she emphasized the last name.

"Would you like to come in?" a faint smile on his face.

She didn't answer but walked in slowly. She may have my eyes, he thought, but she looks just like her mother; olive skin and hair as black as midnight without the moon. Faith looked around the living room. There were pictures of Carol and Olivia on the side tables and a signed painting by Carol hanging over the mantle.

"Who's she?" she asked hesitantly.

"She was my wife."

"Oh, did you leave her too?" she asked, resentment rising in her voice.

"She and our daughter...," pointing to a small portrait of Olivia which Carol had painted, "were killed in an automobile accident almost three years ago."

"I...I...I'm sorry. I shouldn't have said that," Faith said quickly, looking genuinely uncomfortable with her comment.

"That's all right. You didn't know."

He wanted to add other words to help her relax, but he paused and waited.

"Please sit down," he offered. She did, and Peri wrapped his body around her leg.

"That's Peri. He was my wife's cat when I met her. He's about fifteen now, slowing down considerably," he said, relieved that he had something to talk about.

"He's still really pretty," Faith said, petting the cat and becoming less tense. "What kind of cat is he?"

"A Maine Coon. They're very lovable and good natured. He likes everyone, but he misses Rocky. Rocky was my eleven year old Irish setter. He died last month from a bone disease. He was in so much pain at the end. I miss him too. As they say, he was my best friend." Patrick stopped; he was talking too fast.

For a slight second Faith almost let down her guard and allowed herself to feel sorry for him, but then checked her emotions quickly.

"Would you like something to drink? I would," answering his own question. His mouth was dry and felt like cotton. "You drink wine?" he asked, trying to appeal to her adulthood in hopes she would loosen up with the compliment.

"Yes; that'd be nice," she answered, although she had maybe tasted it only once or twice with her girlfriends at a sleepover.

He poured two glasses and handed one to her.

"I thought you were a priest," she said, in an inquiring tone.

"I am a minister, but not a priest, and our religion accepts drinking in moderation."

She sipped her drink and rather liked it. It didn't taste like she remembered, giving him credit for having more expensive taste. "I was raised a Baptist; nobody drinks, in public, that is, except my mom. Well, as you know, she's my aunt, not my real mother."

When she lifted her glass again he recognized the ring on her right third finger, the promise ring he had given her mother nineteen years before.

"But I thought the main reason you left my mother was because you wanted to become a priest," her eyes narrowing again.

"That's true, but that didn't work out like I had planned."

"So you toss away a pregnant woman who loved you and then, pfffft, you don't believe you want to be a priest either. Do you just say too bad Sue? So what if I screwed up your life and the baby's. No big deal. I guess I was trying to find myself!" she asked, angrily.

She was standing now, her face red and the tone of her voice louder.

"Faith, I understand that you are angry, that you hate me for what I did."

"You're correct on both accounts."

"I know that I have no right to ask you if you would allow me to explain, but apparently you came here to understand something," he said softly, in a pained voice.

She sat back down, "Okay, go on," moving her glass away.

"I didn't know your mother was pregnant when I left. Not until she disappeared and the authorities contacted me, did I know anything about you."

"Would it have made any difference?"

"I have asked myself that many times. I truly think it would have. Maybe we wouldn't have stayed together, but I believe I would have married her, saved her the humiliation she must have felt."

"But Alice said my mother asked if anything would change your mind and you said no."

"That's true, but I never dreamed she was talking about our baby."

"Did you ever think about me?" she asked slowly, painfully, without looking up. Her voice was edged with sadness.

"More than you will ever know, and about Sue, too. I kept in touch with the Chief of Police in Townsend for three years until he retired. He said they had no clues, nothing to go on about your mother. The case was at a dead end almost from the start. I knew Alice was raising you, and I knew how Alice felt about me. I believed that if I were not going to try to take you with me, I should stay away."

"I guess I should thank you for that, for not taking me away from Alice, but I don't understand your behavior from the beginning, so nothing makes sense to me. This isn't helping. I need to go," she said, standing to leave.

Patrick stood up quickly. "Please Faith, please don't go," tears welling in his eyes. Just sit here and let me keep talking, please."

He had worried that this day might come, but now that she had found him he didn't want to lose her again. He had lost her once and he had lost his other daughter forever. He didn't want that to happen again, no matter what the risks, no matter what else happened.

"Faith, this is all so much more complicated than it seems on the surface…"

She stopped him before he could finish. "I have one question; did you love my mother?"

"Yes, very much."

"Then how complicated can it be?" she asked with disgust.

Patrick realized Faith was wise beyond her years, yet there was still a hint of a little girl sitting there, a child who wanted to make everything right in a make-believe world. But this was no fairy tale he knew; it was all too true.

"Faith, I want to tell you a long story, but first maybe we need to get something to eat. If I called for a pizza to be delivered, would that be okay?"

"Sure," she shrugged.

While they waited on the pizza, they made small talk. The atmosphere was tense, and he could see that this was not going to be an easy wall to break down. Too many years were between them. He knew she had been hurt, rejected, and the resentment hung in the air as thick as the fog over the harbor on an autumn morning. When the delivery person rang the door bell Patrick was relieved to leave the room.

"Why don't we go outside?" he suggested.

They ate at the veranda table in silence. Having no appetite, he picked at his pizza, but noticed that Faith was hungry as she hastily ate three pieces.

When they finished, he broke the stillness.

"Faith, I have a story to tell you. I knew when you called last week that I needed to do this. It may not make any difference. I know I made many mistakes, and although I take responsibility for them now, admittedly it has taken me a long time to accept that. I have blamed another for my mistakes for so long that it finally feels good to let that go. I am thirty-eight years old and I have never told another soul this story, not my parents, your mother, my wife, no one at the three seminaries where I studied, no one. It is a secret that I have held since I was ten years old, allowing it to haunt me because, I guess, I was weak. In the beginning I was young and confused, but now with age and maturity I realize I could have done things differently, but I didn't and a great many people have suffered."

He began…"I was raised in an Irish Catholic family that didn't believe in questioning anything about the church…"

Almost an hour had passed and Faith had not interrupted a single time. When he finished, they both had tears in their eyes.

"I understand better; but why don't you go to the authorities now, about this priest? I mean, you're a grown man. He can't harm you or anything now."

"No, but it would harm my father, hurt him too much. I just wouldn't do that to him now. He's not in good health. He loves Father Michael, so I'm not sure he would even believe me, and I don't know if I could deal with that. If he did believe me, I'm not sure he would agree that I did the right thing to tell. I think he would say after all these years, what is the point."

"But that's just the point," Faith interjected.

"Yes, I know that and you know that, but you have to understand, my father was born into this culture and it's all he has ever known. The priest is omnipotent to a man like my father."

"So are you ever going to do anything?"

"Yes, when my father dies. I plan to do everything I can to let people know what he did to me. I'm sure I wasn't the only one; that is the worst part of the story to me. I might have saved some other young boy from a similar fate, but only if someone would have helped..." his voice trailing off. "I just never believed that would happen."

"I just hope the jerk outlives your father," Faith said, as only an eighteen year old could.

Patrick smiled to himself. Her East Texas accent and her appearance reminded him so much of Sue. He had never heard the same accent anywhere else. In the aspects of personality her demeanor was not at all like Sue's, more he thought, like Alice, which made sense he guessed. Alice was Faith's role model, the most influential person in her life. Though Alice could be brash, he knew that was what gave her survival skills, and she apparently had passed them on to Faith.

He noticed quickly that Faith was much less reserved than Sue, and like Alice, spoke her mind, not afraid to ask questions if something bothered her and able to take care of herself, physically at least. Emotionally he wasn't so sure, but it was clear she was not the type to run away from a problem, unlike him...and her mother.

"Faith, I never told anyone this story because I was afraid someone would tell someone else and eventually it would get out. That would hurt my father worse. When I go forward with this someday, I want it to be a very organized, calculated effort that catches the priest off guard. I know Father Michael never expects me to do this, but if he knew anything he would begin working the system."

"I won't say anything, I promise. But I sure hope I'm around when all this blows. I want to see the old pervert squirm!"

Surprised with her comment, Patrick could not keep from laughing now.

"Well, I never thought of it quite like that, but that's not a bad assessment. Faith, I hope you're around too, for more reasons than just that."

She looked down. He had not meant to embarrass her with his show of feelings.

"We'll see," is all she said, but she could feel herself weakening, her heart softening. She didn't know whether to fight it or give in.

"I know it might take a long time for us to build any kind of relationship, but I'm willing to wait," Patrick said.

She didn't respond.

"I won't push you Faith. You were a brave young woman to come here. With or without me, you're somebody special. You're a fighter; that much I can tell."

Faith smiled. She liked what he had said.

It was almost midnight so Patrick asked her where she was staying.

"Some little motel near town, I think it is called Fisherman's Inn or something like that. The Ritz, it's not!" she laughed, "although I've never stayed at the Ritz, just seen some magazine pictures.

"If you could stay a few days, I'll move you to the Hilton Harbor. I think that would suit you better."

"I don't know; I really never planned on sticking around, once I met you."

"I would like to know more about your life, Faith. If you would stay, we could go out in my boat tomorrow, maybe have a picnic, watch the lobstermen awhile," he pressed.

"I guess I could, but only for another day. I mean I have paid for the plane ticket and I haven't been to this part of the United States so I might as well see something."

"Can you change your airplane ticket?"

"I'm on a student ticket, so they let you make some changes."

"So, what do you say? I need to go to the office early and then why don't I pick you up about 10:30 a.m. We'll stop at the market before we go to the harbor. Is that too early?

"No, that's fine," she said, wondering if she had made the right choice.

"What will you tell everybody? I mean, who will you tell them I am?"

"I believe it's time for the truth, don't you?"

"I don't know; the preacher with an illegitimate daughter doesn't sound too flattering for you. You might want to just tell everyone I am your niece, sounds a lot safer to me."

He smiled, liking her honesty. He liked her being here.

When he drove up to her motel the next morning, she was standing outside, dressed in Capri pants and a crop top, her long hair in a pony tail. Today she looked like a teenager.

"Good morning," he smiled broadly.

"Hi!" she said, making her southern accent even more notice-able.

"Not a bad New England summer morning, huh?"

"No, this weather is nice. It would already be scorching at home. But you should be there in July and August. You can fry an egg on some of the oil-topped roads." Catching herself, she stopped. "But I guess you know that?"

"I remember hearing that. You all don't eat them do you?" purposely saying you all. "Or is it y'all?"

"No," she grinned. "I mean, no we don't eat them, but yes it's y'all."

"What do you like on a sandwich?"

"Whatta they got?"

"Just about anything; ham, turkey, roast beef, lobster, you name it."

"I think I'll just have ham and cheese," she added.

"What kind of cheese?"

"Huh?"

"American or Swiss cheese?"

"American."

He put everything in the cooler at the harbor. "This way," he said, and she followed him down the long plank.

As he reached down to put the cooler in the dinghy, she said, frowning, "Is this your boat?"

Patrick didn't remember laughing so much in recent years. "No, first we get in this little boat; we call it a dinghy. Then go out to my boat. See," he said, pointing.

"Oh, you mean your boat just sits out there in the middle of the water, bobbing up and down?"

"Well, something like that, except it's anchored."

As the day wore on, talk came easier, seeming to flow with the waves that gently rocked their boat. Faith told him stories of her growing up. When she mentioned her plans to start junior college in the fall, it brought back enough memories to him to sink the boat. He shared travel adventures and reminisced about friendships, giving elaborate details of Carmella and Stefano.

"I just finished my Doctorate at Harvard so that opened up a lot of doors for speaking engagements. That has kept me fairly busy these last few years. I needed that. It has been really lonely."

"So you're Dr. O'Brien, huh?"

"That is what they tell me. They gave me a sheepskin to hang on my wall anyway."

"I'd like to go to Europe someday but first, I want to get rich."

"And how do you propose to do that?"

"I haven't figured it out, but I'm working on it," she said, smiling. "Mom said I needed to have a lot of money to keep her in style as an old woman."

That sounded like the quintessential Alice, he thought, careful not to say it aloud.

"I would like to take you out for lobster tonight. Would you go with me?"

"I guess. I've never tasted lobster."

"Then this should be quite a new experience. You do like seafood, though?"

"Yeah, I've really only eaten fried catfish and shrimp."

He smiled when she mentioned catfish, remembering a tiny restaurant on a lake with her mother so many years ago.

"Well, I had never eaten catfish until I met your mother so I guess we're even." He looked at his watch as they climbed out of the dinghy. "It's four o'clock now, so why don't I pick you up at six? I'm sure you'll be hungry."

"I'm hungry now!"

"Do you want to stop for something?"

"No, I can wait."

"I'll go pay the bill for last night," he said, pulling into a parking space at the motel. "Go ahead and pack and I'll reserve a room for you at a better place."

"Good, but you don't have to pay. I have some money I made last summer working at the pool. It'll be worth it to get out of here. This room is the pits. I think somebody cleaned fish outside my window plus, it doesn't even have air conditioning," she said, frowning.

Patrick smiled, "We rarely need air-conditioning. I asked you to stay, Faith. I'm paying. I'll be back at six o'clock," he said from the car window.

"Okay. Thanks, I'll be ready." She waved her hand in the air above her head, never looking back.

๛

An hour and a half later, she was wearing a light blue summer knit dress and her hair was down. One minute she was a teenage girl and the next a young woman, he surmised.

"Let me help you with your suitcase," he said, taking it. We'll eat first and then you can check in. I called and reserved a room. It's paid for."

"Thanks."

At the restaurant, Patrick ordered clam chowders for them.

"This is really good. Cool little crackers."

He stifled a smile.

When the waiter brought the whole lobsters to the table, the look on Faith's face was more than Patrick could stand. He started laughing and couldn't stop. Finally, she laughed too.

"I don't know what I was expecting, but..."

"Here, I'll show you what to do," Patrick said, demonstrating how to use the lobster tools.

After some difficulty and squirting lobster juice in her eye, Faith finally tasted it.

"This is great, but it's sure a lot of work."

"Next time we'll get lazy man's lobster. That's when they do the work in the kitchen for you, but everyone has to try it like this. Actually, I don't think the lazy man's is as tasty. I'm never sure I get all the best meat."

"I'm glad I don't know anyone here. I wouldn't want anyone to see me in this dumb bib," she said, rolling her eyes.

"Just look around; that's what everyone does."

"What about dessert?"

"Anything chocolate?"

"Sure," and he thought, *maybe she has more than just my eyes.*
"Two chocolate decadences," he ordered.

∾◦๑

When they arrived at the hotel, he said, "Faith, I want to ask a favor of you. You don't have to do this if you would rather not. I'd like for you to stay so I can take you to church with me Sunday. I'd like to introduce you and set everything straight."

She sat silent for the longest time then, "How do you think that will go over?"

"I have no idea. In this church, the congregation has the power, hence the name of the religion. They could tell me to get lost, I guess."

"Are you sure you want to take that chance?"

"I am now. When you called, I admit I was nervous, worried about what would happen. Obviously no one knows about you or any other part of my secret past. Many may wonder just what kind of man I am, what sort of person would do what I have done. I hardly even know myself, so it will be difficult for my congregation, I'm sure. Selfishly, I've been afraid I would lose the church, the only thing I really have left...until," he stopped.

"Faith, I have to come clean. I have to make it right. It may not change the way you feel, but the time for my taking responsibility for mistakes is long overdue."

"Okay, I'll stay," she said softly.

"Would you like to do something tomorrow?"

"I need to buy something to wear if I'm going to church. I didn't plan for that, but I have the rent car so I'll probably do that in the morning."

"I'm supposed to play handball at 8:00 a.m. with my friend Tom, and then I'll be at the house if you want to come by. There is a whale watch excursion at 1:00 p.m. I'd like to take you."

"Do you really see whales?"

"Usually, but this is not the best time of the year. We'll see something interesting. Have you seen a puffin?"

"Apparently not. I've never heard of it. What's a puffin?"

"It's a very small bird. You'll get to see some. There are binoculars on the boat which will help."

"Okay, I'll be at your house by noon."

Patrick took out his wallet and pulled out two one hundred dollar bills. "Faith, use this to buy what you need to wear for church and keep the rest."

"I can't take that."

"Yes, please, I think that is the least I can do. I'll never be able to make up for not providing all these years. Please take this."

"Well, you've gotten off pretty easy, in terms of money so I'll buy a pair of shoes, too," she smiled mischievously.

৵৽

The whale watching turned out to be successful, yielding one humpback, one finback and four Minke whales, plus seals, dolphins and puffins, all relatively close up. Faith could not hide her excitement. "That was pretty cool," she said.

"More lobster tonight?"

"Might as well. I think I've got the hang of it now."

When he started back to her hotel he told her he had to be at the church really early, before 7:30 a.m. "I can tell you where the church is located if you would rather sleep later and come at 10:45."

"Yeah, I'd rather sleep."

"I'll drive you there from the hotel now and show you the best way and then bring you back.

৵৽

The next morning when Patrick walked in the church, he saw her immediately, seated on the second row down front. She looked beautiful, he thought, but he wondered if she were nervous. He knew he was because his palms were wet like they always were when he was worried. Smiling down at her, she smiled back.

Patrick preached a sermon from Hebrews, Chapter II and Faith was touched. As he finished, he paused and looked around at the congregation composed of people who meant so much to him, many a part of his life since he was a very young, inexperienced minister. They had helped him endure his loss of Carol and Olivia and encouraged him to finish his degree at Harvard, at times making sacrifices on their own to help him.

"Ladies and gentlemen, this could very well be my last service here." He could hear mild gasps and even "no, no" from the audience as he continued.

"Since I stood here last week I have thought about how I was going to say this, but there are no eloquent words or delicate phrases for this speech. There is just simple truth."

He stopped, the church was completely still as if people were holding their breath, and then he rushed forward with his words. "As many of you know, when I was a young college student I struggled with becoming a priest. I vacillated, grappling with questions in my heart, changing course time and again, for more than a year and a half. In the meantime, I fell in love. I fathered a child, but I left before I knew of the pregnancy." He hesitated, as if it physically hurt to continue. After the baby was born, the mother disappeared and I was contacted by the police, or I probably never would have known. Her sister raised the baby and the case of the mother's disappearance was never solved. I selfishly followed my dreams and never saw the baby. When I gave up my plans for the priesthood, she was almost five years old and I thought it best not to disturb her life then. I don't know whether that was the right or wrong decision since I made a great many poor choices. I know now there are consequences. My daughter is eighteen years old now and much braver that I. She had the strength, persistence and courage to find me, and she is here today. She has made me realize much more about me than all my soul searching has ever revealed. Her finding me has caused me to admit my weaknesses to myself and now to you. I will not blame you for wanting another minister, a man more worthy of this congregation. I request that after I have completed this speech you stay and discuss your thoughts. When you have made a decision, one of the elders can contact me about my fate, but first, I would like to introduce to you, one very special young lady, Faith O'Brien."

He motioned for her to stand and when she did, the entire congregation stood and applauded. When everyone sat down, Patrick looked out again into the audience.

"I thank you for everything and ask for your forgiveness. He walked down from the pulpit and reached for Faith's hand. They slowly walked out of the church, leaving the congregation behind.

"You were good," she offered.

"Thanks," he murmured weakly not nearly so sure of himself. "I have a light lunch ready at the house. I thought that might save you time before you have to leave to catch your flight."

Long gaps in conversation and a noticeable uneasiness hung over the otherwise pleasantness of fresh crab salad. Faith knew he dreaded her leaving, but sensed there was more. Was he sorry for his admission? As the meal was drawing to a close, Patrick looked squarely into his daughter's eyes and slowly began a sentence, "Faith, there is one more story I have to tell you. I waited until now for fear you would leave." He looked at his watch, knowing this might take some time and worrying about a plane that wouldn't wait.

Even still, he began slowly because he was afraid the words might not come out right and this was not something he could screw up: "Carol was an artist. She lived in New York before we met, and she did some work for magazines, along with selling her art and photographs at a gallery. She did a special assignment called Women of God," He related to her the entire story of the women as Carol had told him, but leaving out the part about Ann having a child.

"I don't understand what this has to do with anything," she said questioningly and with a slight glimmer of exasperation.

"Maybe this will help. I found this in Carol's belonging when I was cleaning the drawers to her dressing table after her death." He handed her a folded note.

Faith took it, opening it slowly and began reading.

Dear Carol,

Thank you so much for the photographs. They forced me to look at myself. I wanted you to know how much I appreciated your listening to me. It was nice to be able to talk to another woman whom I truly believe understood my anguish. As I told you when you were here, I made my decision, and I accept this life. My only regret is that I did not have the opportunity to watch my daughter grow up, to become a woman. I hope she will be braver than her mother if she ever loves a man like I did her father. I hope that she is as strong as her name implies.

Sister Ann

Faith sat looking at the note, appearing still not to understand. She re-read the note, never noticing that Patrick had left and sat back down. He handed her a small, worn and frayed black and white photograph inside a gold money clip, engraved with the words, *I love you, Sue* and then one of the photos Carol had taken.

She looked at one and then the other in disbelief. "Does this...Does this mean my mother is still alive?"

"Yes, Faith, that is what it means."

She stared at the photographs, letting it all sink in. "Do you know where I can find her?" Torn between excitement and total disbelief, she sat silent, trying to tie her feelings together.

"Yes, I have all the information here for you," he said, handing over a tattered folded sheet of paper.

"Why didn't you go there and take her away after your wife died?" The volume and pitch of her voice rose for a slight moment and then she was sorry. She saw the sweat beading on his forehead and his shaking hands and knew this was hard for him.

"I'm not sure. It didn't seem the right thing after all these years. There is a saying in street basketball that I learned as a kid. It's called 'I got next.' That means you stay and keep someone else from getting in the game. If you walk away, you forfeit."

"But you say you loved her, never forgot her."

"Faith, Shakespeare wrote that men at times are masters of their fate. The fault...is not in our stars, but in ourselves. I suppose I could have been cast well for his play. I certainly followed that part of the script."

epilogue

When Faith walked into the convent she blinked and squinted, her eyes adjusting from the sun as she stepped into the dark, subdued foyer. A slight, bent woman in a well-worn, but clean habit appeared and quickly introduced herself as Sister Kathleen.

"Are you Faith?"

"Yes."

"The Reverend Mother is expecting you. She will be right here."

Faith grew more nervous. She had called ahead and explained who she was.

On the phone after Faith had told her story, the Reverend Mother had paused for an interminable minute and Faith was afraid she might refuse to allow her meeting her mother. Finally, haltingly and almost in a whisper, she replied "I will talk with her, Faith, but I cannot know what her decision will be. Although it is not visitation time, if she wishes to see you, I will not stand in her way." Faith wasn't sure if the hesitation in the Reverend Mother's voice was that of understanding or disfavor.

Faith looked around the stark room. Suddenly she heard a clicking noise and looked to the hallway, where she saw who she thought must be the Reverend Mother, upright in her walk and peering straight ahead, a worried frown across her face. Faith looked past her. She knew instantly that the woman following behind was her mother.

The woman's face first broke into a slight smile and then even from a distance, Faith saw tears welling in her eyes and then running uncontrollably down her cheeks. She wanted to run to her, but she steadied herself and stood watching her mother walk closer.

"Mother?" Faith asked slowly. She could stand it no longer. She rushed forward and hugged her. In the embrace each reached to wipe away tears.

"Mother, it really is you, isn't it?"

"Yes, Faith, it really is."

With trembling fingers Sue gently touched Faith's face again and again, as if to be sure this was not all just a dream.

"How did you find me?" Sue asked, softly, her lavender eyes searching for an answer.

Faith paused, not wanting to betray her father but also not willing to hurt her mother. She had anticipated the question, but still it caught her off guard coming so soon. Quickly she regained her composure and looked directly into the eyes of the woman who had given her birth. "Mother, it's not my journey that is important; let's just say for now I was led to you." She reached and pulled her closer. "I'm so happy. I didn't think you were alive. All these years I thought you were dead. I've missed you... Did you ever think of me?"

Sue glanced down, unable to face Faith's questioning blue eyes and youthful innocence, remembering a similar look in a life so long ago. After several minutes of dreadful silence and obvious pain, Sue looked up pleadingly, "Can you ever forgive me, Faith? I may have left, but I always kept you in my heart. I always loved you."

"Oh mother, there's nothing to forgive. You're alive; that's all that matters now."

"Faith, please tell me how you knew I was here."

"Mother, we have so much to talk about, so many years to fill in the pieces..."

∽✑

COMING SOON!

PROMISES KEPT, a sequel to *KEEPING FAITH,* will be available in the spring of 2010.

Determination and grit are the two forces that propel Faith O'Brien. After finding the father she never knew and graduating law school, her focus is centered on bringing to justice the priest who abused her father as a child. As a neophyte attorney she courageously battles a veteran, highly experienced and shrewd Boston lawyer.

Soon, however, she faces a much bigger fight—one that threatens to take the life of the man closest to her heart. But this time intelligence, perseverance and resolve may not be enough.

Keeping Faith cover design by Bill Wilson.

☙❦

☙❦